Cold Chop

PETER
LEWENSTEIN

GET REAL
BOOKS

First published by Get Real Books, London 2024

Cover design by Books Covered Ltd
Typeset on Reedsy

First edition

ISBN: 978-1-0685969-1-9

www.peterlewenstein.com

Edzo bia'a egbe gake me bia'a egbe'a fe ke o

Fire devours the grass but not the roots
(Ewe proverb)

Pronunciation Guide

Akwaaba (Welcome) = ak-QUAH-ba
Ewe (the people and the language) = EV-veh

Names:

Mwinga = M'WING-ga
Kwame = QUAH-meh
Nkrumah = n-KRU-mah (n as in the last n in London)
Osagyefo = os-SADGI-fo
Abotsi = ab-BOT-si
Yawor = YA-wa
Adzowor = AD-jo-wa
(for short) Adzo = AD-jo
Kekeli = keh-KEL-li
Kwaku = QUECK-ku

Places:

Accra = ac-CRAH
Nkroful = n-KROF-ful (n as above in Nkrumah)
Winneba = WIN-eba

Prologue

She's running. Doesn't know where. Anywhere. Get away.

A screech of tyres. She glances behind. Headlights sweep across the deserted road. He's coming after her.

She scrambles into the ditch by the roadside. Squats at the bottom, over a trickle of black water. Panting.

The car approaches, roars past, disappears in the distance. But he'll be back. He won't stop until he finds her, not now she knows.

She can't stay where she is, but she can't catch her breath. Before she has time to think what to do, she hears it returning, getting closer. It slows to a crawl. Stops. A door opens.

She lies by the black trickle, pressed against the side of the ditch, under an overhang. Footsteps approach, scrunches of shoes on gravel. They come to a halt, almost on top of her.

She can hear him breathing. She closes her eyes but pictures him standing there, stroking his moustache with his thumb and finger as he tries to figure things out.

He curses, goes back to the car. Slams the door. Drives off.

She climbs the side of the ditch, panting again. Loses her footing. Slips.

Her bag falls and spills open at the bottom. She drops down, gathers up the contents. The old photograph of her and her

1

sister is soiled. She wipes it on her dress, stuffs it back in the bag with everything else, and clambers back up.

Looks and listens. No cars. Crosses the road – more trees on that side, more shadows. Runs from one to the next, back the way she came, until she reaches the avenue. Looks one way. Can't go there; he'll search for her there for sure. She's got no choice. Looks the other way, the way home. She sets off, keeping to the grassy verge.

Music. An electric guitar, drums. The band at the hotel. She can hide there, amongst the crowd. But her dress, the mud … She'll go home. Tell everything. Do the right thing.

She reaches her turning, but she can't do it. Can't face them. Can't face her uncle, the judge.

She walks. Doesn't know where. Anywhere.

Two cars drive past. The third one doesn't. It slows. She knows it's him. She reaches another turning. Steps out to cross. The car comes round the corner.

She runs. Down the road.

Same screech of tyres. Following her.

She looks back as she runs, staring into the headlights.

GHANA, 2017

He offers his arm for support. She takes it and smiles. A rare instance of recognition. The old songs have roused her. They walk by the river in the bright sunlight until they reach the dam.

The sound of gushing water brings a tear to his eye as he reflects on his achievement and remembers that day … a great day for Ghana but a tragic day for his cousin.

The dam is small, minuscule compared to the one that inspired it. But it's sufficient. It's taken him two years to build. His sweat is as much a part of it as the earth and sticks and stones and concrete. The calluses on his hands bear witness to his effort.

He offers to help her sit on a rock, but she waves him aside with a mutter and a scowl, and he leaves her standing with her crutch.

He goes inside the powerhouse. Picks up the cable ends. Holds them, one in each hand, above his head, in a gesture of triumph.

The speeches from that day are coming back to him, and he shouts through the open door: 'When in a few moments I turn the switch ...'

She's old now, lost in her own world, but if she can hear him ...

'We will dedicate this dam to Osagyefo and to Adzo.'

'And Ofori!' she says, shouting back.

She does remember those times.

He inspects the cables before making the connection. Blows off specks of dust. But he's distracted by his cousin. She's waving her crutch.

'Ofori, come!' she cries. 'Ofori!'

She's confused. It was all so long ago. He nods to her solemnly, hoping to calm her. Raising the cable ends again, he says, 'To those we lost.'

Chapter 1

The plane banked. The rising sun glinted off the wing tip. Patrice Le Congo looked out as the silver surface of Lake Volta came into view, and then the mighty Akosombo Dam, famous the world over, a monument to international co-operation, commercial endeavour and engineering genius that brought light to Ghana and neighbouring countries in West Africa. Tired from a night flight but awestruck by the power – the power of Africa – Patrice thought of the Inga Dams back home on the Congo River, an even bigger project but as yet unfinished, so his people continued to suffer in the dark. He pondered the unfathomable inequalities and unfulfilled promise that still cursed the wretched of the earth.

'Ladies and gentlemen, we will shortly be arriving at Kotoka International Airport. Please ensure your seat belts are fastened …'

Patrice braced himself for the day ahead: a day of speeches and PowerPoint presentations and coffee breaks and break-out groups. But he wasn't complaining. He'd always wanted to come to Ghana, and now he was being paid to do it.

That evening, the conference over, his duty – he thought – done, he observed the Accra nightscape from a taxi window:

a brightly lit six-lane highway, neon-crested shopping malls and high-rise apartment buildings; icons of economic development. He checked the time. His boss had told him to meet her at eight. She'd said she wanted to ask him something – which was ominous. She was a formidable woman and accustomed to getting her own way.

They swept through a set of open gates and onto a cobbled drive and came to a halt outside the hotel. He climbed the carpeted marble steps. The plate glass doors swung open and he walked past two doormen in tunics, standing to attention.

Josie Mwinga was waiting in reception. She was wearing a black evening dress which suited her slender figure, and had had her hair done, straightened. She liked being in this city. Staying in this hotel, she would like it even more.

'Ah, Patrice,' she said. 'Good. Thank you for coming. Come and eat. The food here is excellent.'

Before he had time to return the greeting, she led him through to the restaurant, a large room of pillars and chandeliers.

'I recommend the buffet. I know you like Ghanaian cuisine. They cook your fish fresh, in front of you.'

The chef fried fillets of tilapia and carp. Patrice added jollof rice, grated gari, fried plantain, and boiled yam. He carried his plate to Mwinga's table and sat. His boss had chosen meat. As they ate, he was aware of her small, round, bright eyes watching him.

'Tell me, Patrice, what did you think of the event today? I know you didn't want to come all this way. I expect you're itching to get back to the field?'

'Well, I don't know about that, ma'am.'

'Patrice, please call me Josie – you know me well enough.'

'Yes, ma'am … Josie.' Even making an amicable request, she barked out the words like an order. 'It's true I don't enjoy meetings. I struggle to stay awake, especially after lunch. But I'm happy to be in Ghana. As a matter of fact …'

'You know, the discrimination suffered by disabled people is a serious issue. That's why the Human Rights Commission organised the conference, and why we thought it important that you and the other investigators came.'

'Yes, of course.' He was becoming more suspicious by the mouthful. They'd had a team briefing earlier to discuss "action points". She couldn't have invited him for dinner just to repeat what she'd said then. But the food was delicious.

'Anyway, Patrice, I'm glad you like it here. I need you to do an errand for me.' She took a sip of beer and dabbed her lips with the linen napkin.

'An errand?' He was getting a sinking feeling. 'Actually, I have some plans, I want to …'

'It has to do with the conference, in a way. You know that friend I told you about, George Abotsi, whose cousin suffered all sorts of abuse, because she walks with a limp? Yawor's her name …'

'I'm not sure I do.' Patrice put down his fork.

'Probably you weren't listening to me. Well, it's terribly sad. I rang this afternoon to arrange to go to see him, and his daughter told me he died a week ago. He was electrocuted.'

'Electrocuted?'

'I feel bad I didn't contact him before …'

'What happened?'

'I don't know the details. The line was awful. It didn't really make sense, and I was so taken aback … But one thing I heard clearly: she said it wasn't an accident.'

7

Patrice was pretty sure what was coming next. His boss had no qualms about asking him to do something for her in his own time.

'So, I'd like you to go and meet her. It's not far from Accra … What's the matter? Why are you looking like the sky has fallen down?'

'I was planning to go to western Ghana tomorrow.'

'You can still do that. But go and see this woman first and help her calm down. You have to go because I told her you'd be there in the morning. I would go myself, but I have meetings with government officials here in Accra and it's important we follow up on the conference outcomes while people are still thinking about it. You can be back by the afternoon and set off on your trip then.'

'If there is foul play, she must call the police.'

'She didn't say there was foul play. She just said it wasn't an accident. Please don't be difficult about this, Patrice. She needs someone to talk to. Sit with her, let her say what it is she needs to say; when things are clear to you, you can advise her on the right course of action.'

Delaying his trip wasn't the issue, but with Josie Mwinga one thing often led to another. 'Will I be paid for this? You know I'm on leave …'

'Paid?' Her voice took on a sharpness. 'Well, really, are you adding up your hours? I'm asking you for a favour, and you're asking for money? Do you want double-time, perhaps?'

'A favour. You've used that word before.'

'Yes, a favour. We're a team, we support each other. I want the people in my team to be committed …'

'You think I'm not committed?' He'd risked his life doing favours for her.

'I didn't say you're not committed. All I'm saying is ... well, I'm disappointed. I thought you were motivated by principles, not money.'

'*Mungu wangu!* My God!' He looked at her, dumfounded. 'But no problem. If you have doubts about my motivation and commitment, you won't mind when I'm gone.'

Mwinga took a sip of her drink. 'And what does that mean?'

'I've been meaning to tell you. I want a year off – study leave.'

'What? You're joking, surely ...'

'Not at all. I need some time ... These past years, doing this work, I've encountered too many instances of people doing despicable things to other people, from oppressing them politically to sometimes even killing them with their bare hands – as if they have some God-given right. You cannot comprehend how they can do it, how people can become so dehumanised – or what's behind it, what allows them to justify their behaviour. Tribalism, nationalism, the so-called international order ... I know these are forces that hold us back. But I need to understand how it's all connected, how everything fits together, how it's perpetuated.'

'Well,' she said, after a pause. 'This is a surprise. I was thinking you were dying to get back to the field when what you want is to go back to school. You've been with us no time at all and now you're asking for a year off. I mean, I know your job is not easy, but come on, Patrice!'

'Well, that's fine, ma'am ... Josie, if it's a problem, I can quit.'

The large room seemed to fall silent, like when a waiter drops a tray of plates. He hadn't meant to raise the issue of study leave until he had it all organised. And he hadn't meant to threaten her with his resignation either, but now he'd done it, he felt emboldened. He knew how much the work of the commission's investigations unit meant to his boss, but he had to regain control over his life.

'Listen, Patrice,' she said, quietly. 'There's no need to make a hasty decision. I'm not saying it's a bad idea for the future. But I'd need to discuss it … I don't know if I could keep your post open. I will try. But in return, will you help me, tomorrow? Please?'

'Okay. I'll go and talk to her.'

'Thank you, Patrice.' She clicked her fingers and ordered more beer for them both. 'You know,' she said brightly, as if everything was settled between them, 'the Abotsis are a well-known family. George was a government minister once upon a time and his father was a respected public servant.'

He picked at his food again.

'Anyway,' she said, 'what is it you want to do in western Ghana?'

'I want to visit Nkroful. It's the birthplace of Kwame Nkrumah. He was one of my heroes when I was a student.'

'Oh, for heaven's sake, Patrice! You have the strangest notions. Not even Ghanaians are interested in that man now. They got rid of him, you know, a long time ago. But it doesn't matter. You can still go, after you've seen this poor woman.'

Chapter 2

1966: JANUARY 22

Yawor Abotsi was twiddling a pencil around in her hair. Her hair was short but long enough to pull out curls and let them spring back. Her exercise book lay open on her lap. She looked at her watch and glanced out of the open window. A warm night-time breeze was drifting in, but there was no sign of her sister.

'What's that you're working on, Yawor?' Uncle Joseph asked. He was standing by his old cabinet radio with a glass of palm wine. The radio transmission was swishing in and out.

'It's an assignment for college. I have to write an autobiography. Really, I don't know what I can write about.' She looked at the blank page: a blank blur. All she could think about was Adzo. She should have been home by now.

'Well, is it so difficult? You were born, you went to school, you went to college ... It shouldn't take you long.'

Yawor shrugged. She was squeezed into a sofa with her three young girl-cousins. Her youngest boy-cousin, Charles, was sitting with Aunt Esther in her armchair, wriggling and nagging her to play with him.

'No,' Aunt Esther said. 'Keep still.'

11

'But it's boring.'

'Then you can go to bed. Yawor, where is Adzo?'

Yawor looked at her watch again. 'I don't know, Aunty.' It wasn't a lie, but she crossed her fingers down by her side because it wasn't the whole truth either.

'Anyway, you should know where she is on a Saturday night. She's your younger sister. It's late.'

'She's twenty-two. I cannot ...'

'Shh.' Uncle Joseph had his arms raised like a conductor before the music begins. 'He's starting.'

'Ladies and gentlemen ...'

'The great Osagyefo is speaking.'

'... we are gathered here today to formally inaugurate hydro-electric power from the Volta ...' The fast, forceful and familiar voice of the president, Kwame Nkrumah, cut through the crackle.

Uncle Joseph rolled his eyes. 'Our leader is going to tell us about his latest grand scheme.'

Yawor cringed. She noticed Aunt Esther staring at the floor, which is what she did when her husband was openly mocking the president, which he did frequently.

'... you see, before you, in all its majesty, strength and power, the Akosombo Dam, which has tamed the turbulent waters of the river, turning them into a beautiful vast lake ...'

Uncle Joseph sipped his drink. 'He has no shame. He has his beautiful lake and meanwhile we have to drink palm wine because we cannot afford whisky.'

'Ladies and gentlemen, we live in a word of contradictions ...'

Yawor switched away from the speech and focussed on her assignment, hoping it would take her mind off the tension in the room and her sister. She started to write:

I was born in Ho, the capital of Volta Region. I was the eldest of five; I had one sister and three brothers. Our parents were teachers. They used strong hands on us if we did not behave. At the age of seven I contracted polio and I spent a year in hospital in Accra. My parents came to see me every weekend. They made sure I did not fall behind in my schooling. I recovered and returned home, but my left leg was weak and I had to learn to walk in a different way. Some of the children teased me and shouted things at me. My sister shouted back at them and protected me, which was a comfort. My parents told me I was a good person inside and that was what mattered, and these words helped me. But then one night tragedy befell our family. My sister ...

She paused, thinking how everything always seemed to come back to Adzo.

The president was still speaking. *'... Ghana is a small but very dynamic independent African state ...'*

Uncle Joseph was waving his arm as if he was still holding a conductor's baton. He was a tall, thin man with a bony face. His hair was grey and thinning, in contrast to his eyebrows, which were bushy and jet black and which he arched sarcastically now.

'... we are trying to reconstruct our economy and to build a new, free and equal society ...'

'Why must we listen to this, Papa?' Little Charles had slipped round so that his head was dangling over the floor and his mother was holding him by his legs. 'You don't like Osagyefo.'

'Who says I don't like him?'

'Adzo told me.'

Yawor saw Aunt Esther glance worriedly from her son to her husband.

Uncle Joseph acted as if he was horrified and put his hand against his chest. 'How could anyone not like him? He has come to save us!'

'Joseph!' Aunt Esther cried. 'Mind what you say.'

'Calm yourself, madam, we are safe tonight.' Uncle Joseph winked at Yawor and the girls. 'There are no spies here. You are forgetting, the one who could be minded to betray us is there in Akosombo, at our leader's feet.'

Yawor could feel Elizabeth, who was sitting next her, stiffen; Elizabeth was thirteen and not too young to know what her mother and father were talking about.

'Your voice carries. If people hear …'

'Then let them gossip. Let them run and tell. A man must be able to say what he likes in his own home.'

'… we must free our people from the legacies and hazards of a colonial past and from the encroachments of neo-colonialism …'

Uncle Joseph snarled at the radio. 'God help us!'

Yawor looked back at her page. She altered the last words she'd written:

My parents and three brothers died in a fire. Afterwards my sister and I came to live with our aunt and uncle in Accra. Uncle is a judge and can be strict. Aunty is gentle and more sympathetic. They have treated us like their own children, almost, and have helped us through school and university. But being orphaned made my sister and I closer even than we were before. There is a unique bond between us which is why I become anxious when she goes out in the evenings.

She read it through. She hadn't meant it to be so personal and rubbed out the last two sentences.

The speech was continuing. '… in such a world we certainly need great friends. The United States …'

'The man's a fool! A complete fool. Am I not right?' Uncle Joseph drank some more and looked around the room, like a teacher looking for a child to volunteer an answer.

Yawor looked at her watch again. She'd often wondered why, if he despised the president so much, as he obviously did, why he insisted on listening to all his speeches.

'Yawor? Am I not right?'

She twiddled the pencil around in her hair again as she considered how to reply in a way that neither encouraged nor antagonised him. 'He's a learned man, Uncle. He's written books. I don't think you can believe he's a fool.'

'He must be a fool to trust the Americans. They don't care for his rhetoric, you know. And it's not surprising. The man is deluded!'

'Joseph! Please! You will get us all into trouble.'

As Aunt Esther spoke, a car swung round the bend down the road and the beam from its headlamps flashed around the walls of the room like a searchlight.

'... when, in a few moments, I turn the switch to shed the full radiance ...'

The radio signal was fading in and out and mixing with beeps and whines and other electronic sounds.

'... fruitful collaboration for a better world for all ...'

Uncle Joseph adjusted the tuning dial, frowning, the muscles in his cheeks twitching.

'... our destined and cherished goal: a Union Government for Africa.'

A noise that could have been applause or static filled the room. Uncle Joseph switched off the radio. 'Hal-le-lu-jah!' He took a swig of his palm wine and looked at the near-empty glass in his hand. 'Let them come. Let them put me in jail. I don't care. It won't be for long. It can't be. There's talk all over town. After what happened in Nigeria …'

A knock on the door interrupted his monologue. Yawor, Elizabeth and Aunt Esther all jumped. Now it was Uncle Joseph who looked worried. 'Emmanuel!' He called the houseboy. 'See who it is.'

The boy scurried off and the family sat in silence, listening as he opened the door. He came into the room and bowed. 'Two policemen are here, sir.'

Chapter 3

It was a bright morning. Patrice waited for a taxi outside his hotel. A man was selling sunglasses displayed on three wooden boards by the roadside.

'You want?' the man asked.

Patrice shook his head.

'Latest styles. From Italy.'

Patrice shook his head again.

The man picked up one of the boards and walked over. 'Armani, Versace, Gucci? Look, I have it, for you ...'

A taxi pulled up. Patrice jumped in. 'You know the Dodowa road?'

The driver nodded. 'We can go.'

The sunglasses vendor shouted through the window, 'Wait, my friend!'

Patrice shook his head a third time, and they drove off.

It was eight o'clock and stiflingly hot, even with the windows open. 'The sun is too much,' the driver said, making Patrice glance up and have second thoughts about his decision not to buy a pair of sunglasses.

They drove north, against the rush-hour traffic.

'Where are you from?' the driver asked.

'The Democratic Republic of the Congo.'

'Ah. DRC. That explains the French accent. I thought maybe you are American, because of the Afro hairstyle. But then, I am thinking, you are not so big, and Americans, they eat a lot of meat …'

'We have big people in my country, and people who eat a lot of meat.'

'Of course,' the driver said with a grin. 'When I pick up from hotels, I like to guess where the people are from. It's a game. You like Ghana?'

'Yes.' Patrice smiled back. 'But I've only been here a day, and I spent most of that in meetings. I'm looking forward to seeing more of your country.'

'*Akwaaba!* You are welcome.'

When they reached a crossroads where mattresses for sale were piled up high next to a billboard advertising Heaven Insecticides, Patrice told the driver to pull over. He called the number his boss had given him the night before and passed the phone to the driver, who nodded as he received directions for the last part of the journey.

They carried on towards a line of forest-covered hills, then left the main road and descended into a wide, green valley. They turned again at a Pentecostal church. The road narrowed and after bridging a culvert entered a wooded area and became a potholed dirt track. Low-rise houses sat among the trees. The taxi pulled up outside one, set back from the road behind a lush, wild-looking garden.

A Ghanaian flag – red, gold and green, with a black star – hung from a pole by the porch. Patrice got out and wiped his brow and listened to the birds. He was less than an hour from Accra, but it was another world. The driver wished him a pleasant stay in Ghana.

Patrice climbed the steps to the front door. It opened before he reached it. A woman stepped out.

'Good morning,' she said. 'I'm Kekeli, George Abotsi's daughter. You must be Mr Le Congo.'

'Yes, good morning. Nice to meet you. I'm Patrice.'

They shook hands and clicked fingers - the way Ghanaians do.

'You live in a beautiful place.'

'Yes, we are lucky.'

She looked him up and down, pouting her lips, as if assessing his suitability for a job. She was dressed in a tee-shirt and jeans, like he was, but she didn't look scruffy, like he probably did. Her hair was natural but cut short at the sides and set off her sharp features well. He guessed she was in her mid-thirties, around his age, perhaps older. There was sadness in her eyes but also a shy, friendly sparkle.

'Josie Mwinga said you have helped people in trouble in your home country, victims of war, so I was expecting to see a hardened man bearing the scars of suffering on his face. But I don't see them. Instead, I see light in your eyes, and compassion. I see someone who knows that things can be better.'

'You see a lot. I do have those scars, but they are inside.'

She nodded seriously. 'Well, it's good of you to come. Please follow me.' She closed the door behind her and led Patrice back down the steps. 'The house inside is untidy and my aunt is sleeping.'

He followed her along a path through the plants and bushes to the back of the house, which was shaded by a large bamboo and many other trees.

'My father tended to this. All this land was his.'

Patrice surveyed the garden, which was like a forest. 'It's so green,' he said.'

'Yes, my father installed irrigation. You see here …' Her flip-flopped foot tapped a hosepipe that was delivering a steady flow of water to the nearby plants. 'He was very ingenious.' She glanced at the house, where chairs were set on a wooden veranda. 'It's a week since he died …'

'I'm sorry,' Patrice said. 'Do you want to show me where it happened?'

He turned to make for the house, but Kekeli tugged his arm and said, 'It's this way,' pointing into the garden.

Patrice followed her along another path, through the trees, then alongside a small river, upstream. After ten minutes they reached a clearing, beyond which a dam had been built where the river narrowed. It was a solid-looking structure some three metres high and six across. A sluice at the side channelled water down to a square brick building with a tin roof, and a gush of water exited from below.

'It's a hydroelectric plant,' Kekeli said. 'My father built it to serve all the houses in this area.' She pointed at three power lines that ran from a metal box outside the building to a pylon constructed of two wooden posts and a crossbar and then away through a gap in the trees. 'You can see that everything is in place …'

She led him to the building and they squeezed inside. A blue, box-like piece of heavy-looking metal bolted to a concrete base took up most of the floor space.

'This is what he called the powerhouse. We think he was attempting to connect the turbine here to the transformer, the box outside … He was thrown out of the door. They found him out there, on the grass.'

'Who found him?'

'Well, my aunt was with him, but … well, she … It was when they didn't come back, that's when Gladys, she's a neighbour who cares for Aunty, that's when she got worried and she came with her father, Mr Addo, and they found them …'

'Your aunt was … hurt?'

'No. They found her sitting next to my father. He was her cousin.'

'And what did she say?'

Kekeli looked away. 'She doesn't say much … she's old. So, we're guessing what happened, because my father said before, to Gladys, that he was taking Aunty up here to watch.'

'To watch?'

'To watch the inauguration, that's what he called it. The inauguration of his hydroelectric plant. He told Gladys it would make Aunty happy, but then … it went wrong.'

The sound of the water gushing into the river continued in the background. Patrice looked at the complicated pattern of wires and cables and pieces of porcelain and bits of metal. He knew nothing about electricity and baulked at the idea of constructing a power station.

'Was he an electrician?'

'My father was an engineer, but he went into politics and later became a developer; he bought this land and built houses on it. He knew about all aspects of building.' Kekeli stepped outside.

Patrice followed and found her contemplating the dam. 'My boss said you didn't think it was an accident.'

'My father was being threatened. By people who want this land. They told him he had a choice: to accept their offer of compensation or to fight them, in which case he would lose.

21

That's what they said to him. He was determined to fight them ...'

'How was he being threatened?'

'They said they could make things difficult for him.'

'But the land was his. If he didn't want to leave, these people couldn't take it from him. Could they?'

'You know how things are. With a powerful company, they do what they want. My father said they've already bought up most of the land in the valley.'

Patrice tutted. He did know how things are. He'd come across companies like this – faceless entities, corporate machines whose default position is to crush anyone who gets in their way. 'What do they want to do with it?'

She shrugged. 'I don't know. To develop it, in a different way ... to build more houses, I suppose. It is close to Accra, so the land is worth a lot.'

'Will there be an inquest?'

'Of course not! The police are not interested. For them, the case is closed.' She looked sideways into his eyes, as if gauging his reaction. 'I'm not stupid. I know how it looks ... that he was careless. But that was not like him. If my father was rushing to finish his project, working too quickly, it was because of the pressure they were putting him under. You see? That's what caused his death.'

They set off back the way they'd come, by the side of the river, through the trees.

'Have you raised these concerns of yours with anyone else, apart from my boss?'

'No. But when she called and told me about you being an investigator, I had the idea that you could expose what this company has done.'

'Me? A journalist would be a better person to do that, and a Ghanaian one, someone who knows how things work here.'

'That will be difficult. My father had dealings in the past with the newspapers. They thought he was an old eccentric. They won't take this seriously. But if you make the investigation, people will listen. Josie Mwinga said you've won awards for your work.'

Patrice felt like a fish on a hook being slowly reeled in.

'She said you have a strong sense of justice.'

'Oh, did she?'

'Your boss was a friend of my father's. I met her once. She's forthright. I liked her. I trust her.'

They reached the house. Kekeli turned and looked at Patrice, from one eye to the other. Her own were moist.

'I know you don't know us, but I believe you are our last hope. If you can't help, we will lose this land, we will lose my father's legacy. And Aunty … she's confused, this is the only place she knows.'

Patrice's gaze drifted around the house and the gardens. He asked himself why it was he got talked into these situations. But he knew the answer: the simple reason was, he couldn't walk away. 'My boss knows me too well. I can't promise anything, but I'll see what I can do.'

Kekeli took his hand in both of hers. 'Thank you, Patrice.'

'Are you and your aunt the only family?'

She kissed her teeth. 'My father's family, most of them, they disowned him.'

'Why?'

'This won't mean much to you. But if you want to know, they had a falling out over Kwame Nkrumah.'

Chapter 4

Yawor strained to hear the conversation going on by the front door. Uncle Joseph and the two policemen were speaking in low tones. She got up from the sofa and stepped into the hallway, and saw one of the policemen handing a bracelet to her uncle. It was Adzo's.

'No!' Yawor screamed, a piercing shriek. She stumbled towards them. Uncle Joseph looked at her, fear in his eyes. He held out the bracelet and she snatched it from him.

'She was run over by a car. I'm sorry, Yawor. Adzo is dead.'

She screamed again. 'No!' Her legs gave way. She fell to her knees, sobbing, clutching the bracelet. 'No! No! No! No!' she cried, banging her fists on the floorboards, over and over.

She must have fainted. When she woke, with a thud in her stomach, only Uncle Joseph and Aunt Esther were still up. They were in the front room.

'There, there, Yawor,' Aunt Esther said, her arm round her as they sat on the sofa. 'God has taken Adzo. She is in a good place. We must pray for her.'

Yawor was calm now, numbed. 'What happened, Uncle? Tell me, please.'

'It was only a few streets from here,' Uncle Joseph said, looking up from the glass in his hand. 'But the driver didn't stop. The police found her. They were passing in a patrol car, around nine o'clock, they said. She was lying in the road. Her body was still warm. They took her to the hospital, but she died on the way. They recognised our name on her bracelet.'

'Will there be an investigation?' Yawor asked, though unable to look her uncle in the eye.

He straightened his posture and brought his bushy eyebrows together. 'I will insist there is one. You know what the police are like. They can be lazy. But we will go to the top, to my friend, JWK, the commissioner. We went to school together.' He took a deep, wheezy breath. 'It has not always been easy looking after your sister, but she was a decent girl.'

Yawor bit her lip, feeling more tears coming. 'Is that a good idea? I mean, to go to the commissioner? What can he do? Adzo is gone. The police cannot bring her back.'

'The driver must be found and brought to book. Failing to report an accident is an offence. You must want justice for Adzo?'

'Yes, Uncle.' Yawor hung her head and let the tears fall into her lap. She shuddered at the prospect of an investigation into Adzo's death and the ignominy it might bring on the family who had done so much for the two orphaned sisters.

'Uncle, Aunty ...' She broke off, unable to think of any words that might prepare them. 'You have been so kind to us. I am thankful to you. I lost my parents and my brothers and now I have lost my sister, so you are all I have. Thank you, thank you ...'

Aunt Esther cuddled her some more. 'Go to bed, Yawor. Get some sleep.'

Sleep was a long time coming. The highlife band were playing at the Ambassador Hotel a few streets away, drums and electric guitars. The music made Yawor think of nights when she and Adzo had heard the same band playing and Adzo got out of bed and swirled her hips to the rhythms. 'You try, Yawor,' she said sometimes. And Yawor would have a go, clumsily and painfully twisting her body. Adzo would laugh at her, but lovingly, not like the mocking taunts Yawor used to get at school. *'Ewo ya atsia le asiwo, Sista,'* Adzo used to say. 'You have your own style.'

It was Adzo who'd helped her get through the worst times after she came home from hospital, encouraging her to stand up for herself, telling her to be proud of who she was. 'Nobody is perfect,' she said once, 'but you are clever and strong-minded, and you have smooth rosy cheeks and sparkling eyes and a shining smile – these things more than make up for one bad leg!'

As Yawor lay there in bed now, on her side, squeezing her cheeks in her hands, she couldn't imagine life without her sister. She looked at the dark square shape that was Adzo's empty bed.

'She was a decent girl …' Her uncle's words were ringing in her head. Adzo had gone off the rails, everyone knew that. But everyone knew why: she had blamed herself for what happened to their parents. Her uncle was right; Adzo wasn't a bad person, but she hadn't been able to endure the guilt.

Yawor thought back to the night, six months before, when she'd caught Adzo slipping into their room late. The household had gone to bed. Adzo had been wearing a dress that showed her knees and more. She'd made light of it, saying it was what the girls were wearing in Europe and America, the

26

latest fashion. But the way she'd tugged down on the hem as she spoke had made Yawor suspicious.

Yawor had wanted to shout at her, but she'd held back; she hadn't wanted to make Adzo feel bad about herself. So instead, all she'd said was, 'You don't have to tell me everything you do. But I'm your sister, so you know you can always trust me.'

Adzo had shrugged. 'I'm not hiding anything.'

Yawor had rolled over in her bed and turned her back on her. But Adzo had come to join her. Yawor had heard her sister sniffling.

'I'm not like you, Yawor. You are disciplined and apply yourself to your studies. But I can't do it. I'm not a good person like you. I'm lazy. I don't do this every night, just sometimes, when I need the money.'

'But we're not poor. Uncle gives us everything we need.'

'For you, maybe. I want more than you. I'm sorry, sister.'

Then it was Yawor who'd tried to hold back the tears, and her younger sister who'd been comforting her. Yawor had turned to face her. 'I won't judge you, Adzo. But what you are doing is dangerous. What if you're arrested? What if Uncle finds out?'

Adzo had smiled as if Yawor were a child. '*Mega vorn de nunye o, Sista. Matenu akpor dokuinye dzi,*' she'd said. 'You mustn't worry about me. I can take care of myself.'

That was the one and only time they'd spoken about it. Since then, when Adzo had come in late, Yawor had pretended to be asleep; she'd lost her sister and could only hope that one day she'd come back. Now she never would.

1966: JANUARY 23

The following afternoon, after a tearful morning in church and a heavy lunch of fufu and beef sauce, which the family ate in silence, Yawor sat on the front veranda looking aimlessly at the purple bougainvillea growing on the wall of Uncle Joseph's compound. People said time was the great healer, but she couldn't imagine a time when she wouldn't be feeling the pain of losing her sister. The pastor had told her, after the service, that she would always have her memories. But that was no comfort when those memories would always be painful.

She was wrestling with these sad thoughts when she heard joyful singing from the road. A dozen Young Pioneers were marching in their white shirts and shorts and green felt hats. At the front, holding the Ghanaian flag, was her sixteen-year-old cousin George, and his voice was the loudest as they belted out their song:

Nkrumah, eh, Nkrumah, show boy!
Nkrumah, eh, Nkrumah, show boy!
I want to see you, Kwame Nkrumah, show boy!
I want to see you, Kwame Nkrumah, show boy!
If you follow him, if you follow him,
Osagyefo will make you a fisher of men!

On reaching the house, they slowed to a standing march. George swivelled to face the rest, and on his signal, they stood to attention and saluted. Then they relaxed and exchanged hand-slaps before another boy took the flag, and they set off again. George stayed watching, waving them on their way.

George's enthusiasm for his country and its leader were infectious. Yawor didn't follow politics closely, but she supposed Nkrumah meant well and had Ghana's interests at heart, and sometimes she sang along to the songs. But not today.

The moment George stepped through the gate and saw her, his cheery demeanour vanished. 'What's happened, Cousin?' His eyes darted around. As if he knew, he asked, 'Where's Adzo?'

She tried to get the words out, but they wouldn't come. Her face crumpled. But she shook herself. She didn't want him to hear the news from anyone else. 'She was hit by a car last night and she died.'

They hugged each other. Yawor cried. She could feel George's chest tremble.

'Where did it happen?' he asked, stepping back, holding Yawor gently by her shoulders.

'Not far from here. The driver didn't stop. The police found her. We had been listening to the president's speech at the ceremony when they came with the news.'

'She was out … on her own? What was she doing?'

Yawor looked away. 'I don't know,' she said.

Chapter 5

'It was all to do with the 1966 coup. Something happened that tore the family apart.'

Kekeli Abotsi had made a pot of tea and they were sitting on the veranda steps at the back of her house. The garden was speckled with mid-morning sunlight filtered through the trees.

'My father didn't talk about it. He said it was all in the past, and I suppose now I'll never know the full story. Whatever it was, he and his father never spoke again.'

'It sounds dramatic,' Patrice said. 'But politics can do that.'

'Nkrumah was a divisive figure, but I'm sure it was more than a political disagreement. The family were caught up in the events themselves somehow ...'

'For me, as a young man, the memory of Kwame Nkrumah was a great inspiration: his struggle against colonial rule, being the leader of the first African country to gain independence ... You know, he was voted the greatest African of the last millennium, in a BBC radio poll, even ahead of Nelson Mandela.'

Kekeli smiled. 'You would have got on well with my father. He worshipped Nkrumah – Osagyefo, they used to call him.'

'Osagyefo?'

'From the Akan language. It means something like "Warrior Chief who saved the Nation". My father was a member of the Young Pioneers. Have you heard of them?'

Patrice shook his head.

'They were like Boy Scouts. Their purpose was to support nation-building. They sang songs and cleaned the drains and things like that. Nkrumah's opponents said they were like a young army and claimed they spied on their parents.'

Kekeli said she needed to check on her aunt and went inside the house.

Possibly because of her father's allegiance to Kwame Nkrumah, Patrice felt a connection with George Abotsi and his family and was becoming more reconciled, determined even, to help Kekeli find out what led to his death.

'It's a coincidence,' he said when she came back, 'but I had been planning to go to Nkroful today, Nkrumah's home village.'

'Huh! Like a pilgrimage?'

'In a way, I suppose. It's a starting point for some research I want to do. I'm going to apply to do a master's degree in America.'

'Oh,' Kekeli said. 'I'm sorry if I'm delaying you.' She screwed up her nose. 'But you know, there's not much to see in Nkroful. It's a small place. But while you're here, I can take you to the memorial park in Accra. Nkrumah is buried there. Have you been?'

'No, I haven't had time for sight-seeing.'

'We can go now. Then you can come back and meet our neighbour, Mr Addo, who can tell you about the trouble my father was having with the land developers. He won't be here till later anyway, and to be honest, I don't like being here all

31

the time. It makes me sad. I'll ask Gladys, his daughter, to come and sit with my aunt.'

A short while later, they were driving into Accra in Kekeli's car, an old Nissan Micra. The temperature was rising. A voice on the radio said it was 38 degrees. There was no air-conditioning, so they had the windows open. It wasn't long before they hit traffic. The going was slow. Kekeli tutted and tapped her fingers on the steering wheel. The further they drove into the city centre, the hotter it got. She turned on the fan, which was as cooling as a hair-dryer. She tutted again. Patrice saw beads of sweat forming on her forehead. He wiped his own brow.

'The heat is too much, huh?' she said. 'The rains are late. They say it's because of climate change. But you are an African man, so you are used to this.'

'I'm not complaining. I like it hot. But where I'm from in the hills of eastern Congo, it's not so heavy. The air is fresh. We can breathe there!'

'The hills of eastern Congo. It sounds romantic.'

Patrice chuckled, but sadly. 'It should be. The scenery is beautiful. Looking out over Lake Kivu, you could be in paradise. But years of conflict have taken their toll. Instead of making love, we've made war.'

'And that's why you do what you do, human rights?'

'When people are suffering ... well, we do what we can. It's not much, but it's something.'

'But you want to give it up to study?'

'I need a break. I've been needing a break for a long time ... to sort things out in my head.' He looked out of the window, at the orderly pedestrians walking up and down, at two women laughing together as they inspected shoes for sale outside a shop, at a man sweeping the courtyard in front of a restaurant: people going about their normal everyday business in peace. It was hard to explain to someone from this world how different things could be. 'It's something I've been meaning to do for a long time but haven't got around to. And what about you, Kekeli? You have a job?'

'Yes, I work in human resources in local government. They have given me time off, to deal with things.'

'That's good of them.'

They turned off a wide avenue and into a car park. Kekeli found a space in the shade of a tree, and they unstuck themselves from their seats. They were close to the ocean and there was a comforting breeze. As they were closing the doors, Kekeli got a call. She turned away to take it. From the way she squashed her hand down on the top of her head, it looked like bad news.

'I must go,' she said when she'd finished. 'That was Gladys. We've been served with an eviction notice.'

'What? *Mungu wangu*. My God.'

'You can stay here and look around. Nkrumah's tomb is in these gardens …'

'No, no. I will come with you.'

A girl with cropped hair and wearing a plain brown dress was standing in front of the open front door, a sheet of paper dangling from her fingers, as if she hadn't moved since she'd called Kekeli. But she must have done because one of Patrice's favourite smells, of onions cooking on a pan, was coming from behind her.

'Let me see this, Gladys,' Kekeli said, taking the paper. She tutted as she read.

'My father has the same letter,' the girl said.

'The Addos live that way.' Kekeli pointed beyond the house. She slapped the paper into Patrice's hand and stormed inside.

Patrice read it. All those currently residing at the house were doing so without lawful authorisation and had twenty-eight days to vacate the property, otherwise court proceedings would begin. It was signed by Albert Boateng, General Manager, Sunfall Power Company, Accra.

Kekeli re-emerged with her phone. 'All the houses here have been served with the same notice. Mr Addo says they're in a panic.'

'Who is this company, Sunfall Power?'

'It must be the people I told you about, Patrice, who were trying to get my father out. I told Mr Addo, who bought his plot from my father, that my father would never have sold him land he didn't own. Mr Addo said he knows that, but he's worried. Of course, we all are.'

'But you can prove your father was the owner; there will be documents …'

She shook her head. 'I don't know where he kept the title deeds. I haven't begun to go through his things. But now I think of it, we can go to the Lands Commission, tomorrow. They keep records of everything.'

'Okay. Good idea.'

Visibly cheered by this prospect, Kekeli invited Patrice to stay for food. They went in the house and she showed him into the front room, where there was a dining table. She left him there and returned minutes later supporting a bent-over, grey-haired woman on her arm.

'This is Aunty Yawor,' she said. 'Aunty, this is Patrice. He's from Congo. He's come to help us.'

The woman limped to the table without acknowledging Patrice, and Kekeli helped her sit. He wondered how she'd coped with the walk to the hydroelectric plant.

Gladys had made palava sauce, a mixture of tomatoes and spinach, with chicken, which she served with rice. Patrice cleaned his plate.

'Huh, Gladys, this man likes your cooking!'

Gladys, who looked about sixteen, looked down, shyly.

'It's delicious, thank you, Gladys. You must tell me how you make it. I will take the recipe back to Congo ...'

'You will cook it?' Kekeli asked. 'Or your wife?'

'No, well, I'm not married. But I have a maid who's a good cook.'

'You can cook it yourself! Palava sauce is not hard to cook. I will show you how.'

Aunty Yawor, who up until now had been silent, made a cackling sound. She had keen eyes, but they seemed to be focused on something in the middle distance and it was hard to tell if she was following the conversation or was far away in a world of her own.

Gladys chuckled and said something Patrice didn't catch.

Kekeli laughed. 'She asks me, "You want to cook for this man?" I say, "Why not?" You are helping us, so I want to help you.'

Patrice scratched his head, not sure what the joke was.

Gladys got to her feet and carried out the dishes. Kekeli followed her into the kitchen saying she could manage. The girl nodded and slipped out through the front door. Kekeli shouted after her. 'Tell your father to come, so we can talk.'

Kekeli brought out a bottle of Star. 'Come, Patrice, let's sit outside.'

They helped Aunty Yawor to her feet, and the three of them settled on the back veranda. It was evening now. Apart from the nearby plants and tree trunks glowing in the light from the house, the garden was pitch black. The air was damp and filled with the sound of insects and frogs.

'Aunty, we must tell Patrice the story behind this land, how my father came to buy it.'

The old lady looked blankly into the darkness, leaving Kekeli to tell the story on her own.

'Well, when he came here, twenty-five years ago, there were no houses. Nobody was living here. The city seemed a lot further away than it does now. And that's what attracted him.'

She took a swig from the bottle and passed it to Patrice.

'Before that, he'd been a government minister under Jerry Rawlings. He thought Rawlings was going to be like Nkrumah, but he wasn't, and my father became disillusioned and left. That's when some newspapers wrote bad things about him. They said he was stuck in the past. So, anyway, he came here, with a plan to create …'

A rustling sound in the garden interrupted the story of George Abotsi. A man's head, bearing a thick mop of grey hair, appeared from behind a bush.

'Good evening …'

'Oh, Mr Addo, good evening. Come and join us. We were telling Patrice here about how my father came to buy this land.'

The neighbour nodded to Patrice and glanced at Aunty, who was staring again into the middle distance and seemed not to have noticed his arrival. 'Thank you,' he said and took a seat.

'Would you like some beer?'

'Thank you, my dear. I need it tonight. I tell you, this business, this eviction …' He held up a piece of paper, the same as the one Kekeli had received. 'It's thrown us into a state of confusion.'

Kekeli stepped inside and returned with two more bottles of Star. 'We are all shocked, Mr Addo. Patrice is going to try and help us. He's a renowned human rights defender. He's from Congo …'

Mr Addo raised his bottle to Patrice. 'Thank you, sir,' he said. 'To your good health.' He took a long gulp and looked again at his eviction notice.

Patrice asked to see it. The wording was the same as Kekeli's, signed by the same Albert Boateng. 'Was it this Mr Boateng who delivered the notice?'

'I don't know. It was my wife they gave the notice to. There were two of them. She said they were big men who looked like boxers, but they wore smart clothes. It was actually intimidating for her. Gladys said it was the same men who came here.'

'Do you know who they are, sir, the Sunfall Power Company?'

'They are going to build a solar farm. That's what they told my wife.'

Kekeli grimaced. 'A solar farm?'

Patrice drank some beer and passed the bottle back to Kekeli. He pulled out his phone to search for the company, but the signal was poor and he couldn't connect to the internet. 'Your father didn't know that's what they wanted the land for?'

'He didn't mention it to me.'

'George would have been devastated to know that,' Mr

Addo said, swallowing another gulp of beer. 'It will destroy the valley and everything that lives here, not to mention our houses and his beloved hydro project. Solar farms have their place, in the desert, or you can build floating ones out at sea, but not here, where the land is fertile. Nothing will grow beneath the solar panels.'

They sat in silence for a while. Kekeli fetched more bottles and handed them round. 'You were one of the first people to move here after my father, weren't you, Mr Addo?'

'I was, and I knew your father long before. We studied engineering together. He bought this land from the chief, thirty acres, and built himself a house, and others, which he sold on leases at a reasonable price. He had a dream to build a village that would operate on African socialist principles – that's how he described it – where we would pool our resources, share the work and make decisions collectively.'

'Did it work?' Patrice asked.

Mr Addo looked into the garden. 'George would say it was a work in progress. Accra grew quickly and people came to buy houses here – but mostly because they wanted a convenient commute into the city, not because they wanted to take part in an experiment in communal living. George hoped the hydro-scheme, which he persuaded us all to contribute towards, would show what's possible when we work together. But … well, these days, not so many are inspired by that kind of dream.'

Aunty Yawor was nodding, as if in agreement. Patrice thought she was about to join the conversation, but her eyes were closed, and he realised it was more likely she was dreaming. 'So, the rest of the people living in the houses Kekeli's father built … they'll be happy to move?'

'As long as they're compensated financially. For George, it was different.'

Patrice said, 'It's rare for a person to remain true to their ideals throughout their life. It must have been disappointing to see that others didn't share his vision.'

Mr Addo looked at his bottle of beer. 'He was a hard-working man. And stubborn too. Some might say his idealism was his undoing. In that way, he was like his idol, Kwame Nkrumah.'

Kekeli took the empty bottles inside. Patrice turned to Mr Addo. He kept his voice low. 'When you found Kekeli's father by the dam, was there anything at all suspicious about the scene?'

'Well, of course, it was suspicious. Poor George was lying there dead. But it was clear from the burns on his hands what had happened.' Mr Addo raised his bottle to his lips and was about to take a drink when he stopped. 'What are you getting at?'

Patrice leaned closer. 'Could the powerhouse have been sabotaged?'

'My goodness,' the old man said, shaking his head. 'It's true these people are harassing us, but that would be ... I mean, I don't think things have come to that. I'm afraid George made a mistake. I was there, I saw it. He'd left the master switch on.'

Patrice nodded, but only out of politeness.

Chapter 6

1966: JANUARY 24

On Monday morning, Yawor telephoned the teacher training college in Winneba to tell them she'd lost her sister and would need time off. Then she set off with Uncle Joseph in his car, a black Austin A40. They drove first to the Ridge Hospital, where Adzo had been taken. The sunny morning was in sharp contrast to Yawor's mood.

Uncle Joseph was complaining about the state of the road. 'It's not maintained. You see how bad the surface is? And why is this? In days gone by, we would have said it's because the minister or a civil servant has pocketed the money. Now we know it's because there is no money! The country is bankrupt. You know what I think, Yawor, I've told you before, but things were better when the British were here. Things worked. The roads were good ...'

Yawor watched the steady flow of cars heading down Independence Avenue into town. She could hear her uncle but was barely listening. 'You don't have to come, Uncle. I told you I can make the identification on my own.'

'No, no. Without me, you'll be there all day. Given my standing in the community, we won't have to wait around.'

She looked out of the window. She wanted to see her sister but not with Uncle Joseph. Silently she prayed Adzo would be dressed decently. They parked in the hospital forecourt and walked through a crowd milling around the main entrance. Yawor had been here many times before, for operations on her leg and follow-up physiotherapy. The place stirred up mixed feelings – memories of physical suffering but also of happy times spent with her mother and father, who used to take it in turns to visit. Today it felt dark and solemn.

They were led down a corridor to a part of the hospital she'd never been in before. A door swung open, and they were shown through to the mortuary. The attendant pulled open a drawer. Yawor closed her eyes and prayed again. As it was, a sheet covered her sister from head to toe. The mortician pulled it back enough for them to see Adzo's face. Any make-up she'd been wearing had been cleaned off. She looked young and innocent. 'That is my sister,' she said.

She and Uncle Joseph confirmed the details. The dead woman was Mary Adzowor Abotsi; born in Ho in Volta Region on the 3rd of September 1943; for the last eight years living in Fourth Road, West Ridge, Accra; studying English at the University of Ghana, Legon. Yawor crossed her fingers behind her back.

The mortician said to wait and returned shortly with Adzo's handbag and presented it to Yawor. There wasn't much inside: a handkerchief, a small mirror and items of make-up. She looked for the lipstick, the expensive red one she'd given Adzo for her last birthday, but couldn't find it. She noticed the faded photograph of the two girls when they were young. There were streaks of dried mud over it. She dusted them off and kissed the photo. Tears rolled down her cheeks.

'This is a first-rate hospital,' Uncle Joseph said as they walked back down the corridor. 'But you know that. It was built to treat the British, and they've kept the standards as high as they can, given the circumstances. I'm sure, like they cared for you, they will care for your sister's body.'

In the reception area, they bumped into Doctor Bennett, a kindly man who was among the doctors who'd treated Yawor. It was five years since she'd seen him and his hair was turning grey. He remembered her and offered his condolences when they told him what had brought them to the hospital that morning.

'What dreadful news,' he said. 'I know how close you were to your sister.'

'Thank you, doctor. The driver didn't stop. Perhaps if he had, and sought help, she could have been saved ...'

Doctor Bennett took Yawor's hand. 'Perhaps. But you mustn't dwell on what can't be changed. Nonetheless, it's appalling. Presumably the police are investigating?'

'We're going to headquarters now,' Uncle Joseph said. 'To make sure they do. The commissioner is a personal friend of mine.'

'Well, I won't detain you. But tell me, Yawor, how is your leg? I notice you're not using your crutches ...'

Yawor looked away. 'I prefer to walk by myself.'

'I understand. Only, it would relieve the pressure on your hip, which could help later on in life.'

'That's good advice, Yawor,' Uncle Joseph said, shaking the doctor's hand. 'I've told her that myself, but she's a stubborn young woman. You see, Yawor?'

Yawor glanced at Dr Bennett and he glanced back, apologetically. 'You must do what feels best for you,' he said. 'I'm so sorry for your loss. Please let me know if there's anything I can do.'

It took five minutes to drive to police headquarters on the ring road. Uncle Joseph was waved through at the gate, and various policemen nodded or greeted him with handshakes as they walked through the building. He said he hadn't been there since JWK – as he called him – had been promoted, and he had to ask several times for directions to Commissioner Harlley's office. When they found it, they were told by the commissioner's assistant, a good-looking young sergeant, to sit with him in the ante-room and wait. They had to wait a long time. Maybe, Yawor thought, Uncle Joseph's standing in the community wasn't as high as he liked to think.

The sergeant was busy with paperwork. Yawor noticed sharp creases form at the top of his nose, between his eyebrows, as he concentrated on his job. When he looked up and caught her eye, she blushed and looked away. Eventually, she and her uncle were shown through and welcomed by a stern-looking man with glasses and thin lips.

'*Ei, Ei, Joseph Abotsi. Edzidzi looo* ... It's been a long time.' His greeting was more of a statement than a welcome.

'*Eeeeh! JWK, Amega Polisi Kormishina,* Mr Commissioner of Police! *Edzidzi ntor looo*. A very long time.'

Yawor was surprised to hear her uncle speaking Ewe because at home he insisted that everyone spoke in English. The two men shook hands and Uncle Joseph introduced Yawor. The police chief acknowledged her with a stiff nod of his head. It was a large room, with maps on the walls, a desk at one end, stacked high with papers, and low chairs round a low table at the other. Commissioner Harlley gestured to these and invited them to sit. As they did, Yawor noticed the policeman glance at his watch and then the door.

Uncle Joseph seemed oblivious and complimented his old friend on his promotion two years previously. 'You are doing a fine job, JWK, sir! People say all the time what a good job you are doing in difficult circumstances.'

'It's not easy, I admit.' Even if he was in a hurry to get them out, Harlley spoke slowly. 'Since the restructuring, many of our powers have been transferred to the National Security Service. Our men cannot carry arms. Even Special Branch has been transferred to Flagstaff House, under an appointee of the president … so yes, it is difficult, but we do what we can.'

The police commissioner looked at his watch again; again, Uncle Joseph didn't take the hint.

'You are fighting the criminals with one hand tied behind your back. I hear stories in my court every day, but like you say, you do what you can.'

'And what is it that we can do for you today, Abotsi?'

'Thank you … sir. It's a terrible business. Yawor's sister, Adzowor, is the reason we are here. She was knocked down by a car on Saturday night, close to where we live. Two of your officers found her and came to our house to tell us. She was killed.'

Harlley shook his head. 'I'm sorry.' He was speaking to Uncle Joseph rather than to Yawor.

'But the worst of it is the driver didn't stop. The car had vanished. Your officers … I'm sure they are good men; they didn't ask me for anything … they said it was an accident. Well, of course, I'm sure it was an accident. But the driver should have stopped. So that is why we have come: to make sure, to ask you to make sure, there is a full investigation to find this driver.'

There were two taps on the door. 'Yes ...'

The young sergeant poked his head round. 'The visitor you've been waiting for is here, sir.'

'Please excuse me, Abotsi, I have meetings to attend. But leave this with me. I will set inquiries in motion.' The commissioner rose and beckoned his visitors to the door. 'This is Sergeant Ofori. Sergeant, Mr Abotsi's niece, this young woman's sister, was the victim of a fatal hit-and-run. Take down the details.'

Yawor looked the sergeant in the eye this time. He responded professionally, with a respectful nod.

'Thank you, sir.' Uncle Joseph bowed his head and shook the commissioner's hand again. 'I know you are a busy man. For Adzowor's sake, I thank you. You know, it's strange that our paths have not crossed since you took up your new post, considering we both work in the deliverance of justice ...'

'Yes, yes, it is. But I will keep you informed ... you can rely on me. I will follow this up personally.'

Yawor and Uncle Joseph were shown out. Waiting to see the police commissioner next was a soldier.

'Kwashie!' Uncle Joseph said. *'Oooh, Mawu ... Gododo kae nye sia?* Good heavens! Isn't this a coincidence?'

'Abotsi!' the man replied as they shook hands.

'This is my niece, Yawor. Yawor, this is Captain Francis Kwashie.'

The soldier nodded at Yawor. He was a short, plump man, and sweating a lot.

'Kwashie is another alumnus of the Presbyterian school in Anloga, though as you can see from his youthful looks, he was a few years behind me. Well, I heard you're at the military hospital?'

'Yes, I'm the Secretary … And you? Well, I know, you're a judge. But … but what brings you here?' The captain had a chirpy manner. But the way he kept glancing at the door to the commissioner's office gave Yawor the impression he didn't want to stay chatting for long.

'A personal matter … yes, I don't come here often. And you?'

Captain Kwashie hesitated, staring at Uncle Joseph. 'Meetings!' he said eventually, with a wide grin. 'Always meetings, many meetings! Please excuse me. It's good to see you, Abotsi, and to meet you, Miss Yawor.' And with that, the plump little man saluted and slipped through the door, closing it behind him.

Yawor and Uncle Joseph sat by the young sergeant's desk and gave him Adzo's personal details and told him what they knew about what happened: where and when she'd been run over and where her body was now.

The sergeant scanned his notes, tapping his pencil on the paper as he did. 'Thank you,' he said. 'What was she wearing?'

Yawor's eyes darted around the room. Momentarily lost for words, she could feel Uncle Joseph throw her an impatient glance. 'Why do you want to know that?' she asked.

'So that we can make an appeal for witnesses.'

'A dress,' Yawor said glumly. 'I think she was wearing a dress.'

'Colour?'

'I don't know … I didn't see her leave the house.'

'Don't worry,' the sergeant said. 'I will ask the policemen who found her.'

Chapter 7

Patrice stayed over at Kekeli's house in a musty spare room. In the morning, they drove back into Accra, into the crawling traffic and the rising city heat, and to the offices of the Lands Commission in a district known as Cantonments. They pulled into a large walled compound where the single-storey, tin-roofed colonial buildings were shaded by withered old trees and dusty palms.

Kekeli waved to a young man carrying bundles of files and asked for the office that dealt with title deeds. He directed them along a covered walkway to a door which opened into a hot and stuffy reception area. A stern-looking woman with pulled-back hair sat behind a counter.

'Good morning, madam,' Kekeli said. 'I need a copy of the title deeds to my father's land. He has died recently and I don't know where he kept them.'

'Where is your father's property?'

'By the Dodowa road. It's thirty acres, an area known now as River Valley. He bought the land twenty-five years ago from the Agyeman family.'

'I will need your father's details and your own, and some identification,' the woman said, pushing a form over the counter.

Kekeli filled it in and passed it back with her driving licence.

The woman told them to take a seat and disappeared behind a smoked-glass partition. Patrice glimpsed an open-plan office with wooden desks buried under piles of papers, and walls lined with filing cabinets.

Kekeli pulled out her phone and started playing a game. Patrice went to wait outside, where there was air to breathe. He wasn't there long before she called him back. The woman with pulled-back hair had returned with a perplexed expression.

'Miss Abotsi, I'm sorry to have kept you waiting. I have located the title deeds, but I am afraid I cannot make you a copy.'

'But I need it. We're being threatened with eviction.'

'I'm sorry. The records show this land is not owned by your father.'

'What? Who owns it, if not my father?'

'For that information, you must make a request in writing to the Director of the Lands Registration Division.'

'This is impossible. My father would have told me.'

The woman glanced back into the office. 'I'm sorry.'

'But … but … I don't understand.'

Patrice glared at the woman with pulled-back hair. She tilted her face to the side. Whether she was in on something, or simply being an obedient civil servant, she knew something wasn't right. Patrice resisted an urge to walk round the desk and shake her by the shoulders until the truth came out. Instead, he took Kekeli's arm and led her out of the office and back to the car.

Kekeli muttered a curse but was otherwise silent as she drove the short distance to Patrice's hotel in Oxford Street, in the busy commercial district of Osu. He looked out of the window, trying to figure out what was going on at the Lands Commission, and what to do about it.

He invited her to come in for a drink. They went onto the terrace bar and he ordered two beers. She took a few sips and it seemed to calm her. He did the same and it worked for him too.

'My father would have rather died than give up his land,' she said eventually, staring at the slow-moving traffic below. 'And now he is dead and his land has been ... what? Sold? Stolen?'

Patrice nodded and drank more of his beer. 'We'll sort this out. First, we must find out what exactly has happened.'

'But how? Writing to the Director of the Lands ... how long will that take to get a response?'

'No, no. We must see for ourselves the title deeds they have at that office. We'll go back.'

'But you heard the woman. She will tell us the same ...'

'She won't be there – if we go tonight.'

'What?'

Patrice put a finger to his lips. 'You know, sometimes, when you're dealing with situations like this, you must adapt. It's like a game. If your opponent is not playing by the rules, if they are playing dirty, then maybe you play dirty too. Otherwise, they will beat you, for sure.'

'We're going to break in?'

'Not us,' he said. 'Me. It won't be difficult. The perimeter wall is not so high. The trees will offer cover from the streetlamps. And with the air conditioning not working, there's likely to be an open window.'

She put her hand on his arm. 'I can't let you do this,' she

said, though the way she said it, it didn't sound like she was opposed to the idea.

'Well, you can't stop me, either. Besides, what is the alternative?'

'I know … But what if you get caught?'

He shrugged. 'That place is not well protected.'

'There was a guardhouse.'

'A sleepy night-watchman … You stay outside in your car and keep a lookout.'

'Okay,' she said, slowly breaking into a smile. 'Thank you, Patrice. But promise me you'll be careful. I don't want you getting arrested on my account.'

'Here's to being careful,' he said, smiling back.

He held up his bottle and she clinked hers against it.

That afternoon, with time to kill, they returned to the Kwame Nkrumah Memorial Park to resume the visit they'd abandoned the day before.

'It's the least I can do for you,' Kekeli said when Patrice told her she didn't have to come. 'You are helping me, so I want to help you,' she added, and laughed.

She parked in the same shaded spot, and they strolled through the gardens, enjoying the fountains and the trees and the breeze off the ocean, before entering the pyramid-shaped, marble-clad mausoleum, where they stood before the tombs of Kwame Nkrumah and his wife, Fathia.

It was strange, Patrice thought; he and Kekeli had only known each other a day, yet here she was, acting as his personal tour guide, and that night he was going to break into a government office for her. Somehow, circumstances were drawing them together.

'Come this way ...' She pulled his arm. 'There's a museum which I think you'll find interesting and where it's cool.'

She led him down a slope to a single-storey building. Inside, in a square hall, a group of schoolchildren were being addressed by their teacher, a serious-looking young man with thick-rimmed glasses.

'... Kwame Nkrumah was Ghana's founding father and its most famous son. He was famous all around the world. Here you see important artefacts associated with his life including, over there, the smock he was wearing on the night he declared Ghana's independence, at midnight on March 6th, 1957. Nkrumah ruled Ghana until he was deposed in a military and police coup d'état on February 24th, 1966 ...'

Patrice and Kekeli, and the schoolchildren, walked around the exhibits. Patrice found himself captivated by a series of photographs showing Nkrumah with the world leaders of the time: Kennedy, Krushchev, Mao, Nehru, Tito, Castro, the Pope, the United Nations Secretary General; there was even one of him dancing with the Queen of England, the country against which he'd led the struggle for Ghana's independence. But the picture he looked at most was one, faded and blurred, of Nkrumah sitting with Patrice Lumumba, independent Congo's first Prime Minister.

'I'm named after this man,' he said to Kekeli. 'Seeing these two great men together ... it gives me, I don't how to say it in English, *chaire de poule*, chicken skin?'

'Goose bumps.' Kekeli smiled and patted his shoulder.

'They shared a dream for Africa, for us, to make things better – for Africa to stand on its own two feet. Of course, the Western countries had their own idea about what should happen in Africa. You know, the CIA wanted to kill Lumumba.

They had a plan to put poison on his toothpaste! He was overthrown anyway, and killed …'

'My father said he knew for a fact that the Americans supported the coup against Nkrumah, though I don't know how he knew that.'

They were about to move on when Kekeli said, 'Wait. Look at this photo. It will send a shiver down your spine. Nkrumah's at the airport, about to depart on a peace mission to Vietnam, and these men who are there to see him off are some of those who, days later, led the coup against him, while he was away. The one he's shaking hands with is the commissioner of police, JWK Harlley.'

Patrice studied the men in their high-peaked caps, and uniforms decorated with medals and ribbons. Their stony faces hid their intentions well.

'You see behind them, the children in the white shirts and shorts?' Kekeli pointed at a group sitting among the crowd in the background. 'They're the Young Pioneers. My father could even be there!'

They left the photographs and headed out into the white light of the afternoon. Kekeli stepped aside to call Gladys to check on her aunt. Patrice went to look at a decapitated statue of Kwame Nkrumah – vandalised, according to the inscription, during the coup.

'You know what they say?'

He turned to see the teacher who'd been in the museum. 'What do they say?'

'You don't know what you've got till it's gone. Look at the people we have now. For all his faults, this man was a true leader.'

Patrice studied Nkrumah's face, stained green, the eyes

staring unflinchingly forward. His body, with his right arm raised, stood next to it. 'But his ideas are not so popular now.'

'No,' the teacher said. 'They are out of fashion.'

It was after midnight when they returned to the Lands Commission. Kekeli parked her Nissan Micra past the long-closed entrance to the compound. She pushed a piece of paper into Patrice's hand.

'This is the Land Certificate number to look for. I called Mr Addo. It's what's written on his lease.'

Patrice looked down. 'Good. This gives me something to aim for.'

They walked down the road, away from the entrance, and found a dark corner where some wooden pallets had been stacked against the wall. Patrice climbed onto them, then onto the top of the wall. 'See you later,' he said.

'I'll wait for you in my car.'

He lowered himself to the ground on the other side and checked his bearings. The office building they'd been in earlier was close by. Keeping to the outside wall, he walked further round, away from the guardhouse by the entrance gate, until the office building was between him and the guardhouse. He stepped out from his cover into an open courtyard. Halfway across, he heard a voice. A torchlight flashed on the ground, to the side of the building. It was coming his way.

'... I don't like watching Chelsea. Since Drogba went, they are not the same team for me ...'

It was the night-watchman, not so sleepy, talking on his phone. If Patrice went back to the perimeter wall, he'd be seen. He turned into a shadow and crouched. The torchlight swung round the corner – any further and it would be shining in his face.

'...Arsenal! Ha, ha, ha! They cannot win the title. They lack the players and the mentality...

The night-watchman's torch swung the other way, and his footsteps and football chatter followed.

Patrice got to his feet. He'd been wrong about the night-watchman, but he was right about the windows. One was wide open. He climbed through and found himself in the back office, the room full of wooden desks and walls lined with filing cabinets.

The woman's blurry silhouette had moved to the right-hand side of the room when she'd gone through the door, so that's where he headed. There were a dozen cabinets along the wall, each four drawers high. He pulled them open, one by one. With the light from his phone, he flipped through the file headings, his eyes glazing over phrases such as *Cost Selection*, *Land Sector Agency*, *Spacial Data Infrastructure*. He looked for a reference number similar to Mr Addo's, but there was nothing to show he was in the right area.

He looked around the office, at the filing cabinets and the tables with papers piled high. It would take all night to search the whole room. But he recognised a piece of paper on the top of one cabinet: it was the form Kekeli had filled out earlier. He went through the drawers below. In the third one down, he found the file labelled *River Valley, Dodowa road*.

Kneeling on the floor, he worked his way through the contents. The title deeds stated the land Kekeli thought belonged to her father was registered in the name of Sunfall Power Company. There was a plan of the area, outlining the boundaries. The date on the document was from the week before; in fact, it was the day after George Abotsi died. There was no record of him ever having owned the land, nor of him building houses on it.

Patrice took photos, put the file back, and left by the same window. With no sign of the football-loving night-watchman, he climbed back over the wall. Kekeli was waiting for him in her Nissan.

'Well?' she asked expectantly as he got in.

He brought up the photos on his phone. 'It's not good, Kekeli.'

She scrolled through them. 'They've tampered with the records,' she said. 'They've paid someone to do it.'

Patrice nodded. 'It looks that way.'

Kekeli's head dropped.

He lifted her chin. 'You must find the original title deeds, your father's. I will find out more about this company, Sunfall Power.'

Her eyes were welling up.

'Don't give up, Kekeli. We can stop them.'

Chapter 8

The week passed with no word on the police investigation into Adzo's death.

'JWK's a busy man, Yawor,' Uncle Joseph said as he was leaving for work on Friday. 'But he's a man who keeps his word. We must be patient.'

Yawor had seen how distracted the police commissioner was when they'd met him. For all she and her uncle knew, he'd told the young sergeant to drop the case as soon as they'd left his office. Maybe that would be for the best. Adzo could rest in peace. But something kept nagging at Yawor.

In the afternoon, when her cousin George came home from school, she suggested they go to the street where Adzo had been run over.

'Really, Cousin? Are you sure you want to go there?'

'It will help. I don't like this waiting – leaving everything to others. I feel like I'm abandoning my sister.'

He took her hands in his. 'I understand. Let's go.'

They walked down Fourth Road. As they turned onto Independence Avenue, they passed a woman with two young children sitting by the roadside, all dressed in rags.

A girl held out her hand and said, 'I'm hungry.'

Yawor reached for a coin to give her, but the woman shouted to the girl, 'Don't touch her! She is cursed.'

'What did you say?' George stepped forward angrily. 'She wants to help you.'

The woman yelled some abuse. She got to her feet and pulled her children away down the road.

He shouted after her, 'Stupid woman!'

Yawor sighed. 'Don't mind her. She doesn't know what she's saying.'

He stood there, hands on hips, tutting. 'I know,' he said.

George was a handsome boy, with almond-shaped eyes and prominent cheekbones. He was tall, like his father, but yet to fill out his frame; a boy in a man's body. Yawor had always had a soft spot for him. As he'd grown older and more aware of her disability, he'd become protective of his older cousin, sometimes over-protective. But she was thankful for his support, especially now Adzo was gone.

He held his arm out for her, and they carried on up Independence Avenue, past the junction with Castle Road, until they reached Ninth Road.

'This is the turning,' Yawor said.

It was a quiet residential road, like their own, with the houses set back behind white walls. They walked down it slowly, looking for clues, but there was nothing to indicate where Adzo had fallen.

Yawor asked George to pick a scarlet flower for her from a tree, and she laid it on the grass verge and said a prayer. 'We miss you, Sister.'

By the time they reached home, Uncle Joseph had returned from his day at the law courts. His friend Austin was visiting.

He worked at the foreign ministry, and once or twice a week he dropped by for an early evening drink. They were sitting on the veranda. Uncle Joseph was complimenting his friend on the whisky he'd brought round.

'I tell you, and I'm not exaggerating, you've saved my life. Another evening spent drinking palm wine would have killed me!' They clinked glasses.

Yawor went onto the veranda and sewed buttons on a dress she'd made for her seven-year-old cousin, Anne, who came to sit by her feet, holding the buttons and passing them to her. George was inside, in the front room, doing homework.

A highlife music programme from Voice of America was playing on Uncle Joseph's radio. The two men sipped their whisky and tapped their fingers to a song, *Nsuo beto a, nframa dzi kan*. The words were in Twi, but everyone, including Yawor, knew the meaning ...

Before it starts raining,
The wind will blow.
I told you, but you did not listen.
Before trouble starts,
There is a waving flag.
I warned you, but you did not listen.

'Remember this one?' Uncle Joseph asked, winking mischievously at his friend. 'They don't play it on Radio Ghana these days, which is a pity. It's a catchy one. I like it very much.'

Through the window, Yawor noticed Aunt Esther go to the radio and lower the volume.

'I heard some news today, Joseph, in the office.' Austin leaned forward and lowered his voice. 'They're saying our ambassador in Peking will be going to Hanoi in the coming days to make arrangements for Nkrumah to visit.' The visitor smiled at his host in a way that showed he knew this news would amuse him.

'Ah, wonderful!' Uncle Joseph declared, holding his arms out wide. 'Not content with saving Ghana and Africa, the great Osagyefo is now going to end the Vietnam war!'

The two men sniggered.

'They say President Johnson has assured Nkrumah he won't be dropping any bombs on Hanoi, so it's safe for him to go.'

Uncle Joseph glanced inside, then added, in a whisper, 'What a shame!'

Yawor looked to see if George was listening. If he was, he wasn't reacting.

Austin put his finger to his lips. 'You should know, Joseph, and I have this on authority, there are people in Flagstaff House who are reading more into President Johnson's comment; they see plotting everywhere and they think the Americans would like Nkrumah to leave Ghana for a while, because, you know, when the cat's away ...'

The man was speaking softly and Yawor had to strain to hear him. She could see Uncle Joseph was hanging on his every word.

It was later in the evening, after Austin had gone home and Yawor was sitting in the front room with her aunt and uncle and cousin George, that there was a knock on the door and Emmanuel, the houseboy, announced that Police Commissioner Harlley was there.

Uncle Joseph jumped to his feet. 'You see, Yawor? I told you JWK would not let us down. He has come himself to our house. Show him through, Emmanuel, show him through.'

The others stood to welcome the important visitor.

Harlley appeared in the doorway in full uniform, holding a high-peaked cap in his hands, accompanied by the young sergeant from his office. 'Good evening, Abotsi.'

Uncle Joseph rushed to shake his hand. 'Thank you, sir, thank you. Good evening. This is my family: my wife Esther and my son George, and Yawor, who you know …'

The police commissioner nodded silently at the others in the room before turning abruptly to Uncle Joseph. 'It might be better if we talk alone.'

'Alone? You have news for us? Please, sir, if you have news, you must share it with us all; Adzowor was part of our family. But first, take a seat. Would you like a whisky?'

'No, thank you. I cannot stay long.' Harlley paused, awkwardly, before continuing. 'And very well, if you want me to address the whole family, I will. I appreciate this concerns you all.'

The man's reticence was making Yawor nervous. She turned to Sergeant Ofori for a hint of what was to come, but he was staring at the floor.

The commissioner continued: 'I wanted to bring you the results of the investigation personally. It is a … delicate issue.' Yawor was biting her lower lip. 'We have not as yet found out who was driving the car that ran down your niece. But it appears to us that it was likely someone she was seeking to do business with.'

'Business?' Uncle Joseph screwed up his face and looked around the room. 'What kind of business?'

Harlley threw the briefest of glances at Yawor before turning back to Uncle Joseph. 'I'm sorry, Abotsi …'

'What is it? What are you saying?'

'I'm sorry, Abotsi, there's no other way to put it. Your niece was working as a prostitute.'

The word hung there in the warm evening air. It was as if a grenade had been thrown into the room. Yawor waited for it to explode.

Aunt Esther whimpered, then broke into a sobbing groan. 'No, no, no,' she blubbered, '*Matenu aanye nyatepe o!* It can't be true!'

Yawor stepped across and helped her aunt sit down. George sat too. He looked dazed.

Uncle Joseph was shaking his head. 'It's not possible,' he said. 'Adzo was at college. She was studying English ...'

The police commissioner turned to his assistant. 'Sergeant, tell the family what you found out.'

The sergeant looked at Yawor, raising his eyebrows sympathetically. 'We spoke to the officers who found the young lady, Adzowor Abotsi, and made inquiries at the mortuary. We learned that the night she died, she had been wearing a short dress ...' He glanced at Yawor. 'By that I mean a dress shorter than girls in Accra usually wear. Because of this we made inquiries at hotels and other places where *ashawo* ... where young women do business at night. The owner of a bar by Makola Market recognised her from a photograph we took at the mortuary and confirmed he had seen her walking on the street there.'

'How can this be?' The tone of Uncle Joseph's voice was turning from astonishment to anger. 'So, this is what she was doing! This is why she was not here in the evenings, why she was not coming home till late.' Yawor's head dropped, but she could feel her uncle's gaze. 'You knew, Yawor? You knew what your sister was doing?'

Yawor could hold it back no longer. Like a bursting dam, the tears spilled out. 'I'm sorry, Uncle, I'm sorry. I should have told you and Aunty, but I didn't want to hurt you ...'

'Hurt us! Are we not hurting now? If you had told us, we could have stopped this behaviour. Now look, your sister's dead.'

'Stop it, Papa!' George screamed. 'You cannot blame Yawor.'

Uncle Joseph glared at his son.

The room was stunned into silence.

Yawor and Aunt Esther sniffed and wiped their tears.

Police Commissioner Harlley addressed himself again to Uncle Joseph. 'We understand this is difficult for the family. As I said, for the time being, we do not know the full circumstances of your niece's death. But from what we have discovered so far, we are working on the assumption that it was an accident; that your niece stepped into the road seeking to gain the attention of the driver and was knocked down. We believe the driver panicked, not wanting to be associated with such a woman, and drove off.'

He looked around, as if seeking agreement. 'Of course, we can carry on this investigation. But ... and this is why I wanted to speak to you first, Abotsi, to ask if this is what you wish us to do. Were we to continue and to find the culprit, then the matter would necessarily come to court and the circumstances would become known publicly and, well, given your position and the scandal, this might be something you would rather avoid.'

'What?' Yawor looked from the commissioner to her uncle and back again. Before, she'd been the one afraid of the truth. Now it was there in the open, she saw it differently. 'A crime has been committed,' she said. 'My sister may have made mistakes, but that doesn't mean she doesn't deserve justice.' She looked to the young sergeant, appealing for support. His lips were pursed as he looked from Yawor to her uncle.

Uncle Joseph was running his hand through his hair. 'Not everything is always black and white, Yawor. Adzo has brought shame on this house and this family. But I will not let her be our complete ruin. For that is what it would be if it came out that a niece of mine who was living in my house was a prostitute. I'm a district court judge. I would be forced to resign and we would be disgraced. Is that what you want?'

Yawor hung her head and stared at the floor. She'd said her piece. She couldn't argue further with her uncle. He was in a difficult position, and it was partly because of her. But she couldn't help thinking it was the presence there of the commissioner of police that caused Uncle Joseph the most shame. Aunt Esther was sobbing quietly again. Yawor comforted her with an arm round her shoulders.

'In that case,' Harlley said, for once addressing Yawor, 'we will take the matter no further.'

'Thank you, sir,' Uncle Joseph said. 'Thank you for your discretion.' He showed the two policemen out.

Yawor quietly kissed her teeth.

Chapter 9

Glass-panelled office blocks, construction sites, billboards and signs for banks and phone businesses and restaurants, orderly early morning traffic … Patrice looked down from his second-storey hotel room while he waited for his laptop to fire up. Compared to this modern city, his home town, Bukavu, far away on the shores of Lake Kivu, was like a village backwater.

Even in this modern city, though, the hotel Wi-Fi was erratic. But for now it was working, and he caught up with the international news. The top story was about an attack by Islamist militants in Abidjan, Côte d'Ivoire, next door to Ghana:

Gunmen from al-Qaeda's North African branch have killed at least 16 people, including four Europeans, after they opened fire near several hotels. The shooting came amid fears the jihadi threat is spreading in West Africa …

Patrice read the report through. Only two months before, there'd been a similar event in Burkina Faso, another of Ghana's neighbours. Islamist militancy, it occurred to him, was one thing his country had been spared.

He searched for "Sunfall Power Company". The only reference to Sunfall was a music festival in London. He typed "Sunfall Ghana". Top of the list was a woman selling Ghanaian food at the Sunfall music festival. He tried "Sunfall Power Ghana", which brought up news reports of shortfalls in Ghana's electricity supply and links to one or two solar energy projects in Ghana – but no mention of Sunfall.

An article in the London *Financial Times* about investment opportunities in green energy projects in Ghana caught his eye. A conference of so-called stakeholders in solar power was opening in Accra. It sounded like a good place to get background and ask questions about the Sunfall Power Company, provided he could get in.

He rang his boss. She knew everyone in Accra. It turned out she'd just been speaking to someone who might help. 'He's the son of a friend of mine,' she said. 'Very clued in. He works for the government's electricity regulator, or something like that. He called me to say he'd heard about George Abotsi's death, which was sweet of him.' She said his name was Kwaku Sarpong, and she'd call him back.

Patrice read more about investment in Ghana's renewable energy sector and came across the website of a government agency called the Ghana Investment Promotion Centre. In a section on energy, there was a photograph of a solar farm and the promise of "strategic investment opportunities for power providers to augment Ghana's electricity generation". Out of curiosity, he typed "Congo investment" and was surprised to learn his own country also had a National Agency for the Promotion of Investments. It described Congo as "a land of many potentials and investment opportunities". As far as he was aware, his country's potential had largely been squandered.

He was getting sidetracked. He typed in the name Albert

Boateng, but a message appeared saying he was not connected to the internet. The Wi-Fi was down, again. He was about to call reception to complain, again, but they called him first.

'There's a visitor here for you, sir.'

He went downstairs. A man in his forties with short hair, a trimmed goatee beard, and glasses greeted him with a warm grin.

'Patrice Le Congo? Kwaku Sarpong. Nice to meet you.' He held out his hand.

'That was quick!' Patrice took it and they shook the Ghanaian way.

'Josie called and I was in the area. I hope you don't mind I didn't call you first.'

'Not at all. Thank you for coming.'

'It's my pleasure. A friend of Josie Mwinga is a friend of mine.'

Patrice chuckled. 'She tells me I'm her friend, but really she's my boss. She's always telling me what to do.'

'She tells everyone what to do! But I'm happy to help. I was thinking of attending the solar conference anyway. So if you're ready, we can go.'

Sarpong was of medium build, similar to Patrice, only slimmer. It looked like he worked on keeping himself in shape. He was wearing a sharp, charcoal-grey suit with a perfectly knotted crimson tie. Patrice was in his sandals and jeans. As they walked down the steps to street level, Sarpong swapped his glasses for shades and unlocked the doors of a gleaming Mercedes. The car matched the colour of his tie perfectly. He reversed into the middle of the street and pushed a banknote into the hand of a boy who'd held up the traffic for him. Then they set off.

'Thank you again for this,' Patrice said. 'Madam ... Josie ... said you know everything that's going on ...'

'I wouldn't say that. But as I said, I'm happy to help you any way I can.'

'And you knew George Abotsi?'

'Yes, I knew him. Well, we met once or twice at events. I couldn't believe it when I heard he'd died. Josie told me what you'd found out, about these people wanting his land ... it's mysterious. But what is it exactly you do, Patrice? I know you work for Josie but ...'

'I'm an investigator for the African Union's Human Rights Commission. That's my job. What I'm doing now is not work – it's a personal favour for Josie Mwinga. And how about you? She said you work for the government?'

Sarpong cast a sideways look at Patrice and grinned. 'Really, I work for myself. I work for the government and for lots of other people. I'm a freelance consultant. But one of my clients is the Energy Commission – that's a statutory body that regulates the energy sector in Ghana. They ask me to help them check out proposals for new power projects and things like that.'

'Through your work, then, maybe you've heard of the Sunfall Power Company?'

Sarpong glanced at his rear-view mirror. 'No, no I haven't. Josie mentioned the name to me. It must be a new one.'

He turned off the main road and weaved his car silently through residential backstreets, turning left, right, left again, and right again.

'You know these streets like a taxi driver.'

'If you don't, you'll spend all day in your car. But even this way you get caught at the junctions, because everyone knows these short cuts. But don't worry, we won't be late, we've got plenty of time …'

No sooner had he said this than they came up behind another queue of traffic. He did a three-point turn and turned into another side street. A few minutes later, he pulled out onto a wide avenue by the ocean. Here the traffic was light.

Patrice looked at the white waves rolling in. 'Tell me more about this conference. What's the purpose?'

'It's basically a business networking event. Ghana is trying hard to attract private investment into the energy sector. Demand for electricity is growing at ten to fifteen percent a year and the government is looking for a billion dollars of private investment in renewables such as solar, hydro and wind.'

'I thought the Akosombo Dam provided Ghana with all the electricity it needs?'

'Not any more. But you've heard of Akosombo?'

'I've seen it too, when I was flying in. It's a famous project.'

'Well, yes, it is. But it can't cope with the growing demand, especially with unreliable rainfall. That's why the government has to develop other energy sources. So, this conference is one of many that brings together public authorities looking for new electricity supplies with private companies who can provide them. Anyway, you'll soon see. We're nearly there. This area is called Labadi … there's a beach which turns into a party at weekends, and big hotels.' He nodded at a group of buildings among some palm trees up ahead.

Patrice said, 'I was reading about the attacks near the hotels in Abidjan. Could that happen here?'

'Hey! I hope not.' Sarpong stroked his beard. 'I mean, I guess it's worrying, because this Islamist thing used to be confined to northern Nigeria and now it looks like it could be spreading. But Ghana is a peaceful country. I don't think they'd target us here.'

They left the crimson Mercedes to gleam some more in the car park of La Palm Royal Beach Hotel. They went into a bland-looking block to the side and up two flights of escalators to a landing where groups of mostly men, in suits, were standing and chatting at high round tables, with biscuits and cups of coffee. Along one wall were tables where people with name badges and smiles were handing out glossy brochures. Patrice picked a few at random: one from a Chinese company making solar panels; one from a finance institution promising "A Guarantee for African Growth"; another from a company producing inverters, whatever they were; and one from Germany's Federal Ministry of Economic Affairs and Energy entitled "Making a success of the energy transition – On the road to a secure and affordable energy supply".

Sarpong was talking to a white woman sitting by a table and rows of name badges. He saw Patrice and screwed up his face.

Patrice walked over. 'Is there a problem?'

'I'm sorry, Patrice. They won't let you in.'

'Because I'm not wearing a suit?'

Sarpong grinned. 'No, because you haven't got a ticket.'

'Well, I can buy one, I don't mind ...' He fished out his wallet and started counting out cedis.

Sarpong pulled him to one side. 'You'll need a lot of those.'

'Why? How much are the tickets?'

'Two thousand dollars.'

'*Mungu wangu!*' Patrice stopped counting.

'I'm sorry, I didn't think. I get a pass because of my work with the Energy Commission.'

Patrice looked around. 'These people are all paying two thousand dollars? It must be a good conference.'

Sarpong laughed. 'For the big businesses here, two thousand dollars is small change. For the smaller ones, it's a gamble; if they strike a deal, it'll pay off. But don't worry, a lot of the formal sessions will be technical –you'd be bored stiff. And we can still talk to people out here in the lobby and you'll get a good feel for the renewables market.'

'Hello there!' A man was tapping Sarpong on the shoulder. 'How are things, Kwaku?' It was a white man with greying hair and a South African accent.

'Well, hello, Victor, nice to see you. Things are fine. This is Patrice Le Congo; he's interested in off-grid solutions for some projects he's working on in the DRC. This is Victor Pollock, Africa sales manager for Telstar Solar, a South African photovoltaic panel producer. How's business, Victor?'

The man lowered his voice. 'Seriously, Kwaku, I don't mind telling you, things are tough. The big boys are putting the squeeze on us smaller fellows. It's hard to compete with the Chinese guys, you know.' He nodded discreetly at the brochures in Patrice's hand, the top one of which was the Chinese company's. 'But we're trying. West Africa is a good market for us. The people here trust us to deliver and to follow up. But excuse me, we can talk more later …' With a quick shake of Patrice's hand and a pat on Sarpong's shoulder, he was off to pin down another delegate.

'How's it going?' A sweaty man stuck out a sweaty hand. From the way he shook Patrice's, it was clear he was Ghanaian. 'Ebenezer's my name. I own a panel installation company.

We call it Solar Deity.' He thrust a business card into Patrice's hand. 'We are here in Accra for five years. I trained in the UK. We can handle any job. And you are?'

'Patrice. I'm from Congo. Can you come there to install solar panels?'

The man looked confused, then bust out laughing and slapped Patrice's hand. 'One day, maybe. Give me time! But please introduce me to your friend. I know he is a big man – he can help me.'

Patrice did as requested and listened as Ebenezer asked Sarpong if he could help publicise his business. Then his attention was drawn to two men standing behind Sarpong. One, with a Dutch accent, was talking loudly. '... you know the way things are: Africa is viewed as risky for large-scale projects. It can take twenty-five years to make your money back. People are thinking long term. They're looking at Africa, at Nigeria or Ghana, and they're thinking, "What's going to happen here in the next forty years? Is my investment going to be safe?" That's how it is.'

'Sure, sure.' The other man was nodding. He looked East Asian. 'There's more going on than before, but still very few big schemes. It's not reaching the potential at all, nowhere near. In Dubai, where we've been ...'

A bell cut the man short. The delegates were called to the opening session, and the man called Ebenezer followed the crowd to the main hall.

Sarpong turned to Patrice. 'Let me attend this one and make inquiries about Sunfall Power. There's a nice place to sit out back, a restaurant and bar overlooking the ocean, where they'll serve you a soft drink or coffee. I'll meet you there.'

Patrice went out and wandered along the palm-lined foot-paths, past the swimming pools and through the tidy gardens, and over to a cluster of thatched, open-sided structures. It was early in the day. There were no other customers. A few staff were getting things ready for lunch, wiping glasses and laying tables. Two men were working on a light they'd lowered from the eaves of a large open hut. Patrice ordered a Coke. He watched the men working for a while, then went and stood by the railings overlooking the wide sandy beach and the endless waves, and enjoyed the breeze on his face. Two hawkers headed his way, offering football shirts and kente cloth. He shook his head.

He sat down and pored over the literature he'd accumulated, gaining some basic knowledge about the production of solar energy. An hour later, the men having raised the light back to the ceiling and Patrice having read through his brochures, Kwaku Sarpong joined him and ordered a fruit juice. His broad grin was gone. He looked sullen.

'You're not missing anything, Patrice. It's dull.' He glanced back towards the part of the hotel where the conference was taking place. 'No one will learn anything today they didn't already know. It's like I said, a networking opportunity.'

'Any sign of the Sunfall Power Company?'

'No one's heard of it.' Sarpong said, rubbing his cheek. 'And no one's heard of any project being planned for the Dodowa road area. It's strange. I mean, why would this company be so keen for that piece of land? How big was Abotsi's plot? Thirty acres? It's not such a big area … there's other places they could go looking.'

'Apparently, they've already bought most of the land in that valley; Abotsi's was the last piece.'

Sarpong looked out at the ocean. 'The whole valley? Wow. That's a lot of land, hundreds and hundreds of hectares. A solar farm like that would be … well, one of the biggest in Africa.'

Patrice thought of George Abotsi's little dam and the wooden pylon. 'You know, when Abotsi died, he was working on a small hydropower plant that he'd built himself.'

'Yes, Josie told me. But she didn't tell me what happened.'

'He was about to hook it up, the last stage of the connections, as far as I can make out, when he was electrocuted. Do you know much about electrical work?'

'Well, not really, no …'

'Neither do I, but I've been thinking about it.' Patrice looked over to the hut where the men had been working on the light. 'Anyone with any knowledge, and especially someone who has single-handedly designed and built their own power plant, you'd think such a person would make sure everything was switched off before they touched anything.'

Sarpong nodded slowly. 'What are you suggesting, Patrice?'

'It's just … well, the same people who were harassing him turn out now to be the owners of the land; and the date on the title deeds is the day after he died. I don't want to jump to conclusions that turn out to be false, but I need to go back up there and take another look round.'

They drove back to town. Sarpong dropped Patrice at his hotel. 'It's been nice to meet you, Patrice. Let me know if there's anything I can do for you. And if you want to visit the Akosombo Dam one day, let me know. My father's friends with the head of security up there, so I'm sure he could give you an inside tour. Anyway, take care.'

'Thank you, Kwaku.' Patrice watched the car glide away.

Chapter 10

1966: FEBRUARY 5

Adzo's funeral took place in Ho on an overcast Saturday. Uncle Joseph had suggested only the immediate family need attend, but Aunt Esther pointed out this would invite questions, as no funeral in Ghana was only for the family.

Yawor and her aunt and uncle and cousins drove up the day before and stayed with Aunt Mary, a cousin of Yawor's father. Compared to the usual excitement prior to a funeral, the mood was downbeat. When people came to pay their respects and remarked on Adzo's charm and lively spirit, Uncle Joseph grunted. When they asked what had happened, he told them she'd been involved in a road accident, without further explanation.

'God has taken her for a reason,' Aunt Mary said.

Uncle Joseph didn't comment.

Yawor tried to ignore her uncle's lack of sympathy. She thought of happy times when she and her sister had lived in Ho, when they'd played in the evenings and the long school holidays, and they'd helped their mother with the chores in the house and in the garden.

On the day, a hundred-or-so mourners made their way into

the Evangelical Presbyterian Dela Cathedral for a service to celebrate the cruelly cut-short life of Adzowor Abotsi. They included children from Yawor and Adzo's old school, who sang and danced to greet those arriving for the service. It was not the low-key affair Uncle Joseph had hoped for, but by Ghanaian standards it was a small funeral. It felt smaller still because of the enormous church, which was largely empty.

Yawor and her family were not the only ones who'd travelled from Accra. One of Adzo's tutors at the university had arranged for a minibus to bring a group of students from her course. Yawor wondered how much they'd seen of Adzo during the past six months. She wondered too if there was something to read into their haughty expressions and the way they avoided eye contact that meant they knew why Adzo's attendance had slipped.

The coffin lay at the front, draped in the traditional colours of mourning, red and black. Adzo's university colleagues wailed as they filed past, but only one girl seemed genuinely upset. She stopped at the casket and prayed. When she stood, she used the back of her hand to wipe streaks of eye make-up from her cheeks. Yawor comforted her and gave her a cloth.

'I'm Yawor, Adzo's sister.'

'Thank you, I'm Joanna. I liked Adzo. She made me laugh. I miss her.'

Joanna sat in a pew on her own. She was a tall girl and swung her legs to the side.

Most of the speeches were impersonal. To Yawor's mind, only Mr Francis, a teacher from their secondary school, showed any feeling. An Irishman, now white haired, he spoke fervently about a girl who was quick-witted and kind, lively and generous and popular with her classmates.

75

'It's no secret,' he continued, 'that tragedy struck Adzowor and her sister Yawor at a young age. They lost their parents and their brothers, and it's no secret that Adzowor blamed herself for that tragedy. It was her candle that set their house on fire, an inferno from which only Adzowor and Yawor escaped. We saw a change in her after that. And it's true that she bore some responsibility. But it was not her fault; she fell asleep, it was an accident. I believe the inner Adzowor did not change; there was a goodness in her soul that will live on.'

Tears streamed down Yawor's face. She looked at her uncle sitting beside her. His jaw was stiff. She wondered if he'd ever forgive Adzo.

Throughout the afternoon, visitors came to Aunt Mary's house, where Yawor and Aunt Esther sat under the shade tree and people explained their connection to the family: 'My husband knew your father well, they marked exams together'; 'My uncle used to tend your garden when you were young; he got on well with both your mother and your father'. Afterwards they ate fish and meat and fufu and yam and jollof rice.

The girls from the university left early, as they had a long journey back to Accra. Yawor noticed that when Joanna boarded the bus, she sat apart from the others.

1966: FEBRUARY 6

They were on their way back to Accra and crossing the Adomi Bridge over the Volta River when Yawor's cousin George shouted, 'This is near the dam! Papa, can we visit the dam?'

From the back seat, Yawor saw the side of her uncle's face twitch.

'Please, Papa! Only when you see it close up can you appreciate its full magnificence.'

Uncle Joseph rolled his eyes.

'I would be interested to see it,' Aunt Esther said. 'If it's not far.'

'The distance is not the issue. It is the state of the road. The main road is poor enough. My car will not make it up a dirt track.'

'The road to the dam is good, Papa! They took us there in a bus.'

'But we'd need authorisation. They won't allow us to visit unannounced …'

'They will, they will! People are coming from all over Ghana to visit, and from other countries too.'

They reached the T-junction on the western side of the bridge. Accra was left, Akosombo right. Uncle Joseph's head turned from side to side.

Aunt Esther said, 'It would do us all good to do something nice, Joseph, after the terrible time we've had lately. Come on now …'

Uncle Joseph groaned but turned right. 'I suppose we can enjoy a drink of something, somewhere ….'

They climbed a winding paved road. After the village of Akosombo, they reached the offices of the Volta River Authority, where they booked onto a tour of the dam. They and other visitors boarded a bus and were driven further up the winding road.

'Good afternoon, ladies and gentlemen.' A young man addressed the tour party. 'My name is William Appiah. I am an engineering student at the University of Ghana, Legon, and your volunteer guide. Welcome to Akosombo!'

The bus drove through a checkpoint in a perimeter fence and soon afterwards pulled over by a break in the trees. The guide pointed at a great wall towering behind him. 'There is the marvel that is the Akosombo Dam. It took four years to construct. It is two thousand, one hundred and sixty-five feet long and three hundred and sixty-four feet high. Behind it, which you cannot see from here, but you will see soon, is the great new Lake Volta, the largest man-made lake in the world by surface area. It is this body of water, which accounts for three percent of Ghana's surface area, that brings light to our country.'

As Yawor took in the vast structure, so vast she had to move her head from left to right to see it all, she gasped. 'Oh, my goodness!' she said to her cousin. 'George, you are right. It is beautiful.'

They continued up the road behind the trees, so that the next time they saw the dam, they were level with the top. They got out of the bus and followed their guide to a wall at the back of the dam, from where they could see the new lake.

'Directly below us, this is the intake channel. You can see the water pass through the trash rack, after which it falls at speed through the six penstocks. It is the energy of the falling water that drives the turbines, which in turn drive the generators. The turbines were made by Hitachi in Japan and weigh eighty tons …'

Yawor was looking into the dark water swirling below. It made her feel dizzy, and she stepped away from the wall. The dam was a structure of great beauty, but also of such overwhelming power. 'What if the dam bursts?' she asked.

The guide grinned. 'It cannot burst. The dam wall is thick; it is made of two hundred and eighty million cubic feet of rock and earth and sand; it is so strong it can withstand an earthquake.'

Others in the tour group muttered, sounding impressed. Yawor accepted the guide's assurances. They set off along the road that ran across the top of the dam. Downstream, they could see a fenced-in area of pylons and cables, which the guide explained was the power distribution system.

George offered his arm to Yawor. 'You know,' he said, 'for now, eighty percent of the electricity goes to Kaiser Aluminium's plant in Tema. Osagyefo says that is the price we have to pay for our development. We paid for fifty percent of the construction, but we get only twenty percent of the electricity. An American company takes the rest. It's not fair. We are a poor country ... but one day, everyone in Ghana will have electricity. And I'm going to help make that happen.'

'How will you do that?'

'I've made a decision. I'm going to be an engineer.'

'I thought you were going to be a lawyer?'

George lowered his voice. 'That was not my idea. I want to do something practical. I want to build things. Lawyers spend all their time reading and talking. A lot of them are critical of Osagyefo, you know. They spend too much time thinking and not enough getting their hands dirty!'

'You'll make a brilliant engineer,' Yawor said, squeezing his arm. 'With people like you, Ghana's future is bright!'

'Thank you, Cousin, for your encouragement!'

'I'm grateful to you too, George. You have reminded me it's important to do what you know you should.'

Before leaving Akosombo, Uncle Joseph drove the family

to the new Volta Hotel and ordered drinks on a terrace at the back, which offered a panoramic view of the dam and the lake behind.

George pointed to a white building perched above the dam on the far side of the river, which Yawor hadn't noticed before. 'That is Osagyefo's house,' he said proudly. 'From there he can watch the dam to make sure it is functioning correctly and show important visitors how Ghana is progressing.'

Uncle Joseph looked skyward as he sipped his brandy. 'Really?' he said. 'Visitors to this country may be impressed. But what about the poor people who live in these villages hereabouts? Did you see them as we drove by? They don't have electricity. Are they benefitting from this magnificence?'

George looked at his father with daggers in his eyes.

Chapter 11

The journey to River Valley was becoming familiar. Patrice directed the taxi: up the Dodowa road out of Accra; right at the sign for the herbal clinic with the slogan *Come Sick, Return Healed*; dirt road down to the Pentecostal church; left over the culvert, left again at the end of the track; and there it was, the house the late George Abotsi had built amongst the trees. He told the driver to wait.

Kekeli was out arranging for the funeral. Patrice hadn't told her why he wanted to revisit the scene of her father's death, saying only that he needed to check some details. He didn't want to alarm her.

He walked under the Ghanaian flag and round to the back veranda, where he found Aunty Yawor in her chair, looking out to the garden.

'Hello, Aunty,' he said.

She looked at him but didn't respond. Patrice studied her face. Despite her age and her apparent distraction, her eyes were clear and sharp, inquisitive looking. Her forehead was softly lined, her cheeks smooth. Her hair was a striking silver and pulled back. He guessed she was once beautiful.

He climbed the steps and tapped on the door. Gladys opened it.

'Hello, sir,' she said. 'Miss Kekeli told me you were coming. I will come with you.'

She covered Aunty Yawor's legs with a blanket, which the old lady pulled off.

'It's alright, Aunty.' Gladys picked up the blanket and left it on another chair. 'Come,' she said to Patrice. 'We can go.'

'Will Aunty be alright on her own?'

'You don't mind if we go for a short time, do you Aunty?'

Aunty didn't answer.

'Does she ...' Patrice turned to the old lady. 'Aunty, do you remember the day your cousin George died?'

The old lady blinked but didn't speak.

Gladys squatted down next to her. 'Do you remember, Aunty? You went with him to his dam? He was singing: *Nkrumah never dies, never dies, never dies ...* Remember?'

The girl sang more of the song and as she did, Aunty Yawor's eyes lifted, and she joined in: '*Nkrumah never dies, he lives for ever more!*'

'Aunty, that's right, that's what he sang.'

'We went to Akosombo. I went with George.' Aunty Yawor hummed more of the song, quietly, and closed her eyes.

'We can leave her,' Gladys said. 'She's sleeping.'

'Akosombo?' Patrice scratched his head. 'Is that what Mr Abotsi called his dam?'

'I never heard him call it by any name, sir.'

Patrice and Gladys walked through the garden and continued along the path up the forested valley.

'Is it unusual for Aunty to speak?' Patrice asked.

'Sometimes she says things, but you can't always understand her. She used to be a talkative person. Now for some time she has been quiet. And more so since last week.'

82

'Do you think she follows what people are saying?'

'No, not really. She heard the song and sang along, but – you saw her – I don't think she knew why she was singing.'

'She seems frail. How was she able to walk with Mr Abotsi that day? It's steep.'

'Actually she is strong. She has crutches, though she doesn't like them, but she was using one that day.'

The scene by the dam was as Patrice remembered it: the small brick powerhouse with the transformer outside. 'So, Gladys, where were they when you found them, Mr Abotsi and Aunty Yawor?'

'It was in the morning. They were there …' She pointed to the building. 'Outside. My father said straight away that Mr George was dead. His face was grey. There were marks like burns on his hands.'

'And you didn't see anyone else here that morning?'

'No. There were children playing in the river further up, I could hear their voices. But there was no one here.'

'Okay. I'm going to look around.'

Patrice went inside the powerhouse first. The cables and machinery were as he'd seen them the last time. Only now, having called up Ebenezer – the solar panel installer and, he learned, trained electrician – he knew what to look for. And he saw it on the wall on the other side of the room, next to a back door: a row of switches, including a large lever – the master switch. It was up now, switched off; presumably, Gladys's father, Mr Addo, had seen to that. Yet George Abotsi hadn't noticed it was down and switched on. Ebenezer had also said, without prompting, that no one who knew anything about electricity would set to work on a project such as this without checking the supply was off.

Gladys was standing at the door, peering inside.

'Is there another way to get here,' Patrice asked, 'other than walking up by the river?'

She looked at him incredulously. 'There is a road. Mr George could not carry this machinery here on his head. He had a truck for that.'

Patrice looked at the heavy-looking pieces of equipment. He saw what she meant. 'Where is the road?'

'Behind.'

'You should have told me; we could have come in my taxi.'

'It takes a long time on the road – it's winding and in poor condition. When it's raining, you cannot use it.'

'Show me, please, where it is.'

She led him behind the building and up a short path shaded by trees to a clearing, which was a turning circle at the end of a dirt track.

'When did Mr Abotsi finish the construction work, Gladys?'

'It was some months ago. It took a long time to connect it all together. He complained about that to my father.'

The track was dry. 'Has it rained at all since last week?'

'No, sir, not at all.'

Patrice stepped carefully, bent over, examining the ground, and spotted a pattern in the dusty earth. He got down on all fours. It was a tyre track, sharply defined. He took photos.

After taking more photos, inside and outside the hydro-plant, he headed back with Gladys, down by the river and through the trees, to the house. Aunty Yawor was in her chair, her eyes still closed.

Patrice asked to see George Abotsi's truck. It was a pick-up, parked under a shelter at the side of the house. He looked at the tyres. The tread was well worn.

He thanked Gladys for her time, returned to his waiting taxi, and woke up the driver. They set off for town but didn't get far before they saw, by the side of the road, close to the culvert, a dark blue shipping container being lowered to the ground by a truck crane.

'What's this?' Patrice asked.

'Police,' the taxi driver said, slowing down. 'You see?' He pointed at a police pick-up parked further down the road.

Parked next to the pick-up was Kekeli's old Nissan. Patrice told the driver to pull over. He walked across to the container as the chains were being uncoupled from the corners. Voices were coming from behind it, among them Kekeli's, raised.

'We didn't request a police post here,' she was saying, 'and we don't need one. Let me see your ID. I want to see your ID.' She was talking to a policeman. 'What department are you from?'

'Calm down, miss. We are a Swat unit.' He held up an ID card.

'But you can't do this. This land is my father's and now he's dead it will pass to me. Patrice,' she said as she saw him approach, 'look what they are doing ...'

'We are doing what we've been requested to do,' the policeman said. 'We have our orders.'

'Orders from who?'

'A private company has commissioned this post ...' He unfolded a piece of paper. The name at the top was SUNFALL POWER.

The truck crane drove away. The container it had left behind had windows cut on one side, and in white lettering below, the words GHANA POLICE.

'What's a Swat unit?' Patrice asked.

85

The policeman answered. 'Special Weapons and Tactics.'

'And private companies hire you?'

'Yes, all the time.'

'But why do they want you here? Is there much crime?'

'Our job is to protect their property.'

'Can I look at that paper?'

The policeman held it up. Patrice squinted at the small print and spotted an address: 3rd Floor, Kente House, Kente Street, Accra. 'Where is Kente Street?'

'That place is by Kwame Nkrumah Circle.'

A smaller truck arrived, delivering a desk and chairs. The policeman went to supervise the setting up of the furniture in the newly installed police post.

Patrice turned to Kekeli. Her eyes were wet. 'It's like I said,' she said. 'With a powerful company, they do what they want. My father is not even in his grave and they've stolen his land. I'm glad he didn't have to see this. Where he's going, it must be a better place.'

'They haven't got you out yet, Kekeli. You must find your father's title deeds. But bury your father first.'

'Yes. Thank you, Patrice.' She took his hand. She forced a smile, squeezing out a tear.

Patrice watched it trickle down her cheek.

'Will you come to the funeral? It's on Saturday. It'll be here.'

He nodded. 'I'd like to. In the church?'

'No, on his land. My father was a humanist. He wouldn't have wanted want a religious funeral. The ceremony will be here, then we will take his body to the crematorium.'

Patrice saw Kekeli to her car, then he got back in his taxi and set off again for Accra. On the way, he made a call to Kwaku Sarpong, to ask a favour.

Chapter 12

There was the Adzo she knew, and the Adzo she didn't; if she found out more about the latter, perhaps she'd find out who killed her. That was Yawor's reasoning as she rode in a bus to the University of Ghana in East Legon, in the northern outskirts of Accra.

The bus dropped her at the campus gates. It was early afternoon. The sun was shining as she walked across the familiar gardens, past the Great Hall with its whitewashed walls and red-tiled roof, and headed for the English department. She found Miss Mawson, her old tutor, in her office and said she'd come to inform her of her sister's passing.

Miss Mawson said she'd heard about Adzowor and offered her condolences. 'It's a terrible, terrible thing. She was a promising student. Though I never taught her myself, I could see by the sparkle in her eye that she had a sharp mind, like her sister.'

'Thank you, miss.'

'So, you have not yet returned to your studies?'

'No, miss. I was at home the weekend she died and I have not felt ready to return. I will go soon.'

'And how is it going in Winneba? Are you enjoying this new adventure?'

'Yes, miss. We work hard and I get good grades. My only complaint is about the living conditions. We are seven in our room and it is cramped. And we have to queue in the morning for the bathroom.'

'It's new. It will take time to build it up. But it's progress. Ghana has its own teacher training college. Soon you won't need people like me to come from England!'

'Yes, miss. Thank you.' Yawor paused, weighing up how to ask what she wanted to ask without arousing suspicions. 'We held the funeral on Saturday. Students from Adzowor's course came. I wanted to say thank you to them. Do you know where I can find them?'

Miss Mawson opened a file. 'Monday afternoon ... they'll be in the lecture hall till four.'

'Oh, good. I'll wait for them. Thank you, Miss Mawson.'

'Goodbye, Yawor. And stick with the studies. You'll make a wonderful teacher!'

Yawor sat in the shade of a tree, in sight of the clock tower. At four o'clock she went to the lecture hall. She watched as the students streamed out and spotted two who'd attended the funeral. But Joanna was not amongst them.

She hobbled after the girls she recognised. 'Hello,' she said. 'I was looking for you. I didn't get a chance on Saturday to thank you for coming to the funeral. It meant a lot to me and my family that you travelled so far.'

The girls nodded. 'It's okay,' one said. 'Funerals are important.'

'Yes. Tell me, is the girl Joanna at college today? I didn't see her coming out of the lecture hall.'

The girl made a face like there was a bad smell in the air. 'You won't find her here much these days. Like it was with your sister.'

A lump rose in Yawor's throat. She looked away.

'Bye, then.' The girls walked on.

Yawor let them go. She knew where she'd have to go to find Joanna, and she knew there'd be no point going there before nightfall.

To fill the time, she went to the library to read the *Daily Graphic*. A report on the front page confirmed the news that Uncle Joseph's friend Austin had mentioned:

Osagyefo Dr Kwame Nkrumah, President of the Republic of Ghana, has been officially invited to pay a state visit to North Vietnam. The dates for the visit have been tentatively fixed for February 26th to March 4th. It is expected that the president will make stopovers along the way; in Cairo, he will brief his close friend President Nasser on the efforts to end the war in Indo-China; and in Peking, he will meet Chairman Mao, before travelling on to Hanoi ...

Yawor knew this meant the talk of plots against the president would intensify, much to the delight of her uncle.

At half past six, the night sky black, the air still hot, she caught a bus going back into the centre of Accra, past the airport, past Flagstaff House, the seat of government, where she imagined the president sitting at his desk writing one of his speeches, past West Ridge, all the way to the downtown area of the city. She got off at Makola Market and headed for a street behind it which she'd heard of by reputation – a street she'd never been to before and one she'd never, ever, intended to visit.

As she turned the corner she felt scared, not for herself, but for Adzo, wondering how she must have felt the first time she came here. It was not well lit, but a dim glow spilled out from the small bars and chop houses along the road – dim but enough to show the shapes and shadows of the *ashawo*, as the women here were called. She walked towards the dim lights. A wigged shape appeared out of nowhere.

'What are you doing here? This is where I stand.'

'I … I … I'm not stopping. I'm looking for a friend. Joanna? Do you know her? She's tall …'

The woman spat on the ground. 'No. Move along. You'll put off my clients.'

Yawor carried on. At the first light, there was a ramshackle bar with a tin roof. Two men sat at a table with two girls who looked young, despite the thick powder and rouge caked on their faces. Yawor tried not to stare. She could feel their eyes on her limp.

'What are you looking at?' one of the men shouted to Yawor. 'You want to join us?'

The other laughed. 'You'll have to pay us!'

They both laughed. The two girls smirked. Yawor stiffened and walked on. A man walked past. As he did, he brushed himself against her and groped her buttock.

'Leave me alone,' she said as she shook him off.

'Hey, what's your problem?'

She didn't answer. A car approached from behind. She heard it slow down, as if it was following her. She was feeling scared again – but now for herself. The darkness, the eyes, the muffled calls and hisses; it was only a mile from the safety and comfort of Uncle Joseph's house, but it was another world, an underworld.

The car edged past her, then stopped, pulling over so she

had to squeeze by. The window was down. She smelled stale armpits.

A squeaky voice called out, 'How much for a short time?'

Yawor glared at the sweating, slobbery face inside.

'Don't play hard-to-get. You won't get many stopping. How much?'

His hand moved and she noticed something shiny. She realised he was rubbing himself. 'I'm not working,' she said. She wanted to add that if she was, she wouldn't want to work with him, but had second thoughts. For all she knew, he had a knife in there as well. 'Look for someone else.'

The car drove on. Its lights revealed more girls on the roadside up ahead. Even from a distance, Yawor could tell from the long legs that one of them was Joanna, in a short black dress.

The car that had stopped by Yawor stopped by Joanna. Yawor prayed she wouldn't get in. She didn't like to think of her getting into any car, but please, not that one, and not now. Joanna bent over and talked through the open window, then abruptly walked away, tutting. The car drove off.

Yawor went after her. 'Joanna.'

The girl turned.

'It's me, Yawor. Adzo's sister.'

'Oh ...'

'I came to find you. I wanted to talk.'

'But ... but here?'

'Please, Joanna. I want to find out what happened to my sister.'

'I thought she was run over?'

'Yes, but I want to find out who by. You know, they didn't stop?'

Joanna looked up and down the street. There were no cars coming. 'Come …' They crossed the road to another shack, another two tables under a tin roof, and a bar hidden in the darkness behind. The owner came and asked what they wanted. Yawor shook her head.

'We have to take something,' Joanna said. 'Otherwise, we can't sit here.'

Yawor wished they could go somewhere else, away from this street. But she realised Joanna was taking time out to talk to her. 'I'll take Star.'

'Two Star.' Joanna sent the owner off with their order. 'How did you find me?'

'The girls at the university said they hadn't seen you around much lately … like Adzo.'

Joanna squeezed her plum-coloured lips. 'They sneer at me.'

'Is this where you met Adzo? On this street?'

'We met in class, in lectures. I was studying English too. I was a year behind Adzo, so we didn't know each other well. Then I stopped going … and the next time I saw her was on the first night she came here. It was six months ago …' Joanna let the words hang, as if waiting for a sign from Yawor that she should continue.

Their bottles arrived and they each took a sip. 'Please go on,' Yawor said.

'She was nervous that first night. We all are. She saw me and she stayed close to me. I don't mind. I prefer to stand with another girl. We are safer in pairs.'

'Safer?'

'There are strange men that come here.' She gestured at where the car had pulled up by her minutes earlier. 'That last man, he didn't even want to go with me. He's just excited to be here. Men like that are harmless. But there are dangerous ones. Adzo wasn't the first girl to get herself killed.'

Yawor shook her head. 'I don't know how she ... how you can work here; it's so intimidating.'

'Like anything, you get used to it. What's strange at first becomes normal after some time.'

Two men stopped as they walked past and stared at the two women. Yawor's stomach tightened.

'Ignore them and they will go away,' Joanna said. 'Anyway, I'm taking a break.' She smiled, revealing a gap between her front teeth.

Yawor smiled, relieved. 'You were saying about the first night Adzo came?'

'She was nervous. But she was determined too. She had an attitude. She asked lots of questions about it: how the business worked; what she should do in certain situations, like if they asked her to do something she didn't want to do, or if the police came ...'

'Was she ever caught by the police? I asked her once what would happen ...'

'They don't arrest you ... They say, "Let me feel free," so you let them ... and they leave you.' Joanna shrugged and drank her beer. 'You know, Adzo was different from a lot of the girls. She didn't do this because she needed to. It was a choice. She wanted to save money, so that she could go to America.'

Yawor shook her head. 'She never told me that.' A few things fell into place, like how Adzo had been so keen to follow European and American fashion trends. 'When was the last time you saw her?'

'It was before Christmas.'

93

'Did she ever talk about any problems she had with a client? If she had been threatened, for instance?'

Joanna shook her head. 'She never said that to me.'

'Where did she go with her clients?'

'It depends, it's the same for all of us. If the man is on foot, usually we go with them behind a wall. If they have a car, sometimes they drive somewhere quiet, a quiet street, and we do what it is they want in the car. Other times, if they want more, there are small hotels where we go.' She pointed a finger down the road. 'There is a place two streets away where Adzo went. But she only took them for a short time, she never stayed a night with them.'

Yawor shuddered at the thought of what kind of hotel that might be: dark corridors and rats, creaking bed frames, stinking, damp mattresses ...

As if Joanna could read her mind, she added, 'I rent a room there, above the hotel. It's where I live for now.' She shrugged. 'It's not so bad.'

'Did Adzo ever walk ... try to find clients ... in other parts of town?'

'I don't know. I don't think she did.'

Yawor pictured the road where Adzo had been struck down. 'Where she was found, that's a quiet street. The police said she was trying to solicit business and stepped in front of a car. But why would she do that in a quiet side street?' New possibilities occurred to her as she spoke. 'What if she'd been driven there by a client, driven to a quiet street, and they had an argument, over money perhaps? It was in West Ridge.'

Joanna looked down the road. Yawor followed her eyes. Two cars were approaching, slowly. Joanna gulped down her beer.

'You know, some clients, they like to drive around for a while first, talking. I say if they want to talk, they have to pay for that too. But maybe they know that area, so they feel more comfortable there, and they know the places they won't be interrupted. Adzo never told me of anyone taking her to West Ridge ...' She tailed off as if a thought had occurred mid-sentence. 'She had one client who was regular, a white man. I don't know where he lives, but it is likely to be a wealthy area.' She checked her face in her mirror and got to her feet. 'I must get back to work.'

'Wait! A white man? She saw him more than once?'

'Yes. He came usually on Saturdays ...'

'It was a Saturday when she died. She never spoke of any trouble with this man? Did she say anything about him?'

'No, no. The opposite. She liked him, or something about him. She said he said he could help her.'

'To do what?'

Joanna was following the progress of the cars. One had stopped. The other was coming their way. 'I don't know. Some men say things like that, pretending they're big men, to impress.'

'Did she tell you his name?'

'Uh-uh. But I saw him once or twice in his car. He had black hair, straight, parted on the left, and a moustache. And I can tell you the car he drives: a red Ford.'

'Have you seen him since Adzo died?'

'No.' And with that, Joanna stepped up to the roadside in time to tempt the passing car to pull over. After a brief conversation, she got in and was driven off, calling out to Yawor, 'Good luck!'

Chapter 13

Kwaku Sarpong lived in a modern complex in Cantonments, near the Lands Commission offices. He was, as Patrice suspected, a man who owned many suits, and he was happy to lend one out when Patrice said he needed to look smart for an unexpected meeting with international donors. Sarpong suggested navy – black would be 'too formal' – with a white shirt, yellow tie, and brown shoes; they had the same shoe size. Patrice hadn't worn a suit and tie since the funeral of his wife and son six years previously. As he stepped outside Sarpong's apartment block, the heat of the Accra afternoon reminded him why he found them so uncomfortable.

He took a taxi to Kwame Nkrumah Circle and walked the short distance to Kente House, a bland three-storey block clad in white tiles on a street off Kwame Nkrumah Avenue.

A glass door opened into a gloomy reception area. Inside, a young woman sat behind a counter. She popped the gum she was chewing and said, 'Can I help you?'

'Sunfall Power?'

She pointed a finger upwards. 'Third floor.'

Patrice headed for the lift.

'The lift is not working. No power.'

'I see. And a power company has its offices here?'

The young woman shrugged and popped her gum again.

Patrice passed an armed guard recumbent on a chair by the out-of-order lift and climbed the concrete stairs. On the third-floor landing there were two doors; a small plastic plaque stuck to one said *Sunfall Power Company*. Wiping his brow, resisting the urge to loosen his tie, he entered a small lobby with plain white walls, where a woman in a tight-fitting, emerald green dress sat at a desk, a laptop open in front of her.

'Good afternoon, Vera,' he said, noting the name on her badge and smiling. 'I've come to see Mr Albert Boateng.'

The woman didn't smile back. She was as unwelcoming as the receptionist downstairs. 'Your name?'

'Étienne Kabanda. From Congo.' He passed her a business card he'd had printed at a place next to his hotel less than an hour earlier, which described him as an Energy Consultant.

'You have an appointment?'

'No.'

'Mr Boateng doesn't see people without an appointment.'

'Okay. I'd like to make an appointment to see Mr Boateng, please.' He smiled again.

Again, she didn't. Nonetheless, while suggesting it was an act that required great effort, she picked up a phone on her desk. 'There's a Mr Kabanda here to see Mr Boateng.'

There was a pause, during which she avoided eye contact. Her screen was at an angle and revealed a selection of red dresses. She put the phone down and announced, 'You can wait.' She pointed at two chairs.

'Thank you, Vera.' Patrice took a seat and flipped through the leaflets and trade magazines piled on a table, which were like those he'd picked up at the solar power conference.

Curiously, there were no brochures for Sunfall Power. In fact, apart from on the plastic plaque outside, the name was nowhere to be seen, even in their own offices.

Vera was tapping the mouse by her laptop.

'How long have you been working here, Vera?' Patrice asked.

She looked up blankly. 'A few weeks. The company is newly established.'

'Is it interesting for you?'

'It's a job.'

The minutes passed. Patrice was preparing himself for a long wait when he heard voices coming from the other side of an internal door. The door opened and he caught the end of a conversation.

'… I'm sure it will be only a matter of days before we get a response.'

'Good. We hope to hear from you soon.'

'We'll keep in touch.'

Two men emerged: a Latin-looking man with a moustache, and an East Asian with a young, clean-shaven face, who Patrice recognised from the solar conference the previous day. The man looked at him, as if trying to figure out if he knew him. They were followed by an African, a short, skinny man with big eyes. He shook the other men's hands vigorously as they said their goodbyes, and the two non-Africans left.

Patrice got up. 'Mr Boateng?'

The man looked him up and down. Sarpong's suit seemed to impress him. It was a tight fit, but Patrice could blame Ghanaian cuisine for that.

'Yes. That's me.'

'Étienne Kabanda, from Congo.' Patrice handed over

another of his cards. The man looked at it without reacting.

'What can I do for you, Mr Kabanda?' His voice was high-pitched but neutral, neither friendly nor hostile.

'I was hoping we could talk. I have come to Accra to do business.'

Boateng looked at the window. It was after five and the sun was sinking into the hazy horizon. 'It's late in the day. Why don't you come tomorrow?'

'Oh, but I am leaving tonight. I won't take much of your time. Just to introduce myself and to see if you are interested in what I have to say. If you are, then we can meet again. It's okay?'

Boateng sniffed out through his nose, squeezed his lips and threw a glance at Vera. 'Come through. I have an engagement this evening. But we can talk briefly.'

The inner office was sparsely furnished: there was a desk and three chairs and lots of bare, hard surfaces. Boateng gestured to the chairs and they sat either side of the desk. 'So, tell me, Mr Kabanda, what do you wish to talk about?'

'Thank you, Mr Boateng. I will get straight to the point. I have a client in my country who is in land acquisition. He has a large site which he thinks would be suitable for development as a solar power plant. Currently, my country has poor electricity connectivity, owing to poor distribution and lack of generating capacity. Most of the renewable effort is relying on hydro supply; I'm sure you have heard of the Inga Three dam project on the Congo River? But the government is also seeking to diversify, and my client believes large-scale solar plants would get official support.'

From the lack of reaction, Patrice couldn't be sure the man on the other side of the desk had heard a single word. 'So,' he concluded, trying to sound businesslike and direct, 'this is what I would like to discuss with you.'

'How did you hear about Sunfall Power, Mr Kabanda?'

'Someone at the solar power conference at La Palm Royal Beach Hotel recommended your company to me.'

'Who was that, may I ask?'

Patrice smiled apologetically. 'You know, I don't remember the man's name. He gave me his card, but I have misplaced it. He works for the Ministry of Energy here in Accra ...'

Boateng frowned and looked far from convinced.

Patrice gambled on flattery. 'This man told me he'd heard your company has put forward a bold and impressive proposal for a new solar plant here in Ghana that would be among the biggest in Africa.'

Boateng's big eyes lit up. 'Hmm, well, it's not official yet. That is why I was interested to know who'd spoken to you, Mr Kabanda. But we are hopeful. But Congo? It is not a stable country. You have had a war ...'

'Mr Boateng, there would be risks. But great rewards too. The war is over more or less, except for a few skirmishes in the East.' Patrice winced as he heard himself play down the continued insecurity at home. 'As you know, Congo is a large country. The land my client proposes for this scheme is far away from that area. And there is plenty more ...'

'How big a plant is your client envisaging?'

'This is what he wishes to discuss with you, the possibilities. The land is two hundred hectares, which he understands is space enough for a plant to supply electricity for one hundred thousand homes. And near to this land is a city of that size, where up till now the people are relying on diesel generators. You see the potential?'

Boateng's big eyes grew bigger. 'We are talking about one hundred and fifty megawatts, six hundred thousand panels. It's a big project.'

'My client is ambitious. But if the project is too big for your company to manage, I understand.'

For the first time, the man smiled. 'Mr Kabanda, I didn't say it is too big. I can tell you, what we are planning here is bigger than that.'

'Bigger?'

'Yes. For your client's information – and please don't repeat this publicly until the official announcements – the River Valley farm will be two-hundred and fifty megawatts, a million solar panels. But it is a considerable investment: five hundred million dollars.' He paused, as if Patrice would need time for the scale of the venture to sink in.

Patrice responded with a long, quiet whistle.

'The new government here in Ghana is pro-business,' the man continued. 'They've said they will support private sector investment in utility-scale solar projects and we intend to take full advantage of that. But you can understand, with this scale of enterprise, why investors need to be reassured … about security and stability.'

'And they can have that reassurance, Mr Boateng. Because what my client envisages is a joint venture. He is well connected. He has friends in government who will want to invest. And because of their positions in government, they can guarantee security. You see what I mean?'

Boateng pursed his lips and nodded. Glancing at his watch, he said, 'Why don't we arrange a meeting? It would be good to meet your client face-to-face …'

'We can arrange that, definitely. But before I report back

to him, there are some things I need to ask you. I have been forthcoming, I hope you agree. So, please, tell me more about Sunfall Power. I was wondering why, for instance, you did not have a presence at the solar conference here? That was an opportunity for you to let people know about your company, which I understand is quite new ...'

'We are new, but we prefer to work quietly, behind the scenes, through contacts – perhaps like your client's – in government and other areas of influence.'

'That is good. I can tell my client that he can rely on discretion in his dealings with you. But there is something else he will want to know, and that is, who are the partners of Sunfall? Who are the main suppliers and installers? Are they names my client will know?'

'If your client knows anything about this industry, he will know these companies. The contract for construction and maintenance is with Desert Power, Arizona, while the panel manufacturer is Blue Electric, from Guangzhou.' Boateng paused again, and Patrice tried again to look impressed. 'Again, this information is not yet public.'

'Thank you. Of course, this is between ourselves and our respective clients. And indeed, my client knows of these companies. Finally, there is one further matter, and that is if you could give me an understanding of the financial resources of Sunfall Power? You are proposing a large project ...'

Boateng pursed his lips and stared at Patrice. He didn't offer an answer.

Patrice pressed him. 'I will have to say something about your company's credentials. If my client asks me about the Sunfall Power Company, it won't sound right if I say, "All I know is there's the general manager, Mr Boateng, a nice man, who has a small bare office, with a small plastic sign outside … and few people have heard of his company." You see? If I go back to Kinshasa with just this …'

'Mr Kabanda, the names of those we are working with should be enough to reassure your client. I can tell you, Sunfall is a Ghanaian venture with big partners and big plans. But I am not going to open the company's books to a total stranger who has walked in off the street …' He smiled, but not warmly.

Patrice held the man's gaze.

Boateng leaned forward. 'Now it's my turn. I have supplied you with a lot of information. So I would like to know, in order that I can have confidence to make recommendations about any venture in your country, who is your client?'

'I understand.' Patrice nodded seriously. 'Like you, I must ask that the information I am about to give to you goes no further than your immediate colleagues.' He drew closer and whispered a name. 'He is a senior official in the National Agency for the Promotion of Investments, with responsibility for the renewables sector. I was not exaggerating when I said my client has good contacts within the government.'

Boateng sat back. He looked out of the window again and then at his watch, and rubbed his hands together. 'Well, Mr Kabanda, very good. Let's see where this leads. I will report to my board, you to your client, and we will keep in contact.'

He led Patrice to the door and shook hands, but without the enthusiasm he'd shown to his visitors earlier. Patrice threw Vera another smile and left the unimpressive offices of the Sunfall Power Company. As he walked down the three flights of concrete stairs, he loosened his tie and undid the top buttons of his shirt.

The main reception area was dark. The gum-chewing receptionist had left. He stepped past the armed guard and out into the dusk and walked to Kwame Nkrumah Avenue to look for a taxi.

The hotel maid said she'd have Sarpong's suit dry-cleaned the next day. Back in his jeans and tee-shirt and sandals, Patrice ate dinner at an Ivorian restaurant up a side street behind the hotel. The tilapia was well cooked but lukewarm. He picked at it half-heartedly, leaving much of it on his plate. He rated the meal the same as his meeting with Albert Boateng: some potential but not fully realised.

He drank a bottle of Star with his food and another afterwards. He paid and left and strolled down the dark, unpaved road. The warm evening air and the beer were comforting. A couple holding hands passed by, chatting and laughing. He looked back and saw them silhouetted beneath the yellow glow of a streetlamp. Accra was a city where the streets felt safe at night.

A screech of brakes spoiled the moment. A car turned into the road, driving too fast, almost crashing into a wall and spewing up a cloud of dust. It steadied itself in the middle of the road but didn't slow down. It was heading in Patrice's direction. Patrice guessed the driver was drunk and stepped to the side. As he did, the car altered its course. It was still coming towards him and still speeding. He pushed himself against the pulled-down shutter of a shop-front. But the car was about to crash – into him. He swivelled into the recess of a door next to the shutter. The back wheels skidded as the car swiped against the shutter, missing Patrice by the width of a grilled tilapia. Before he had time even to swear out loud, the car pulled away in another cloud of dust and disappeared beyond the streetlamp under which seconds earlier the couple had walked holding hands.

'Idiot!' he said, to himself, as there was no one else around.

He brushed the dust off his clothes and carried on down the road. He didn't feel so safe now. There were two streets more to the main road, which he could see up ahead, marked by a red neon casino sign and a steady flow of cars passing in each direction. At the first junction, he looked in all directions and listened carefully. All was quiet. At the second, a short block away from the main road, he wasn't so cautious. He was halfway across when he heard the screech of tyres again. Same screech, same reckless turn into the side road, same headlights shining in his face.

This time he ran, making for the main road. Another screech followed him round the corner. There was a long wall on one side of him and the side of the casino on the other, and no doorway. No escape. The car was closing down on him fast. Its lights made shadows of his legs on the road in front. He looked again for an exit. All he could see were walls on either side. He was close to the main road but not close enough. Then, just as he was expecting the impact, a car turned into his road from the main road. Without thinking, he jumped in front of it with his hands in the air. The car skidded to a stop. The car behind braked sharply and swerved, and swept past him.

Patrice watched it turn sharply into the main road. When he looked back, two women in the car in front of him were staring at him and screaming.

Chapter 14

The Paris Hotel stood near the bottom of Independence Avenue. From the terrace café at the front, Yawor could see the T-junction with 28th February Road and High Street, and the Accra Club and Golf Course beyond. It was a well-known landmark and as good a place as any to look for a white man driving a red Ford.

The café in the early afternoon was busy. Most of the customers were white, and she felt as uncomfortable as she had the previous evening in the street behind Makola Market. She ordered a pot of tea. She took a college exercise book and a pencil from her bag and watched the traffic drive by. Unfamiliar with the different makes of car, she planned to take down the registration numbers of all the red ones driven by white men. She sat there for an hour and didn't see any.

She ordered more tea. While she waited for it, she over-heard a conversation between two men at a table behind hers.

'... three months, no more.'

'Wishful thinking. The people might want him out, but who's going to do it? He rules with an iron grip. As soon as he suspects anything, they're all locked up.'

'I'll bet you ten pounds he'll be out by the first rains.'

'Ten pounds? You're on!'

The men laughed and clinked glasses.

Yawor kissed her teeth.

She drank her tea and continued her watch. She saw several red cars, but none with a white driver. After another hour, she called it a day.

The tea cost more than she'd expected, leaving her no fare for a taxi. Stressed and despondent, she set off on the long walk home, sweating as she hauled herself up Independence Avenue, her hip hurting more than usual.

She'd stopped to rest against a tree when a car horn startled her. She turned and froze. It was a red car. It was pulling over. At the wheel was Doctor Bennett.

'Hello, Yawor! Where are you going? Can I give you a lift?'

She stared at him. 'It's alright, doctor, thank you. I'm enjoying the exercise.'

'Are you sure? You look worn out. It's no trouble for me. Please, get in ...' He leaned across and opened the passenger door.

She was trying frantically to identify the make of car. She'd spent two hours looking for a red Ford and now she was praying she hadn't found one. Doctor Bennett was giving her a curious look. The cars behind were beeping.

'Thank you,' she said, and got in.

'Are you alright, Yawor?' he asked as he drove off.

'Yes, yes, thank you, doctor. I was hot, walking.'

'If you used your crutches ...'

'Yes, thank you for stopping. You have a nice car. What kind of car is it?'

Doctor Bennett looked at her out of the side of his eye. 'A

Triumph Herald. I had it shipped over from England. I'm glad you like it.'

Yawor almost cried with relief. 'Yes, I do,' she said, the breeze from the open window cooling her face pleasantly. How could she, even for a second, have suspected Doctor Bennett?

'I haven't seen you since that day at the hospital. I heard you buried poor Adzowor.'

'Yes, on Saturday, in Ho. It made me feel better, to lay her to rest.'

'Have the police made any headway, finding the driver?'

Yawor looked down. 'No. I ... I don't think they're likely to, it's sometime past.'

'I see. Mind you, they work slowly sometimes.' The doctor had his eyes on the road but his lips were pursed. 'I thought the result of the post-mortem might have added some urgency to their investigation.'

Yawor pricked up her ears. 'Post-mortem? I didn't know there was a post-mortem.'

'I'm sorry, Yawor, I assumed ... It's routine in the case of an unnatural death.'

'But for what purpose? We know she was run over.'

'Yes, she was. The cause of death supports that; she died of multiple injuries to her head and internal organs. But there was also severe bruising to the back of her legs, which suggests the car struck her from behind.'

'From behind?' Yawor was trying to work out why he was telling her this and what else a post-mortem examination might have revealed. She was relieved to see they were pulling up outside Uncle Joseph's compound. As she was opening the car door, the doctor turned to face her.

'Yawor, I know what the police think and about what Adzowor was doing.'

She looked away. Her ears were hot.

'I don't mean to upset you, but the point is this: if she was struck from behind, it's unlikely she was attempting to solicit business with the driver of that car. I'm not a pathologist, but it sounds more likely she was running away.'

Yawor's head was spinning as she watched Doctor Bennett drive off in his red car. She went through the gate and found her uncle on the front veranda, drinking palm wine with his friend Austin. The sound of the radio was coming through the open window behind them – the president was delivering another speech.

'We welcome foreign investment provided that there are no strings attached to it and also provided that it fits in with our plans for national development and our socialist policy.'

'Here he goes!' Uncle Joseph said. 'Perfect timing, Yawor. He's addressing the opening session of the National Assembly. I bet he'll say "neo-colonialism" in the next sentence …'

'And we insist that foreign investment should not interfere or meddle with the political life of our country.'

A mushy sound of applause followed.

'Well, I was close …'

'I'll go inside, Uncle.'

'Careful, Yawor, you don't want the neighbours to think you're not interested in what our great leader has to say!' Uncle Joseph winked at his friend and they sniggered.

Yawor tutted to herself and went to her room and washed and changed. The sound of Nkrumah's speech was still coming from the front room. She went through and sat with the men on the veranda. The president had turned to a different subject.

'... it is not the duty of the army to rule or govern, because it has no political mandate and its duty is not to seek a political mandate. The army only operates under the mandate of the civil government.'

'Ooh, I say, Austin. The man is worried. He thinks he's next.'

'If the national interest compels the armed forces to intervene, then, immediately after the intervention, the army must hand over to a new civil government elected by the people and enjoying the people's mandate under a constitution accepted by them.'

'I believe you're right, Joseph. He hears the rumours. It's as if he's talking to the soldiers, not the members of the assembly.

'If the army does not do this, then the position of the army becomes dubious and anomalous and involves a betrayal of the people and the national interest.'

Uncle Joseph lowered his voice. 'The sooner things get sorted out, the better, my friend. Then this country can get back to normal.'

'You mean you'll be able to buy your whisky again?'

The two men laughed.

'But it's not just whisky. We can't even buy sugar. Can you fathom it, Austin? No sugar! This is what this man has reduced us to: a one-party state where the people can't afford sugar.'

'Joseph, please!' Aunt Esther was at the doorway. 'Keep your voice down. I can hear you in the kitchen.'

Austin leaned across. 'Your voice does carry. Be patient. I'm sure you can't have long to wait.'

'Agh ... it's hard not to speak out. You only have to look

around and see the way the people cower. This is part of the problem. But yes, I'll do as you both say, keep my head down. Luckily, I have something to anaesthetise the sense of frustration …' He winked at his friend and topped up their glasses.

Yawor waited until they'd had a sip. 'Uncle?'

'Yes, my dear, what is it?'

'I was wondering if you'd heard anything more from your friend, the police commissioner … if he had any news?'

'Why would he have any news?'

'I don't know.'

Uncle Joseph tutted. 'He's a busy man, Yawor. He hasn't got time to be socialising with all his old friends.'

'Yes, Uncle.' Yawor clenched her fists and went inside to help her aunt.

Chapter 15

Patrice looked absent-mindedly down the menu: grilled chicken; grilled fish; jollof rice with chicken or fish; palm oil beans stew with beef, served with fried plantains ... He was in the restaurant at his hotel waiting for Josie Mwinga to join him for lunch, but he wasn't thinking of food. He was mulling things over. He didn't know the full story yet, but he did know he was getting drawn deeper and deeper into it.

Before his boss arrived, Kwaku Sarpong dropped by to collect his suit. 'How did it go with the donors?' he asked with a grin as he inspected the dry cleaner's work. 'I hope you made a suitable impression.'

'Actually, that meeting didn't happen. I went to meet Mr Albert Boateng at the offices of the Sunfall Power Company instead.'

'Oh, really?' Sarpong took a seat, laid his suit carefully over the one next to it, and poured himself a glass of sparkling water.

'I pretended I was an energy consultant from Congo. I didn't want to tell you in case you thought it was a bad idea. Apologies for the deception.'

Sarpong chuckled. 'It's no problem. But how did *that* meeting go?'

'He confirmed they're planning a massive solar power plant, two hundred and fifty megawatts.' Patrice summarised the conversation he'd had with Boateng.

'That is an ambitious plan,' Sarpong said, sounding genuinely impressed. 'Sounds like you wore my suit well, for him to be so forthcoming!'

'Yes. But he must have checked out my story, because later on they tried to kill me.'

Sarpong spluttered. 'What? Who?'

'Sunfall. They sent a car after me and tried to run me down. Last night, when I was walking back after dinner.'

'Jesus! That's insane. I can't believe it …'

'I'm not joking, Kwaku. It was two streets from here. It was about to hit me when another car came round a corner. If it wasn't for that, I wouldn't be here talking to you.'

'Oh my God. Did you get the registration number?'

Patrice shook his head.

'What make of car was it?'

'I don't know. It was a dark colour …'

'Sure, of course.' Sarpong nodded sympathetically. 'But why would they do that?'

'Boateng must have seen through my disguise.'

'And sent out a hit-squad?'

'Well, who else could it be? And don't forget, they killed … or might have killed George Abotsi …'

Sarpong looked at Patrice over his glasses. 'I know from what you told me it's possible, but his death could also have been an accident. I mean, think about it. Why would they kill him?'

'Because he didn't want to sell his land.'

'I don't know …' Sarpong turned his glass of water round on

the table. 'I can't see it. If you want to do business in Ghana, there are plenty of ways to do it without killing people – especially if you're in with big partners like the two Boateng's told you about. They are really big ...'

'Well, we know for a fact someone's tampered with the records at the Lands Commission. They're up to something and they don't want me snooping around. If they weren't trying to kill me last night, they were sending me a warning.'

Patrice caught sight of Josie Mwinga coming through the doors. He leant forward to finish what he was saying. 'Either way, they don't know me well. The more they want me to go away, the more I want to stay.'

Sarpong looked pained. 'If you're right about this, you should be careful.'

'Don't worry about me. But let's keep this between our-selves for now. My boss is inclined to blow things out of proportion.'

'Well, hello, young men.' Josie Mwinga approached in a blue and white patterned top with puffed shoulders and a matching full-length, narrow skirt. She sat down next to Patrice and placed her bag on the table. 'Good to see you, Kwaku. It looks like life is treating you well. You're looking smart, I must say.'

Sarpong smiled but looked embarrassed. 'Thank you, yes. Likewise, you look well yourself.'

'What news, Patrice?'

'Well, ma'am ... Josie, I've been telling Kwaku what I was able to find out about the Sunfall Power Company ...'

He repeated the summary of his meeting with Albert Boateng.

Mwinga listened intently, her hands in a prayer position,

the tips of her fingers tapping against her lips. 'And you really think George Abotsi's death is linked to this?' she asked when he'd finished.

'Yes, definitely. But I need more time to investigate, to gather more evidence.'

'But shouldn't you go to the police with what you know so far?'

'That's a problem. They've got the police working on their side. They've hired a Swat unit to protect the land up there. We must tread carefully.'

'Thank you, Patrice. I appreciate your efforts, and I promise I'll look into your request for study leave when I get back to Banjul. Kwaku, there's no talk about this deal at the Energy Commission?'

'Not that I've heard of, but I'm an outsider so I don't hear everything.'

'I read there was a limit on the size of privately owned power stations?'

'Well, yes, on some. The government's actually reviewing its entire energy policy. For the time being, there's a cap on the size of utility-scale solar projects, and the one Patrice has been told about far exceeds that, ten times over.'

'So, they won't get a licence?'

'That's up to the Energy Commission. The idea behind the cap was to give them time to assess the impact of electricity generated by solar, and of wind, on the national grid. But they've made exceptions and granted licences to a couple of big solar projects. The thing is, the power sector needs investment and it's the private companies who've got the capital.'

'Well, please keep your ear to the ground, as they say. Now,' she said, looking around, 'let's have lunch. Kwaku, will you join us?'

'Well, I …'

'Jolly good. Waiter!'

Any sorrow Josie Mwinga was feeling over the death of her friend wasn't going to spoil her meal. She ordered chicken in groundnut sauce and a bottle of Star. Sarpong ordered the same. Patrice wasn't in the mood for a heavy lunch and asked for fresh fruit. The food came and they talked about other things.

'You know, Kwaku,' Mwinga said, 'Accra is one of my favourite cities. I have so many friends here, I never want to leave. People like your father, people I've known a long time. But Accra has changed a lot. It's a modern city now. Skyscrapers, shopping centres … Patrice, what do you think Kwame Nkrumah would have made of Accra today?'

Patrice had actually been asking himself why his boss was still in Accra. She'd had plenty of time for her post-conference follow-up discussions. Her question took him by surprise. 'How do you mean?'

'Come on, Patrice, all this business activity and private investment … Kwame Nkrumah would be turning in his grave, wouldn't he?' She grinned at Patrice and winked at Kwaku Sarpong.

Patrice answered straight. 'I don't think Nkrumah was against private investment or private enterprise; he was pragmatic about that kind of thing, despite his talk of African socialism.'

Mwinga cackled and turned to Sarpong. 'Patrice here is a great fan of your Kwame Nkrumah. He wants to visit his birthplace. I told him Ghanaians got rid of him …'

116

'Yes,' Patrice interrupted. 'And there are Ghanaians now who regret that.'

'Oh please, Patrice! Kwaku, put this man straight, will you? How many people vote for Nkrumah's party these days?'

Sarpong looked ill at ease being put on the spot. 'Well, barely any. But listen, people accept that in some respects Nkrumah was a great man. He led our country to independence, the first African colony to win its freedom. But what he did afterwards? One-party rule, locking up his political opponents, letting them die in prison?'

Josie Mwinga snapped her fingers and shouted for the dessert menu. 'The service here is slow ...'

Patrice wasn't finished. 'I'm not saying Nkrumah was perfect. But for the rest of us in Africa he was a hero. He inspired other countries to fight for their freedom too. He wanted Africa to take its place at the world table ... and saw the only way to do that was through a united Africa. And when he was overthrown, that dream went with him.'

Sarpong grinned. 'Patrice, are you a Pan-Africanist?'

'Of course. Many of us are, at heart.'

'But how would it work? Look at your own country, Congo. It's not even united. How could the whole of Africa be? I mean, can you imagine, Africa is one country and the president of Africa is barking off instructions from Addis or somewhere? You think anyone here, thousands of kilometres away, will be listening?'

'That depends on what the president of Africa is saying, not where they are. I think Africa as it is, arbitrarily carved up into fifty-odd countries, is not working. Nationalism is another form of tribalism. It divides us. I don't like borders, especially ones drawn by colonialists.'

The other two were silent.

'Well, you asked me what I thought.'

Mwinga tutted. 'I have to say I agree with Kwaku. You are a dreamer, Patrice, if you don't mind me saying. A united Africa was an idea of the 1960s. Times have moved on ...'

Patrice shrugged and smiled – he was used to such comments. 'So you won't be joining me on a trip to Nkroful?'

The three of them laughed. 'No,' Sarpong said. 'But I can recommend a hotel near there. There are nice ones on the coast.'

Josie Mwinga ordered ice cream and coffee. Sarpong looked at his watch and said he had to get going.

'Okay, Kwaku, nice to see you. Keep us posted, please.'

'Yes, I will.'

They watched him leave with his suit.

'You know, Patrice, there's one friend of mine here, a very good friend, who's well connected with the government. I'll ask him if he's heard about this Sunfall Power Company and their plans. And let me know if you need him to ... well, make discreet inquiries, further down the line.'

'Thank you, ma'am ... Josie.' She really did have a lot of friends. 'What does he do, this very good friend of yours?'

'Right,' she said, ignoring his question. 'And please go and see Kekeli Abotsi soon, will you? I spoke to her this morning on the phone. She needs reassuring that someone is on her side.'

'Well, I saw her yesterday, but not for long. I'll go this afternoon. I can help her look for her father's title deeds.'

Chapter 16

1966: FEBRUARY 9

There was a scene at breakfast when Yawor's cousin George announced that he no longer wanted to be a lawyer, that he wanted to be an engineer instead.

Uncle Joseph stared at his son. 'What, may I ask, has prompted this decision?'

'I have been thinking about this since we went to Akosombo. The construction of the dam has inspired me. I want to contribute to Osagyefo's plans for national development and his socialist policy.'

'Oh, God help us!' Uncle Joseph held his head in his hands. 'If Osagyefo told the Young Pioneers to jump off a cliff, you'd be first in line ...'

'He's not telling us to jump off a cliff. He's telling us to build our nation.'

'And a developing nation doesn't need lawyers?'

'I am not someone who can bury their head in books. I want to do practical work.'

Yawor noticed a vein pulsing on the side of Uncle Joseph's forehead. He finished his omelette, put down his knife and fork, and thumped the table.

'No! I cannot accept it. Your father trained as a lawyer and is a district court judge; your grandfather did likewise. You shall do the same.' He glared at his son. 'Do you hear me?'

George stared back at his father. 'I hear you, but my mind is made up.'

Uncle Joseph rose from the table and left the room. George's jaw was trembling. His brother and sisters were looking at the table. Aunt Esther told the younger children it was time to get ready for school and shooed them out. Emmanuel, the houseboy, came to clear the dishes.

Yawor patted George on the back. 'I'll come with you to the bus stop,' she said.

George offered his arm to Yawor as they walked to Independence Avenue. 'I don't care if my father doesn't show respect for Osagyefo,' he said. 'He never will – his politics are old fashioned. But it hurts that he has no respect for me. He treats me like a fool.'

'He won't now, not after today,' Yawor said.

'You think so?'

'You stood up to him. You showed you're ready to make decisions about your life and will not be bullied. It was a brave thing to do.'

'Thank you, Cousin. My father thinks he knows what's best for everyone, as you know.'

'Yes, he does ...' Yawor was thinking things over. 'I need to be brave like you, George.'

George squeezed her hand. 'What do you mean?'

'I should have spoken to your father last night, but I didn't.'

'About what?'

'I met Doctor Bennett yesterday – you remember him, from the hospital? He told me a post-mortem was carried out on

Adzo's body. He said one of her injuries suggested she was running away from the car that hit her.'

'That's not what the police told us.'

'I know. Doctor Bennett said they work slowly, so they might not have known about it then. The thing is, I was afraid to tell your father because I thought he'd get angry.' They'd reached the main road. Yawor pointed at the traffic. 'Your bus is coming, George.'

'But what will you do? About what the doctor told you?'

'I'm going to ask the police if they know about the post-mortem now, and if so, what they make of it.'

'Who? The commissioner?'

'Not him. I'll talk to Sergeant Ofori, who works in the commissioner's office, the one who came to our house with the commissioner. He looks like an honest man. I feel like he will help.'

The bus had pulled up and a crowd of passengers were pushing to get on. 'You can't go there alone, Cousin. I will come with you.'

'But you'll miss school.'

'I'll go afterwards. Today we'll be mostly preparing for a Young Pioneer camp that's starting tomorrow. Besides,' he added, 'there's no space in that bus.'

They set off along Independence Avenue on foot. The bus overtook them with passengers bulging out of the doors, making it tilt to the side. Thick black smoke followed it up the road. Behind it, a minibus taxi was coming.

'We can take this *trotro*,' George said.

'No, I want to walk. I want to tell you something else.'

'Oh? What is it? I'm listening.'

He held out his arm again and Yawor linked hers round

121

it. She told him about her visit to the street behind Makola Market, and what Joanna had said about the white man and the red Ford. She winced, expecting him to shout at her for being so reckless.

'My God!' he said, sounding more astonished than angry. 'And you say you're not brave!'

There was the usual hubbub outside police headquarters, with cars and people jostling to get in and out of the forecourt. Yawor led the way to the commissioner's office. 'I hope the commissioner is not around,' she whispered.

The door to the ante-room was open. She marched in, George behind her, but the room was empty. She was weighing up whether to wait, when the door to Harlley's inner-office opened and the young sergeant stepped out, closing it behind him.

'Miss Abotsi. Good morning. How are you?'

'Good morning, Sergeant. I'm well ... thank you. How are you? How is everything? How is the commissioner?' The words dribbled out uncontrollably.

A smile showed at the corners of the sergeant's mouth. 'All is well here, thank you, Miss Abotsi. What can we do for you?'

'I ... I wanted to ask you about something.' Yawor felt her mouth drying and swallowed. 'This is my cousin George. You met him at our house ... he's a senior Young Pioneer ...'

The sergeant nodded at George. He held up his fist and said, 'Nkrumah does no wrong!'

George held up his fist and responded, 'Nkrumah is our leader! Nkrumah is our Messiah! Nkrumah never dies!'

The two of them slapped hands and grinned. 'Were you a Pioneer?' George asked.

'I was too old, but my brothers, of course, and my sister.' The sergeant smiled at Yawor. 'You are welcome, both of you. Please take a seat. The commissioner is busy with visitors. Is it urgent?'

'No, no. We don't need to trouble the commissioner.' Yawor and her cousin sat in the seats she and her uncle had sat in on her previous visit. 'I was thinking we could talk to you and see what you think?'

'I am at your service. But ... what is it?'

'Well, I understand a post-mortem was carried out on my sister's body. I was told this yesterday. Have the results been passed to the police?'

Sergeant Ofori looked up from the notebook he'd opened and put down the pencil he'd picked up. 'Miss, the case of your sister's death was closed ... you must remember?'

'Yes, I know. But the post-mortem suggested the car struck her from behind – this is what I was told – which raises the possibility it was a deliberate act, which changes everything.'

The sergeant went to a filing cabinet and pulled out a sheet of paper. The creases appeared between his eyebrows as he studied the document. 'Who told you about this?' he asked.

'I don't want to get anyone in trouble. A friend of mine works at the hospital.'

'Well ...' The young man frowned. 'Miss, I know you want to do right by your sister, but may I ask why you have come with your cousin today and not your uncle?'

Yawor's lips tightened into a thin line as she considered how to reply. 'Sergeant, it's difficult. You saw how my uncle reacted. I don't want to upset him unnecessarily. So I was thinking ...'

'You haven't told him about the post-mortem?'

Yawor shook her head.

The sergeant sighed. 'I don't know ... I mean, this doesn't prove your sister was deliberately run down ...'

'But in normal circumstances you would investigate this further, wouldn't you? Couldn't you and your colleagues make more inquiries, discreetly? I've already found out some information about one of her clients ...'

'But this is not normal circumstances.' He glanced at his boss's door. 'Your father went to the commissioner, and the commissioner went to your house. Please, miss, I can't re-open the investigation behind their backs.'

Yawor cast her eyes down.

'Cousin.' George had been silent up to now. He placed his hand on Yawor's. 'The sergeant here believes this new information is important. What it means is we must tell my father before ...'

Before George could finish the sentence, the door to the police commissioner's office opened again. Yawor held back a squeal.

'Sergeant, get these processed immediately ...' Harlley came through and handed some documents to Sergeant Ofori, but he cut short his orders when he saw who else was there. 'Miss Abotsi. Is everything alright? What brings you here?'

'Yes, sir. It is. I ...' The police chief's eyes were fixed on her, pinning her to her chair. It was like she'd been caught stealing mangos from a neighbour's garden. 'This is my cousin George, my uncle's son; he's in the Young Pioneers ...'

The police chief's eyes flashed from Yawor to George and back. 'I remember him from your house. But what can we do for you here? Has something happened?'

'No. I ... it's just I didn't know who to come to with this

information …' In her panic Yawor said the first thing that came to her. 'I have in recent days overheard disturbing conversations – people suggesting there are plots afoot to overthrow Osagyefo! So I thought I must report this, and George, being a Young Pioneer, well, he's concerned too, so that's why we came …' Out of the corner of her eye she could see Sergeant Ofori's face; he was staring at her. She couldn't see George's, but she could imagine his look of anguish. 'Well, I didn't know who to trust, so I came here, to your office …'

Creases formed at the edge of Harlley's eyes. His face looked as hard as stone. 'Where did you hear these conversations?'

'Well, yesterday I was on the terrace at the Paris Hotel and two men, white men, were having a bet. One bet the other ten pounds the president would be out by the first rains. Those were his exact words …'

'Miss Abotsi, don't concern yourself with the idle gossip of foreigners. These people have nothing better to do. We know they don't wish our country to succeed. I thank you for coming, but I can assure you the country and our leader are safe in the hands of the Ghanaian police force.'

Yawor made to get up. 'Thank you, sir. I'm sorry to …'

'Wait,' the police commissioner snapped. His eyes were fierce and still narrowed as they moved again between the two young visitors. 'I may be old like your uncle, but I'm not a fool. Such talk as you've reported has been going round Accra for the past five years, as you and I well know, so a silly bet by two white men is unlikely to make you come to the office of the commissioner of police. So, Sergeant Ofori, perhaps you will tell me what brought these two here today?'

Yawor closed her eyes in shame.

Before the sergeant had time to reply, George spoke up. 'Sir, we came because my cousin found out her sister may have been murdered.'

The commissioner turned to Sergeant Ofori.

It dawned on Yawor that her carelessness could cause trouble for the young sergeant. 'I'm sorry, sir,' she said. 'Please forgive me for not being straight with you. As you know, this has been a traumatic business for our family.' She had the commissioner's attention, but he was frowning. 'Since you came to our house, I have learned that a post-mortem found my sister had bruises on the back of her legs ... as if she was running away from the car. For her sake, I had to see what the police thought about this, so I came back here, because Sergeant Ofori knows the case. I thought we should ask him what he thought ...'

'And what do you think, Sergeant?' the commissioner asked, still looking at Yawor.

'Well, it could be significant.' The sergeant passed the post-mortem report to his boss. 'But I reminded the young lady of her uncle's position on the case, and I think she was about to go and consult him before asking us to pursue this matter ...'

'That's a good idea. Well done, Sergeant. Good advice.' The police commissioner looked from Yawor to George again, to confirm they agreed.

Yawor nodded. 'Yes, we were just leaving ... Thank you, sir, and Sergeant. I'm sorry we've wasted your time.'

As they turned and walked out of the office, Yawor could feel Harlley's glare burning a hole in the back of her neck.

Chapter 17

The mid-afternoon streets were quiet, as if the city was sleeping off its lunch. Patrice guided the taxi up the Dodowa road and down to River Valley. The driver pulled over when the police post by the culvert came into view.

'Where is your place?' he asked.

'It's not far.'

'Okay, good, I will leave you here.'

'Why?'

'I have temporary papers while I wait for a new licence. These people will ask for money ...'

Patrice paid the fare and walked the rest of the way. It was a beautiful, peaceful afternoon in the hills. Birdsong and insect sounds filled the air. A lone policeman was sitting in the shade by the shipping container. He lifted his heavy-looking eyelids as Patrice passed and let them close again.

The Ghanaian flag hung outside the Abotsi house but not as high as before. The pole was buckling and looked like it might break any minute. He looked back down the valley, reflecting on the scene. If the Sunfall Power Company got its way, the trees and the house and the flag would all be flattened.

He knocked on the door. No one answered, so he went to the back. 'Hello,' he called as he rounded the last corner.

'Huh! You made me jump.' Kekeli was there, her hand gripping a single piece of blue patterned material wrapped around her body. 'I wasn't expecting you so soon.'

He guessed she'd just had a shower. 'I can wait at the front.'

She smiled. 'It's no problem. I'm glad you're here. You can help me make dinner. Remember I said I'd teach you how to cook palava sauce?'

'Okay, but what about the title deeds?'

'We can look for them later. Aren't you hungry?'

He smiled. 'I am.'

She went inside and returned with bowl containing spinach and onions and various bags, and a chopping board. 'Come and learn,' she said, sitting at a low table. She passed him an onion and a knife. He hesitated, and she took them back.

'Men! Ugh!' She cut the onion in half, peeled it, and began chopping. 'Tell me about yesterday,' she said. 'Did you find those people?'

He told her about his meeting with Albert Boateng but not about his encounter with the car later. 'And what about you? Did you make the funeral arrangements?'

She shook her head. 'Not the way I was hoping to. I can't find anyone to perform a non-religious funeral. No one knows what I'm talking about when I say that's what my father wanted.'

'What will you do?'

'We'll hold the funeral at the church. I'll bring his ashes home and scatter them here in his garden.'

She turned to a small iron stove and blew on the charcoal. 'You can tend the fire ... take this.'

She passed him a fan made of woven palm leaves. He looked at it. She laughed. Her face lit up in a way Patrice hadn't

128

seen since they'd met. Her eyes sparkled and her teeth shone brightly. It was impossible not to laugh with her.

'Do it like this,' she said, taking back the fan and busily fanning the charcoal so it was glowing orange. 'Okay? Can you do that?'

She smiled again as she passed it back again, and Patrice set to work.

'Where's your aunt?'

'She's gone with Gladys to the Addos' house. Are you afraid to be with me alone?'

Patrice chuckled and carried on doing as he was told. If she was flirting with him, she was doing a good job.

Kekeli put a tin pot on the stove and added a large handful of spinach and a couple of tablespoons of water. 'Not so much water,' she said. 'Because there is water in the spinach, see …'

When the spinach had cooked to her satisfaction, she put the pot to one side and replaced it with a shallow frying pan and tipped in a bowlful of chopped tomatoes. She added a spoonful of garlic, then ginger, chopped onions and salt and pepper.

Patrice's mouth was watering. His arm was tiring. Close to the fire, he was sweating.

Kekeli noticed. 'Aha, you see, you are doing real work!'

She was sweating herself, her smooth, moist skin catching the light around her collarbones and arms. The way she moved – picking up the jars, spooning them out, adding them to the pan with a simple flick of the wrist – so naturally, with such poise, it was like she was performing a dance. The smell, the crackling sound, the whole scene, was intoxicating. Patrice closed his eyes and breathed in, savouring the moment.

129

'You know what the Ashanti women of Ghana say about cooking for a man?'

'No.'

Kekeli laughed again as she gave the mix a stir. 'One day I'll tell you.'

Patrice swallowed. Something stirred below. The pan hissed as she added the spinach and more water to the tomatoes. Then she sprinkled chilli pepper over it and spooned in some palm oil. Finally, she broke two eggs into the mix and stirred them in, completing the plate, a sweet-smelling dish of green, yellow and red, like the colours of the Ghanaian flag.

'I'm using eggs because you didn't bring me meat.' She patted him playfully on his head. 'Next time, bring me meat! But now, it's ready: palava sauce.'

'Kekeli, it looks and smells amazing ...'

'You can stop fanning the fire,' she said, smiling, holding his arm.

He hadn't realised he was still doing it. He smiled back, dropped the fan, and pulled her towards him. She pressed against him and he leaned down to kiss her. She tipped her head up and their lips met.

'We don't have to eat it immediately,' she said. She put a plate over the pan and led him indoors.

The meal tasted as good as it looked and smelled.

'So now you know about the magic of palava sauce,' Kekeli said as they mopped their plates with bread.

'Yes,' Patrice replied, looking across at her. 'Thank you for the lesson. I like the flavours. One day I'll make it for you.'

'I would like that.'

They grinned at each other.

They went to sit on the back veranda, sharing a bottle of Star.

'You're a beautiful woman, Kekeli, and a great cook! But you don't have a husband?'

She tutted. 'I did, but he left me. Because I couldn't have children. He said a wife cannot be barren. That's when I came back to live here. Now I don't have much to do with men – you are a rare exception.'

'Then I'm lucky!'

'But you too are not married.'

'No. I was, also, but my wife died in childbirth, our baby too. It was some years ago … since then, I've been busy with my work, so …'

There was a rustle of leaves. They stopped talking. Aunty Yawor appeared, walking with a single crutch, followed by Gladys. The old lady looked from Kekeli to Patrice and back.

'Hello, Aunty.'

Aunty Yawor raised her crutch and pointed it at them, and cackled. She pulled herself up the steps and went to her chair. Gladys was staring at the ground.

'How are you, Gladys?' Kekeli asked. 'And your father?'

The girl took a few moments to respond. 'My father says we must leave our house. We are packing our things to go. Within a week we will be gone.'

'But why? We have more time than that – not much, but you don't have to go yet. Where will you go?'

'He says he doesn't want to stay to the end. We will drive to his sister's house in Koforidua. It is not so far.'

Gladys looked from Kekeli to Aunty Yawor and broke into tears. 'What about Aunty? Who will look after Aunty?'

Kekeli put her arm round the girl. 'Don't worry about Aunty. I will look after her. We're going to look for my father's title deeds. If we find them, maybe you and your father, and all of us, can stay.'

'I will pray for that.' Gladys wiped her cheeks and went back through the bushes.

'Agh! Ek!' Aunty Yawor was muttering. She seemed more restless than usual. Her eyes were narrowed, as if she was trying to remember something. Out of the blue, she said, 'A red car. He was driving a red car.'

Kekeli stared at her aunt. 'Who was?'

The old lady didn't answer.

'Aunty?' Patrice tried to coax her. 'Who was driving a red car?'

The concentration that had briefly shown was gone. She was looking vacantly into the middle distance.

Patrice was thinking about the tyre marks on the track above George Abotsi's hydro-plant. 'Is she talking about the day your father died?'

Kekeli looked at her aunt. 'I don't know. She hasn't said a word to me about that day. But I think with you here asking lots of questions, it's jolted her memory.'

Chapter 18

1966: FEBRUARY 9

Yawor walked with George from police headquarters to the bus stop on Independence Avenue. She wondered what she was getting herself and her cousin into: potentially a lot of trouble. They agreed to wait for him to get back from school, then together they'd confront his father with the news of Adzo's post-mortem.

'He'll be furious we went to the police behind his back,' Yawor said.

'Yes, but it was the commissioner himself who said we should talk to him.'

'That will make him more furious.'

George caught his bus and Yawor walked home. Shortly after lunch, she was surprised, and alarmed, to hear Uncle Joseph's car outside. She went to meet him at the top of the front steps.

'Uncle. You're home early.'

'Yes. I need to talk to you, Yawor.' He looked and sounded like he had bad news.

'What is it, Uncle?'

'Come …' They sat on a cane sofa on the veranda. 'Yawor,

133

I had a visit from Commissioner Harlley. He came to the courthouse with his sergeant.'

Yawor tensed up.

'He told me you went to his office this morning with information about Adzo ...'

'I did, I ... I wanted to talk to you about it but I was afraid you'd be angry. It was about the post-mortem ... Dr Bennett told me about it ...'

'I know, I know. It's alright, Yawor. You did the right thing. And the police will make further inquiries.'

'They will? What if there's a scandal?'

'It's the right thing to do. When I spoke before, it was in anger. I was upset and shocked ... to hear what Adzo had been doing. But if she was run down deliberately, we can't ignore that.'

Yawor put her arms round her uncle. 'Thank you, Uncle, thank you.' She'd never been close to Uncle Joseph, but now she felt sorry for him, for putting his reputation at risk. 'There's something else,' she said, sitting back, 'something I haven't told the police yet.'

'What is it?'

She hesitated. If she told her uncle about Adzo's client who drove the red car, she'd have to explain she'd gone to Makola Market on her own, after he'd said the investigation should go no further. 'Oh, nothing.'

'What haven't you told the police, Yawor?'

'Well, I ... the thing is, Adzo had been doing this business, this work, for six months, at least ... she told me six months ago. It occurred to me the police should know that ...'

Uncle Joseph patted her hand. 'I'll pass that on. But Yawor, listen to me. Since this happened you've been upset, and that's natural. But now you must return to Winneba. It's what Adzo would have wanted. Applying yourself to your studies will help you get over this tragedy.'

'But I can't ... not while this is going on, while we don't know what happened ...'

'The police will find out what happened. That's their job. Pack your bag. Tomorrow morning I'll take you to the bus station.'

It was her uncle's house. She couldn't argue with him, so she did as she was told. Afterwards she took one of her college books onto the veranda. She tried to read, but it was impossible to concentrate. Before she'd reached the end of the first line, she was thinking about something else: a letter. She'd write an anonymous letter to Police Commissioner Harlley about the red car.

When George came home, she went to greet him at the gate. She embraced him and whispered in his ear. 'The commissioner went to see your father and told him we'd been to see him.' Her cousin's body stiffened. 'He says they'll carry out more inquiries into Adzo's death, but your father's told me to go back to Winneba.'

'George!' Uncle Joseph was calling from the open front door. 'Come here, my boy.' George looked up.

Yawor held on to him. 'George, wait, I didn't want to tell him about the red car, but I'm going to write an anonymous letter to the commissioner. Please don't mention it. I'm sorry, George, for getting you involved in all this.'

'Don't worry, Cousin. I'm on your side.' He puffed out his chest and marched up the steps and followed his father indoors.

Yawor slid a sheet of plain paper into her exercise book and composed her letter. She wrote in pencil: TO POLICE COM-MISSIONER HARLLEY. INFORMATION RELATING TO THE DEATH OF ADZOWOR ABOTSI …

To her surprise there were no shouts from inside. After a few minutes her cousin emerged, shrugging his shoulders. 'My father told me families should not have secrets. He said he was sure everything would turn out for the best. He asked me to think again about my choice of career, but he said he would respect my decision. He's a different person to how he was this morning – and he hasn't been drinking!'

'You see, he respects you now!' Yawor showed him her letter.

He nodded his approval. 'Give it to me. I'm staying at my friend Kwabena's tonight, before we go to camp; I can post it on my way over.'

They sat in the dusk together. Insects were chirping. The buses and cars rumbled in the distance along Independence Avenue.

'It doesn't feel right to be leaving,' Yawor said. 'I promised I wouldn't abandon Adzo. But now I'm going …'

'You haven't abandoned her. Because of you, the police are going to reopen their investigation.'

At dinner that evening, and after glasses of palm wine, Uncle Joseph was in a jovial mood. Instead of becoming morose and complaining about the state of the country, the bad roads, the lack of basics in the shops, he was entertaining the younger children with stories from his own childhood. Then, out of the blue, he surprised everyone by saying he intended to take the family to England for a holiday. The young children shrieked with delight. Aunt Esther looked like she'd misheard.

'Can we afford to do that?'

'Don't you want to go?'

'Well, yes, I do. But …'

'Nonsense. No buts! It's time the children saw there is a world beyond Ghana. We can take them to see Buckingham Palace and the Houses of Parliament.'

Yawor assumed she would not be joining them, but she didn't mind. She had no great desire to travel to Europe.

George said, 'Papa, as this is Yawor's last night with us for another term, shouldn't we be wishing her well?'

'We should, indeed! And the future is bright for Yawor. She's had a difficult time, like we all have, but she can look forward now to becoming a teacher, imparting knowledge on the nation's children.' Uncle Joseph raised his glass. 'To Yawor!'

The younger children looked sad. Yawor put on a brave face for them. 'Thank you, Uncle, and thank you, Aunty, for having me in your house and for being so kind to me these last weeks.' She raised her glass of water.

After dinner, George left for his friend Kwabena's. Yawor saw him down to the gate and hugged him. 'I'll miss you, George. You are a real friend.'

'Goodbye, Cousin. Be strong and study hard.'

Yawor wasn't sleepy that night. When the family went to bed, she went out onto the front veranda. A bright moon was up. The bougainvillea looked jet-black against the white wall. The highlife band was playing at the Ambassador Hotel. She was thinking she'd miss their music in Winneba, a small sleepy town along the coast, when she heard a hiss coming from close by. Someone was outside on the road.

Herbert, the guard, was sitting by the gatehouse. He didn't stir. From the way his chin rested on his chest, Yawor could tell he was asleep. The house was still and quiet. She eased herself down the steps and made for the gate. The hissing had stopped. She slid aside the peephole cover. Looking into her eyes from the other side was Sergeant Ofori.

Yawor took a sharp breath. Sergeant Ofori put his finger over his lips.

'What is it?' Yawor whispered.

'I must talk to you.'

'But ... but ...' She looked round at Herbert. He was still sleeping. She lifted the bolt and pulled the gate open to before the point where she knew it squeaked, squeezed through, and pulled it back.

'Come,' the sergeant said softly. He was still in his uniform. 'I'm sorry for the secrecy. But we must be careful.'

He took her hand and they walked away, keeping close to the wall of her uncle's compound, and further, to a tree where they could stand in the shade, out of the moonlight. His grip was firm but reassuring. Her heart fluttered. She shook her head, rebuking herself for being silly.

At last, he spoke. 'Miss, I ... I shouldn't be doing this – if the commissioner knew, he would sack me on the spot, maybe worse. But ...' He was looking at her intently. '... but I believe you are a good person. And what I heard today ... I had to tell you, because it is not right ...'

'What? What did you hear?'

'When you came this morning with your cousin, the commissioner was in a meeting. Normally these meetings are long, but after you left, this one ended quickly. He told me to drive him to the district court and to find your uncle. We arrived as your uncle was preparing to go into the courtroom. The commissioner said for him to wait, and told him that you and your cousin had come to his office and had heard about the post-mortem.'

'I know, my uncle told me.'

'Wait, let me finish. The commissioner said, "Abotsi, this has to stop." Before your uncle could respond, the commissioner said, "I can't explain everything to you. But there is an ongoing matter of national importance which cannot be disrupted." Your uncle looked surprised. The commissioner called him by his first name. He said, "Joseph, we are old friends, we may not have kept in touch, but we know each other and I'm asking you to trust me." Those were his words.'

Yawor was lost. 'A matter of national importance? What does this have to do with Adzo?'

'Your uncle asked the same. The commissioner said, "I cannot go into details, Joseph, but what I can say to you, between us, is that if everything goes to plan, there will soon be a major reorganisation of the judicial system. And when it comes to new appointments, I can ensure that your name will be at the top of the list." When he said that, your uncle stood up straight and said, "I have full trust in you, sir."

'Then, and this is where it connects to your sister, the commissioner said that in the meantime, with resources being stretched the way they are, he could not allow his men to be sidetracked by other matters. That was the word he used: sidetracked.

'Your uncle said, "If this is the situation, and it's a matter of national importance, it must take precedence. I understand. And you can rely on me." He said he would send you back to college in Winneba tomorrow morning.'

Yawor put her hand over her mouth as the sergeant's words sunk in. 'So, they won't be investigating Adzo's death. My uncle said they would … he was lying. And that's why he was so cheerful tonight. And why he said he wants to take the family on holiday to England.' The implications hit her like a brick. 'Because he's going to get a promotion. He'd put his own career ahead of justice for Adzo.'

Sergeant Ofori lowered his eyes. 'It seems so.'

'What can be so important that all other police work has to stop? I don't understand.'

'I don't understand either, miss. The commissioner hasn't said anything to me. But I hope you don't mind that I came to tell you. I thought you'd want to know.'

She was shaking her head, reeling from the news. 'No, yes, thank you. But you shouldn't have taken such a risk on my account …'

She looked up into his eyes. He was staring down into hers.

'You took a risk,' he said, 'when you came to headquarters today. I saw again how much its means to you to help your sister.'

'It means everything to me. But now, what should I do?'

'How do you mean?'

'I can't help Adzo if I'm in Winneba.'

'You've done everything you can, and more …'

'I made a promise to Adzo that I wouldn't abandon her. And I won't. But will you help me?'

'I would like to, but how?'

'I don't know yet. But there's something you should know. I met a friend of Adzo's … from the university. She said Adzo had a regular client, a white man who picked her up in a red car. I was going to tell you today. Then, this evening, after my uncle said I was going back to college tomorrow, I wrote an anonymous letter to the commissioner with that information. If he has no intention of continuing with the investigation, I don't want him to know that others have not forgotten. But my cousin took the letter to post ...'

Sergeant Ofori nodded. 'With that I can help. I open all the commissioner's post, unless it's marked "confidential", so he will not have to read your letter.'

'Really? You'd do that? What if ... you got caught?'

He shrugged.

She took hold of his hand again. 'Do you agree it's important? I mean, how many white men drive a red car in Accra? And he used to pick her up on Saturdays, which is the day she died.'

'There cannot be many. I have a friend who works in the vehicle licensing department. I will ask him what records they keep. Miss, you should be a detective!'

They set off back towards Uncle Joseph's house, still holding hands, but differently, more like friends. They reached the gate. Yawor peered through the peephole. Herbert was still sleeping.

'Goodnight,' she whispered. 'Thank you for coming and for everything. But I don't know your first name.'

'It's Anthony.'

'Anthony Ofori. Sergeant Anthony Ofori. But I will call you Ofori. I like that name. You may call me Yawor. I will keep in touch somehow ... discreetly.'

'Take care, Yawor.'

They clicked fingers quietly before Yawor sneaked back into her uncle's house and went to bed. It was late but she still couldn't sleep. Her mind was racing in all directions.

141

Chapter 19

George Abotsi had lived in the house he built in River Valley for twenty years, and in that time he hadn't thrown away a single scrap of paper. That's how it seemed to Patrice as he helped Kekeli search for her father's title deeds. Every shelf, every surface, was buried under piles of books and notebooks and diaries and stacks of newspapers.

They started in the room Kekeli called his office. It was a large room overlooking the back garden. There were two desks set at right angles, a sofa, and upright chairs, all covered with files and envelopes, and sheets of paper with sketches and mathematical calculations.

Patrice's eye fell at random on a cardboard box on the floor. He blew the dust off the lid and opened it. It was stuffed full of old photographs. 'Look at this,' he said.

Kekeli flipped through the prints. 'I've never seen these before. Look, here he is with the Young Pioneers.'

A black and white image showed twenty boys in three rows, wearing white shirts and shorts.

'That's Papa.' She pointed at a boy with an upright posture and a proud smile sitting in the middle at the front. He had the same sharp features as his daughter and the same glint in his eye. 'He must be about fifteen. And look at this one; he's older, perhaps when he was at college.' It was a head-and-shoulders shot, but the facial expression was serious.

Kekeli skimmed through the photographs, tutting. 'I don't know who half these people are.'

'Your aunt might recognise them?'

'Yes, that's true. That's a good idea, Patrice. One day, when we've got time, I'll sit with her and we'll look at them together. It may help her with her memory.'

All morning, they worked through the boxes and papers. They found a folder containing a map of the valley, with plans and drawings of the plots and houses and bills of sale for building materials, and another with papers relating to George Abotsi's hydroelectric scheme: drawings, invoices from European and Japanese companies for the components, and quotes from local construction companies for the damming work. But no title deeds.

They took a break for lunch and sat on the back veranda. Patrice could tell from Kekeli's sagging shoulders that she was losing hope.

'I don't know,' she said. 'We could pack up and leave, like the Addos. Aunty has some small savings, and my ex-husband owes me money. We can find somewhere in Accra.' She looked at her aunt, who was gazing into the garden. Then she looked at the garden herself. 'My father had a dream for this place, but I don't know how we can save it ...'

She went over to the old lady. 'Are you hungry, Aunty? Let me heat the palava sauce for you.' She snuffled and wiped a tear and headed for the kitchen.

Patrice looked from Kekeli to Aunty Yawor and then, like the old lady, gazed into the garden. Was this, he asked himself, how things were always going to be? Good, honest people getting trampled on by the rich and powerful, while others just sit and watch and hope their turn isn't coming next?

'No!' he said as he smacked the armrest of his chair. 'Kekeli, don't give up!' He sprang to his feet and skipped down the steps.

'Where are you going? Don't you want to eat?'

'I'm not hungry, thank you. I'll see you ...'

He walked to the main road and boarded a *trotro* back to town. He went to his hotel and showered. Then he took a regular taxi to Kwame Nkrumah Circle. If he had any doubts about the moral correctness of what he planned to do, they vanished when he passed a news-stand and saw the headline: *GIANT SOLAR POWER PLANT PROPOSED*.

He got out at the traffic circle and walked the rest of the way, down Kwame Nkrumah Avenue and into Kente Street. There was an alleyway opposite Kente House, and that's where he waited, leaning against a wall in the shadows.

It wasn't long before the Sunfall Power Company's receptionist, Vera, left the building and walked to the main road. A while later, Albert Boateng emerged. He stood in the doorway and looked at his watch. The sky was darkening. There was no one else around. As he stepped away from the entrance, Patrice called after him.

'Mr Boateng!'

The man swivelled round. It took him a moment to recognise Patrice. 'Mr Kabanda. I wasn't expecting to see you here again. I thought you were going home.'

'Change of plan.'

'And change of clothes, I notice.' He smiled smugly. 'Where's your beautiful suit?'

'I've had enough of that game.'

'In that case, what are you doing here?'

'Unfinished business.'

Boateng glanced back at the entrance to Kente House. 'I don't believe we have any business to discuss.'

'Oh. You don't want to invest in my country?'

Boateng's smug smile was fading. 'I admit you had me fooled at first. But, of course, we checked your story and discovered your client doesn't exist and you turn out to be someone quite different: not an energy consultant but a human rights investigator called Patrice Le Congo. So please don't waste any more of my time. Besides, there must be many things for you to investigate in that messed-up country of yours. Goodbye, Mr Le Congo.'

Boateng turned to go, but Patrice jumped forward and slapped his hand on the man's shoulder. 'Uh-uh. Not so fast.'

He swung him round and grabbed hold of his jacket lapels and looked him hard in the eye. 'Now come with me. We're going to have another chat.'

The short, skinny man with big eyes looked like a frightened child. 'Let go of me.' He tried to wriggle free, but his resistance was feeble.

'You leave the rough stuff to others, don't you, Mr Boateng?' Patrice dragged him sideways and pushed him backwards into the alleyway and up against a wall. Playing the tough guy wasn't in Patrice's nature, but he sensed it would yield quick results with this coward.

'What do you want?' the man was trembling.

'It's payback time.' Patrice shoved his fists against Boateng's neck. 'The thing is, I don't have thugs to send to your house

145

with an eviction notice. And I don't have money to pay for police protection. And I don't have a car, so I can't run you down. So, I'll do this myself, hand-to-hand combat, the way the people in my messed-up country have shown me …'

He pressed harder with his fists. Boateng's eyes were popping out of his head.

'Stop, Le Congo,' he said, gasping. 'Is it money you want? I can get you money …'

'Money! You think everything's about money?'

'Please, please … Le Congo … what do you want?'

Patrice let go of Boateng's jacket lapels but he still had him pinned against the wall. 'You do, you think everything's about money. And when George Abotsi said he didn't want your money, you killed him.'

There was a pause. Boateng was panting. 'I didn't kill him.'

'Who did?'

'I don't know. It was an accident …'

'You're lying!'

'I swear …'

Patrice slapped him hard on his cheeks.

Boateng squealed. 'No, please … that's what I heard. But I don't know. I deal with the business side of things …'

'The business side of things? You mean like altering records at the Lands Commission? Well, that's good. You can alter them again and give the Abotsi family back their land.'

'Please, I can't do that. It's not me … I do what I'm told.'

'By who? Who runs this company?'

Boateng hung his head.

Patrice raised his open hand again. With his other, he yanked the man's head up. 'Last chance, Boateng. Who gives you your orders?'

Boateng was whimpering, but his lips were closed tight.

'Talk to me or I'll smash this sick head of yours against this wall.'

'Alright, alright ... stop! I don't know how it all works. There's a man ... a senior official in the Energy Commission. His name's Mensah. Victor Mensah.'

Patrice let go and stepped back, wiping his hands on his jeans. 'You're a worm, Boateng.' He left the general manager of the Sunfall Power Company snivelling and quivering, slumped against the wall.

Chapter 20

The bus station at dawn was half hidden in a haze of smoke from cooking stoves and vehicle exhaust. Uncle Joseph manoeuvred his car over the potholes and between the pedestrians, and up to the Winneba stand, where three or four buses were touting for passengers.

The drivers' mates called out, 'Winneba, Winneba-a-a!'

Uncle Joseph bought Yawor a ticket for a bus that was nearly full and supervised the loading of her bag.

'Thank you, Uncle, you don't have to wait.'

'No, no, I said I'll see you off. You never know with these people.'

'You never know what?'

Uncle Joseph grunted. 'For all you know, they'll sell your seat to someone else.'

They ate rice water porridge, sitting on a bench. Uncle Joseph slurped. The noise irritated Yawor. She shifted away from him. She despised everything about him now. But at least he'd given her some money.

When the bus was ready to leave, she climbed aboard and took her seat, which hadn't been sold to someone else.

148

Uncle Joseph walked round and called through the open window. 'Have a safe journey, Yawor. Work hard and we'll see you at Easter.'

He held up his hand. Yawor didn't want to touch him but forced herself to shake it. 'Thank you, Uncle,' she said through gritted teeth.

He waved goodbye. She watched him get in the Austin A40 and drive out of the station, beeping at pedestrians to get out of his way.

There was a jolt and a rumble and more smoke as the bus driver started the engine. With a grinding clunk, he forced it into gear. But before he moved off, Yawor shouted, 'Driver, wait, let me down!'

Two minutes later, she was standing outside the bus station. There was shouting all around. Early morning travellers and traders crammed the streets. A policeman said she was causing an obstruction and told her to move. Her bag was too heavy to carry far, so she hailed a taxi to take her to Makola Market.

She directed the driver to the road behind the market and told him to slow down while she got her bearings. It looked different in daylight, like a normal street in downtown Accra. Women were cooking over small fires, offering breakfast. She recognised the spot where she'd talked to Joanna. Two blocks further on, she told the driver to pull up outside a three-storey clapboard building. A sign in peeling paint welcomed patrons to the Black Star Hotel.

'You're staying here?' the driver asked.

'Do I look like I'm staying here?'

'No.'

'Then mind your business, please.'

149

Yawor paid her fare and watched him drive away. The stairs to the porch creaked and a musty smell of damp carpet greeted her as she opened the door into the lobby. A young woman sat at the front desk. Her head was resting on it, and she was snoring.

Yawor coughed to get her attention. 'Good morning.'

The woman snorted and raised herself. Her eyes were tired and red.

'I'm sorry to disturb you. I'm looking for my friend, Joanna … She rents a room here.'

The tired eyes blinked as they looked Yawor up and down. The woman pointed at the door. 'You go that way, the stairs outside. Top floor. Room eleven.'

Yawor lugged her bag up several flights of worn wooden steps. By the time she reached the top, her hip was burning and she was sweating and out of breath. She walked down the open landing, found the door and knocked. She knocked twice more. Eventually, it squeaked open. Joanna was looking sleepy and dishevelled but wearing no make-up, which gave Yawor hope she was alone.

'Yawor! What are you doing here? What time is it?'

'I know it's early. I'm sorry. I wanted to ask you a favour … a big favour.'

'What is it?'

'Can I stay with you? For a few days? A week maybe?'

'Well, I … I don't know … I mean …'

'I don't know where else to go. I need to hide. My uncle thinks I've gone back to college. But I can't leave Accra.'

Joanna rubbed her face and looked back into the room behind her. 'You'd better come in …' She opened the door wider to let Yawor pass.

Inside, it was dark. The bed was unmade, but it didn't stink and there were no rats.

'What I mean is, sometimes I work here, Yawor ... I bring clients ... sometimes for a whole night.'

Yawor blushed. 'I know. I understand. I can wait outside when that happens. It won't be for long, I promise.'

'You can't do that!' Joanna took her hand. 'But I want to help you. There is a small room where you can sleep when I have a client.' She pointed at another door. 'If you don't mind sleeping on the floor, and the noise.'

'Thank you, Joanna. Thank you so much.'

They sat on the bed and Yawor explained her situation. 'The police have called off their investigation, but I'm not giving up. I'm going to find that red car.'

'The police will never care if someone kills an *ashawo*,' Joanna said. 'Oh! But I forgot, the car came back. I saw it two nights ago.'

'You saw it?' Yawor grabbed Joanna's arm. 'The red Ford? The same one?'

'I think so. It was down the street ...'

'Was it stopping for girls?'

'Yes ... a girl got in, but I didn't recognise her.'

'Did you see the driver?'

'No. Sorry ...'

'Don't be sorry. If he came back once, he may come again. I will wait for him every night ...'

'But what will you do if he comes?'

'Well, for one thing, I'll get the registration number. There's a policeman I know who ... who will help me. Perhaps he can find out who the driver is.'

Joanna showed Yawor the room off the side, small and bare,

more like a walk-in cupboard, with no bed or other furniture. 'I have a blanket you can use.'

'Thank you, Joanna. I will pray that God rewards you for what you are doing for me.'

Yawor stepped out to buy the *Daily Graphic* and spent the day in Joanna's room reading the paper from cover to cover. Most of the reports were about development projects: a new school opening; how to improve crop yields for yams; the need for children to get vaccinated. The opinion articles focussed on community issues and the importance of the country working together. There was one that criticised the international financial system for a fall in cocoa prices, which it said was at the root of Ghana's economic problems. There was no news of any police operation that might be connected to a matter of national importance.

At dusk, she walked with Joanna down the road and found a seat in the bar where they'd talked before. While Joanna went about her business, Yawor observed the activity out on the street: young women appearing in doorways; men hovering; cars crawling past. Now and again, Joanna took a break and came to join her. The longer Yawor sat there, the less threatening she found the whole place. Really, she thought, it was a market, like any other. The women had something to sell and men came to buy. The difference was that trading took place under the cover of darkness.

The red Ford did not appear that first evening. Afterwards Yawor spent the night on the floor of the little room, listening to one of Joanna's clients groaning and snoring. She reminded herself she was doing this for Adzo.

1966: FEBRUARY 12

Two nights later, her hopes were higher. It was a Saturday, the day of the week the man in the red Ford usually came to the street - the day of the week, three weeks earlier, that Adzo was killed. More women were out than on the previous evenings and more cars driving slowly past. But still no red Ford. It was getting late, and less busy, when Joanna came and sat with her. She was grinning.

'I've had three clients. All quick.' She counted her earnings, discreetly unfolding the banknotes and checking their value under the green neon light. 'It's my lucky day!'

'Not for me,' Yawor said. 'It's three nights I've been sitting here. The bar owner knows me well.'

'Yes, you're the girl who takes five hours to drink one beer and never gets up to do any work!'

They laughed. Yawor was so grateful to Joanna. She wouldn't have felt safe but for her. Even if Joanna wasn't always there, the bar owner and the other girls knew Yawor was her friend and let her be. Throughout those long evenings, no one ever asked her why she was there. 'Thank you, Jo,' she said, 'for helping me.'

'You know, for me, it's nice to have a friend. Apart from the girls here, no one wants to know me. When people see me coming, they cross the road.'

'I know that feeling too,' Yawor said. 'We are both pariahs.'

She passed her bottle and Joanna took a sip.

'Thank you, Yawor.'

At that moment Yawor froze, her eyes fixed on the scene twenty yards away, where a car had pulled over beneath a streetlamp.

153

'What is it, Yawor?'

It wasn't the car that concerned Yawor but the woman talking to the driver through the window. It was Beatrice Ansah, the daughter of Uncle Joseph's friend Austin. The last time she'd seen her was in a lecture hall three years earlier.

'I know that girl. If she sees me and tells her father ...'

'Hey, don't worry. She won't tell, or else she'll have to explain what she was doing here too!'

'Her father knows my uncle. He comes to the house all the time. He could mention to Beatrice in passing that he heard I was going back to Winneba and she could let it slip ... she could say she saw me at the market ...' Yawor turned in her chair. 'Tell me when she goes.'

'She's not going anywhere. She's arguing with another girl.'

Yawor could hear their raised voices.

'It's a mistake to stand with a girl who's not your friend,' Joanna said. 'The client won't like a scene like that, it'll draw attention to him ... you see, he's driving away with neither of them. And the girl you know is walking this way.'

'Oh no!'

'She's looking at this place. She's coming to sit here ...'

Yawor heard the footsteps approaching. She buried her head in her shoulders. But then she heard a car reversing quickly and a man shouting, 'Come, get in.' And she saw from the smile on Joanna's face that Beatrice Ansah wouldn't be stopping for a drink after all. She let out a long breath. 'That was close!'

Joanna slapped her playfully on the thigh. 'Huh! You should have seen your face, you looked like you'd seen a ...' She stopped sharp, mid-sentence. And it was Joanna who looked like she'd seen a ghost.

Yawor swung round. A car had pulled up. A red one. Reflected in the green neon light, the chrome letters on the front of the bonnet spelled out F-O-R-D.

She felt a sudden, uncontrollable rush of heat. Her fists were clenched tight and hard as bullets. 'Murderer!' she shouted. Without knowing what she was doing, she pushed herself out of her chair and started for the car, off balance, swaying, swinging her arms.

A woman was talking to the driver. Yawor could see the driver was a white man, with straight dark hair and a moustache. All she could think of was pushing aside the girl, opening the door, and strangling that man.

'Yawor! Come here!' Joanna had both her arms around Yawor's waist and was pulling her back to the bar. 'For God's sake!' she whispered sharply into Yawor's ear. 'You want to get killed too?'

Panting, Yawor came to her senses and let Joanna lead her back to her chair. She shook her head, dismayed at her recklessness. She fumbled in her bag for her pencil and paper so she could write down the registration number. But her hands were trembling so much she couldn't hold the pencil.

Joanna patted her gently on her shoulder. 'Calm down. Leave this to me …'

Yawor watched Joanna stroll up to the car, have a word in the woman's ear, and slip her some banknotes. Then it was Joanna bending over and negotiating with the driver. Before long she returned to Yawor.

'He wants to drive somewhere,' she said. 'But I told him, first he must buy me a drink at the Black Star.'

'What? But Jo …' Yawor glanced back at the driver. He was looking at Joanna, stroking his moustache, parting it with his thumb and finger. She hated to think what was going on in his mind.

'That way he has to leave the car outside. And while we're having a drink, you can get a good look at it.'

'But Jo, if it's him ... look what he did to Adzo. Where's he going to take you?'

'Don't worry about me, Yawor. Follow us to the Black Star but be quick.'

Moments later, Joanna was getting into the red Ford.

Chapter 21

A taxi dropped Patrice outside his hotel. He bought a copy of the *Daily Graphic* and stood below a streetlamp reading the front-page story:

A Ghanaian company has applied for a licence to build one of the biggest solar power stations in the world. If it gets the go-ahead, the plant will generate enough electricity to power 150,000 homes. But the proposal poses a dilemma for the government, because the output of 250 megawatts is above the maximum allowed for independent power projects ...

Sunfall Power had made their move, and he was going to have to watch his step. He checked out of the hotel, crossed the road, and checked into another. It was similarly bland, a little cheaper, and also had a terrace bar above the street, which is where he headed. He drank a bottle of Star, watching the traffic, contemplating his next move.

Further on, past a bank, he noticed the casino. Bright lights from inside flooded the pavement outside. Two young men entered, patting each other on their backs. An older man left, looking downcast.

Patrice called Kwaku Sarpong, thinking he must know the senior official at the Energy Commission that Albert Boateng had told him about. The call went to voicemail, so he ordered another Star. As he was putting the bottle to his lips, another man stepped out of the casino down the road who, strangely, resembled Kwaku Sarpong. He was standing with the light behind him, so it was hard to be sure. The man rubbed his brow. It looked like he was having a bad night. He pulled out his phone, held it for a moment, then put it to his ear.

Moments later, Patrice's phone rang. Kwaku Sarpong's name was showing. Patrice was about to answer but let it ring out instead. The man put his phone back in his pocket and retreated into the casino.

Patrice abandoned his little-drunk second bottle of Star, left the hotel, and walked down the road. Chandeliers, a loud carpet, and men sitting at machines were visible through the casino's glass door. Two besuited bouncers stood guard. He didn't go in but made for another bar, up a side street, where he ordered a replacement bottle of Star and returned Sarpong's call.

Sarpong picked up on the first ring. 'Patrice, are you okay?'

'Yes, yes, I'm good. I'm sorry I missed your call. How are you?'

'I'm fine. But I wondered … because I went to your hotel and they said you'd checked out?'

'Yes, I didn't like it there. The Wi-Fi is weak, and it's expensive.'

'I'm sorry about that. Did you hear the Sunfall project has been submitted?'

'Yes, I read it in the newspaper. Where are you? We could meet up?'

'Good idea. I'm finishing work. Where are you?'

'You know the Republic? It's a bar round the corner from my old hotel, where people sit out on the street.'

'Yes. I can be there in ten minutes.'

Patrice drank his beer, and considered why Sarpong hadn't wanted him to know he'd been at the casino. Perhaps he thought Patrice would disapprove. It didn't matter, but he'd lied without hesitating.

Five minutes later, Sarpong came walking up the street and joined Patrice at his table. They shook hands and Sarpong smiled in his usual way.

'You didn't drive?' Patrice asked.

This time there was a split-second pause. 'Yes, I parked round the corner. This road is dusty.' He smiled again. 'So where are you staying now, Patrice?'

'Another hotel, near here.' Patrice pointed vaguely towards Oxford Street.

'Oh, right, the Milano?'

Patrice nodded. 'It's pretty much the same, but it's cheaper and I want to keep out of harm's way.'

Sarpong looked at him like he was considering what Patrice meant. An eyebrow lifted a fraction. 'And reliable Wi-Fi? Well, good.' He snapped his fingers at a waitress and ordered a 7up.

The bar was busy. Young people were sitting and chatting at the tables spilling onto the street, wearing jeans, drinking beers and cocktails. Patrice and Sarpong waited for the drink to come, not talking, as if once their conversation started, they couldn't be interrupted.

The 7up came.

'Cheers, Patrice.'

'*Salut.*'

They raised their drinks and took a sip.

'So, Patrice, the Sunfall proposal ...'

159

'Do you think they'll get the licence?'

'I don't know. But they must have a reason to be confident about it. You know how things are, Patrice. Sometimes an offer is too big to turn down. The Energy Commission has set a limit, but if it comes under pressure ...' There was no trace of a smile on Sarpong's face now.

'What kind of pressure?'

'I don't know ... who knows? These multinational companies are formidable. And an investment this size? The government could say it's in the national interest to make another exception ...'

'But Sunfall Power is a Ghanaian company, right?'

'Well, yes, apparently.'

They had more of their drinks.

Patrice said, 'You look worried.'

'I think the government should be careful. I support the cautious approach.'

'I thought you were all for the free market?'

This elicited a brief smile. 'Within the rules. They've set a cap. Let's see how it goes. If it works well, if investment comes and the power supply is increased, and the national grid is also improved, then they could review the limit ...'

'What happens with the Sunfall bid now?'

'The Energy Commission board has to respond to the application within sixty days.' Sarpong looked down and played with his fingers.

'Do you know if a man called Victor Mensah will have anything to do with that process?'

Sarpong shot him a panicked glance. 'You know this man?'

'No. I heard his name today for the first time. But you know him?'

'Yes. I do.' His voiced was hushed. 'Stay clear of him. If he's involved in this … it's not good.'

'Why? What's he done?'

'It's not one bad thing you can point to. He's got his fingers in a lot of pies. He scares people and takes advantage of them to …'

'To what?'

'I don't know. To further himself? To make himself richer? More powerful? With people like this, you don't know really what their motives are. But who told you about him?'

Patrice puffed out his cheeks. 'I had a chat with Albert Boateng.'

The same eyebrow lifted, higher. 'A chat?'

'Um … not exactly a chat. Actually, I roughed him up a little, and to get me to stop he told me he gets his orders from Victor Mensah.'

'Patrice!' Sarpong's hands were on his head, like he was trying to squash it. 'Why? Why did you do that?'

'It's a thing of mine. Like a crusade, to bring down the bullies.'

'But Patrice, really. These people … I mean, if Victor Mensah … they could come after you.'

'Well, I'll keep my head down for a while.'

'They can find you, Patrice, if they want to. And after what you've done, they'll want to.'

'I just slapped him a couple of times. It was nothing serious.'

'You must leave Accra, please. What's happening with George Abotsi's land, you can't stop it on your own.' Sarpong looked into Patrice's eyes, like he was pleading with him.

A car was coming down the road. Patrice could hear it behind him. He turned. It wasn't swerving across the road recklessly, but it was going too fast for the dusty side street, where people were sitting at tables to the side. He looked back at Sarpong, who looked, almost literally, like a rabbit in the headlights.

A drinker at the next table stood up, waving a fist. 'Hey, crazy driver!' A young woman screamed.

The car drove past.

Sarpong gripped hold of Patrice's arm. 'Look what happened to you the other night, Patrice. If that was a warning, like you said, they'll see you've ignored it … and more. You need to leave, really … go now, to the airport. It's not safe for you to stay.'

'Thank you for caring. I appreciate it.' Patrice patted Sarpong's hand. 'But I can't go. I won't let them chase me out. You know, there's a famous saying: "All that is necessary for the triumph of evil is that good men do nothing". I don't know who said it – Martin Luther King? Anyway, it's true, don't you think?'

Sarpong hung his head like a man who was having a very bad night at the casino.

Patrice walked back to his hotel. He bought a couple more bottles of Star at the bar and took them upstairs. His room was at the back of the building. The window overlooked a piece of grassy waste ground, beyond which he could make out the shadowy shapes and silhouettes of a construction site: wooden scaffold and exposed concrete staircases.

He opened his laptop and joined the hotel Wi-Fi and searched for the name Victor Mensah. It was a common name. There was a Victor Mensah playing professional football in Thailand; another was a rapper from Chicago; but there was no mention of anyone with that name working at the Ghana Energy Commission.

He spent a while reading up on the two companies Albert Boateng had told him about at their first meeting, Sunfall Power's partners:

Desert Power was established in 1985 near a town called Carefree, in Arizona, by two electricians who installed solar panels on residential houses. In 1999, they won a sub-contract with a company building a shopping mall. Six years later, Desert Power was bought by ArizOil, a mid-size petroleum company with its head office in Phoenix. Now Desert Power claimed to be one of the world's biggest builders of solar farms, with projects in thirty countries.

Blue Electric, the Chinese panel manufacturer, also appeared to be a subsidiary of a larger company, in its case, a construction conglomerate. Its website described it as a world leader, with commercial and residential customers in virtually every continent, employing ten thousand people at five production facilities, in China (two), Vietnam, Spain and Mexico. Patrice glazed over a lot of the more technical-sounding information.

Neither company was free of controversy. Environmental campaigners in Vietnam had accused Blue Electric of polluting a river with its production waste, while in the United States, a group of indigenous Americans claimed Desert Power had built a solar farm in New Mexico to conceal an underground chemical weapons facility run by the Department of Defense.

Patrice closed the laptop and rubbed his eyes and drank some beer. He took a sheet of paper and drew a diagram: at the top was the name *Victor Mensah*; below, linked by a line,

Albert Boateng; below that, a line to *Sunfall*; branching out
from either side of that, lines to *Desert Power* and *Blue Electric*.
Then, as if his hand had a mind of its own, because he hadn't
thought about it consciously, he wrote – separate from the
rest – *Kwaku Sarpong?*

He took a shower and tried to remember what exactly Josie
Mwinga had said about Sarpong when she'd put them in
touch. He cast his mind back ... she said she'd just been
speaking to him: 'He's the son of a friend of mine. Very clued
in. He called me to say he'd heard about George Abotsi's
death, which was sweet of him.'

He paced around his room, towel round his waist. To settle
his curiosity, he picked up his phone and called his boss.

'Patrice!' Her voice came booming down the line, though
there was chatter in the background.

'Hello, ma'am ... Josie. I hope I'm not disturbing you.'

'I'm at the opening of a new art gallery, but it's okay ...'

'I wanted to ask you something. I could ring another time.'

'No, it's okay ... let me move away from these people ...'
The background volume reduced. 'This is better. What is it,
Patrice? Is everything alright?'

'Well, not exactly. I've made some progress since yesterday,
and I went to see Kekeli, but the more I find out, the worse it
looks for her and her aunt. You must have seen the news – the
solar company have put in their application for a licence ...'
Patrice was still on his feet, speaking as he walked round the
room, and was looking out of the window again. He saw a car
pull into the empty plot of land below and pulled the blind
down. 'Well, powerful people are involved in this business,
I'm sure of that.'

'Oh dear,' Mwinga said. 'I feared as much. Is there anything

I can do to help? I hope you're being discreet and careful …'

Patrice smiled. It was nice she cared about his safety, but he knew she also meant *carry on with your investigation.* 'Come to think of it, ma'am, you said you knew someone with contacts in the government?'

'Yes, he used to be a presidential adviser. He still has his ear close to the ground.'

'It would be good to have inside information on how this licence application is dealt with.'

'Come and see me tomorrow and we can go through this in more detail. The speeches are about to begin …'

'Okay. Before you go, quickly, I wanted to ask you about Kwaku Sarpong.'

'Kwaku? What about him?'

'I was wondering how well you know him?'

'Well, I don't know him well … but I've known his father for many years; he's a successful businessman. He runs Black Star Telecoms, one of the mobile phone operators here. Why, Patrice?'

'Oh, it's nothing …' His phone vibrated; Kekeli was calling. 'Anyway, ma'am, I'll leave you to your speeches. I have to go too.'

'Hang on, Patrice. Is there a problem with Kwaku?'

'No, it's nothing …'

There was a knock on the door and a voice called out, 'Room service!'

'… I'll see you tomorrow, bye.'

'Okay, Patrice, good night.'

Patrice looked at his phone as he walked across the room. He'd missed the call from Kekeli. He'd call her back in a minute, he thought, as he opened the door.

Chapter 22

The bar at the Black Star Hotel was in a garden to the side. A tin roof sheltered the far end. The tables at the front were open to the night sky. It was at one of these that Yawor spotted Joanna. She'd arranged it so the white man had his back to a gravelled parking area where he'd left his car, the red Ford.

The car looked modern. Even under the dim streetlamps, the paintwork was shiny. Yawor steeled herself and approached, and saw something that made her feel sick to her stomach: a dent on the bonnet, a small but distinct kink between the O and the R of FORD. Beneath it a chrome horse-shaped emblem was squashed against the radiator grille.

'This is the car that killed my sister,' she said to herself.

She checked Joanna and the man were still at their table. Then she peered through the driver's window, her hands cupped against the glass. It was tidy inside. There was no briefcase, nor papers, nor any rubbish – no clue as to the owner's identity. She glanced down the street. Two women were standing by the roadside nearby, not paying her any attention. Her heart was pounding. It felt like it was inside her head.

She tried the door handle. It opened. She looked round again. Joanna was staring at her. Yawor herself couldn't believe what she was doing as she shuffled into the driver's seat.

It was cramped inside, with a heavy smell of leather. The steering wheel was made of polished wood, with three shiny metallic spokes and, in the middle, a badge with the words *Ford Mustang*. She looked at the passenger seat and pictured Adzo there: that's where she'd sat, more than once – where she'd been sitting when an argument broke out, and she got out of the car, and ... She noticed the glove box. Leaned over, pressed the button. The cover dropped open, making her jump. A tap on the window made her jump again. Joanna was there.

'He's gone to relieve himself, then we're going.'

'Oh God!' Yawor fumbled through the contents of the glove box: two packets of Winston cigarettes, a book of matches, sticks of chewing gum. Her hands were shaking. She pulled out some papers: receipts for petrol and one for a meal at the Ambassador Hotel - she could find out who'd eaten dinner there that day, but there was no date. There were documents relating to the car's registration, but she couldn't see a name. But she found something: a stamp for *Barry's Motors, Baltimore, MD*.

'American,' she said.

'Yawor! Come! Please!' Joanna was tapping at the window again.

Yawor put the papers back, but in her rush one tore. 'Oh God!' she said again. She was sweating and her fingers were wet. She slid the torn sheet between the others. As she did, she saw it was an import licence. At the bottom was a stamp:

Ghana Customs, Tema Port; and next to it, a scrawled signature above a printed name: *Howard Bane.* She put the papers back and threw the other items in on top, closed the flap, turned and pulled herself out of the door.

'Okay, baby, let's go.'

The man's voice sounded American. Yawor couldn't see his face. But she could see Joanna staring down the pathway behind the parked cars.

'Are you sure you don't want another drink?'

Yawor closed the door as quietly as she could and coughed at the same time to conceal the clunk.

'Oh!' Joanna shouted. 'I didn't see you there. Are you alright?'

Yawor went down on her knees. 'Yes, I'm fine, thank you. I dropped my bag under this car, but I think I've got everything.'

She stood up. She wanted to scream 'Thank you!' to Joanna, but that wasn't possible because the driver of the red Ford had joined her. Yawor's stomach seized up, but she forced a smile as she asked, 'Is this your car?'

'What's it to you?' The man didn't seem to recognise her from earlier, when she'd wanted to strangle him and Joanna had dragged her away.

'It's beautiful,' Yawor said, feeling calmer and more confident. 'Is it American?'

His eyes narrowed. 'Uh-huh.'

'It's beautiful, but you don't look after it.' Yawor pointed at the front of the bonnet. 'There is damage. It's a shame.'

'That's nothing,' he said. 'A scratch. Don't worry about it.' He turned to Joanna. 'You know this cripple?'

Yawor winced.

'She's my friend,' Joanna said.

He stroked the two sides of his moustache with his thumb and forefinger. 'I don't like her.'

'So? You don't need to be rude.'

'She snooping around?'

'She's not snooping. I thought you wanted to go? Are we going?

'Get in the car.' The American was speaking to Joanna, but he was looking at Yawor.

Yawor backed away. 'Bye, Jo,' she said as her friend obeyed the instruction.

The man gave Yawor a last, suspicious look, got into the car himself and started it up. As he was pulling away, he called through the window. 'Be careful with that bag of yours. Crawl under a car again and you could get run down.'

Yawor watched the car head off down the road and prayed Joanna would come to no harm.

She went to Joanna's room and lay on the bed, watching shadows move across the ceiling as cars passed by below … *She heard Adzo calling to her: 'Sister, sister, don't worry about me, I can look after myself.' Adzo repeated the phrase, again and again, but as she did, the words became fainter, like she was walking away down the road. There was a screech of car brakes and a scream …*

1966: FEBRUARY 13

Yawor woke with a start. It was she who'd screamed. A door opened and Joanna walked in.

'Yawor! Are you alright?'

169

'Oh … I was dreaming.' She blinked a few times as she remembered where she was. 'But you, Jo, you're alright? He didn't hurt you?'

'No, he hardly touched me. All he wanted … well, I won't tell you the details. But we were in the car the whole time; it was easy money for me.'

Yawor fetched cups of water. She was wide awake now. 'Where did he drive you?'

'Not far at all. A quiet road.'

'Weren't you scared?' Yawor was picturing the quiet road near her house where Adzo was found.

'At first, when we drove off. But it seemed like he'd enjoyed my company in the bar …'

'What was he like, to talk to?'

'He was boastful. He talked about himself all the time. "I'm a businessman, I'm important, your people love me." Bla bla, bla bla.'

'Poor you, having to listen to that and … to go with him. I don't know how you do it, Jo.'

'I think of the money. Like lots of people who do jobs they don't like. My father was a civil servant, until they fired him, and he was always complaining. He said it was boring. He spent his working day looking at the clock. So he was doing it for the money.' Joanna shrugged.

'Why was he fired?'

'A big man offered him money if he helped him with a contract, to make it happen quickly. My father refused and reported the man to his superior, and the next day he lost his job.'

'I'm sorry, that's bad. Is that when you started … to work here?'

'Yes. My father couldn't find another job. But he kicked me out of his house when he found out what I was doing, so I don't shed tears for him.'

'I think my uncle would have kicked Adzo out of his house had he known what she was doing. But what about your studies?'

'University is not for me, that's what I can say.'

'That's what Adzo said.' Yawor fiddled with the hem of her nightshirt. She'd never been able to put herself in Adzo's shoes, to imagine how being an *ashawo* could be preferable to college. 'But one day I'm sure you'll find other work ...'

'Maybe. But you don't need to worry about me, I'm happy. For now, I don't mind this.'

'Well, I do worry. I was worried when you went with that American. Look what he did to Adzo, and she said the same to me, not to worry.'

Joanna took Yawor's hand in hers and smiled. 'I came back, didn't I?'

Yawor nodded and did her best to return the smile. 'I wonder what led to them arguing, Adzo and that man?'

'I don't know. If he is a successful businessman, it wouldn't be about money. He paid me with no problem. Unless Adzo asked him for more, but I don't think she'd have done that.'

'Did he say what business he does?'

'Importing ... things, equipment, that's what he said. From America.'

'Equipment? His car's imported from America. I saw the documents.'

'Agh, Yawor! You gave me a scare. You nearly got caught in there!'

'It was close!' Yawor opened her mouth and fanned herself

171

with her hand and they laughed and slapped hands. 'But I saw his name. Howard Bane. Is that how you say it? Like pain, but with a B?'

'He told me his name was Steve.'

'You see, he's lying. But if he's lying about his name, he could be lying about other things too.'

They went to bed. As they lay there, Joanna asked, 'So, now you know his name, his real name, what are you going to do?'

'There's a man I know, a friend, who can help me, I hope. I mentioned him to you before – he's a policeman.'

'What? Please don't bring him here, Yawor!'

'I won't. But he's nice, and sympathetic.'

'I never met a sympathetic policeman. So I say the same to you as you say to me: be careful!'

Chapter 23

The door flew open. Two men barged in, big guys with shaved heads, dark suits, and black gloves. In another life they'd probably been bouncers on a casino door. Before Patrice had time to utter a word, one of them shoved him hard on the chest, sending him staggering backwards onto the bed.

'Get dressed,' he said. 'You're coming with us.'

'Who are you?'

Neither man answered. Both of them were twice his size. The one doing the shoving was shorter and rounder than the other. He had a squashed face and a crooked nose. The other man was at the desk, looking at the diagram Patrice had drawn. Patrice pulled on his clothes.

They took the service stairs, left the building by a back door, and walked to a car parked in the darkness – the car Patrice had seen from his window. The man with the squashed face had a hand clamped round Patrice's arm. He pushed Patrice into the back seat and got in next to him. The other jumped into the driving seat. Patrice noticed a third man, sitting in the front passenger seat.

'Is this him?' the driver asked.

The man in the passenger seat said, 'Yes.' It was Albert Boateng.

The driver set off with a screech of tyres that sounded familiar. He drove up Oxford Street and onto the ring road.

Boateng stared straight ahead in silence.

It was late. There wasn't much traffic. They turned onto the airport road, then again down a side street. It was an upmarket residential area, leafy and quiet, the houses hidden behind high walls. After several more turnings, Patrice was lost. He didn't ask where they were going – he'd find out soon enough. And no one, it seemed, was in the mood for conversation.

They pulled up outside a heavy-looking metal gate. A night guard with a scarf draped over his head opened it and waved them through, and they parked inside. Patrice was pulled out of the car by his escort and greeted by two huge dogs, barking but chained to a post. He was led up three steps and into a modern-looking house, painted white, and through into a large, air-conditioned living area. Boateng followed. The second thug stayed behind.

The three of them sat on an L-shaped sofa. The silence continued, cold and hostile. A door to the side opened. Boateng jumped to his feet. The thug stood too and lifted Patrice up with him. A tall, lean man wearing a night-robe walked in. He looked Patrice up and down and slowly shook his head.

'This is him?'

'Yes, sir,' Boateng answered.

'This scruffy little man beat you up and tortured you?'

'Sir. He ambushed me outside the office.'

'What's his name again?'

'Le Congo.'

'Ah yes. Le Congo, Patrice Le Congo, the human rights

investigator with high principles but prone to moments of madness.' The tall man brushed an invisible speck of dust off his sleeve. He had a hard, bony face. His short hair was greying at the sides. His eyes were narrow and narrowed further as he studied Patrice. 'I understand, Mr Le Congo, you've been behaving unpleasantly to Mr Boateng here and generally making a nuisance of yourself.' His lips squeezed together into a thin smile.

Patrice was glad he'd had a few beers – to numb him against whatever was coming next. He was quite sure the evening was not going to end well, for him. 'Actually, it's Mr Boateng who's been behaving unpleasantly and making a nuisance of himself. He needs to learn to respect other people.'

The man didn't react.

'You must be Victor Mensah. The man who tells Mr Boateng what to do.'

The man glanced at Boateng but didn't speak.

'Mr Boateng said you'd be able to tell me who killed George Abotsi.'

The man looked again at Boateng.

'That's not true, sir.' Boateng looked more scared now than he had in the alleyway earlier.

'Mr Boateng said he deals with the business side of things and not the other stuff, and that you're in charge. So tell me, Mr Mensah, what happened to George Abotsi?'

The man briefly examined his other sleeve. He seemed to care a lot about the appearance of his night-robe. 'Is this really why you are causing all this trouble, Mr Le Congo? If so, you have been wasting a lot of your time and energy. George Abotsi had an accident, with electricity. It's a sad story.'

'A fairy tale, more like.' Patrice was aware the alcohol was

175

loosening his tongue, but the man's callous complacency was getting to him. 'George Abotsi refused to give up his land to the Sunfall Power Company, and next thing, he dies. Within days, his family and all the other people living on his land receive eviction notices signed by Mr Boateng. His death was very convenient.'

'The police investigated the matter ...'

'The same police who are in the pay of the Sunfall Power Company? Who've set up a post on Abotsi's land? It's clear what's going on: no one can get in the way of your plans to build a solar farm; if they won't get out of the way willingly, they'll be forced out, even if that means in a coffin. This is the way for people like you: profit is all that matters.'

Mensah clapped his hands slowly three times. 'Thank you, Mr Le Congo. I was waiting for the speech. Perhaps you'd like to sing us a song too? "Nkrumah never dies, never dies, never dies ..." You know that one? They used to sing that here. George Abotsi used to sing that song. Well, they were wrong about Nkrumah, as you are wrong about George Abotsi. I'm afraid your principles are impairing your vision.'

'Rubbish!' Patrice couldn't contain himself and lurched forward, but the hand on his arm pulled him back. 'My vision was clear enough to see that someone's tampered with Abotsi's title deeds at the Lands Commission.'

The tall man smiled another of his thin smiles. 'We were prepared to wait for him to come round. Because everyone has their price, and even an old Nkrumahist like George Abotsi would have sold in the end. But he pushed his hand too far. In attempting to frustrate us, he played with fire, with electricity in this case, and he got burned. But not by us. He did it himself. He was a fool. And his death was an accident. If you have evidence to the contrary, bring it forward, likewise if you have proof about his title deeds. If you don't trust the police, take your evidence to your boss, Josie Mwinga. She is well connected, I believe. Which is as well for you.'

Patrice shook his head. 'All this … for a solar farm. The man didn't want to sell. You should have let him be.'

'Don't lecture me, Mr Le Congo.' The smile had gone. 'And stop poking your nose into other people's business. It's time to go back to your country.'

'I'm not finished here.'

'Finished what? Trying to turn back the tide of progress? To stop my country from developing, because you don't agree with the political direction? Ghana needs electricity, Mr Le Congo. We will provide it. And, yes, we will make a profit. That is the way the world works, now.'

'You can all go to hell.'

'Enough.' The tall man walked up to Patrice and pointed a finger at him. 'You're a rude little man. It's you who needs to learn some respect. Good evening.' He stepped back, nodded to the thug, then turned and walked out through the side door.

Patrice was led outside. For a brief moment he savoured the warm night air. Then the thug stepped behind him and grabbed both his arms. The other thug appeared from somewhere, stepped forward and dug a rock-like fist into Patrice's stomach. Patrice buckled. He couldn't breathe. His hands went to the pain. The man behind held him up. Another blow came, this one on his side. Then another, on the other side. Then another into his stomach. Gasping for air, he looked up and saw the fist close up, firing towards him. Something cracked and everything went black.

177

Chapter 24

1966: FEBRUARY 14

Unrecognisable, she hoped, in an old dress and headscarf, Yawor bought two dozen oranges in Makola Market, then took a *trotro* up Independence Avenue to the ring road. From there she walked to police headquarters. It was early afternoon and burning hot. Beads of sweat tickled her face. A small tree across the road from the entrance offered some shade. She sat beneath it, pulled her headscarf forward, and arranged half her fruit in pyramids of four in front of her. As she finished laying them out, a policeman from the gatehouse walked over. He was wagging a finger.

'You cannot sit here,' he said. 'Not in front of police headquarters.'

'Where can I go?'

'You can go anywhere but not here.'

'I'm not making trouble. Let me do my business.'

Another policeman came over. He stooped to pick up an orange and sniffed it. 'How much?'

Yawor stared at him, speechless; she hadn't thought how much she'd charge. 'For a policeman,' she said eventually, 'two pesewas each, or four for seven.'

'If you want to stay here, you must give me two.'

Yawor scowled and tutted. The policemen took the oranges and gave one to his colleague, and they walked back across the road. She replaced the fruit with two from her bag.

She sat for two hours under the tree, watching the comings and goings at police headquarters. Two pedestrians bought a single orange each, but she didn't have many customers.

Around five, with an orange sun sinking behind the clouds, the doors to the main building swung open and the rigid figure of Police Commissioner JWK Harlley stepped outside, placing his cap on his head. He looked around and seemed to pause as his gaze focussed on Yawor. As he turned back to the door, it opened again and a tall white man with thinning hair emerged, followed by Sergeant Anthony Ofori. Yawor tried not to stare. Sergeant Ofori glanced in her direction but didn't stop to look more closely. The commissioner spoke to him. The sergeant saluted and went back inside. Yawor's heart sank.

The commissioner and the white man walked behind the parked cars, talking, until they stopped by one and parted with a handshake. Harlley looked around again. Yawor dipped her head. Glancing up, checking her scarf was in place, she saw he was making for the gatehouse. He spoke to the men there, whereupon the policeman who'd taken the oranges earlier came walking across the road. Yawor could see Harlley following him with his eyes. She lowered her head further, her hand on her forehead. The policeman took an age to reach her. Despite the traffic, she could feel his footsteps approaching as he came – she was certain – to apprehend her and drag her back to present to his boss. She tried to think what she'd say, but her mind was a messy blank.

'Don't be shy,' the policeman said. 'You won't sell anything that way. Give me four. The commissioner is paying.'

Yawor gulped. She picked up the oranges, her hands shaking as she held them out for him. The policeman gave her a puzzled look before taking the oranges, dropping some coins into her lap, and crossing back over the road. The police commissioner in turn took the oranges and walked back to the building and disappeared inside. Yawor's heart now was crashing against her ribs.

Dusk was falling, and she was on the verge of packing up, when Sergeant Ofori appeared outside again. Yawor clapped a hand over her mouth for fear of calling out his name. He stood by the entrance for what seemed like an age. As if God himself had told him where to go, he walked to the main gate and out and across the road.

'My boss says your oranges are sweet,' he said.

'Very,' she said and peeked out from under her scarf.

He grinned at her. 'I thought it was you,' he said, bending down to inspect the fruit. 'But I couldn't believe it!'

'I'm glad to see you, Ofori!'

'Me too!' He picked up an orange. 'But you're in Accra!'

'I didn't go to Winneba. I've been hiding. But listen, I've found out the name of the man who killed Adzo.'

'Really?' Ofori leaned closer. 'We can't talk here. You know the Holy Spirit Cathedral? Go there and I'll meet you after dark.'

'Yes, I'll be there.'

He got up to leave.

'Hey!' she shouted. 'Two pesewas!'

He grinned and gave her the money, then returned to his

work. Yawor collected up the fruit and caught a *trotro* back down Independence Avenue to Castle Road. She was a couple of streets from Uncle Joseph's house. She did her best to conceal her limp by taking more weight on her knee. The pain made her flinch, but it subsided once she was safely inside the cathedral and seated on a pew at the back.

There were few people inside. The light outside the tall, narrow windows faded. Shortly after it had disappeared completely, Sergeant Ofori slipped in beside her. He was out of breath, as if he'd run from police headquarters, but he was smiling.

'My God, Yawor, you don't give up! But what have you been doing these last days? Where are you staying?'

'Please don't tell anyone. I'm staying with Adzo's friend, the one who told me about the white man in the red car …'

'You're staying at the university?'

'Well, no, they met at the university, but … now, she … she does what Adzo was doing, so I'm staying with her in a room she rents … near Makola Market.' Yawor paused, expecting a reprimand or a look of disapproval but none came. 'She was worried when I said I knew a policeman who might help, but I said you would be sympathetic. Ofori? You won't make trouble for her, will you?'

'I won't say a word. I'm on your side, Yawor. But you must be careful.'

'That's what Adzo's friend said. Thank you, Ofori. But listen, on Saturday … we saw the car, and while she had a drink with the man, I looked inside.'

'Eeek! Yawor! You really are like a detective. What if he caught you?'

'I didn't care. I was so angry.'

He took her hand. 'You are crazy, but you did it for your sister.'

'And I found papers in the car with his name. Howard Bane. He's American. So I was thinking, you said you have a friend at the vehicle licencing …' She didn't finish her sentence because of the look of astonishment on Ofori's face. 'What is it?'

'Howard Bane?'

'Yes. Howard Bane. You know him?' Her eyes widened in anticipation.

Ofori's eyes were moving one way then the other, as if he was making sure what he was going to say was correct. 'Howard Bane is head of the CIA in Accra.'

'Head of what?'

'The CIA. The American Central Intelligence Agency, their secret service. He's the station chief.'

'What does that mean?'

'It means he's like a spy. But also, he's an important person.'

Yawor reeled. 'A spy?'

Ofori nodded, looking apologetic.

She looked him in the eye. 'Is this why the commissioner didn't want to continue the investigation into Adzo's death? Because he knows the man who killed her is an American spy?'

'I don't know.' Ofori knitted his brows. 'But anyway, they couldn't arrest him; he has an official position at the American embassy, so he will have diplomatic immunity. But perhaps, to avoid a scandal …'

'Adzo's client, her killer, was an American spy. It's … unbelievable.' Yawor looked around the vast interior of the cathedral and felt very small.

'He's even friends with my boss, the commissioner. He sees him regularly ... But Yawor, you must have seen him – he was there today.'

She shook her head. 'I saw the white man, but that wasn't him. Adzo's client is not tall. And he's got a full head of hair and a moustache ...'

'That man with the commissioner was Howard Bane. There is only one Howard Bane.'

Yawor felt deflated, as if her prey had escaped. 'Well, another man is driving his car and using it to ... to pick up prostitutes.' She thought hard. 'The man told Joanna his name was Steve. Perhaps that is his real name after all ...'

'Steve? With a moustache? And his hair, is it like this?' Ofori arranged his hands to form a parting to one side of his head.

'Yes, like that.'

'There's another man from the embassy, called Steve Krieger. He's been to headquarters recently with Bane. He looks like that.'

'Another spy?'

'I don't know. I mean, if they work together, and he's driving Bane's car ... But if it is him, he will have immunity too.'

'So, he couldn't be prosecuted?'

'No. Not unless his government waived his immunity. But if they didn't, it would cause an incident. He would be shamed, and our government could order him to leave.'

'Then, at the very least, we must expose what he's done.'

'But Yawor, you don't know for sure ...'

'There was a dent on his car. And ... he was not a pleasant man. It's him, I'm sure.' She looked into Ofori's eyes, and he nodded, showing he believed her. 'We must find out more about him, this Steve Krieger. What do he and Howard Bane talk to your boss about when they come?'

Ofori shrugged. 'I open the door for them, let them in and show them out. I don't hear their conversations.'

Yawor shook her head. 'I can't believe Adzo was involved with a man like that. Joanna said she liked him and went with him several times, that she knew of, and maybe many more times she didn't know. Did Adzo know he was a spy?'

'I didn't say he was a spy. But he could be. If he was, he would pretend to be someone else. A businessman, or anything.'

Evening service was beginning. An organist was playing hymns. More people were entering the cathedral, mostly heading to the front.

'We should leave,' Yawor said. Ofori nodded.

Outside, in the warm night, they walked further down Castle Road, away from the cathedral and from Uncle Joseph's neighbourhood, but heading nowhere in particular.

'What can we do?' Yawor asked.

'I don't know. It's dangerous. These people are powerful.'

'How do you know Howard Bane is a spy? Surely that is a secret?'

'Not with Howard Bane. He boasts about it. That's one thing I have heard him talking about, openly, with the commissioner. He throws parties and invites all sorts. He wants people to know he's head of the CIA here, so if they have information, they know where to go, who to tell ...'

'What kind of information?'

'You know, things about the government, business contracts, things like that.'

'You seem to know a lot about this business. How do I know you're not a spy?'

He feigned a look of outrage. She chuckled.

They found themselves at the junction with Kwame Nkrumah Avenue and walked towards the circle. Highlife music was spilling out from a nightclub.

'Do you like dancing, Yawor?'

'I do, but ... I'm not able to dance well.'

'Let's try.' He pulled her towards him and they swayed gently together. 'You are not so bad,' he said.

Yawor's feet felt light. Her hip hardly hurt at all. 'My sister is the only person who has ever wanted to dance with me. But I am sure you have danced with many girls, Ofori.'

'I have danced with some. But I am sure I have never danced with anyone as brave as you, Yawor!'

She smiled, lost in the moment.

The song ended. They stayed, standing by the tree. Ofori was looking down at her. 'When this is all over,' he said, 'when things are settled, I should like to come to your uncle's house to ask properly if I can take you dancing. I hope you won't mind.'

'Of course I won't! I should like it very much. But when *will* this be all over? I was forgetting about Adzo.'

He looked away, thoughtfully. A nearby streetlamp high-lighted the creases at the top of his nose, and his smooth cheeks. His face was young-looking, his eyes bright and expectant. He was a police sergeant, but there an innocence about him. 'I must become more like a spy,' he said earnestly. 'From now on I will listen carefully when these Americans come to talk to the commissioner.'

'You must be careful, Ofori.'

'They're meeting again tomorrow night.'

'Who?'

'The commissioner and Howard Bane, and Krieger will be there too. But not at police headquarters. At the commissioner's residence – he often holds meetings there.'

'How do you know that? It sounds like you're already listening carefully.'

'They agreed it when they parted this afternoon. Bane said Krieger will bring what the commissioner asked him for.'

'What's that?'

'I don't know.'

'Something to do with Adzo?'

Ofori shrugged.

'I know the commissioner's residence. It's in Cantonments. My uncle pointed it out to me once.'

'It's a big house. I've driven the commissioner there many …' He stepped back. 'What are you thinking, Yawor? I hope it's not something crazy.'

Sweet guitar notes heralded the start of another song. She held up her hands for him to take. 'Let's dance some more. I liked that.'

Chapter 25

His face was throbbing. He reached for his nose and winced as his fingers landed on something sticky and tender. He remembered the fist and opened his eyes. A blurred structure assumed a square shape. He wasn't in Mensah's courtyard any longer.

Patrice recognised the back of his hotel. A square of light was his window. He attempted to sit. A searing pain tore through his ribs like a bolt of electricity. Blood dripped from his nose. Dizziness took hold. He started swaying, and everything went black again.

Next time he woke, he was in a bed, surrounded by bright lights and white walls and cupboards. He reached again for his nose and found a bandage.

'Hello, he's awake.' A woman dressed in white came into view. 'How are you feeling?'

Patrice had to think about it. 'Sleepy.'

'You've had painkillers. Let me know if you need more.'

'Where am I?'

'Accra, Ghana. The Sisters of Mercy Clinic.'

'Are you one of them?'

'Who?'

'The Sisters of Mercy? Did you bring me here?'

The woman smiled. 'No. I'm Nurse Agnes. It was your friend …' She turned and called out. 'You can come.'

Josie Mwinga appeared at the door. She was shaking her head. 'Patrice! Dear oh dear …'

'Hello, ma'am, yes … I walked into a tree.'

'Really? A tree with knuckles?'

'Don't worry – it's a few scratches, that's all.'

'Your nose is broken. From what the doctor told me, you're lucky your brain's still inside your head. And the rest of your body's not much better.' She sat on a chair by the bed.

'How did you find me?'

'I was trying to call you last night but, for reasons that are obvious now, you weren't picking up. So I called Kwaku and he told me you'd moved hotels. And when I got there, a passer-by had found you lying unconscious at the back. They thought you were dead.'

'Yes. Kwaku Sarpong knew I'd moved. I wasn't comfortable where I was, and the Wi-Fi …'

'I'm not interested in your Wi-Fi connection, Patrice. Who did this to you?'

'I didn't get his name. He didn't talk much, nor his friend, who was holding my arms behind my back. But like Albert Boateng, they take their orders from a man called Victor Mensah, who works in the Energy Commission – and told me I was being nosy.'

His boss stared at him.

'This is a sort of joke,' Patrice added, pointing at the bandage.

'What on earth is going on?'

'I don't know. But I feel like we're only scratching the surface.'

'I agree. It's got to be about more than a few solar panels.'

'Well, a lot of solar panels. But still …'

'Have you talked to Kwaku? What does he think?'

Patrice cleared his throat, and another fifty thousand volts shot through his ribcage. 'I told him I'd moved hotels. A short time later, Mensah's thugs came knocking on my door.'

Mwinga screwed up her nose. 'You can't think … surely …'

'Sarpong's involved, I'm not sure how. But leave him to me. What were you calling about?'

'Calling?'

'You said you were trying to ring me.'

'Oh, yes, I heard some disturbing news that, indirectly, has a bearing on this business. After we spoke, I called my friend, the one who used to be an adviser to the president, and he said he'd find out what he could about the Sunfall proposal. He called me back to say the president was in an emergency meeting with his senior ministers and military advisers. They've been informed of a serious security threat. It's all hush-hush, but apparently there's a plot to blow up the Akosombo Dam.'

'What?'

'I know, it's shocking. But it does mean …'

'Wait, hold on a minute. Someone wants to blow up the Akosombo Dam? Who?'

'Islamists. My friend says the tip-off came from the Americans. They've been interrogating two operatives of a group affiliated to al-Qaeda in the Maghreb, who were stopped at a checkpoint by French troops in Mali. Details of the plot aren't known, but the government suspects it's being orchestrated by the same people who planned the attacks in Côte d'Ivoire and Mali and Burkina Faso.'

His boss was speaking quickly. Patrice was struggling against the sedation to make sense of what she was telling him. 'But those attacks were on hotels and cafés, places where Westerners go,' he said. 'Why attack the dam? Because the Americans helped to build it?'

'Who knows, Patrice. These people are terrorists. Their aim is to kill as many people as they can, in the most dramatic way possible.'

'It's terrible. I mean, it would be catastrophic.'

'Yes, well, anyway,' she said, calmer, 'one thing's certain for now: the government won't be thinking about anything else till this situation is resolved, so nothing will happen to that solar farm planning application.'

'Yes, it may give us more time. Thank you for letting me know. Maybe your well-connected friend knows of Victor Mensah? Mensah seemed to know about you.'

'Really? I'll ask him.'

Josie Mwinga left, saying she had to get ready for George Abotsi's funeral. Patrice called Kekeli to explain he wouldn't be able to come, as something had cropped up. She said it sounded like he had a cold.

After lunch, Nurse Agnes came with an orthopaedic surgeon who introduced himself as Mr Shah. The nurse administered a local anaesthetic. The surgeon produced what looked like a pair of pliers and began manhandling Patrice's nose. Sometime later, with a new bandage in place, Mr Shah declared the procedure a success. 'But take it easy,' he said. 'No running around for two weeks and no contact sports for six.' Nurse Agnes gave Patrice a sympathetic smile, and he dozed off.

When he woke, it was evening. The anaesthetic had worn

off. His nose ached like he'd been punched again, only harder. He was trying to work out how to sit up without his ribs tearing him apart, when the door opened and the nurse said he had visitors. Two men entered, one short with grey hair, the other tall and young-looking.

'Mr Congo?' the older one asked.

'That's me.'

'Forgive us for disturbing you. I am Christian Iliasu. This is my son, Joseph. We have been at the funeral of George Abotsi, where we met your employer, Madam Mwinga. She told us to come.'

Patrice shuffled backwards up the bed. The young man stepped forward and arranged the pillows to support him.

'Thank you. And no, sir, you are not disturbing me. I hope the funeral went well.'

'Yes, many people were there, and will be for some time. George Abotsi was well liked. We couldn't stay. We are from Northern Region and must take an overnight bus home. But madam said to make sure we see you before we leave.'

'You're welcome. Please …' He gestured at the chair.

'Thank you.' The father accepted the invitation to sit. 'I hope my information is of some use. George Abotsi and I met when we were in the Young Pioneers. That was many years ago. Afterwards we lost touch. But when I heard he had died, I wanted to pay my respects. It was when I was talking to madam that I learned that his daughter and her aunty are being threatened with eviction. I told her that was an unfortunate coincidence. Because we too have been served with notices to leave our land.'

'I'm sorry.'

'Well, madam said you would want to know.'

'I see. Yes. That's terrible. Why are you being evicted?'

'They offered us compensation, but we don't want to leave. So we are being evicted.'

'But by who?'

'It is a company that wants to build a solar farm.'

Patrice sat up straight, causing his nose to throb and a stabbing pain in his chest. 'That is a coincidence, like you say. What's the name of the company?'

'It is called Northern Light. It is based in Tamale, the capital of Northern Region. When they handed us the letter, they said if we have complaints, we should direct them to the Energy Commission of Ghana.'

'And did you do that?'

'Yes, we wrote and were told this was a matter for the courts.'

'Did you appeal to the courts?'

Christian Iliasu looked away. 'You know, with the courts, we cannot pay for a lawyer, so it is difficult ...'

'I'm sorry. Tell me, who signed the eviction notice?'

The man shook his head. 'I don't remember the name.'

'Who at the Energy Commission were you told to write to?'

'That one I know. It was Mr Victor Mensah.'

Patrice left the Sisters of Mercy Clinic the following afternoon and headed straight for the casino on Oxford Street. Outside, the sun was shining more brightly than usual. Inside, the chandeliers were dim in comparison. He walked through the lobby. There were few customers. It didn't take long to find Kwaku Sarpong, sitting at a machine, swiping his credit card, pushing buttons, looking miserable. Patrice approached him from behind.

'Looks like your luck's out.'

Sarpong swung round on his stool, but his face didn't betray his surprise or discomfort. He was a man used to lying. He even managed half a grin. 'Patrice, I didn't know you liked to play the machines ... but my goodness, what happened to you?'

'They didn't tell you?'

'Who?'

'The people you invited to my hotel.'

Sarpong's eyes flitted from side to side. 'Patrice, you've got this wrong ... I don't know which people you're talking about.'

'I think you do.' Patrice snatched the card from his hand. 'They're the people, I suppose, who pay for this.'

Sarpong's resistance didn't last long. His head sunk. 'How did you find me here?'

'I saw you leaving this place the other night, from the bar of my new hotel. It's just down the road ... but you know that. That's when I called you, but I wish I hadn't. If we hadn't met up, my face would still be in one piece.'

'I ... I didn't realise ... Boateng said they wanted to talk to you, that's all.'

'Oh, really? You thought they wanted a friendly chat? Over bottles of beer, perhaps? We could talk about football and music and the state of Africa today and all get to know one another. Well, we did talk. Mr Mensah lectured me on the ways of the world and the naivety of principles – he seemed to know me well; I would say he was well briefed. He told me to stop being nosy. They have a sense of humour, your friends.'

'They're not my friends.' Sarpong glanced at the machine

beside him, its lights flashing. It seemed like his big grin could be lost for ever. 'I owe them money, a lot of money.'

'Oh, I see. So in order to play your games here, you betray people who trust you.'

'I'm not a bad person, Patrice. I got into trouble ...'

'Why did you call my boss the other day, the day she asked you to take me to the solar energy conference?'

'I ... to offer my condolences, after I heard what happened to George Abotsi. To ask if there was anything I could do ...'

'You're lying again. You got her to talk. You wanted to know what I'd found out. Didn't you?'

He hung his head again. 'Mensah's men saw you up there, leaving George Abotsi's house with his daughter. They were delivering the eviction notices. They asked at the house who you were. So Mensah called me ... He knew I knew Abotsi, and Josie Mwinga. Then he saw me at the solar conference with you ...'

'He was there?'

'He was in the hall. I told him you were asking questions about Sunfall ...'

'Jesus.' The more Sarpong babbled his confession, the more Patrice realised how completely he'd been deceived.

'You told me you'd never heard of Sunfall.'

'I didn't think it would lead to this.'

'Well, it did.'

'I tried to warn you ...'

'Oh, so that makes it okay. You can rest easy. The doctor says I should rest for two weeks, but I can't do that because for all I know, more people will be getting their faces smashed in while you sit here putting money into this machine. Now, tell me what else you've done for these people.'

'What do you mean?'

'That nice car of yours …'

'My car?'

'It's quite conspicuous.'

'What are you talking about, Patrice?'

'I'm talking about the morning George Abotsi died. Was killed.'

'What … what about that morning?'

'There are tyre tracks on the road above Abotsi's hydro-plant. And someone saw a red car.'

Sarpong's eyes bulged. 'A red … Patrice, what are you saying? You think that was my car? That I was up there?'

'Was it? Were you?'

Sarpong's mouth was moving, but no words were coming out. He waved his hands and gulped for air. 'My God,' he said eventually. 'Patrice, you think I killed George Abotsi? Okay, I've done some stupid things, some bad things. I know that. But I'm not a murderer. You must believe me.' He was panting and pressing his hands together.

Patrice narrowed his eyes. 'It's hard to know when to believe a liar. So, who did kill him?'

'I don't know, Patrice. It was an accident, that's what I understood.'

'What you understood? What does that mean? Come on, Kwaku. A man you know dies, a man who you also know owns a piece of land that's wanted by a gang of criminals, and you didn't question that?'

Sarpong was rubbing the top of his head and grimacing. 'I did ask, Patrice. I asked Boateng what happened. He said he heard they sent a couple of guys up there, people Mensah knew …'

'Those two thugs …'

'He didn't say who they were. The idea was to lean on Abotsi. That's what he said. But when they got there, Abotsi was dead. He was on the ground outside his power station. There were loose cables and a smell of burning inside – he'd suffered an electric shock. But it was an accident.'

'That's a lot of detail, Kwaku – like you were there. Maybe one of those guys they sent to lean on Abotsi was you.'

Sarpong shook his head. 'Patrice, I swear …'

Patrice grabbed hold of Sarpong's tie below the perfect knot and held it up against his chin. 'And I swear, if you're lying again …' He took a couple of breaths as the throbbing in his nose and pain in his chest reminded him why he'd been advised to take it easy. He let go and pushed Sarpong away. 'You need to pull yourself together. This gambling, look what it's doing to you.'

Sarpong looked away.

'I will talk to your friend Josie Mwinga. I'm sure she can help you.'

'Patrice, no, please, you mustn't tell Josie. She will tell my father …'

'Maybe that would be a good idea. You have a problem.'

'I know I have a problem. But I will deal with it. If my father finds out, he'll disown me … please, I'll do anything …'

'Like arrange to have Mr Mensah's nose broken?'

'Patrice, I didn't arrange for that, I didn't know …'

'You didn't know, you keep saying. So why did you warn me to leave Accra?'

He didn't answer.

Patrice slapped a flashing button. Part of him felt sorry for Sarpong. But the fact was the man had played him for a fool.

The wheels spun round and stopped one after the other with three clunks. The signs didn't match.

'Oh. More bad luck for you, Kwaku. But, since you offered, there is something you can do for me. I want a list of all the solar companies Mensah's running.'

Sarpong's face turned stone grey. He looked like he'd aged ten years in two seconds. 'I don't know about other companies. Only Sunfall.'

'There are more. Northern Light is one, based in Tamale. I want to know how many more, and what their proposals are.'

'How will I get this information?'

'From the Energy Commission. If not from their official records, then from somewhere or someone in Mensah's office.'

Sarpong swallowed. 'But ... I mean, look what they did to you. You want to carry on ... with this investigation?'

'It's not finished yet, so yes. And now I've got you to help me, it should be easier.'

'But what if they find out ... if they catch me? They'll tear me apart.'

'Don't worry,' Patrice said, pointing at the bandage over his nose. 'I know an excellent clinic where they can repair the damage.'

He slapped Kwaku Sarpong on his back and left him to his spinning wheels and flashing buttons.

Chapter 26

It was early, still dark. The air in her room was thick and
stale. A client of Joanna's was snoring in the next room.
Yawor was lying on the blanket on the floor wide awake;
even without the noise, she'd couldn't have slept. She got up,
put on the smartest outfit she had, a Western-style floral dress
that she'd made herself, and slipped out. Downstairs the hotel
receptionist was sweeping the courtyard. A neighbourhood
cockerel crowed. A smell of sour porridge was in the air. She
walked to the end of the road and hailed a taxi to take her to
Fourth Road.

It pulled up outside the Abotsi family compound shortly
after dawn. It was less than a week since Uncle Joseph had
driven her from here to the bus station. The gate was open.
Everything inside was unchanged: the bougainvillea spilling
over the wall, Herbert sitting on his chair by the gatehouse,
the path leading up to the house, and the steps to the veranda
where she'd spent so many hours of her life. And yet it was
different: a place where now she couldn't show her face.

She passed a letter to the driver to give to the guard while
she waited in the taxi. Then she told him to drive her to the

198

Paris Hotel. On the way, by chance, they passed the American embassy. It was near where she lived, but she'd never paid it much attention. Now, as they sped past, she looked out for a red Ford Mustang. She couldn't see one.

At the hotel, she took a *Daily Graphic* onto the terrace. There was nothing in it to suggest any untoward activity requiring a major police operation. The main news was that Osagyefo was busy preparing for his peace mission to Vietnam. The report said he'd locked himself in his study to read up on the history of the region and the conflict.

Two hours later, the terrace having emptied after breakfast, George entered the hotel. Yawor got up to greet him with a hug, but he pulled away.

'Cousin,' he said, 'what's going on?'

'George, I had to see you ...'

'You took a risk giving the letter to Herbert. You know he's loyal to my father.'

'I didn't give it to him. I told the taxi driver to ... anyway, you got it and you're here. And thank you for coming.'

'And? So?'

Yawor clutched her hands together. 'I didn't go to Winneba.'

'I know. And my father knows. He's furious. The college telephoned to ask where you were ... All of us were worried.'

'I'm sorry, George. It's a long story. Would you like breakfast? A cup of tea?'

'I ate at home. I'm not hungry.'

'I understand. I will explain everything.'

He sat with his arms crossed, and listened, his jaw dropping further with each new episode of Yawor's story. When she finished, it was some time before he spoke.

'I am ashamed of my father. How could he sell himself like

that? Where's his honour? But Cousin, I'm sorry I was short with you. I'm proud of you! I don't know if you are brave or crazy or both, but I admire you. You are the one with honour.'

'I should have let you know I was safe. Everything has been so hectic. That's why I wanted to see you today. So that in case something happens to me, you'll know why.'

'Like what?'

'For instance, I could be arrested.'

'You must take care!'

'I will. Thank you, George.' She took his hand. 'Are you sure you won't take something?'

'No. I have to go to school. Also,' he said, 'I don't like this place, I don't feel comfortable here.'

'We can go. I don't like it either. I only chose it because it's close to your house.'

They walked down the steps to the road and headed for a bus stop.

'That's where you heard the men making bets about the president, isn't it?'

'Yes.'

George shook his head. 'Now everybody seems to think there's a plot to remove him. Even among the Young Pioneers, we have heard the rumours that it will happen soon. They say Osagyefo knows about these rumours, but he dismisses them. It's like we're waiting, helplessly …'

She patted his arm. 'Commissioner Harlley said there was nothing to worry about.'

'After what you've told me this morning, I don't know if I trust what he says.'

She looked up Independence Avenue. 'No. Me neither.'

They waited together at the bus stop. Other people were

waiting too. The traffic moved past in an orderly fashion. Everything looked normal.

'How will we keep in touch?'

'I can get a message to you, George. Or you can come to Joanna's room ...'

'Please, Cousin, I'm not going to that street!'

She hugged him.

George caught his bus. Yawor watched it disappear up the road before setting off on foot and taking a turning that led to the American embassy.

It was an unusual-looking building, a single square storey supported by white stilts, set back from the road. Yawor had intended only to walk past, but the quiet, ungated driveway lured her in.

'I want to apply for a visa,' she told the guard standing by a sentry box.

'Write your name here.' He gestured to a register. She wrote the first name that came to mind: Beatrice Ansah.

'That way, miss.'

She walked through to a central courtyard, noticing more cars parked in the shade beneath the building, but no red ones. She climbed the stairs and followed a sign for the visa department. As she reached the end of a corridor, a door opened and a tall man with thinning hair stepped out. Yawor drew a sharp breath. It was the man she'd seen with Commissioner Harlley the day before: Howard Bane.

'Hello,' he said. 'Are you lost? May I help you?' He was wearing a white shirt with a silk cravat.

Yawor gulped. 'No, er, well ... thank you. I'm looking for the visa department.'

'Sure, come with me, I'm headed that way. Howard Bane's my name.' He smiled warmly and held out his hand.

Yawor shook it loosely. She could hardly breathe. 'Nice to meet you. I am Beatrice Ansah.'

'You looking to study in the States?'

'Study?'

'A study visa? Is that what you're after?'

'Oh, yes. I want to do a master's degree in English.'

'Great idea. Let me know if I can help.'

'You can help me get a visa?'

'Maybe. I deal with information. Hear anything interesting, let me know!'

He put his hand in his shirt pocket and pulled out a business card. Knowing his actual job, she blinked as she read the bland description: 'Howard Bane, Second Secretary, United States Embassy, Accra'.

'Thank you,' she said. 'You're kind.' Her mouth was so dry she could barely get the words out.

'My pleasure, Beatrice. Here's the visa office. Good luck and have a nice day.'

He went on his way. Yawor pushed through the double doors and fell into a seat, trying to compose herself.

A woman behind a desk looked up. 'Yes, miss?'

'Oh, please, I want to apply for a student visa.'

The woman held up a form.

Yawor collected the form and left through the double doors. She glanced along the corridor, wondering where Howard Bane's office was and if he shared it with the man who drove his car, Steve Krieger. It occurred to her she could spy on the spies, but she wasn't that brave or crazy, and went back the way she'd come.

As she was walking down the stairs, she noticed a group of men at workbenches below the far side of the building. They were making up placards. She looked around. No one was looking at her. She walked between the posts that supported the building until she got close enough to read the slogans:

LONG LIVE NEW GHANA

NO MORE ANIMAL FARM

LONG LIVE NATIONAL LIBERATION COUNCIL

The words made no sense to Yawor.

A man approached the workers, clapping his hands enthusiastically. His back was to Yawor, but there was no mistaking it was Howard Bane. She had the feeling she shouldn't be there. She hurried to the exit. The guard at the sentry box asked her to write her name again. Outside, she turned down a road shielded from the embassy building by a wall.

It was midday. The now-hazy sun was overhead. There was little traffic. She was trying to work out how to get round to Independence Avenue when a glint at the bottom of the drainage ditch between the footpath and the road caught her eye. She stopped to look more closely. Next to a trickle of dark water, she saw a tube of lipstick. She clambered down and picked it up, and wiped it clean. She recognised the make and the red colour: the red she'd given her sister on her last birthday. And she recognised the dried mud on the casing: the same as on the photograph she'd found in Adzo's bag.

Adzo had been in that ditch. Before Yawor could think why, she heard a car pulling up and a door slam. She looked up. Standing above her with his hands on his hips was Uncle Joseph.

Chapter 27

The last part of the taxi ride, over the potholed track, sent jarring aftershocks through Patrice's battered body. It was a relief to reach the house and to place his feet on solid ground. He had to step around the Ghanaian flag to get to the back of the house – the pole was bent nearly at right angles now so that the faded red, gold and green stripes drooped like a sad curtain. He found Kekeli and Aunty Yawor on the veranda. Two boys were with them.

'Patrice!' Kekeli got to her feet. 'Oh my God, what happened to you?'

He'd forgotten about the bandage on his nose. 'Oh, this … I walked into a tree. Which reminds me, you need to fix that flagpole. It's becoming a hazard.'

Kekeli rolled her eyes. 'Come,' she said, like there were more urgent matters. 'Come and meet these boys.'

They looked like brothers. Teenagers. They looked from Kekeli to Patrice nervously.

'They were at the funeral yesterday. They say they were playing near my father's hydro-plant the day he died.'

'Oh, really?' Patrice sat on the steps.

'Boys, Patrice is my friend. Tell him what you've been telling me and Aunty. Start from the beginning.'

The older one spoke. 'We live behind that side.' He pointed up the valley. 'But far. We didn't know her father had died until yesterday, when we saw people dressed for the funeral. We didn't know whose funeral it was, we just came …'

Kekeli patted him on the shoulder. 'It's alright to say – lots of people come to funerals. You were welcome.'

The boy nodded. 'So we came, and they said the man died at his electricity station two weeks ago, and we realised it was the day we were there. We were swimming in the river and playing …'

He broke off and looked down again.

'Thank you for coming to speak to us,' Patrice said, trying to put the boy at ease. 'This is important. So, the two of you were swimming and playing …'

The boy sucked in his cheeks.

'There were others? It's okay, you can tell us. You won't get into trouble.'

The boy dropped his voice. 'Two girls were with us.' The boy looked at his brother, who was looking into the garden as if he wasn't listening.

'That's not a problem.' Kekeli smiled. 'Tell Patrice what you saw.'

'From where we were, we couldn't see the electricity station, not the whole building, just the roof. We were in the water above the dam. We heard voices singing, and we saw a man and the old lady walking …' He nodded at Aunty Yawor. 'She had a crutch. The man turned to her and held up his hand, like he was saying to wait. He walked to the building, but, like I said, we couldn't see it all, so we couldn't see if he went in. But we could see the old lady. She was standing by a rock.'

'Aunty?' Patrice turned to her. She was in her chair, staring

into the garden in her usual way. 'Do you remember this?'
She didn't answer.

The boy continued. 'The next thing, the lady was shouting
and waving her crutch. We heard a cry. And we saw a man
running away from the electricity station, to a car on the road
above.'

Patrice hardly dared ask the next question. 'What colour
was the car?'

'It was behind the trees. I don't know the colour. We didn't
see it.'

'How do you know there was a car?'

'We heard it drive away. And we saw dust from the road. It
was a car.' He looked at his brother, who nodded.

'You didn't go to see what had happened?' Patrice asked,
trying not to sound accusatory.

'It didn't occur to us,' the older one said. 'We thought the
man ... the man who has died ... we thought he had scared the
other man and the other man ran. We didn't know anyone
was hurt.'

Kekeli nodded. 'We understand. And there's nothing you
could have done.'

The boy chewed on his lips.

'How far away were you?' Patrice asked. 'Did you get a
good look at the man who ran away?'

'We were not close.'

'Would you recognise him again?'

'I don't think so.' The boy looked again at his brother, who
shook his head. 'We couldn't see his face.'

'Was he big or small?'

The boy shrugged. 'The same size like you.'

'What was he wearing?'

'Like jeans. And a sports top, black, with a hood.'

It didn't sound like either of Mensah's thugs, or Boateng, and it was hard to imagine Kwaku Sarpong wearing jeans.

'It was a white man.' It was Aunty Yawor speaking. They all turned. Her eyes were wide open.

'The man who was running away?' Patrice asked. 'Who got in the car?'

'A white man in a red car.'

'You saw him? You saw the car? Aunty?'

Her eyes glazed over again.

'Boys? Could it have been a white man?'

They both shrugged. 'We could see only his back. He was carrying something in front of him, like a bag or a box.'

'Did your aunt really see those things? For a moment it seemed like she was with us, but then she slipped away again.'

'I don't know, Patrice. She says these words out of the blue. It's frustrating.'

It was later and they were lying in bed. Kekeli was fiddling with her hair, pulling at twists of it. 'She likes you. She knows you want to help us. So, is she trying to help too? Since you came, she's come out of her shell a little. She has been withdrawn for a long time now.'

'That's what Gladys said. Is it dementia?'

'That is part of it. She can be forgetful and confused. But I believe also she has a condition called delayed-onset PTSD.'

'Delayed what?'

'Delayed-onset Post Traumatic Stress Disorder. Aunty's early life was beset by tragedy. She lost her parents and brothers in a fire and then she lost her sister. But she got on with her life, apparently normally, working as a teacher.

The trauma struck when she retired. That's when she went into herself and stopped communicating. I read books in the library and articles on the internet, and they gave me the idea she might have this condition. But these things she's saying now … the white man, the red car? I don't know what to make of it.'

Patrice shifted gingerly on the bed and turned to face Kekeli. 'There's something you should know about this man, Kwaku Sarpong.' He'd told her how he'd got his nose broken and what Sarpong had told him about the day her father died – which didn't quite match the boy's evidence. 'I didn't want to tell you before, but you should know.'

'What is it, Patrice?'

'He drives a red car.'

She stopped twiddling with her hair and stared at him.

'It's … well, it might be coincidence, there are many red cars. But these people, they've got a hold over him, they could have …'

'But he's not white.'

'I know, and he denies he was there. But that's why I was asking you about Aunty. Could she be right about the red car and wrong about the white man?'

'Would he have told you what he did, about what happened that day, if … he was there?'

'Kwaku Sarpong is a tortured soul. He knows he's done wrong and wants to put things right. Perhaps he told me those things because he wants to help me, but only so long as it won't land him in further trouble.'

Kekeli found a fresh twist of hair to twiddle. They were silent for a while. Then she asked, 'Do you think my father was murdered, Patrice?'

He sighed. 'Honestly, I don't know. But we know, even if it was an accident, someone else was there.'

'Perhaps we should go to the police, after all?'

'At some point. But we must be careful. The way Victor Mensah spoke, he has nothing to fear, which means his contacts inside the police have the influence to prevent a serious investigation.'

'So what do we do?'

'I will talk to my boss. She also has connections, which Mensah seemed to know about. But first, I want to confront Sarpong again. He's a coward but he's a good driver. Aunty might be right about the white man and the red car; Sarpong could have been sitting in it, ready to make a getaway with the man in the hooded top.'

'But you talked to him before, so why would he say anything different?'

'Because you'll be there too. He can lie to me, and he could lie to the police, but if he sees George Abotsi's daughter … perhaps, somewhere deep down, hidden beneath the dollar signs, he has a conscience.'

Chapter 28

1966: FEBRUARY 15

Uncle Joseph's form was silhouetted against the glare of the sun, but Yawor could see he was shaking. His jaw was clamped tight. His eyes were narrow slits, as if it was painful to look at her.

'Don't expect me to get you out of there,' he said. 'Do it yourself. Now!'

There was no escape. She crawled out of the ditch on her hands and knees, and struggled to her feet. An open hand slapped her hard across her cheek.

'Get in the car.'

She sat in the back, smarting, holding back the tears. He hadn't hit her since she was a girl. The last time was when she was fifteen. She'd come home from school with a B in mathematics. She'd arrived the same time as Uncle Joseph on his return from work. He'd seen the worried look on her face and the piece of paper in her hand and slapped her. But that slap was not hard like this one.

'I should have left you in that ditch. That's where you belong. In a sewer, like a rat. Do you hear me, Yawor?'

She didn't answer.

'Do you want to make me a laughing stock? Do you want to ruin me? Is that what you want? You've lived in our house all these years. We've sheltered and fed you and your sister. And now you turn against us? Why, Yawor?'

Yawor wanted to shout and scream at him and tell him to his face he was a liar. And she would have done – she didn't care if he hit her again. But she knew she could land Sergeant Ofori in trouble. So she kept her silence.

'I told you the police will continue to investigate your sister's death, did I not? But you, it seems, do not trust our police force. Because, it seems, you are carrying on your own investigation. I know you've always had a chip on your shoulder but ...' He pulled up at a junction and looked for an opportunity to pull out.

Yawor wished she could tell him Adzo's killer was an American spy, and see the look on his face. That would stop him in his tracks. But she stayed quiet. The less he knew about how much she knew, the better. She was learning how to play this game. Lesson Number One: it was about who you could trust. And she couldn't trust her uncle.

They turned onto Independence Avenue and the barrage continued.

'Stupid, stupid girl. You think the police are stupid, but it's you. They saw you outside police headquarters yesterday selling oranges. You think you're Sherlock Holmes, putting on a disguise? So stupid. And today they get information that you're snooping around the American embassy. JWK himself called to tell me.'

So, she thought, Howard Bane must have recognised her. He's a spy, a professional spy. He must have noticed her selling the oranges, then recognised her when she went to

211

the embassy and called the commissioner. Lesson Number Two: she needed to be a lot more careful.

'I said it can't be true. I had to pretend I thought you were still in Winneba. But the last place I expected you to turn up was the American embassy. What were you doing there? Do you think he hasn't got more important business to attend to? The police commissioner? Than chasing after a stupid girl? And what kind of fool do you think he thinks I am?'

They pulled up at the house. Herbert opened the gate, looking from Yawor to Uncle Joseph. She held her hand up to cover her cheek.

Aunt Esther opened the front door. 'Yawor, what's happened?'

'Plenty.' Uncle Joseph pushed Yawor into the hallway. 'All sorts of fun and games. She seems to have lost her tongue, but no matter; she can tell us her story in her own time. And she'll have a lot of that. She's to be confined to her room.'

He marched Yawor to her room and closed the door behind her and locked it. She couldn't remember that door ever being locked. Like the prisoner she was, she went to the window and wrapped her hands round the bars of the security grille. It was fixed firmly to the wall outside. She sat on her bed, her head in her hands, staring hopelessly at the floor.

At dusk, Aunt Esther came with a tray of food: fufu and goat stew.

'Your uncle's very upset,' she said as Yawor ate. 'You might think he's being unfair, but this is his house …'

'I know, Aunty. It was rude and ungracious of me. And I'm sorry that I've upset and disappointed you as well.'

'Can't you talk to him? Explain to him why you didn't go to Winneba?'

Yawor knew her aunt hated conflict in the house. 'I'm sorry, Aunty, I don't want to talk to him.' She added, casually, 'Where's George?'

'He's with the Pioneers. They're arranging a send-off for the president when he leaves for Vietnam.'

Yawor wiped her mouth and pushed the unfinished plate away.

'Eat your food, Yawor. You must look after yourself. It's not pleasant being confined to your room, but at least it's comfortable.'

Yawor glanced around and noticed the window. 'Thank you, Aunty. I know you'll look after me. But I'm scared.'

'Why? You are safe.'

'What if there's a fire? I won't be able to get out. It reminds me ...' She looked down and put her hand to her head.

'Oh, Yawor ... I don't know ... what can I do?'

'Please Aunty, don't lock the door. I won't leave.' She glanced up at her aunt who was looking at the door, doubtless contemplating how far she could trust her suddenly wayward niece, fearing maybe the wrath she'd incur from her husband if Yawor didn't do as she said.

Aunt Esther stroked Yawor's hair. 'Alright, my dear.'

'Thank you, Aunty. I'll sleep now. Goodnight.'

'Goodnight, Yawor.' She left without locking the door.

Yawor reflected on how easy it was to get away with a lie when somebody trusted you.

She waited until eight o'clock before she slipped out. Highlife music was coming from the radio in the front room. She could picture the scene: Uncle Joseph in his armchair, reading; Aunt Esther and the older girls on the sofa, sewing or doing homework. Yawor went the other way, tiptoeing, trying not to drag her bad leg. She sneaked past the kitchen, where Emmanuel was clearing up, and out the back door. Herbert the guard was dozing by the gate. Making sure it didn't squeak, she squeezed through.

The police commissioner's residence was in Cantonments, an area of leafy streets and grand houses. Yawor caught a *trotro* up Independence Avenue to the Achimota Road and walked the rest of the way. She'd changed into a loose-fitting black dress, but it was a warm evening and she arrived dripping with sweat.

The front gate was high, as was the perimeter wall. She followed the wall round a corner. A tree branch hung over it, from which, she thought, she could view the lay-out inside the compound. But she was a hopeless climber. She stretched and grabbed hold of a lower branch and tried to pull herself up, but she couldn't lift her feet off the ground. She rubbed her hands and made a second attempt. Leading with her good leg, she got a foot up. But she couldn't lift the rest of herself. She was stuck, and she was like this when she saw a figure turn the corner and walk, then run, towards her.

She held back a scream. But as the figure approached, she recognised the slender shape of Sergeant Ofori. Relieved but embarrassed, Yawor swung her foot off the branch. Her hands lost their grip and she fell – into the arms of the young policeman.

'I've caught you red-handed!' he said with a smile.

She chuckled. As he let her down, she smoothed her dress and tried to regain her dignity. 'Thank you, Ofori. You gave me a fright, that's why I slipped ...'

'I thought I might find you here, like I thought I knew the

orange seller outside police headquarters. I know you well!'

Yawor hung her head. 'I feel like a fool. And I was lucky it was you who came round the corner and not one of your colleagues.'

'Come,' he said. He took her hand and led her past the tree and further up the turning. 'From there you cannot see much – the house is far away. I know a better place ...'

'Ofori, if I get caught, I'll be in a lot of trouble – so much, they may not even call my uncle. But if you get caught, it will be much worse.'

'I have to see what's going on. I'm beginning to suspect ...' He cut himself off mid-sentence, putting a finger to his lips, and beckoned her to crouch next to him.

They were near the top end of the compound. The street was dark, with many trees. A small wooden gate was cut in the wall, from which a slat was missing. Through the gap, they had a clear view of the first-floor veranda on the side of Commissioner Harlley's house. It was close by and illuminated by a single bulb, which gave enough light for them to make out six men seated around a table.

Harlley was at one end. He was sitting upright, his chest puffed out. He was in uniform, his peaked cap on a bench to the side. To his right was Howard Bane, wearing his cravat and flicking at a mosquito. Next to him was another man Yawor recognised, the soldier who'd been waiting to see Harlley when she and Uncle Joseph had first visited his office, Captain Francis Kwashie. To his right, at the end opposite Harlley, was another soldier.

'Who's that?' Yawor whispered, pointing.

Sweat was glistening on Ofori's forehead. 'That's Colonel Kotoka. He's Commander of Second Brigade ... he controls half the army. I don't know the man sitting to his right with his back to us, but the man sitting between that man and the commissioner is Deputy Commissioner Deku. They are all friends …'

'… one company to take Ghana Radio.' Colonel Kotoka was speaking. 'Then one company to take Flagstaff House, supported by another who'll occupy the security flats overlooking the entrance and another who'll take up position in the Information Services compound next door.' The eyes of the other men were fixed on the colonel. 'That's the plan.'

Yawor and Ofori looked at each other, mouths wide open.

Harlley stroked his chin. 'In total, six companies?'

'Six hundred men.'

'We're entrusting our future to six hundred soldiers. Are they enough?' He was addressing the colonel.

The colonel's face muscles twitched. 'So long as Second Battalion don't interfere. If they come with their heavy weapons from Shai Hills, we could be in trouble. So we must make sure Major Tetteh, their commander, is on our side, and I believe he will be. And Ocran at Burma Camp will um and ah, but he will join us once he sees which way the wind is blowing. So, Harlley, you make the civilian arrests and we can deal with any military resistance we meet at Flagstaff House.'

Their voices carried clearly through the still night air, the bare lightbulb under which they sat intensifying the moment. From the little Yawor and Ofori had heard, it was clear these men on Harlley's veranda were finalising the details of a coup d'état.

The police commissioner nodded. 'Good, but what about Barwah? You know how loyal he is to the president. He

accuses you of tribalism. He doesn't like us police either ...'
Yawor had heard Uncle Joseph talk about Major General
Charles Barwah, the chief of army staff; he called him one of
Nkrumah's lackeys. 'If he gets wind of this and sends orders
to Second Battalion, Tetteh may buckle.'

'Don't worry about Barwah. We'll send an advance party.
They'll take him out before he knows what's happening.'

Yawor glanced at Ofori. He was glowering at the scene
in front of them. The creases above his nose had formed a
zigzag. It was a look she hadn't seen on his face before – one
of unmitigated anger.

'And the date. You can be ready by then?'

The colonel tutted. 'Relax, Harlley. Provided the president
leaves for Hanoi as planned on the 22nd, we will be ready.
We cannot move until he is in the air. Then we need two
days to get our men in position. Operation Cold Chop can
commence on the morning of the 24th.'

'Very well. In the meantime, we must be careful who we
speak to. Only those who have to know can know. What will
you tell the men?'

'We'll tell them we're moving to the Accra Plains for a
training exercise in case they are called upon to go to Rhodesia
to fight against the breakaway government there.'

Harlley snorted. 'Will they believe that?'

'Oh yes. The president has talked about such a possibility.
And the Accra Plains resemble the topography of Rhodesia.
It's very credible.'

There was silence, the men perhaps reassuring themselves
that nothing was being left to chance. Then Captain Kwashie
spoke in Ewe. '*Me ngble dem be mi atenu aka de wo Yevu-velia
sia dzia.*'

217

Ofori whispered to Yawor, 'What's he saying?'

'Wait …'

'*E se miafe dodoawo fuun eza ya.*'

'He says he hopes they can trust Harlley's white-man friend because he's heard a lot about their plans.'

The police commissioner chuckled. '*Aleke wor. Xorse de edzi.*'

Yawor translated: 'But of course. We can trust him.'

'*De 'ye wova be yea kpe de mia nu.*'

'He is here to help us.'

Bane was looking from one man to the other.

'It's alright, Howard, he's asking if you're ready for the party afterwards. I told him you won't let us down.'

'Oh, sure, that's taken care of. It's all at the embassy, out of sight.'

'Good. It should stay there for now.'

There was a satisfied murmur around the table. Harlley raised a glass. 'To Operation Cold Chop!' The others joined in the toast.

Chapter 29

The Addos' house was similar to George Abotsi's: a wood-frame structure built among the trees with steps up to the front door. The hallway was full of boxes stacked up ready for moving. Gladys said Aunty could sit undisturbed on the back veranda, where she had a favourite chair. Patrice and Kekeli settled her and headed for Accra.

The aim was to get to Kwaku Sarpong's apartment early, to catch him off guard. But the city-bound traffic was moving at a snail's pace. After half an hour, it ground to a halt. Drivers got out of their cars to see what was going on. It was a good morning for the water sellers; the higher the sun rose, the faster they handed out their bags.

Kekeli tapped the steering wheel of her old Nissan. 'This is not normal. Perhaps there is an incident at the airport.'

She dialled through the radio stations, searching for news. Mostly she found commercials, for banks, for new apartments, for cars and formula milk. Eventually, on *Joy FM*, she found a traffic report: an overloaded truck had lost control, skidded onto its side, spilled its load of yams, and blocked all three lanes at Tetteh Quashie.

The reporter was at the scene. 'From where I'm standing, I can see the truck and the traffic stretching back bumper to bumper. It is before the roundabout, so there's no alternative exit for these commuters. They're going to be late for work.'

'And we'll be late too,' Patrice said.

Kekeli tutted. 'Welcome to Accra.'

Listeners were calling into the station. A young-sounding woman said, 'This is the twenty-first century. We cannot be having farm vehicles driving into Accra in the morning traffic. I'm telling you, it should not be allowed ...'

As they sat there, stationary, Patrice looked at the advertising hoardings: mobile phones, nappies, noodles. He noticed a small sign for The Chop Bar at A&C and remembered something. 'Kekeli, what is *cold chop*?'

'Cold chop is fast food. Are you hungry? That place is good, but how do we get there?'

'No, I'm not hungry. I was reading about the coup against Nkrumah. It was called Operation Cold Chop. Do you know why?'

'Huh! That's nothing to do with food. Cold chop can also mean a thing you can get easily, with little effort.'

'Ah, so they were confident.'

'Or they wanted to think they were.'

'I must do some more research. You know, it's said the CIA were in close contact with the coup plotters. American policy on Ghana at that time will make an interesting case study for my master's application, if I ever get round to making it.'

After an hour, *Joy FM* reported that the road was clear of yams and the truck had been pushed aside. And after another half-hour, Kekeli drove past the wreckage. The driver was leaning against the upturned vehicle, talking to two policemen. He was in worn clothes, in stark contrast to the people on their way to work in their fine suits.

'9.33,' Patrice said, reading the time off the radio. 'If he's going to work, we'll miss him. But maybe he's planning a day at the casino ...'

'Cantonments is not far.' They passed the airport and a new-looking shopping mall, then turned off. 'The Lands Commission is down that road, Patrice. Where do we go?'

'One more street and turn ...'

Kekeli followed his directions. Patrice recognised the street, and moments later they were parking outside Sarpong's apartment complex.

'This is a nice area,' Kekeli said as they approached the gate. 'But an apartment here, even a small one, will not be cheap. If your friend has money problems, he should look for somewhere else.'

'He's not my friend.' Patrice pointed at his bandaged nose.

A guard said to ring the video intercom. There was no answer.

'Did you see Mr Sarpong leave this morning?' Patrice asked.

'No, sir,' the guard answered, but with a shrug that suggested he hadn't paid much attention to who'd been passing in and out.

Patrice tried the intercom again. Again, no answer. They were turning to leave when the gate opened. A four-by-four was coming out. Patrice noticed a janitor was cleaning around the entrance to Sarpong's block and had propped open the door with a bucket. He glanced at Kekeli. She nodded. They walked through the gate, across the forecourt, and into the building. The janitor was doing a good job. The white marble floors and white walls looked spotless, as they had before, when Patrice had come to borrow Sarpong's navy suit.

They climbed the white marble stairs. 'I'm hoping he's

221

overslept after a late night,' Patrice said. 'Let me do the talking to begin with, then I'll introduce you and we'll see how he reacts.'

They reached the first-floor landing. Sarpong's front door wasn't fully closed. Patrice's stomach muscles pulled tight. He leaned in close and listened. All he could hear was the janitor's mop downstairs and a distant rumble of Accra traffic. He knocked. No answer. He pushed the door and called out, 'Kwaku! Get up!' Still no response.

He stepped inside, Kekeli behind him. More white marble floors and white walls greeted them, and more silence. They walked down the hallway to the living area: black leather sofa, glass-topped coffee table, flat-screen TV. Kwaku Sarpong's bachelor apartment – but minus Kwaku Sarpong.

They went through to the kitchenette. A glass was on the counter, smelling of whisky. It didn't look like anyone had had breakfast there that morning.

Another short corridor led off the living area. The bathroom door was open, the room empty. The bedroom door was closed. A range of extreme possibilities ran through Patrice's mind: the best, that Sarpong was tucked up in bed, fast asleep; the worst, that he'd seen who was at the gate through the intercom, had looked out of his window and seen Patrice and Kekeli walk in, had left his front door open, and was waiting for them in his room with a gun in his hand.

Patrice gripped the handle and opened the door.

Kwaku Sarpong was in his room with a gun in his hand. But he was dead – lying on his bed with a hole in the top of his head and blood splattered across the wall behind.

Kekeli looked in. 'Oh my God!'

Patrice touched the body. It was warm. 'He must have seen

us coming and … shot himself.' Instinctively, hopelessly, he felt Sarpong's neck for a pulse. There wasn't one. 'Jesus.'

Kekeli was staring at the corpse. 'Now we really must call the police.'

'Yes, you're right.' Patrice fumbled for his phone. 'What's the number?'

'What?'

'The number for the police?'

'One nine one.'

Before Patrice could finish dialling, he heard footsteps coming up the stairs, then voices on the landing.

'… is it the place?'

'Why's the door open?'

It was two men. Patrice recognised their voices - at least, one of them. 'Shit!' he whispered.

'Who is it?'

Patrice pointed again at the bandage on his nose.

'Shit!'

The footsteps entered the apartment.

'Where is he? Sarpong?'

The men clattered about. It sounded like they were emptying drawers and cupboards.

'They're looking for something,' Patrice said, stating the obvious, his eyes darting around the bedroom.

One of them called out again. 'Search the whole place. I'll watch outside …'

A set of footsteps went to the front door; another approached the bedroom. Patrice and Kekeli looked at each other and, as one, stepped behind the bedroom door. A tall shape passed behind the crack between the door and the frame. Patrice was weighing up the options when Kekeli

223

flung the door back. The edge swung round and smacked against a face. There was a heavy crack and a cry. The man tottered into the room with his hand on his head. Patrice slipped past Kekeli and punched him low in the stomach, and as the man coiled over, gripped hold of his head and kneed him in the face. There was another cry and the man collapsed.

'Come, Patrice, let's get away from here.' Kekeli skipped round the heap on the floor and started down the hall.

Patrice restrained himself from giving the man another kick. He picked Sarpong's phone off the bed and went after Kekeli. She was at the top of the stairs, with one finger over her lips and another pointing down. Footsteps were coming up. Quickly, quietly, they walked up past the next half-landing. They watched the other man go back into Sarpong's apartment, then made their move, running down the stairs and out of the building. The gate to the street was open. They ran through, got into the old Nissan, and drove off at speed. Patrice glanced behind. There was no sign of the two men who worked for Victor Mensah.

'I can't believe we did that, Patrice!' Kekeli said as she steered round the first corner. 'We're quite a team, huh?'

'Really!' Patrice said, his ribs burning, his nose throbbing, despite the rush of adrenalin. 'That was some trick with the door!'

'I wasn't thinking. I just pushed it as hard as I could.'

'Well, he had it coming to him. An eye for an eye.'

'And a nose for a nose!'

Patrice laughed, which made him wince. But as he looked through the messages on Sarpong's phone, he soon forgot about his physical discomfort.

'At 9.07 he sent a text: *Patrice, I've got what you wanted.*'

'What did he mean?'

'I asked him to get me a list of all the companies these people have set up … it must be that. That's what those men were looking for.'

'But did the text come through? We were stuck in the traffic then.'

'That's the problem – he didn't send the text to me. He sent it to Albert Boateng. It must have been by mistake …'

'Oh my God. And then he shot himself?'

'Wait. Before he sent the text, he received one from Boateng. It says, *Sarpong, where are you?* And then …' Patrice checked the calls. 'Before that, there are three missed calls from Boateng. Sarpong knew they were onto him. He said if he got caught, they'd tear him apart. He was desperate.'

They drove on in silence, numbed by what had just happened. Kekeli kept to the side streets, avoiding the worst of the traffic. 'You can't blame yourself for this,' she said after a while. 'The man was obviously unstable.'

'Yes. He was, I suppose. But we may never know now if he had anything to do with your father's death. I'm sorry, Kekeli.' He picked up his own phone. 'I must call my boss. Sarpong was her friend's son. We'd better meet up with her.'

'What about the police?'

Patrice looked at Kwaku Sarpong's phone in his other hand. 'I'm not sure now. It's getting complicated. They'll have questions. It'll take a long time.'

Kekeli kept her eyes on the road and turned another corner.

Chapter 30

1966: FEBRUARY 15

Under the single bulb on the first-floor veranda of the police commissioner's residence, the six men discussed their plans to overthrow the government.

'To think how the commissioner patronised me in your office,' Yawor said, whispering to Sergeant Ofori. 'Remember what he said? "The country and our leader are safe in the hands of the Ghanaian police." Huh!'

'That's what all the meetings have been about,' Ofori said, shaking his head. 'While I sit on the other side of the door filing pieces of paper, they have been plotting ... right under my nose. I feel ashamed. The commissioner takes me for a fool!'

'You cannot blame yourself for any of this, Ofori. But why did the investigation into my sister's death have to be ...'

'Shh.' Ofori held his finger to his mouth. 'Listen.'

'... to other details. Howard, where is your friend? We have to know what's going on in Flagstaff House.'

'He's on his way.'

The American craned his neck to look down the driveway. As if on cue, the gate at the bottom opened and a car drove in. The red paint looked different in the silver moonlight, but Yawor recognised the Ford Mustang as if she'd seen it a thousand times before. Her fists tightened into balls. Ofori put his hand on her shoulder.

The car pulled up by the house. Howard Bane and Police Commissioner Harlley left the veranda and reappeared below as the driver's door opened and a man with parted hair and a moustache got out – the man Yawor had last seen driving off with Joanna.

'Good to see you, Steve. The commissioner was worried you weren't going to make it.'

'I didn't say that, Howard …'

'It's okay, buddy, I'm only teasing, you know me! Steve, show us what you got.'

They went to the back of the car. Krieger opened the trunk and pulled out a box. Harlley called up to the others. 'Come and help.'

Yawor and Ofori watched them carry a dozen boxes into the house and out onto the veranda. Krieger opened them one by one and listed the contents as he held them up for the others to see. 'Headphones … receivers …antennae … and these little cuties …'

Yawor strained her eyes. It looked like he was holding small coins tied to pieces of string.

'Microphones,' Ofori whispered.

'… plant these in Flagstaff House and it'll be like you're there.'

Harlley took them in his palm and admired them. 'Deku, this is your job. You can get them in?'

'Yes. I have a man on the Flagstaff House security detail. He will install them. Even tomorrow he can start.'

227

Harlley nodded his approval. 'So, Kwashie, you take the receivers to your house. Living so close to Flagstaff House has its advantages.'

'Yes, sir.'

Colonel Kotoka clicked a handshake with the captain. 'I want Kwashie's house to be headquarters for the operation; its location is ideal, and with this equipment there it makes even more sense.'

The men nodded.

'Agreed. Good.' Harlley wiped his brow and took another sip of his drink. 'Well done, Howard. With these things, we are safe. We will know in advance if they're onto us. And for us, that can mean the difference between life and death. You follow me?'

Bane nodded and said, 'Well done, agent,' as he patted Krieger on the back.

Harlley continued. 'You know, I went to the British, but they turned me down. I asked Thompson, the MI5 man, and he passed on my request, but it was declined. Apparently Prime Minister Wilson wouldn't approve. It was Thompson who said I should go to you …'

'Happy to oblige, John.' Bane held out his hand and they shook. 'It's all for our mutual benefit. Pity we've had to cancel the sideshow at the Chinese embassy. It was a perfect opportunity.'

Harlley smiled knowingly. 'Your superiors may have had to face some awkward questions.'

'No one could have proved a thing. Steve here's the man who'd have pulled it off. Which reminds me, John,' he said, speaking to Harlley but glancing at Krieger, 'thanks for the favour.' Krieger was looking at his shoes.

Yawor's head was burning. She looked to the sky. 'Why doesn't God strike these people down?' she said, still whispering, but not as quietly as before.

'Shh,' Ofori said again.

The group on the veranda broke up. Harlley and the two Americans stepped away and reappeared at the front of the house. Bane and Krieger got into the red Ford, Krieger on the driver's side. Yawor saw them exchange a smile. From inside her somewhere, she heard Adzo scream. A fiery heat rose to her head. She raised her fists and made to thump them against the wooden gate. Ofori caught her wrists just in time.

'Let's go,' he said, and pulled her away. She took a moment to catch her breath, then turned too quickly. Her leg gave way. She slipped, and her foot kicked against the gate. The voices coming from the first-floor veranda fell silent. The car doors that had been opened didn't close.

'What's that?' Harlley called out.

'Over there ...'

Ofori took Yawor's hand and yanked her up. 'Come,' he said urgently, as he arranged her arm over his shoulder.

'... it came from there.'

Footsteps approached the gate from inside. Ofori moved forward, Yawor clinging to him, a sharp pain shooting through her hip. The two of them were just a few steps from the corner of the compound. The men were at the gate.

'Open it ...'

There were sounds of scraping and banging, then a sliding bolt. Yawor and Ofori reached the corner. As they turned, her arm slipped off his shoulder. He grabbed her round her waist and hauled her forward. The next thing she knew, they were lying on the grass in the darkness.

'There's nothing there. It must have been a cat.'

The gate slammed shut. The voices on the other side of the wall returned to normal. The car doors closed, and the car drove off.

They got to their feet, dusted themselves down, and walked away from the residence of the commissioner of police.

Yawor was still in a daze after what she'd heard. 'So that's it,' she said.

Ofori said, 'He takes me for a fool.'

'Adzo was just a pawn in a much bigger game. And her killer will go free.'

'He has underestimated me.'

It seemed they were having different conversations. 'What are you saying, Ofori?'

He turned to face her. 'We can stop them!'

'Ofori, how can we do that?'

'We can raise the alarm.'

'But you said Colonel Kotoka controls half the army! And who will listen to us? We are small people. No one will believe us.'

'We must warn Major General Barwah. We know he is on the president's side. And he is the chief of army staff. He can stop it with a phone call to Second Battalion, with their heavy guns, that's what they said.'

'Ofori, you cannot go to him. You heard the commissioner saying Barwah doesn't like the police.'

'We will get a message to him, with all the details, so he can see this is not idle gossip.'

'But if you get caught by the commissioner …'

'Not me.'

'Good, but Ofori, I can't go. I'm sorry, I don't know how I could …'

'Not you, Yawor. Your cousin, George. He can help us.'

'George? But he's … he's a boy!'

'He's a Young Pioneer. He's going to be at the airport when the president leaves. And for sure, Barwah will be there too. He can pass him a note.'

She thought about it. It was desperate. But it might work.

'Yawor, one thing I know about you is that you don't give up. If the coup fails, there's a chance that Krieger can be brought to justice.'

They carried on walking, avoiding the main avenue, as if they feared the plotters might be out looking for them.

Yawor said, 'I will speak to George and ask him if he is comfortable with such a plan. He will need to be so careful.'

She took Ofori's arm for support. It was a long walk. She was limping badly. They parted outside Uncle Joseph's house. She looked through the peephole to confirm that Herbert was sleeping, squeezed through the gate, and went into the house by the back door.

It was late. The house was quiet. She went to her room. Nothing had been disturbed. She sat at her desk and wrote down, to the best of her recollection, the details of Operation Cold Chop, as outlined by Colonel Kotoka and the others that evening, and the names of those she knew to be involved. Then she went along the corridor and quietly opened the door to George's room.

He was sleeping. Gently, she shook him awake. 'Shh,' she whispered when his eyes opened. 'George, we need your help. Listen …'

They sat on the bed and in hushed tones she told him

about the meeting she and Ofori had witnessed at the police commissioner's residence.

'So, it's all true,' he said dejectedly. 'The rumours.'

'Yes,' Yawor took his hand. 'But maybe we can stop it.'

'How? Tell me what to do, Cousin. I will do anything.'

She handed him the notes she'd written. 'Ofori says Major General Barwah will be at the airport when Osagyefo leaves next week. Can you pass this to him?'

'Yes, I can. I will!' He held up his fist. 'Nkrumah is our leader! Nkrumah is our Messiah! Nkrumah never dies!'

Yawor placed her hands on his fist. 'George, this is serious. You must be careful. No one must see what you're doing. If you are caught …'

A loud knock cut short the whispered conversation. They looked round and saw the tall, menacing figure of Uncle Joseph framed in the doorway.

'Wife!' he called. 'The prisoner has escaped.' He snatched Yawor off the bed, dragged her down the hall, and pushed her into her room, slamming the door behind her and turning the key.

Yawor fell onto her bed. She heard her uncle march back down the hall and then return. The key turned again. He walked in, a leather belt in his hand.

Chapter 31

The hotel receptionist, a deadpan young woman called Heaven, told Patrice his friend was waiting in the coffee lounge.

'Did you have an accident, sir?' she asked.

'No, I wouldn't call it that.'

'I'm sorry, sir.'

He hurried through with Kekeli. They were safe for now, but it wouldn't be long before Mensah's men came looking for them.

Josie Mwinga, in a dark linen trouser suit, rose to greet them. She looked pale. 'Hello, Kekeli, Patrice … I can't say good morning. I mean, since you called … my goodness, what a shock.'

They sat and ordered drinks – the women coffees, Patrice a black tea. He explained how they found Sarpong's body and how they weren't the only visitors to the apartment that morning.

Mwinga shook her head. 'What do I say to his father? You know, he lost his wife only recently, poor man.'

'Say nothing.'

'Patrice, he's a friend of mine. I can't not speak to him.'

'Hold off for now. The police should be the ones to tell him.

Besides, if he heard the news from you, you'd have to tell him we were there.'

'He'll have to know sooner or later.'

'Of course. But later would be better.'

His boss heaved a sigh.

Patrice sat back in the round armchair and sipped his tea, observing the surroundings, thinking hard but not coming up with much. It was a dark room with soft lights hanging over the tables. A thick carpet absorbed the sound. Other conversations were taking place, but all he could hear was a murmur and the tinkle of a teaspoon in a cup.

'Have you heard any more about the plot to attack the Akosombo Dam?' he asked.

Kekeli looked at him, looking startled. He hadn't mentioned this to her; there'd been too much going on.

'Well,' Josie Mwinga said, almost excitedly, as if it was a relief to talk about something else. 'My friend says the president has discussed the matter with his cabinet.' She leaned in closer and kept her voice low, despite the soundproof acoustics. 'Everyone is sworn to silence. But there are divisions. Some believe it's a hoax and should be ignored. Others say at the very least it's a reminder that the country should not be so reliant on the dam for its power generation.'

Patrice thought some more. 'It would be interesting to know who those others are – and if they have any connection to people within the Energy Commission.'

Mwinga snorted. 'What are you suggesting, Patrice?'

'Don't you see? Who stands to gain if Ghana starts looking for alternative sources of electricity?' The two women stared at him. 'Large-scale solar farms, for one. And we know of at least two that are ready to exploit such an opportunity. This so-called threat against the Akosombo Dam is convenient for them.'

'Hang on, Patrice. This is no time for conspiracy theories. You're forgetting this information came from two members of a group affiliated to al-Qaeda in the Maghreb. Are you saying al-Qaeda is moving into solar energy production? It would be quite a change of direction.'

Patrice shrugged.

'Really, Patrice.'

'What's the president's view?'

'He's pointed out a review of Ghana's energy policy is under way, and it won't be influenced by unconfirmed rumours. But he's ordered security at the dam to be stepped up, as a precaution.'

'That sounds sensible.'

'Good, well, there we are. I must be on my way.' Josie Mwinga got to her feet and picked up her bag. 'I will go later to talk to Kwaku Sarpong's poor father. Please be careful, both of you.'

Patrice watched his boss walk purposefully out of the lounge. He supposed she meant well. It occurred to him that he'd spent more time in her company on this trip than he had ever done in the past – they lived in different countries and communicated mostly by emails and texts. 'She's a good boss, generally,' he said, turning to Kekeli. 'Demanding but loyal to her staff and decisive. But there's something about her here in Ghana … like she's distracted …'

'It's no wonder if she is,' Kekeli said. 'After what happened to my father, and now to her friend's son.' She tapped Patrice's knee. 'We should go. Those people will be looking for you, and me.'

235

They headed out of the hotel and into a wall of hot air. But before the automatic doors had closed behind them, the receptionist called out. 'Mr Le Congo, you have a letter.'

He spun round. She was holding a large manila envelope. He went back and took it from her and peered inside - briefly but long enough to see there were thirty-odd pages of photocopies and a cover sheet with a hand-written note: *I'm sorry, Patrice. I hope this helps. K.*

Patrice swallowed.

'Thank you, Heaven. It's good of you to remember. Have a nice day. If anyone comes asking for me, tell them you haven't seen me.'

'Yes, sir,' she said, blankly.

He followed Kekeli to her car. 'I need somewhere to read all this. Somewhere we won't be disturbed.'

'I know a place. Come.' They got in the old Nissan.

'A friend of mine works for the government ...' Kekeli was driving and bringing up a number on her phone at the same time. 'She has her own office. It's not far from here. She won't mind us ... Valerie? Yes, it's me ...'

Patrice was flipping through the pages in the envelope. 'This is it ... all the solar companies applying to the Energy Commission for licences to build power plants. There are ten ... twelve names: Solar Glow, Kumasi; Bright Dawn, Sunyani; Radiance Systems, Ho ... it goes on. Incredible ...'

'Valerie says it's fine. She'll be going for lunch, but you can sit in her office.' They turned into a wide driveway. Ahead of them was a square-shaped single-storey office block, raised off the ground as if it was on stilts. 'This used to be the American embassy. It was built in Nkrumah's time. Now it's a ministry ...'

They parked, and walked under the building to a central courtyard, then up a staircase and along a bright corridor. Patrice agreed it was a good hiding place.

'Her office is this way,' Kekeli said, turning down another corridor. 'There she is …'

An attractive woman in her forties, in a green and red dress and matching headscarf, was standing by a door, talking to a man with a clipboard and a tape measure. Kekeli waved. Her friend waved back and mouthed 'Hello.' The man disappeared through the door, and she came over, arms out wide.

'Kekeli!'

'Valerie!'

The women embraced, and Kekeli introduced Patrice to Valerie Asamoah, Assistant Permanent Secretary at the Ministry of Women and Children's Affairs. She could have been Kekeli's sister: older and plumper, but with the same shaped face and shine in her eye.

'Come,' Valerie said, as they followed her down the corridor. 'We are having works done. They are going to convert two store cupboards into an office. Personally, I don't think it will be a pleasant environment to work in. It will be too small. And the works will be noisy …'

She led them into a large square office with windows on two sides. Patrice could understand why she wouldn't want to work in a converted cupboard. She gestured for him to sit on an L-shaped sofa in a corner and ordered an assistant to fetch cold drinks.

'Anyway,' she said, 'make yourself comfortable. This sounds exciting, though I won't ask what it's about.' She took Kekeli's arm and led her over to a desk in the opposite corner of the office. 'Now, my dear, how are you doing …'

Patrice pulled out the papers from the manila envelope and laid them out on a low table. Sarpong had stapled together several pages for each bid, with details of the number of panels, output projections, installation and maintenance costs, and maps showing the proposed sites and access roads. He'd printed out emails as well. The man must have been up all night – what turned out to be his last night.

At the back of each bid was a final page listing persons objecting to the proposals. He picked up the pages relating to Sunfall Power and turned to the last one. George Abotsi's name was there. A pencil line ran through it.

'... Patrice?'

He looked up. Kekeli and Valerie were walking out of the office.

'We'll see you later.'

'Where are you going?'

'I said, we're going for lunch.'

Valerie smiled. 'You can stay here. Please ask my secretary if you need anything. We can bring sandwiches for you?'

'No, thank you.'

The women left. He continued with his reading. At first glance there was nothing to link the applications, but then he noticed the signature at the end of each one: they'd all been approved in principle by Victor Mensah. He studied the proposals in more detail. Soon another connection emerged: in every case, the contract for the construction and running of the solar farm was with Desert Power of Arizona. He collected up the papers and was sliding them back into the envelope when he noticed a couple of loose sheets still inside. They were hand-written tables, in the same writing as Sarpong's note.

On one page, he'd listed all the companies and their investment and output estimates. If he'd got his sums right, the companies were making a combined bid of two billion dollars to produce more than a thousand megawatts of electricity. All the bids were above the output limit set by the government. On the other page, Sarpong had drawn a diagram in the shape of a clock face, listing the bidding companies around the edge. Lines connected all of them to a single name in the centre of the circle: ArizOil.

Patrice wrote out the sums. If the suggestion was that ArizOil owned all the companies, and he knew it also owned Desert Power, it meant a single American oil company was in effect bidding for a twenty percent stake in Ghana's power sector. Mensah's job was to make sure the bids got government approval; doubtless his reward would be a massive kick-back.

Kekeli returned from lunch with her friend. 'Okay, Patrice?'

'Yes,' he said. 'And thank you, Valerie. You can get back to your work.'

Valerie smiled another smile. 'It's no trouble. But young man, you must be careful! That bandage on your nose can only hide so much. Let me know if I can be of any help.'

Patrice's hand went to the bandage. He kept forgetting it was there. 'There is something. Could you look after this for me?' He held up the envelope.

'I can keep it in my safe.'

'Thank you.'

They drove off in the old Nissan. Patrice was telling Kekeli what he'd discovered when his phone rang. It was Josie Mwinga. 'It'll be interesting to hear what my boss makes of all this,' he said. 'Ma'am, I was ...'

'Hold on, Patrice, let me speak. I've spoken to John Sarpong. He says the police believe his son was murdered.'

'That's ridiculous. What about the gun in his hand?'

'The police were called by a janitor. When they arrived, there was no gun. The apartment had been turned over. They think it was a robbery.'

'Jesus! Those thugs must have taken it. But someone will have seen them leave – one of them had a bloody nose.'

'The janitor saw two people, Patrice. One did have a bandage on his nose. The other was a woman. Are you following me? Apparently, there are fingerprints in the apartment. I hope they're not yours.'

Patrice didn't reply directly to that. 'Does Sarpong's father know me and Kekeli were at the apartment?'

'No. Not yet. But Patrice, I can't stay silent about this, you understand that? John Sarpong is my friend. He knew Kwaku had problems, but he was his son. And I can't pretend I don't have important information about his son's death.'

'I don't need long.'

'I can't hide you, Patrice. I can get you a good lawyer, but you must go to the police.'

'I will, I will, but I'm close to cracking this …'

'You've got … precisely three and a half hours. I'm going to John Sarpong's house this evening to pay my respects. If you haven't been to the police by then, I'll tell him what I know and go to the police myself.'

Chapter 32

A week had passed, a week incarcerated in her room. Yawor sat on the bed and for the hundredth time read the letter that George had slipped under her door that morning.

Dear Cousin,

I hope you are not suffering too much. I am sorry I have not written to you before. It did not occur to me.

My father has imposed a reign of terror in the house. Everyone fears if they step out of line, even by one inch, they will be beaten. The girls are crying all the time. We feel for you and miss you.

But what my father did to you has strengthened my resolve. I want you to know I am ready. Yesterday we held a rehearsal at the airport. I saw a list of the VIPs expected to attend Osagyefo's departure, and Major General Barwah's name was on it. So today I will hand him your note.

Cousin, have faith in me and pray for me! I am doing this for you and your sister and for Ghana!

Please take care.

Your loving cousin,

George.

Yawor looked over at Adzo's empty bed and through the window at the dusk sky outside. She was exhausted, physically and mentally. She'd spent much of the day pacing – hobbling – across her room, fretting about her cousin. She had no idea what had happened at the airport. It was hours since Osagyefo was due to have left for Vietnam. The longer she heard nothing, the more she feared the worst. He was just a boy, she thought, and hung her head guiltily.

Her back and the back of her legs were still sore. Twenty-four lashes. Uncle Joseph had counted them out. One, he said, for each year of her miserable life. Since then, she'd had one meal a day, a portion of cold fufu. Only Uncle Joseph had the key to her room. He came each evening to open the door and allow Emmanuel to replace her bowl – and bucket.

Yawor had spent seven days cut off from the outside world, reading her college books and trying not to think of George and the task he'd taken on with such enthusiasm. Now she could think of nothing else. But she heard nothing more that evening.

1966: FEBRUARY 23

Still no word from her cousin. She barely got out of bed. She barely touched her food. When night came, she couldn't sleep, aching with anxiety and waiting helplessly for Operation Cold Chop to take its course.

It was late when she heard the tap on the window.

'George?' she whispered, daring to hope he was safe. She pulled aside the thin curtain. It wasn't George.

'Ofori!'

He held a finger to his lips, like he'd done the night he came to her house before. In his other hand he was holding an iron bar, and in less than a minute he'd levered off the metal grille. Yawor fetched a chair and climbed out.

'Ofori!' she whispered. 'What are you doing here?'

'Shh,' he said. 'I'll explain. Come.'

She took his hand. His grip was tight and tense. They slipped past the sleeping Herbert and out onto the street, then walked in silence close to the outside wall. Only once they were past the next house did Ofori stop and turn to face her.

'I had to come and see you tonight.'

'But what's happened? How did you know I was locked in my room?'

'I saw your cousin yesterday. He told me. That was after ...'

'After what? Ofori, what's happened to George?'

He cupped his hands round her shoulders. 'Your cousin's in jail.'

'What?'

'They arrested him at the airport. I saw it with my own eyes.'

'Oh, George! Where, which jail?'

'The prison.'

'The prison? But he's a boy!'

'I know. It's not right. It's my fault.'

'How can it be your fault?'

'It was my idea. For George to pass the note to Major General Barwah.'

Yawor gripped Ofori's hand. 'Please, Ofori, tell me what happened.'

The young sergeant looked tortured as he related the previous day's events. 'The president went to the airport, and the ceremony went ahead as planned. The Young Pioneers marched and the band played. But the atmosphere was ominous, perhaps because of what I knew. To be honest, it was hard to watch – to see the commissioner shake hands with the president and wish him well …'

'Horrible man.'

'After the president's plane took off, the dignitaries dispersed. The Young Pioneers were positioned between them and the terminal building. As Barwah walked past, your cousin stepped forward and called out, "Major General!" He made to shake hands, but as he did this, the commissioner shouted, "Arrest that boy!" Immediately, three policemen blocked his path and led him away.'

Yawor gasped. 'Oh no!'

'Shh, Yawor …'

'But poor George,' she said. 'Was he hurt?'

'No, they didn't hurt him, but he was shouting, "Let me go! I have important information!" The commissioner went to Barwah and said he knew this young man, your cousin, that he was an agitator who would be dealt with. He knew … he had been warned.'

'Warned? By who? About what?'

The street was deserted, and they were standing in a shadow, but Ofori lowered his voice. 'Listen. They took your cousin to headquarters. It was while he was waiting in my office that I asked him what had happened to you. At the same time, the commissioner was in his office telephoning your uncle. The door was open. I heard him say, "Your son has been arrested for disorderly conduct at the airport." Then he said, "Thank you for alerting us to his state of mind." Those were his words. George was sitting with me. He heard them too.'

'My uncle found us together … he must have heard us talking. And he betrayed his son!'

'There's more. The commissioner asked your uncle if he wanted to come and get him. I couldn't hear what your uncle said, but the commissioner replied, "That's a good idea. It will be only for a few days." He came out and told me … he told me to arrange for your cousin to be taken to the prison.' Ofori's face was crumpling.

Yawor stroked his head. 'Ofori, you could not refuse.'

He looked up but avoided Yawor's eyes. 'Yawor, I was not looking forward to telling you this news. The whole day … it was a difficult situation. I wanted to help your cousin, but if I did …'

'I know you would have, if you could.'

He turned to her. 'This is why I came – to talk to you and explain everything, before I go, in case …'

'Go? Where?'

'It's my duty. To do what I can.' He stiffened his frame. 'I have found out where Major General Barwah lives. I am going there now to warn him … to do what George tried to do, what I should have done before, instead of putting a boy in danger.'

'But, Ofori …' Yawor glanced back at her uncle's compound. 'I asked George to do it, I wrote out the note for him. I will go with you.'

'Yawor, you can't. It will be dangerous. There is sure to be fighting later, gunfire …'

'It will be better if I come. You heard the commissioner say it: Barwah doesn't trust the police, and you are a policeman. So we can go together.'

'No, Yawor.'

'Yes, Ofori. I owe it to George and to Adzo.'

He took her hand. The creases above his nose tightened. 'If you are sure, let's go. His house is not far. We must hope we are not too late.'

They reached Independence Avenue. There were no cars about. The city was quiet. Yawor looked down the road. A mile away, her cousin was sitting in a prison cell. She looked the other way. Outside the city, the rebel army units would be assembling, ready for their advance on Flagstaff House.

Ofori offered his arm and she held it. As they set off up the wide, deserted street, she remembered his words: "When this is all over …" Fate, it seemed to Yawor, was in their hands.

Chapter 33

They were heading out of town on the airport road, Keleli
with her foot down, Patrice scrolling through the texts on
Kwaku Sarpong's phone. The messages only went back a
week. Sarpong must have deleted the older ones. Patrice
switched to the call register and made a note of the numbers.
He looked out of the window as they sped past the now-
familiar billboards for nappies and noodles and mobile
phones ... Then he pulled out his own phone and brought up
Sarpong's number.

'Hey, Patrice!' Kekeli nudged him with her elbow. 'You've
got three hours to save your neck and you want to compare
phones?'

'024 is which network?' Patrice was thinking aloud.

'MTN. It's the one you're on, remember?'

'It's strange ...' Patrice went back to the texts on Sarpong's
phone and brought up the last one received. 'And 022?'

'022 is Black Star. What's strange?'

'... that Sarpong's contract was with MTN, yet his own
father runs a mobile phone network.'

'Perhaps he didn't like his father.'

'I don't know about that. Anyway, it's not important ...'
Kekeli shrugged.

Patrice called Josie Mwinga. 'Hello, ma'am … Josie. I wanted to ask you about Kwaku Sarpong's father.'

'What do you want to know, Patrice? Like I said, he's upset.'

'Yes, I appreciate that. I was wondering, as you said he was an old friend, would you say he was a patriot?'

'A patriot? The man's lost his son in terrible circumstances and you want to know if he's a patriot? Of course he's a patriot. He named his company Black Star, after the star on Ghana's flag.'

'And he's a man you trust?'

'Yes, Patrice.'

'Good. Because I'd like to tell him everything – and let him decide what he wants me to do.' His boss was speechless for once. 'I was thinking I could accompany you when you go to his house. If it's not improper of me to impose … on his grief.'

'I must say, Patrice, you can be unpredictable. But that's a good idea. He will have many visitors today expressing their condolences. I will tell him you have information about his son's death and he will welcome you. It's only fair he knows everything. Bring Kekeli. She was there too, in Kwaku's apartment. Pick me up at my hotel at seven.'

'Yes, ma'am.' Patrice ended the call and turned to Kekeli. 'She'd like you to come too, to see Sarpong's father. Do you mind?'

'What about Aunty? We have to get back.'

'Gladys will be with her, won't she? We'll be back tonight.'

Kekeli gave him a sideways glance. 'I hope you know what you're doing, Patrice. We could both end up in jail tonight and not get back to Aunty for a long time …' She U-turned at the next junction and they headed back the way they'd come.

They collected Josie Mwinga from her hotel as arranged. She was waiting in reception, pacing up and down.

'I feel uneasy about this,' she said to Patrice as they descended the carpeted marble steps. 'I've deceived an old friend. We should have gone straight to the police.'

'He'll understand why we didn't, and he can choose, like I said, ma'am.'

'Please stop calling me that, Patrice. I told you to call me Josie.'

'Yes ...'

They got in the car. His boss told Kekeli to head for Airport Residential. As they turned off the airport road and down a side street, Patrice recognised the neighbourhood as Victor Mensah's. He reached to his nose. The bandage was still in place, the nose still sore.

They drew up outside an iron gate. Mwinga got out and addressed an intercom; the gate opened and Kekeli drove through. John Sarpong's house was large, white and modern-looking, with plate-glass windows and a balcony on the upper floor. The man himself greeted them at the front door.

Josie Mwinga offered her condolences, then introduced Patrice and Kekeli.

Sarpong senior was an imposing figure, two metres tall, with big hands and a powerful grip. 'It's a pleasure to meet you,' he said. 'I wish it could be under happier circumstances.' His voice was deep and measured, but quiet.

'We're sorry for your loss,' Patrice said. 'I got to know your son a little over the past couple of weeks. He had his troubles, but I believe, ultimately, he meant well.'

'Thank you. Come through, please.'

They followed the big man down a wide hallway that

opened into an enormous living area, with two groups of sofas and chairs, a TV in one corner and a wall lined with bookshelves from floor to ceiling. The décor was expensive but not ostentatious: wooden flooring, elegant tables with vases of flowers, abstract paintings on the white walls. Sarpong gestured to a sunken seating area, asked them what they'd like to drink, and snapped his fingers. A house girl appeared and he told her to bring three beers and a whisky.

'So, Josie tells me you may have information about my son's death.'

Patrice glanced at his boss, then addressed John Sarpong. The man had a large head, which made his features look small. His wide-eyed expression suggested he was apprehensive about what Patrice was going to tell him. 'The first thing to say is your son was not murdered. But he feared he might be, and he took his own life.'

John Sarpong's large head sank. When he looked up, he said, 'Please tell me what you know.'

Patrice told him about his investigations and how he came to know Kwaku Sarpong, from their first meeting and their visit to the solar power conference, to his gambling problem and dealings with Albert Boateng and Victor Mensah, to the documents from the Energy Commission he'd copied in order to make amends, to their finding his body in his apartment with a gun in his hand. The only thing he didn't mention was the red car. There was no proof it was Kwaku Sarpong's and it was unfair to burden his father with an unproven suspicion.

When he'd finished, he pulled out Kwaku Sarpong's phone and placed it on the glass coffee table between them. 'This is your son's. It's not locked. The messages and calls explain what happened to him.'

John Sarpong sat shaking his head. He hadn't touched the glass of whisky in front of him, but now he picked it up and downed it in one, snapping his fingers immediately afterwards to order another. He downed that one as well. Then he got to his feet. 'Please excuse me for a minute.'

The two women and Patrice exchanged uncertain glances as Sarpong left the room. He returned looking ashen-faced and dazed, and sunk back into his seat.

'Thank you, Patrice, for speaking to me honestly. And do not blame yourself for anything. In fact, some of the blame – maybe more – lies with me. Because, to begin with, I believe the gun Kwaku used was mine.'

There was a momentary shocked silence before the big man continued, clasping his big hands together.

'He dropped by last night. He was agitated and didn't stay long. Now I understand the purpose of his visit. I have kept a gun for many years. It was given to me by a friend who was in the army. It was 1982, at a time of political upheaval. Things were uncertain. There were those who feared Rawlings' revolutionary government might turn against the business community. This friend gave me the gun for my protection. Ghana is not like that today, but I keep the gun in a drawer in my desk – because, well, you never know. Just now, when I looked, it was not there. I see why Kwaku came round last night. He planned to take his own life.'

'I'm so sorry.'

'Please, Patrice, it's not your fault. But I must ask, why have you not been to the police?'

'Sir, your friend, my boss, Madam ... Josie ... doesn't like this word, but there is a conspiracy afoot, one that seeks to undermine your country's control over its energy resources.

251

And there is every reason to believe that senior police officers are involved. Only once this conspiracy is exposed will it be safe to reveal what happened to Kwaku.'

'But in the meantime, the police will be investigating his death. And these people will no doubt be leading them in your direction ...'

'Yes. We must act fast.'

'What is it you propose to do?'

Patrice took a sip of beer. 'This is partly why I came here tonight. I want to ask for your help.'

The man and the two women stared at Patrice. John Sarpong asked, 'How can I help you?'

Patrice looked around. The fewer people who heard what he was about to say, the better. He kept his voice down. 'Albert Boateng's phone is on the Black Star network. If we could look through his texts and see the calls he's made ...'

'Patrice!' Josie Mwinga threw up her arms. 'That is illegal. You can't ask John to ...'

'It's okay, Josie.' Sarpong cut her off. 'These people drove my son ... to kill himself. I'm with Patrice. Please take some food with me, then we can go and sort this out.' Ushering his guests to the adjoining dining room, he pulled out his phone and made a call. 'Michael. Meet me at the office in an hour.'

They ate fish stew and jollof rice. John Sarpong talked about his son. 'It's no secret that Kwaku and I did not get along so well,' he said, wiping his mouth with a serviette. 'He felt a sense of entitlement ... and didn't take kindly to my insistence that if a man wants something, he must work hard to earn it. Perhaps I was too hard on him ... perhaps I made him feel inadequate ...'

'Not at all, John.' Mwinga touched him lightly on the

shoulder. 'It's a father's responsibility to set an example and that's what you did.' She turned to Kekeli. 'Did you know John knew your father?'

'No, I didn't know that.'

Sarpong nodded. 'It was a long time ago. But I heard about his passing. And to learn it's tied up with this business, well, it's terrible. You have my sympathy.'

'Thank you, sir. You have mine too. We are connected in this.'

'John and your father were in the Young Pioneers together, isn't that right, John?'

'Yes, it is.' The big man smiled ruefully. 'As I said, it was a long time ago.'

'That sounds like quite a journey,' Kekeli said. 'From Young Pioneer to telecoms mogul.'

'I wouldn't say mogul, I'm not quite in that league. But yes, I changed. When I was young, I was like your father, rebellious and full of radical ideas. After the overthrow of Nkrumah, and as I grew older and more realistic, and more confident I could succeed … well, I suppose I moved on …'

'It's human nature, John, to want to succeed and to get to the top.'

Patrice thought the beer must be going to his boss's head. Either that or she was flirting with a man who'd lost his son that same day.

'Don't you agree, Patrice? Patrice still has those old ideas. George never lost them either. But it's about human nature; you can't change the way people are.'

Patrice took a sip of his beer. It didn't seem like the right time at all for a philosophical discussion, but the others were looking at him expectantly. 'The way I see it, human nature is a convenient excuse for a lot of bad behaviour, but it's not a fixed state. It reflects the environment through which we've evolved. Take greed, for example. After tens of thousands of years in caves, competing with wild animals, it's no surprise people still feel insecure and grab as much as they can, sometimes more than they need. But this can change over time. Through education, we'll learn to see there's enough on this planet to go round for everyone.'

'Hear, hear, Patrice!' Kekeli gave him a supportive pat on the back. 'Greed cannot sustain a healthy society. Look at these people and their solar farms. That is greed for you.'

'Oh, what it is to be young,' Josie Mwinga said. 'But John here is not greedy. And he's actually being modest, because he's worked his way up to become one of Ghana's most respected businessmen.'

'Well, to say I worked my way up is giving me more credit than I'm due, Josie. My father gave me a good start. All I did was use what he gave me wisely and work hard ... there I go again, lecturing on the merits of hard work.'

The modest telecoms mogul arched his eyebrows and glanced down at his expensive-looking watch and said it was time he and Patrice went to his office. 'Please wait here, ladies. Make yourselves comfortable. We won't be long.'

John Sarpong told Patrice to wait by the front door. Moments later, he pulled up in a car Patrice had seen before, a crimson-coloured Mercedes.

Patrice got in. 'Is this Kwaku's car?' He had to ask.

'He used it. A lot. Did he tell you it was his?'

'No, he didn't. I assumed ...' Patrice was thinking about the tread on the tyres, but this was not the time for that.

'As you discovered, money slipped through Kwaku's fingers like sand. He never owned a car, as far as I know.'

'Did you know about his gambling problem?'

They were at a red signal, waiting to turn onto the ring road. Sarpong was looking out of his window. 'Yes, we knew. We found out five years ago. His mother and I returned from a weekend away and half our furniture downstairs was missing. He'd sold it to pay a debt he'd incurred during two days of gambling at a casino. After that, he never asked to borrow money from me again. I allowed myself to believe he'd quit the habit, but I see now he hadn't ... he'd simply gone elsewhere to sustain it.' The lights changed and they moved off. 'They say it's a disease, an addiction like alcoholism. Once you've caught it, the only cure is total abstinence. I guess he wasn't strong enough.'

They rode across the high flyover above Kwame Nkrumah Circle. Patrice saw a light in an office window a few streets away and wondered if it was Albert Boateng's. Soon afterwards they turned off the ring road, down a dark street, past warehouses and light industrial units, until they reached a large compound surrounded by a high white wall, behind which a mast stretched into the night sky, white dishes attached to all sides at the top.

A guard opened a gate and they drove in. Before them were six white, two-storey buildings, standing two by two. It looked more like an old military camp than a modern communications centre.

'We're building a new headquarters,' Sarpong said. 'For now, this is still our home. We've been here fifteen years.'

They parked by one of the buildings. A man appeared out of the shadows wearing jeans and trainers.

'Good evening, Michael. Thank you for coming.'

'Yes, sir. Good evening.'

'This is Mr Le Congo, he's an investigator.'

'Yes, sir.' Michael nodded at Patrice.

'Michael is our chief engineer. Let's go in here.' Sarpong led them through a metal door into an area containing rows and rows of metal cabinets. A low hum filled the air.

'Michael, I need you to bring up the data for a Black Star number.'

Michael glanced at Patrice.

'It's alright,' Sarpong said. 'But I must ask you not to mention this to anyone. It is a matter of national security.'

'Yes, sir.' Michael nodded and they followed him to a desk. 'What is the number, sir?'

Patrice passed it to the engineer, who brought up pages of lists onto a computer screen.

'This is the call register,' he said, pointing. 'Like on your phone, you can see the numbers and the time and date. This goes back a year. And here …' He brought up another page. '… here you can see the texts. These are kept for thirty days.'

The engineer made way and Patrice slipped into a seat. He searched first for the evening he'd waited for Boateng outside the Sunfall office. As he expected, there was a text, sent at 20:47: *On our way with the Congolese.* He checked the recipient's number. In the call register, he saw a call had been made to that number at 18:33, which would have been shortly after he'd left Boateng. That number had to be Victor Mensah's. He couldn't help noticing a call shortly after that to Kwaku Sarpong's number, and one received from Sarpong an hour later. Once again, his hand went to the bandage on his nose.

Next, he checked more recent exchanges. He found the text he'd seen earlier on Sarpong's phone. Looking again at the calls, he saw that one had taken place between Boateng and Mensah two minutes before the text had been sent. Everything Boateng did, he seemed to check with Mensah. There was nothing in his messages to suggest he had a love life – perhaps he used a different phone for that.

There'd been a flurry of calls later in the morning, presumably to discuss what to do about Sarpong's death. Perhaps also to consider how to deal with Patrice. Only one text had been received by Boateng since then – from Mensah, at 13:49: *No change, still on.* Boateng had forwarded it to another number. Patrice went back through the messages, looking for a similar pattern. A week earlier, a text from Mensah had been forwarded to the same number by Boateng. It read: *Operation Jumbo next week Thursday. Stand by.*

'Operation Jumbo?' Patrice turned to John Sarpong. 'Does that mean anything to you, sir?'

Sarpong shook his head.

Patrice was at a loss too. But given when the text was sent, next week Thursday was the day after next. It was possible they were meeting for a drink, but he doubted it.

Meticulously, he worked his way back through Boateng's texts, crosschecking them with calls, noting down numbers. Looking at the dates, there didn't seem to be any contact with Mensah's two thugs; most likely they took their orders only from Mensah.

Another text caught his eye, from Mensah to Boateng: *Andoh and Kwakofi are with us.* He showed it to John Sarpong.

'My God!'

'Aren't they …?'

'Yes. They're both in the cabinet. Anthony Andoh is among the president's closest confidantes.'

Patrice checked one last thing before they left. He went back to the day George Abotsi died, two weeks earlier. There were no texts sent or received that morning. And no calls to or from Kwaku Sarpong. But there was a call received from the number Boateng had been forwarding Mensah's messages to. And a call made minutes later from Boateng to Mensah. It didn't prove anything, but it made Patrice wonder if he'd been too quick to suspect Kwaku Sarpong of being the man who drove away from the scene in the red car. He drew a circle round the number from which Boateng had received the call.

They drove back round the ring road in silence. John Sarpong parked the crimson-coloured Mercedes by the side of the house and they went inside.

The women were sitting on a sofa. 'Well, Patrice?' Even Josie Mwinga seemed now to accept he might be onto something. Perhaps Kekeli had put in a good word for him.

'Ma'am, it is possible an attack on the Akosombo Dam is being planned. And is imminent. But it's not al-Qaeda. I don't know the details, but as I said earlier, we're dealing with a high-level conspiracy. It involves senior people in government as well as the police and others, possibly international business interests.'

Mwinga frowned as she reached for her phone. 'I'll call my friend. He can alert the president.'

'With respect, ma'am, I'm sure we can trust him; but even government ministers he knows may be part of this. And there's nothing specific you can tell him. The president is aware of the threat ...'

'Well … well … what will we do?'

'I will go there, to Akosombo.' Patrice turned to John Sarpong. 'Sir, Kwaku mentioned to me that a friend of yours is head of security at the Volta River Authority. Is that correct?'

'Yes, it is. I know him well.'

'You need to be ready to call him, at short notice but not yet. Wait till I have concrete information.'

'Call me then, Patrice, and I will call him.' John Sarpong punched his right fist into his left palm. 'They are well trained up there. They will go into action fast, I am sure of that.'

'In that case,' Patrice said, turning to Kekeli, 'we must go now.' He shook hands with the big man and nodded to Josie Mwinga. 'I'll be in touch.'

Chapter 34

1966: FEBRUARY 24

The early hours were warm and dark and quiet – like the early hours of any other day. No traffic, nothing untoward. The calm before the storm.

Yawor and Ofori made their way up Independence Avenue. After a week confined to her room, her hip was stiff and ached. Before they reached Flagstaff House, they turned down a side street to the chief of army staff's residence. Two soldiers were sitting at the entrance, looking sleepy.

Yawor addressed them. 'We wish to talk to Major General Charles Barwah. We have important information.'

The soldiers looked her up and down. 'It's late,' one said. 'He's in bed. Come in the morning.'

'This cannot wait. It's a matter of life and death. His life and death.'

The soldiers looked at one another. The one who'd spoken got up slowly and went through a doorway cut in the gate. He took his time, but he returned to say the major general would see them. Yawor exchanged a nervous glance with Ofori as they followed the soldier into the compound.

The chief of army staff was standing in the doorway of his

bungalow. He was in a tee-shirt and shorts. He looked young for his senior rank.

'Well, yes, what is it?' He spoke English with an English accent.

'Sir, there is a plot to overthrow the government!' Yawor was so relieved to tell someone in authority, and someone they could trust, that she shouted the words.

Barwah rubbed a hand through his hair and yawned. 'Do you know how often people come to tell me that? If I had a cedi for every time in the past two years I have heard those exact same words, I would be a rich man! But ...'

'Sir, it's true. It's ...'

'Calm down, young lady. Let me finish. But, I was going to say, never before has anyone come to me in the middle of the night to tell me such a thing. So I thank you for your concern, but now go home to your beds. Because, I can assure you, we are all safe. Everything is as it should be.'

'But it won't be for long. The operation is planned for this very morning.'

'Now please! Enough! Rumours, rumours, rumours! It seems there is nothing else to talk about these days. Only last evening, the head of military intelligence called to say he'd heard a column of troops was moving south from Kumasi. So you see, you have heard the same rumour. That is all. It's all nonsense!'

Yawor clasped her head in her hands. She wanted to scream. Instead, calmly, she said, 'With respect, Major General, this is not a rumour. We saw the plotters discussing their plans. We heard what they said. With our own eyes and our own ears. My cousin attempted to warn you at the airport, but he was arrested.'

A frown on the major general's face was the first sign that he was taking them seriously.

Ofori cut in. 'Sir, what this lady is telling you is true. I was with her. Please listen to us. The leaders of the plot are Police Commissioner Harlley, who is my boss, and Colonel Kotoka, commander of the ...'

'I know who Colonel Kotoka is, young man. He reports to me ...' The major general's steadfast tone couldn't conceal the growing look of concern on his face.

Ofori continued. 'They are going to take over the radio station and Flagstaff House. And you should know, sir, they want to kill you. They say you are too loyal to the president.'

Barwah laughed dismissively. 'Let them try! Harlley and Kotoka can plot all they like. The army will defend the president and the government against any rogue elements, have no fear. Colonel Zanlerigu is at Flagstaff House with the Presidential Guard ... But thank you for your information. I will pass it to my head of military intelligence. Brigadier Hassan is a good man. We shall investigate what these clowns are up to ... In fact, I will call him this minute; perhaps his report of troop movements was not so far off the mark ...'

The major general disappeared indoors. He returned minutes later, pulling on his clothes. He wasn't laughing any more. 'Brigadier Hassan has been detained by soldiers. His son was about to call me. Now my line's been cut. I will go to Flagstaff House and call in Second Battalion ...'

'Oh God ...' Yawor looked at Ofori. 'It's started.'

Barwah was setting off down the path when the compound gate swung open and twenty soldiers marched in. He stopped in his tracks.

'Major General Barwah?'

'Yes, that's me. Who are you?'

The young soldier at the front of the column of troops raised a pistol and shot the major general in the forehead.

Yawor watched in disbelief as he fell.

The young soldier ordered his men to take the body away. It was a few moments before he sent others to search the major general's bungalow, enough time for Yawor and Ofori to edge backwards to the side of the bungalow and slip out of the way and out of sight.

'Oh my God,' Yawor said, stumbling across the garden. 'He shot him, the chief of army staff!'

'We must get out of here,' Ofori said, finding a gate and a path that led back round the outside of the compound. 'That's the advance party.'

Visions of the bullet entering the major general's forehead were flashing in front of Yawor's eyes. 'That's it,' she said, following Ofori again but not knowing where he was leading her. 'Our only hope is lying dead. There's nothing more we can do …'

'Yes there is!' Ofori said, turning while he moved to face her, sweat shining on his cheeks. 'We can go to Flagstaff House ourselves and warn Colonel Zanlerigu. He can call Second Battalion.'

The creases had formed again above Ofori's nose, but there was something desperate, out of control, about the way he now stared fixedly ahead. He was walking quickly. Yawor was struggling to keep up.

'Ofori, is this a good idea? It can't be long before the main force arrives and attacks Flagstaff House. We'll be trapped.'

'It's our last chance,' he said. 'Come on, Yawor, for your sister and your cousin, and for Osagyefo!'

They reached the road. They could see the gate to Barwah's residence. The troops who'd murdered the major general were milling around. Ofori turned to walk the other way. Yawor couldn't risk going back past the soldiers. She had no choice but to keep following Ofori.

The streets seemed even darker and quieter than before. Yawor could hear her shoes scraping on the ground and a strange animal-like noise, which she realised she was making herself as she panted.

They reached Independence Avenue and peered round the corner. Flagstaff House stood up ahead in peaceful silence.

'You see,' Ofori said. 'There's still time ...'

They ventured out. The road was deserted but for them. But there was no cover, no shadows to hide in. Suddenly the silence felt dangerous and Yawa felt vulnerable.

A single armoured vehicle, like a small tank, was parked across the entrance to Flagstaff House. White lettering on the side identified it as *President's Own Guard Regiment*. Sentry boxes were positioned either side of the gate. Ofori approached one and spoke to the soldier inside. Yawor followed.

Breathless and dizzy, she looked up at Ofori. She could see his lips moving, she could hear his voice, but she couldn't hear the words, like she wasn't really there, like she was in a dream. 'When this is all over,' she said to herself, shaking her head.

The soldier was wagging a finger. Ofori was shouting and waving his arms. As if she'd suddenly woken, Yawor was alert – and scared. The soldier from the other sentry box was walking over. He had his rifle raised.

'Ofori, come. We must leave ...'

Ofori turned. 'They won't let us through,' he said, his face twisted and pained. 'Their orders are not to let anyone pass and not to leave their posts.'

Yawor held out her hand, urging him to follow her. 'You've done what you can, Ofori. Come with me, while there's …'

There was no time. Approaching down Independence Avenue, from the north, came the ominous rumble of engines: a column of vehicles. The coup was under way.

'Oh my God! Quick, Ofori, we must go.'

She made to cross the road, but instead of following her, Ofori stepped back towards the sentry box. 'You see,' he shouted at the soldier. 'They are coming!'

Yawor kept moving, heading for the other side of the road. 'Ofori, come with me …' There was a low wall. They could get behind it, out of the way. '… Ofori, come.'

He wasn't hearing her or wasn't listening. She reached the wall, climbed over, and crouched behind it. She heard herself panting again, but not for long, as the column of vehicles came trundling and clattering down the road. Peeping over the wall, she saw the first of them, small ones with mounted guns and larger ones, troop carriers perhaps, pass by the gate. They were going to the radio station, she supposed, remembering the plans spelled out on Commissioner Harlley's veranda. Through the gaps between the vehicles, she saw Ofori was still on the other side of the road with the soldiers. He seemed rooted to the spot, as if hypnotised by the scene in front of him.

Yawor shouted. 'Ofori! Run! Run!'

He looked at her. He saw her. But he didn't move.

Inevitably, the sound of gunfire and explosions followed. Flashes of light and puffs of smoke emanated from the windows of Flagstaff House, as loyalist troops mounted their defence.

The front vehicles continued on their way, but those outside Flagstaff House pulled up, and the mutinous troops began returning fire. Ofori was caught in the middle of the battle. At last he made to run, but it was too late. He was struck on the shoulder. His body whipped round and fell.

'Ofori!'

He was struck again as he lay on the ground. And again.

'Ofori! Ofori!'

And again. His body flipped over. Then it lay still.

'Ofori … Ofori …' She carried on calling his name, but by now her cry was a whimper. She was lying on the ground behind the low wall. Bullets and shells were whistling overhead, the sky was filled with orange flashes and soon the air was thick with smoke. She wanted to lie next to Ofori, but a life-preserving reflex made her pick herself up and crawl along on the grass.

She crawled as far as the radio station, where the low wall ended. There was no fighting here, just three army vehicles stationed by the entrance. Yawor got to her feet and walked past them. Soldiers watched as she went by. They didn't seem interested in her and didn't try to stop her.

She made her way down Independence Avenue, turning often to look back as she walked. The sky stayed lit up. She couldn't tell who was winning the battle. But the fact it was continuing meant the troops loyal to the president hadn't been able to put down the rebellion.

Dawn was breaking when she arrived at Uncle Joseph's house. The battle was still going on, in the distance and in her head. She'd resigned herself to another beating and she didn't care. Nothing could ever hurt her now. She was numb to everything.

As it was, as she was climbing the front steps, Uncle Joseph opened the door with a broad grin on his face.

'Ahh, there you are. What a wonderful morning! Listen. The sound of freedom! What Ghana has been waiting for!'

Yawor's despair was his joy. She followed him into the front room and collapsed onto a sofa.

The news that morning on her uncle's radio sounded different. No praises for Osagyefo. Instead, military music and then an announcement:

'I have come to inform you that the military, in co-operation with the Ghana police, have taken over the government of Ghana today.'

Yawor recognised the voice. She'd heard the same voice at Police Commissioner Harlley's residence a week before. It was Colonel Kotoka.

'The myth surrounding Kwame Nkrumah has been broken. Parliament is dissolved and Kwame Nkrumah is dismissed from office. All ministers are also dismissed. The Convention People's Party is disbanded with effect ...'

Sergeant Anthony Ofori had tried to stop them, and lost his life.

'Hallelujah!' Uncle Joseph shouted. 'We are saved!'

'And the killer of Adzowor Abotsi will go free,' Yawor said to herself.

Uncle Joseph seemed oblivious to her mood. He was dancing and clapping his hands.

'You got what you wanted, Uncle,' she said, out loud.

He seemed not to hear.

Later that day, crowds came out to celebrate the fall of Kwame Nkrumah. Uncle Joseph insisted his family went to Independence Avenue to watch. Women dressed in white were dancing. Yawor recognised some of them as fruit sellers from Makola Market. They carried placards. Yawor recognised some of those too – the ones she'd seen being assembled at the American embassy. A group of women approached some soldiers standing by an armoured vehicle and put chains of flowers round their necks. The Americans now were nowhere to be seen.

Soldiers fired bullets in the air. The crowds cheered. But Yawor was back peeping over that low wall. With every shot, she saw Anthony Ofori's body flip up in the air and crash back to the ground with a heavy thud.

'When this is all over,' she said. And she knew, as she said it, that it was never going to be all over.

Chapter 35

Aunty Yawor was dozing in the chair she liked on the Addos'
back veranda, under a dim solar lamp. Kekeli woke her gently.
Patrice offered to help her up. The old woman snarled and
waved her crutch and got to her feet unaided.

'Come,' Kekeli said, 'I've got your things.'

They led her aunt to the car and manoeuvred her into the
back seat.

'We're going on a trip. We're going to stay by the river, near
Akosombo.'

Aunty Yawor blinked, as if a distant bell had rung. But her
eyes soon closed and she was sleeping again.

Kekeli drove them off into the darkness. 'We will take the
main roads. I don't like the small roads at night.'

They headed towards Accra, turned east towards the port
of Tema, then north. After that, the road was unlit. There
were few other cars.

A sign flashed by for Shai Hills Resource Reserve. Kekeli
slowed down. 'There are animals here.'

The road was clear but sets of eyes twinkled to the side.

'Are there elephants?' Patrice asked.

'No, I don't think so. Monkeys and antelopes, I believe, and
many birds, of course …'

'I was thinking about that name. Operation Jumbo. What can it mean? Jumbo was a famous elephant ...'

'Jumbo is something big.'

'An attack on the dam would be big ...'

'A jumbo jet? Oh my God, a suicide attack on the dam with an aeroplane!'

'Hang on, Kekeli. If it was al-Qaeda, maybe – they've got their cause and people willing to die for it because they think they'll go to paradise. But Mensah and his gang? They're not martyrs. They're in it for the money.'

Kekeli pursed her lips. 'The name may not mean anything. Have you heard of Operation Guitar Boy?'

'No.'

'It was a year after the overthrow of Nkrumah. Young soldiers attempted a counter-coup against the National Liberation Council. They failed, but they assassinated one of the leaders of the 24th of February coup, Lieutenant General Emmanuel Kotoka. They shot him at the airport.'

'And they called it Operation Guitar Boy?'

'Yes. Guitar Boy was the name of a popular song, but I don't know why they chose it for their operation.'

'Perhaps it was playing on the radio when they were making their plans ... What was it about?'

'It was by a Nigerian. I can't remember his name. In the song, he's given a guitar by the water goddess Mami Wata, who asks him to play nice music. That's it. After the failed coup, it was banned from the radio in Ghana.'

Patrice was none the wiser.

The old Nissan Micra rattled its way on towards Akosombo. An hour later, well after midnight, they turned down a track and pulled up outside a wooden gate. A million insects danced in front of the headlights, which shone at a hand-painted sign welcoming them to the Waterside Hotel. Kekeli beeped the horn. A sleepy receptionist let them in and helped carry their bags through the moonlight to two chalets built on the grassy bank of the Volta River. Each chalet had its own private deck floating on the water, accessed by a gangway.

'It's a secluded place,' Kekeli said.

Patrice agreed. 'It's perfect. How did you find it?'

'I came here once with my father. He took me to visit the dam.'

Warbling frogs and rippling water were the only sounds. Down river they could see the arch bridge over which the road from Accra continued to Ho. The dam was upstream, out of sight.

The morning revealed the full beauty of the setting: the wide river with the green hills beyond, the trees shading the hotel buildings, and the bright flowers all around. They breakfasted on a floating platform that served as the dining room.

Afterwards Patrice set off to make a reconnaissance of the dam, leaving Kekeli with her aunt. He took a taxi to the Volta River Authority offices in Akosombo town and boarded a tour bus with a group of American students.

On the way to the dam, the bus stopped at a checkpoint where the road passed through a perimeter fence. Two guards got on and walked down the aisle, prodding rucksacks and checking under seats. A guard outside used an extending mirror to inspect behind the wheels and the underside of the bus.

The tour guide, an engineer who worked for the Volta River Authority, said security had been tightened in recent days.

271

'But the dam is well protected,' he added, laughing. 'We will look after you!'

Some of the students sniggered. A woman sitting next to Patrice snorted. 'Well, really,' she said, 'I should hope so!' She smiled at him, rolling her eyes.

'I think he just wants to reassure us.'

'Oh, sure. I was only kidding. They don't want to take any chances. But up here, well, I've been coming here six years and it's usually pretty relaxed.'

'Good. I hope it stays that way.' Patrice returned her smile.

She responded by holding out her hand and introducing herself. 'I'm Professor Elsa Henderson,' she said. She had short, straight, black hair. 'My students are on an exchange programme from the University of Louisiana with the University of Ghana, Legon.'

Patrice tried not to show his surprise; he'd never met a young woman professor before. 'It's nice to meet you. I'm Patrice Le Congo, from Congo.'

'Oh, that's an intriguing name. I mean, when you think of Patrice and you think of Congo, you think of Patrice Lumumba ...'

'That's right. I was named after both: the country and its first prime minister.'

'Wow, how cool is that! I mean that, really ... I hope you don't mind me asking about it. I teach political science.'

'I see.'

'And how about you? Are you here on vacation? Did you have an accident?' she added, looking at his nose.

'Yes, unfortunately. But I'm here to do research. I'm going to apply to do a master's degree in your country.'

'Oh, really? Interesting! What subject?'

'I don't know exactly the subject, but I want to study the influence of Western capitalism on the direction of economic development in Africa. Something like that.'

'Awesome! Which college are you applying to?'

'I'm not sure. I haven't had time to consider that ...' He was distracted as the bus swung round a corner and the dam came into view. 'Oh, that is impressive. I knew it was big, but from here you can really see it.'

'It's pretty big, there's no denying that ...'

'But?'

'I'm sorry?'

'I thought you were going to say more ...'

'Only that it came with a heavy price tag, you know. Like, eighty thousand people were displaced when they created the lake, and to begin with, most of the electricity was taken by Kaiser Aluminium ...'

'But those people, they were rehoused, weren't they? And now more of the electricity is for Ghanaians. That's what I was told. But it's true, you can't make an omelette without breaking an egg.'

She looked at him and smiled. 'I should have guessed, with your name and all, and being in here in Ghana; you're an Nkrumahist.'

'I don't know about that. I like him, and I think he was doing what he believed was best for his country and for Africa. But I know he made mistakes too.'

The bus climbed a winding road and parked in a turning circle by the top of the dam. Patrice stepped out with the professor and her students; there were about twenty of them, mostly in jeans and trainers, a couple of boys wearing baseball caps back to front. Professor Henderson was wearing a tee-shirt and floral skirt, and sandals that looked like they were made from old car-tyres.

The guide brought the group together by a low wall at the back of the dam, which overlooked the intake channel; the water here flowed towards six tunnel entrances, the penstocks, into which it drained sharply and out of sight. He recited facts about the amount of rock, earth and sand used to make the main dam wall. Being of this material, the guide said, it could withstand an earthquake. Patrice nodded in approval. The structure was so immense, so wide and sturdy, appearing as solid as the surrounding hills, that it was hard to imagine how anyone could seriously damage it.

'Before we walk across, are there any questions?'

A boy stuck up his hand. 'What if someone fell in here? Would they be swept into one of those tunnels?' This prompted a few chuckles.

'No,' the guide said. 'There is a trash rack. You see the bars? They prevent debris from entering the penstocks.'

With no other students having questions, their teacher asked one. 'The water level looks pretty low … is that a problem?'

'In recent years the level has reduced, because of climate change. Currently it is two hundred and forty-four feet, which is enough. The minimum is two hundred and forty.'

'And if it reduces to that level?'

'In those circumstances the turbines inside the power station cannot operate.'

'Has that ever happened?' a student asked.

'Yes, it happened once, some years ago, when too much water was diverted from the river upstream. We hope it will not happen again. Now, please follow me …'

The tour party walked along the road across the top of the dam. From here Patrice could see how the giant penstock pipes channelled the water down steeply into the power station below the dam, beyond which a network of pylons carried the electricity off in different directions.

At the far side of the dam were the spillways, which the guide said opened when the water level became too high. He said the highest water level ever recorded was two hundred and seventy-seven feet, in November 2010.

'And there on the hill,' he said, pointing, 'is the house built by Kwame Nkrumah so that he could look at the dam and entertain distinguished visitors. Now it is used by the police.'

Professor Henderson turned to Patrice. 'That kind of says it all, huh? Up there in his villa, Nkrumah had no idea how his people were feeling. Five weeks after he opened the dam, he was overthrown. He was thinking about his Pan-Africanism and about Vietnam, but not about Ghana. He'd become completely detached.'

Patrice looked up. 'That's what people say.'

'Time to walk back, everyone.' The guide was waving to the group and they set off again.

'Hey, Patrice …' Professor Henderson tapped his arm as they approached the other side. 'We're going to the Volta Hotel for a drink on their terrace. Would you care to join us?' She gestured at a grey stone building down the valley, in the hills beyond the power station. 'You get a great view.'

'Yes,' he said. 'I can see that. I'd like to come, thank you.'

They climbed back on the bus and rode down the winding road and out of the dam security area, then turned up a winding road, and a winding driveway, to reach the hotel. The wide terrace was at the back. The professor was right about the view. Yet surprisingly, from this vantage point, almost face on, the dam didn't look so big: still wide and solid, but not as high as it had felt walking along the top.

Patrice ordered a pot of tea, Professor Henderson a Coke. Apart from the students, the other tables were mostly occupied by tourists. A man with a loud American voice was recounting a visit he and his wife had made to the Hoover Dam.

'... oh my God, it was hot there! Remember, Alice? We got out of the car and shouted "Help!" I'm not kidding ...'

Two women in hiking boots were sitting at another table. Patrice thought they were speaking German.

Professor Henderson was telling him how she first came to Ghana when Jerry Rawlings was in power. 'JJ, they called him. He staged two coups, shot three judges after one of them. He was wild – he used to parachute out of a plane, even when he was president – but he brought stability after years of turmoil. Just goes to show ...'

She tailed off and Patrice noticed she was looking at something behind his shoulder. He turned and saw two white men at the back of the terrace.

'I know those guys ... well, one of them,' she said, keeping her voice low, rolling her eyes. 'He works at the embassy – our embassy, in Accra.'

'You don't like him?'

'He's a creep. He made a drunken pass at me once, at a function they laid on for students who were finishing their semester. I told him to get his hand off my butt or I'd scream. He claimed he wasn't doing anything. Asshole!'

'Did you complain officially?'

'You can't complain about that kind of thing. Well, you

couldn't then. I never told anyone. I mean, it was no big deal. Jerk.'

'What's his job?'

'He's got a title, Second Secretary, something like that. Probably means he's a spy.'

'You think so?'

'Only kidding. But you never know with these guys.' She glanced in the man's direction again. 'Looks like he's brought his pop here for vacation.'

Patrice looked again at the two men. The older one was wearing a straw hat that shaded his face and a check shirt. The younger was in jeans and a tee-shirt, and was staring straight back at Patrice. 'I think he remembers you too,' he said. 'He looks hostile.'

'For sure he's spotted me. Loser! Anyway, I'd better round up my students. We're going to a village on the lakeside where people were resettled when the dam was built. Come to think of it, you might find this place interesting – you could come with us if you like? And after that, we're going on to the Wli falls ... I mean, I don't mean to push ...'

Patrice smiled. 'I would find it interesting, and I've heard the falls are beautiful. But I'm staying here with friends, not here but in a small hotel down by the river, and I have things to do, so ...'

'Hey, no problem. Do you want a ride back to the VRA offices?'

'No, thank you, I'll sit here a little longer ...'

'Okay, sure. Well, it was really a pleasure to meet you. And have a good trip.' She patted her pockets. 'I'm all out of cards, but give me your number and I'll text you my details. If I can be of any help with your application, get in touch ...'

Patrice read out his number.

'Who knows,' she said as she sent the text, 'maybe you'll come to the University of Louisiana!'

'Thank you, I'll let you know if I do.'

She got up and clapped a couple of times and led the students off the terrace.

Patrice ordered more tea and sat watching the dam. The weakest point appeared to be where the narrow intake channel steered the water towards the penstocks, but even here the dam wall was thick. An attack on the power station was another possibility, but it was well protected by high fences. He looked at Nkrumah's villa, a white speck high on the other side of the river, and wondered what the view was like from there.

He paid his bill and asked the waiter if the hotel had a business centre.

The waiter nodded. 'Ask at reception.'

Patrice walked back through the hotel. The receptionist said the business centre was for guests only. He told her the Wi-Fi connection was bad at the Waterside Hotel, so he was thinking of changing if it was good in her business centre. She handed him a slip of paper with the code.

The business centre was empty. He sat at a computer and searched for "Akosombo Dam map". When the image came up, he saw something he hadn't noticed when he'd flown in over the dam. His heartbeat quickened. He chose the satellite option and zoomed in. Viewed from above, the curved shape of the intake channel, where he'd been standing an hour before, resembled an elephant's trunk. Operation Jumbo? It was obscure, but it made sense. As much sense as anything else did.

278

He logged off and went out through reception. As he did, he noticed the man from the American embassy and his companion standing at the front desk. The older man was talking to the receptionist. The embassy man was looking at his watch. He glanced in Patrice's direction and looked back at his watch.

Patrice left the hotel and walked to the road to wait for a passing taxi. It was around noon. The sky was overcast, the air muggy. There was little traffic. He was about to set off on foot when he saw a black four-by-four coming down the hotel driveway. The American was at the wheel. Patrice thought about asking for a ride. But at the junction it turned the wrong way for him. He walked on.

Presently a taxi came by and picked him up. 'It's a long walk in the middle of the day,' the driver said with a grin as they wound their way back down the road. 'You'll be sweating too much if you walk all this way.'

'Yes. Tell me, what's the other way, where you've come from?'

'That way is Marine, the port.'

'Oh. Can I get a boat there to cross the lake?'

'You want to hire a boat?'

'No. Is there a passenger service?'

'Yes, it goes to Yeji, but not today. Next boat is Saturday.'

'So, you weren't taking passengers there today?'

'To Marine? No. I went to the market, for yams. You want to go?'

'No, thank you.' Patrice shook his head. 'I was curious, that's all.'

Chapter 36

Kekeli and Aunty Yawor were eating lunch on the floating dining room.

'It's our favourite, Patrice: palava sauce!'

Kekeli was smiling. The way she smiled made Patrice smile too. Coming here had been good for her, just to get away. Even Aunty Yawor seemed more relaxed, less jumpy.

'There's a plate for you.' Kekeli pulled out a chair next to hers and Patrice sat down. 'It's not as good as mine,' she added. 'Too much oil.'

Patrice ate. It seemed delicious to him.

She looked at him expectantly. 'So? How was the dam? Did you find what you were looking for?'

'I'm not sure. I hope so. I'll go back tonight.'

'You must call Mr Sarpong so he can alert his friend at the Volta River Authority.'

'Not yet. I've got nothing to tell them. I'm acting on a hunch, that's all. When … if … things start happening, then I'll call.'

'You're taking a big risk, Patrice. If you get this wrong, the consequences could be disastrous.'

He looked out over the river. Kekeli was right. It was a dangerous game, but he couldn't think of any other way to play it. So for now he kept the doubts that preyed on his mind to himself. 'The view from the Volta Hotel is spectacular, you know. You should take your aunt there.'

'I've been there!'

Patrice and Kekeli turned together. Aunty Yawor was grinning back at them.

'Really, Aunty?' Kekeli said.

'George was there. We went to the inauguration.'

'Did you?'

'Your father was in the Young Pioneers.'

'Yes, Aunty.'

'Your grandfather ...' Aunty Yawor kissed her teeth. 'He didn't like Nkrumah. He didn't know about the Americans. Ofori knew. He tried ...' She tailed off, not finishing what she was saying.

'What about the Americans, Aunty? Who's Ofori?'

The old lady had slipped back into her closed world, taking her memories with her. After lunch, she went to her chalet to rest. Kekeli asked Patrice if she should come to his. As she took off her clothes, he forgot everything else. She was offering him a brief respite from the tension, from the threat he was to face later. It was hot in the chalet and the sweat on her skin glistened.

Afterwards they lay side by side, her head on his shoulder.

'I know a lot about your father, Kekeli, but what happened to your mother?'

'She died when I was young. I don't remember her at all. My father raised me. I was an only child. And you? What about your family?'

'I never knew my birth parents. I was brought up in an orphanage, run by a woman we called Mama. And she was like a mother to me, and to all of us. She fed us, she taught

281

us, she sent us to school. She lived humbly herself. All she wanted was to give us a chance in life. It's actually people like her who give me hope for the future of humanity. For every evil man like Victor Mensah, there are a hundred good people like Mama. I hope I'm right about that ...'

He drifted into a deep sleep. When he woke, it was dusk. He showered and found Kekeli with her aunt on the floating platform at the back of the chalet. He walked along the gangway to join them, noticing how rickety the structures were: planks of wood knocked together with a hammer and nails, tied over four barrels. A waiter brought a bottle of Star. As they clinked glasses, there was a flash of lightning above the hills that lit up the river. The temperature plummeted and the wind picked up.

'We must go inside,' Kekeli said. The floating platform was beginning to rock. She offered to help her aunt to her feet, but the old lady shook her off and pulled herself up, leaning on the table and placing her crutch under her arm.

A large drop splashed on Patrice's cheek, then another – then the heavens opened. As they struggled along the gangway, the rain was swirling down. The palms on the bank were swaying wildly.

'Quick, Aunty ...' Kekeli was ahead, reaching back with one hand, clutching the rail with the other, shouting to make herself heard over the wind. Her light dress was wet through and stuck to her body. Aunty Yawor was too far behind. She was bent forward, holding her crutch with both hands but unable to place one foot ahead of the other. Her head tilted back and she was thrown off balance. Patrice ran to catch her before she fell.

There was another flash of lightning and the hotel lights

went out. A torchlight shone in the open-sided reception area, but everywhere else was in darkness. Patrice helped Aunty Yawor along. Kekeli had made it to the bank. A man appeared behind her. Patrice thought a member of staff had come to help until he saw, incomprehensibly, it was one of Mensah's men, the shorter one with the squashed face.

'Look out!' Patrice shouted into the wind and rain. Kekeli turned. The man swiped her face with the back of his hand. She yelped and fell, slipped on the wet grass, and slid into the water. Patrice pressed Aunty Yawor's hand onto the rail and cried out, 'Hold tight!' He leapt forward, but his feet slipped on the planks. As he stooped to regain his balance, a fist came crunching into his cheek. He saw stars and sunk to his knees, and over onto his side. When he looked up, the man was on top of him with a knife in his hand.

The man grabbed Patrice by his shirt and held the knife to his throat. 'Today's your last day!' He was shouting and snarling, rain streaming off his face. 'Say your prayers!'

Out of the corner of his eye, Patrice saw Kekeli climbing out of the water. She was safe. But he was trapped. He saw the muscles in the man's forearms flex as he tightened his grip on the knife. He felt the cold wet steel on his neck ...

'Eeeaak!' Aunty Yawor screeched. She was standing above them. The man looked up. The old lady brought her crutch down, like a fisherwoman spearing a fish, and rammed it into his eye. He screamed and toppled over. Patrice swung a forearm, knocked the knife from the man's hand, then pulled himself up and pinned his attacker down.

Kekeli appeared at the end of the gangway. 'Aunty!'

The old lady was leaning on her crutch, staring at her victim.

283

The man was struggling feebly and moaning. His eye socket was filled with blood. Patrice shouted to Kekeli to get some rope. She came back with the receptionist and the waiter, who hauled the man away.

No other guests were staying at the Waterside Hotel that evening. The man with the squashed face and bloody eye was slumped on the floor in reception, his wrists bound behind him round a pillar.

Patrice took the man's phone from his trouser pocket. The screen was cracked and wet but it worked, and he scrolled through the call register and texts. He was expert at this now. He recognised a number as one he'd seen on Boateng's phone records – it was Mensah's, and it had sent a text two hours earlier: *Confirm when it's done.* After looking through a few other messages and confirming that the owner of this phone was a man of few words, Patrice replied: *Done.*

The man looked dazed. His eye was swelling up. Patrice knelt in front of him and lifted the man's chin. 'Now it's time for you to listen to me. We can fetch salt water to treat your eye. It may be the only way to save it …'

The man groaned.

'But first, to get this treatment, you need to tell me what the plan is for tonight. When are they going to attack the dam?'

'I don't know what you're talking about.'

'How did you know where to find me?'

'Mr Mensah.'

'But who told him?'

'No idea.'

Patrice clenched his fist. He was debating whether to use it when he saw Kekeli approaching, Aunty Yawor at her side.

'I don't mind if you punch him, Patrice. He can drown in the river for all I care. He would let me drown there.'

'The moment's passed. I won't let this clown make me angry.'

The storm was over. Water was dripping from the gutters and the trees. They sat at a table in the bar area. They didn't feel like eating, but ordered another drink. The waiter said the police were coming.

Patrice glanced at Kekeli. 'I must go before they get here.'

'Why? You're a witness. He was trying to kill you!'

'It'll take too long. And what if he starts talking about Kwaku Sarpong? If he suggests they compare my fingerprints with those at Sarpong's apartment?'

'I'm scared.'

'You'll be safe here.'

'Not for me. For you.'

'Don't worry about me. I'll be back later.'

Patrice got up before she could raise more objections and left the hotel by a back entrance. He walked into town and took a taxi back to the Volta Hotel. He told the driver to drop him at the bottom of the drive. As soon as the taxi was out of sight, he walked back the way they'd come and turned up towards the dam.

When the checkpoint in the perimeter fence came into view, he cut off through the bushes, crawling and climbing through the thick, rain-soaked vegetation until he reached the river. The water was flat and slow-moving under the night sky. He wrapped his phone in a plastic bag, stuffed his sandals into his back pockets, and waded in. Swimming breaststroke silently against the current, he kept close to the overhanging foliage. Eventually, he came to a clearing where the perimeter fence entered the water. He swam round the fence and back to the bank and pulled himself out. Then he squeezed out his clothes and sat naked in the warm evening air, waiting to dry.

The cloud was breaking up. A bright moon was rising. Nearing midnight, he got dressed, found his way back to the road, and headed for the dam. No cars passed. The area around the power station was floodlit, so he kept to the shadows. There was no sign of extra security, no sign of anyone. All was quiet except for the hum of the turbines and the relentless croaking of the frogs.

Rounding a bend, he reached the turning circle where the tour bus had parked in the morning and saw the top of the dam. There were streetlights on the road across it. Beneath one of them, halfway along, two security guards were walking on patrol and heading his way. He lowered himself into a ditch and kept his head down. Footsteps and voices approached. They got closer. They can't have been more than ten paces away when they stopped. The men carried on talking, but turned, and Patrice watched them stroll back across the top of the dam.

When they were out of earshot and passing under a light, he climbed out of the ditch and ran, stooping, to the low wall where he and the other visitors had listened to the guide earlier. He peeped over; the guards were still walking away. He looked into the intake channel. Now, at night, the water below was black and calm, with gentle ripples showing silver under the moonlit clouds. But where it approached the dam wall, it swirled menacingly before disappearing down into the penstocks.

He had a good view from this point, but anyone coming up the road would have a good view of him. He crawled alongside the wall, away from the road that crossed the dam, and came to a path above a scree bank which curved round parallel to the intake channel, towards the main part of the lake.

He headed for a bush a little way along and sat down next to it. All he could do was wait some more. His cover was good. He was hidden from the dam, and anyone approaching down the channel would be unlikely to pick him out against the bush. With the moon passing in and out of the clouds, he could see the flow of water pass below him. Upstream, he could make out the point where the intake channel began, beyond which the lake widened out. In the open water, lights flickered on small fishing boats.

He must have dozed off, because the moon had moved across the sky. It was 2am. Everything else looked the way it had before. Except that a small boat was entering the channel from the lake. It looked like a canoe. It had no lights. He could make out two figures, each with a paddle. If Patrice moved, he'd be seen. He sat still and watched as they floated down the channel, silently but for the soft splash of their paddles and the slap of ripples against the bank.

At the point where they passed Patrice, with the canoe a stone's throw away from him, the moon came out. He could see the man in front wore an open shirt. Beads of sweat sparkled on his chest. The man behind wore a dark hooded jacket. He had a bag at his feet. Patrice couldn't see his face but he could see his hands – a white man's hands.

Patrice pulled out his phone and called a number he'd noted while looking through Boateng's call register, the number that called Boateng the morning George Abotsi died. A second later, the man in the canoe with the hooded jacket reached into his pocket and pulled out his phone. It was on vibrate but Patrice could hear it. He cut the call and the phone stopped vibrating.

The man muttered a curse. Patrice could see him clearly now, and he recognised him: it was the man Professor Henderson had pointed out at the hotel, the man from the American embassy.

The canoe was heading down the centre of the intake channel, towards the penstocks. Patrice watched the men float by and waited for them to get closer to the dam – so that once the alarm sounded, they'd be too far down the channel to turn and make their escape. Then he rang John Sarpong.

'Sir, they're here. The intake channel. Two men in a canoe. Please call your friend immediately.'

'Okay, Patrice. But stay out of the way. Your boss gave me strict instructions: you're to leave this to the professionals.'

'Yes, sir.'

As the canoe approached the end of the channel, the men turned it side-on and allowed the current to pull it towards the trash rack in front of one of the six penstocks. The man in front held on to the vertical bars to steady the boat. The man in the hood, the American, opened the bag and brought out some kind of tool, which he placed between two bars at water level. It was a car jack. He turned the lever, prising apart the bars.

Patrice checked the time. He hoped John Sarpong hadn't been exaggerating the security team's ability to respond quickly to an emergency.

The canoe made its way alongside the trash rack, pausing by each penstock while the American widened the gap between the bars. As it reached the sixth and final penstock, a siren blasted and floodlights illuminated the area. From the top of the dam, half a dozen men in black overalls and balaclavas were abseiling down the wall, above the penstock openings.

The men in the canoe looked at each other. The man in front pushed away from the trash rack. The American shouted at him, 'Stop, you fuck!' He pulled them back to the last gap he'd made.

Two of the security men had lowered themselves onto the top of the trash rack, where it fixed into the wall, but to reach the canoe they had to step awkwardly along the top of the metal bars, and it was slow going.

The American lifted a box from his bag, fiddled with something on it, and pushed it through the gap in the bars. The current dragged it towards the penstock. It slipped down and out of sight, like a matchstick washing into a drain. Within moments there was a rumble like a clap of thunder. The ground shook. The men in the canoe paddled together now, away from the dam, as a flash of steam and water and fire erupted from the penstock.

The men were paddling hard. The canoe was heading out of danger. But abruptly, as if it had hit an invisible wall, it came to a halt. Swivelling out of control in the current, it was pulled back. The American shouted, 'What the fuck?' A section of the trash rack had swung open. Nothing could stop the boat passing through. The two men dived off as it plunged into the abyss.

The man who'd been in front reappeared, grabbing hold of the bars. The security men on the bars above lowered themselves and grabbed hold of him. The American was nowhere to be seen.

A horn blasted. A motor launch with a mounted searchlight was sailing up the intake channel. Patrice looked back at the dam. Above it, the sky was red. In the black water below, close by, a hooded head bobbed up – and the American pulled himself onto the bank. The security men were too far away to stop him, the motor launch too.

Patrice skidded down the scree slope. The man was clawing his way up. Patrice went below him and pulled him back by his legs. Security men were on their way, running down the path. But the man was putting up a fight. He caught Patrice on the nose with an elbow. Stunned momentarily, Patrice couldn't prevent him wriggling free. He reached out and caught hold of the man's ankle. Together they slid down and splashed into the water.

The American kicked with his free leg, catching Patrice on his head, but Patrice didn't let go. They were underwater. He pulled the man forward, ducked beneath him, and locked his arm round the man's neck. The man flailed around. Patrice held him tight. He came up for air. Both men gasped. But they were drifting away from the bank. The current was pulling them towards the penstocks, and getting stronger.

Patrice tried to steer a course away from the section of trash rack that had been blown open, but it was hopeless as he was grappling with the American at the same time. They were being sucked ever faster towards oblivion. He could see where the water dipped into the penstock and away.

He had one chance as they passed through the gap in the trash rack: lunging to the side, he caught hold of a bar. A heavy elbow jabbed him in the ribs. He cried out and lost hold of the man. The American was taken by the current and vanished down the dark tunnel.

The force of the water was pulling Patrice's legs in the same direction. He clung to the bar. It was impossible to draw his legs up. His arms were tiring, his fingers straining as they gripped the metal. Water was smashing into his face. He was spluttering, exhausted, unsure how much longer he could hold on, when he heard a shout.

'Take this!'

A rope was thrown. He stretched out an arm and gritted his teeth as he clutched the lifeline. The rope pulled. In his confusion he didn't let go of the trash rack, so that his body was being torn apart. Then he realised. His fingers sprung off the bar, and he was dragged clear of the penstock and the roaring water.

Chapter 37

He didn't know where he was, but he knew he'd been there before. A face appeared, adding to the mystery: a woman he knew but didn't know. She smiled and he recognised her. Nurse Agnes at the Sisters of Mercy Clinic in Accra.

'Hello,' she said. 'How are you feeling?'

'I feel … drowsy. Like the last time you woke me.' He wheezed and coughed. 'But I must go.' He made to get out of the bed, but his limbs were too heavy to move.

'I don't think so.' The nurse placed a hand on his chest, and he gave up trying. 'You've got pneumonia.' She pointed to a drip attached to his arm. 'You're on anti-biotics. You nearly drowned.'

It was coming back to him: the dam, the canoe, the explosion. The pull of the water, the dark tunnel. He put his hand to his face and felt a new bandage on his nose, and closed his eyes.

When he woke the next time, his head was clearer. Josie Mwinga appeared at the door, looking at him pitifully.

'Oh, Patrice, you had us worried. But, my goodness, what a business! What a business!' She sat on the chair by his bed.

'Yes,' he said. 'What a business.' He turned to take a drink of water and propped himself up. His body ached all over.

'You know, Patrice, the president himself wants to come and thank you for what you've done. You averted a catastrophe.'

'But what about the explosion? Is the dam ... safe?'

'The dam is safe. One turbine is out of action. It will take months to repair. But that is the limit of it. No one working at the dam was hurt. They found a bag in the water with five more explosive devices. They were planning to blow up all six turbines. You can imagine the effects of that. The dam was saved and it's thanks to you.'

'Thank you, ma'am. But it was actually the security men. And they saved me too.'

She patted his shoulder. 'I thought you'd like to know, the man they caught led them to Boateng, who's made a full confession. He and Mensah are in jail, along with that man who attacked you at your hotel by the river, and the one who thumped you on the nose before. And I can tell you, Patrice,' she added, leaning forward, 'other arrests have been made, though because of their sensitivity, these won't be announced until all the facts have been established. Two cabinet ministers and an assistant director general of police.'

Patrice's head was swirling. He tried to clear his throat. It felt like his chest was exploding.

'Please, Patrice, don't worry yourself. But let me say this, because, well, you were right. It was, as you said, a conspiracy. I was wrong. I should have listened to you.'

'What about the American? The man who slipped down the penstock?'

'There was not much left of him, I understand, after what happened. According to the other man in the canoe, he was an explosives expert.'

'He worked for the American embassy.'

'No, Patrice. He'd been working in the gold mines in Obuasi. Why would the American embassy employ an explosives expert?'

The conversation was making him dizzy. He wiped his forehead. 'Someone I met recognised him. I knew there was an American angle to this. The American parent company, the information about al-Qaeda coming from the Americans, which means the CIA ... it's all adding up.'

'Oh, do stop that! There's no American angle, as you call it. The person you met must have been mistaken. The man's background has been checked.'

'And the older man, who he was travelling with?'

'He was a business associate who knew nothing about what his colleague was doing. He thought they were on a fishing holiday.' She smiled at Patrice, shaking her head. 'The danger to the dam is over. That's the important thing. All you need to do is rest and get better.'

Nurse Agnes came and pressed a thermometer into Patrice's ear. 'You need to listen to your friend here. Your temperature is still high.'

Patrice rolled his eyes as the nurse left, which made his head hurt. 'Well, if the Sunfall proposal is off the table, at least Kekeli and her aunt can stay in their house ...' He caught his boss looking away. 'Please tell me the deal is off.'

'You know, I've spoken to Kekeli myself. I felt I should, to see how she is. She says she's thinking of accepting an offer of compensation.'

'What offer? There was an offer, but her father rejected it.'

'Yes, well, it seems the offer has been renewed. Not compensation exactly. But a gesture of goodwill, to help her and her aunt resettle.'

'Resettle? Goodwill?'

'Yes. With Mensah and Boateng exposed, and in jail, a new management team has been installed at Sunfall ...'

'I hope you're joking, but I don't think you are.'

'The thing is, as Kekeli doesn't have the original deeds, the ownership is in question. To be honest, Patrice, I think she's had enough of all this. And it's a generous gesture. You see, as you discovered, Sunfall Power was one of several companies with proposals for solar farms ...'

'Yes, and Mensah and Boateng were pulling the whole deal together.'

'But the parent company, ArizOil, had no idea what Mensah and Boateng were up to, the underhand tactics they were using. It would still like to proceed with its plans if the Ghanaian government agrees.'

'I bet it would!'

'Look, obviously, given everything that's happened, the government would be reckless and foolish if it didn't consider diversifying its sources of electricity generation. The country's energy strategy is crucial to its development.'

'But the dam! These people tried to sabotage the Akosombo Dam.'

His boss took a deep breath. 'As I said, the people responsible for that are in jail, and will be for a long time. The Ghanaian justice system is robust. I know awful things have been going on, but we've got to be level-headed about this, Patrice. The government believes it's in the national interest to continue to consider these proposals.'

Patrice couldn't stop shaking his head. 'I'm sorry, ma'am, I didn't realise you had taken on a new job as spokesperson for the Government of Ghana. Congratulations.'

'There's no need to be facetious, Patrice. You nearly lost your life. You deserve a full explanation and that's what I'm trying to do, to explain, if you like, how some good might come out of this terrible business.'

He touched the bandage on his nose and looked at the antibiotic drip. 'How can the government fall for this? Don't you see? They've been blackmailed into thinking this way ...'

'Circumstances have changed. The fact is, with climate change and less reliable rainfall, the government has to look at alternatives to Akosombo. It has to be flexible and be willing to adapt ...'

'By allowing a foreign company to take over a large share of the energy sector?'

'These are Ghanaian companies, Patrice. The parent company may be American, but they are Ghanaian.'

Patrice's brain was burning, his body exhausted. 'It's a con, ma'am.'

She pursed her lips. 'When it comes to development, as someone once said, it doesn't matter if the cat is black or white, so long as it catches the mouse.'

'Deng Xiaoping.' He tutted and sighed. 'It's the same old story. These people will take Ghana's sunshine for next to nothing, process it, and sell it back to Ghanaians as electricity. It's neo-colonialism – ironically, a term coined by Kwame Nkrumah.'

'What's done is done, Patrice. It wasn't planned this way, but you can't blame the government for attempting to make the most of this situation.'

Patrice was beginning to think someone had spiked Josie Mwinga's tea with a drug that shrank the brain. 'So your friend George Abotsi died for a good cause?'

Mwinga turned her face as if she'd been slapped. 'That's unfair, to suggest I don't care about what happened to George.'

She squeezed her lips. He thought she might cry. They were silent for a while. The nurse came again and said Patrice needed to rest. His getting excited wasn't helping, she said.

Josie Mwinga got up to leave and wished him well.

A doctor told Patrice he'd be there at least another two days, depending on how he responded to treatment. For most of that time, he dosed and drifted between dreams and dazed moments of consciousness.

On the second day, Kekeli visited. She looked tired. She said she couldn't stay long; Aunty Yawor was with Gladys, but the Addos were busy with their move. Aunty herself seemed none the worse for the incident at the Waterside Hotel.

'What about you?' Patrice asked. 'How are you feeling? My boss says they've made a new offer for your house?'

'Yes, it's true, a reasonable one. I don't want to go. I'm sure Aunty doesn't want to go. But I can't prove the house is ours. And also … I don't know … We can move on, let Aunty live out her life in peace. Even Josie Mwinga said we'd be better off moving. She said it might be best for Ghana.'

Patrice scowled. What was happening was wrong. But it was Kekeli's choice. And he couldn't blame her.

She took his hand, smiling resignedly.

He wanted to say more to encourage her, but sleep was overwhelming him. All he came out with was, 'I understand.' And he drifted off.

When he woke, she was gone. But he felt better. The fever had gone too.

Chapter 38

It didn't seem likely Professor Elsa Henderson had been mistaken about the man she saw on the hotel terrace. Not likely at all.

Patrice would have called her, but he'd lost his phone and her number somewhere in Lake Volta. So he went to see her instead. With an all-clear from the doctors and an assurance the coughing and breathlessness would improve, provided he didn't exert himself, he took a taxi to the University of Ghana in Legon.

The taxi dropped him at the main entrance. It was a nice day, sunny and hot but not humid. He followed some students up a wide stone staircase and into a white colonial-style building and asked a receptionist for the Department of Political Science. As he followed the directions across the grassy campus, it occurred to him how he might enjoy being a student again himself; to have time to think and not to have to deal with people who thumped him on the nose or tried to blow up dams.

The Department of Political Science occupied a low-rise building with a tin roof. Patrice stepped inside and asked a man sitting behind a desk if he knew the professor's whereabouts. The man told him to wait.

He sat on a chair and picked up a copy of the *Daily Graphic*. The front page showed a photograph of Victor Mensah and Albert Boateng being led into court. The headline asked: *Who else was involved?* A report said police had been unable to verify the identity of the man who died during the attack on Akosombo.

'You wanted to see Professor Henderson?' A middle-aged man with glasses and a craggy face was standing at the entrance to a corridor.

'Yes, is she here today?'

'You are a friend?'

'Not exactly. We met last week. She said if ever I needed her help, to contact her ...'

'Please come with me ...'

'If she's in class, I can wait.'

The man led him into an office and offered him another chair. '... I'm Professor Kwesi Stevens, a senior lecturer.'

Patrice introduced himself.

'Mr Le Congo. I'm afraid you can't see Professor Henderson, today or any other day. She died. Just days ago.'

'Died? But ... I saw her, just days ago, at the dam ... she seemed fine.'

'She had an accident. She was taking her students to a village by Lake Volta ... it would have been directly after they visited the dam. It's a terrible business.'

'That's awful. She invited me to go to the village with her and the students ... I can't believe it.'

'To be honest with you, neither can we. She was a dynamic professor. She brought her students here and took ours to America. The exchanges have been of great benefit. She was full of life. It's hard to believe she's no longer with us.'

'How did it happen?'

Professor Stevens took off his glasses and wiped them. 'The village chief says he was explaining to the students how life has been for the people since they were relocated there, when the dam was built and the lake was created. At some point, Professor Henderson stepped behind a house by the lakeside and must have slipped and fallen into the water. She knocked her head on a rock and drowned.'

'*Mungu wangu.*'

'They found her when the chief took the students to the water's edge to show them how the level of the lake rises and falls. She can only have been dead a matter of minutes.'

'How terrible, for the students and everyone.'

'Yes, absolutely. The students were very fond of her. I am sorry to be the bearer of such bad news. But you said you needed Professor Henderson's help? Is it something I can help you with?'

'No … She saw someone that morning. I wanted to know his name, that's all.'

The professor got to his feet. 'In that case, if you don't mind, I must return to my class. You are welcome to sit here for some time if you wish.'

'That's alright, thank you. I will go. I'm sorry for your loss.'

Patrice left the university campus and wandered the streets, thinking how to proceed. He found himself at a corner where there were bars and food stalls. He sat and drank a Coke.

A young woman in a short, tight, black dress sat at his table. He looked around and saw other young women, walking the street – students, he supposed, working in their spare time to help pay for their fees.

The girl said, 'Hello. Shall I sit with you?'

Patrice said, 'Hello and goodbye. I'm leaving.'

'You don't want me to sit with you?'

'You don't know the meaning of goodbye?'

The girl shrugged.

'It's okay.'

He got up and hailed a taxi.

That afternoon, he returned to Akosombo. He caught a bus to Atimpoko and a taxi to the Volta Hotel. It was only a few days since he was there last, but it felt like a month. The same receptionist was on duty. He introduced himself. 'Maybe you remember me?'

She nodded and looked away.

'Unfortunately, my stay in Akosombo was cut short. But now I'm investigating the death of a man who was staying here last week, an American man ...'

'The police have been to discuss that matter.'

She was about twenty-five and serious looking. She wore a black jacket over a white blouse and tied her hair in a tidy bun. The name on her badge was Rachael.

'Yes. It seems there's confusion over the man's identity.'

'My manager told them the man's name.'

'What was it?'

'I cannot tell you that. But I was here. There was no confusion. It was in his passport.'

'Can you show it to me, his passport?'

'How can I do that? We don't have his passport now.'

'I know, but you photocopy all the passports, so you can show me that.'

The look on her face was hard as rock.

'Rachael, I think you owe me?'

She bit her lip, averting her eyes.

'You told that man where I was staying.'

'I … He asked me …'

'I understand. I don't blame you. But he and his associates wanted to kill me. So that's why I want to know who he is.' He looked into her eyes, which were staring at his nose. 'Please help me, Rachael.'

She pursed her lips. Glancing around, she tapped her computer and turned the screen so Patrice could look. The name was Martin Daley. Born in Texas in 1985. There was nothing to indicate it was a diplomatic passport.

'Did the police ask about the other man, who he was staying with, the older one?'

'They took his details.'

'Would you mind showing me his passport too?'

She tapped on the keyboard again. 'I shouldn't be doing this. If my manager comes …' She turned the screen again for him. It was another American passport, but they weren't travelling as father and son. The older man's name was Joseph Horst. Born in New Jersey in 1941.

'Thank you, Rachael.'

'You're welcome,' she said, breaking into a shy smile. 'I hope it helps you.'

'Did they say where they were going, that day when I was here?'

'They said they were going fishing in the lake. The older man said he was looking forward to it because normally he fishes in the ocean, so this would be different. He lives in Ghana, that man.'

'Where? How do you know?'

'He was forward – I didn't like him. He said he owns a hotel

302

on the coast, in Western Region. He said I could come to work for him there, but he was not polite.'

'How was he not polite?'

She gestured to the top of her cleavage and said, 'He was looking all the time down here.'

Patrice grimaced. 'He's old enough to be your grandfather.'

She kissed her teeth.

'Did he say where his hotel was exactly?'

'No, and I didn't ask that. To be honest with you, I was glad when he checked out. I'm sorry if …'

'It's okay, don't worry about it. But could you print me a copy of his passport, showing his photo? I want to find him.'

'Rachael!' A man was calling across reception.

She glanced up. 'My manager is coming now. Come back in a few minutes.'

Patrice went to the business centre. He switched on a computer, and searched for the two names, Martin Daley and Joseph Horst. It didn't take long to find them: sole directors of a company called Blast Mining Solutions, with an address in Charleston, West Virginia.

Their website stated: *Our services include all aspects of mine design, feasibility studies, blast optimization, environmental impact. Our motto: No problem too small; no challenge too big!* Daley was described as *Lead Explosives Expert*, Horst as *Chief Geologist and Strategist*. There was no information about specific projects they'd worked on and no mention of Ghana.

He got up and stretched, an act that tore his chest apart, and went back to Rachael at reception. She handed him an envelope and smiled. He thanked her and went out on the terrace to study Joseph Horst's passport photograph: small, dark eyes, straight nose, clean shaven, thinning grey hair, parted to one side. An unremarkable face, but one that shouldn't be hard to find among the coastal hotels in Ghana's Western Region.

Setting off down the hill on foot, Patrice called Kekeli on a cheap phone he'd bought in Accra. She asked when he'd be coming to see her and he said that evening, after he'd followed up one more thing in Akosombo.

He waved down a taxi and got a ride to the Volta River Authority. When he walked through the door of the front offices, the four members of staff stood and applauded. Patrice looked behind him, but there was no one there.

'You don't remember us?' one of them called out, and they all laughed. 'They brought you here after they rescued you from the lake.'

'You are our hero!' another one said. 'The man who saved the dam!'

Patrice recognised a couple of faces from his first visit to the dam, when he'd taken the tour bus. He laughed and waved. 'You guys! You're embarrassing me!'

'Who's embarrassed?' A bald man with a big grin walked in. 'You should be proud of what you've done for us.'

There were giggles around the room.

'Come, Mr Congo, come and have a cold drink in my office.' The man introduced himself as the acting director and led him down a corridor and into a small office with shelves stacked with papers and books. He poured Patrice some water.

'We were not expecting to see you so soon. We heard you were not well?'

'Yes, I had a cough. I'm pretty much recovered, thank you.'

'Well, as you can see, we are all pleased to see you. You are our guest of honour and we are here at your disposal. What can I do for you?'

'I wanted to check something, something unpleasant. I hope you don't mind.' The man looked puzzled. 'It's about the man who slipped down the penstock. I was told not much remained of him, but was there enough to make a formal identification?'

'Of course not, there couldn't be, after that ...' He went over to some diagrams on the wall. 'That man fell here ...' He pointed at a cross-section drawing. '... and down towards the turbine at speed – like a turd being flushed down a toilet. Excuse me. The turbine was not working because of the bomb, which badly damaged it, mangling the blades. But for that man, it would be like passing through a shredder. We found an arm and a foot ... The turbine itself will have to be replaced; it is beyond repair.'

'Did they take fingerprints?'

'It was an arm but without a hand, so no. They established his identity when his friend reported him missing the next day. He thought he'd gone fishing.'

'I see.' Patrice sighed.

'We did find something else.' The man grinned again. 'As a matter of fact, I thought this was why you had come.' He reached down and pulled open a drawer, and handed Patrice a bowl of uncooked rice.

Patrice screwed up his face.

The man laughed out loud. 'Have a look inside!'

Patrice dug his fingers in – and pulled out his phone. 'That's amazing. How did you find it?'

'The divers did, three days ago, when they were inspecting the damage to the trash rack. I don't know if it can work, but

305

one of my colleagues said to try this, to dry it out. Perhaps the information will be retrievable?'

'Thank you so much.'

It was early evening when Patrice arrived at Kekeli's house. The sad flagpole had almost snapped in two. The top half was bent so far over that most of the flag itself was lying on the grass.

He found Kekeli with her aunt on the back veranda. They embraced.

'You must fix that flagpole,' Patrice said. 'Even if you're not staying. It's too sad to leave it like that.'

'Well, perhaps you could do it. You saved the Akosombo Dam from being blown up, so I'm sure you can fix a broken flagpole.'

Patrice laughed. 'Okay, I will. But look what I've got.' He held up his phone. 'Recovered from the depths of Lake Volta. Can I charge it here?'

Kekeli nodded and he plugged it into the solar-powered charger.

'And look what I've got,' Kekeli said, showing him a type-written manuscript. 'It's my grandfather's, my father's father's. I was having a last look for the title deeds and I found this.'

Patrice read the title: *A Memoir: The life and times of Joseph Abotsi, Humble Servant to the Public.*

Chapter 39

The air was dry and warm, the kind of warm that's so perfect you can barely feel it. Insects were reciting their night-time chorus. Patrice was reclined in a comfortable chair, a bottle of beer within reach. Was there a better way to spend an evening than sitting peacefully on a veranda in tropical Africa? If so, he'd like to know about it. He'd spent a year in Europe as a student. If he went to the United States to study again, he'd have to endure another cold winter in a place where people walked around hunched and shivering and had no time to stop and talk, and spent a fortune on fuel bills … In Ghana, he reflected, heating was free.

Kekeli was reading out extracts from the pages of her grandfather's memoirs. Now and again, Aunty Yawor cackled and muttered things like, 'Humble? Huh! Humble bumble!'

'Aunty, is this upsetting you? Do you want me to stop?'

There was no response.

Kekeli carried on:

I turn to the events leading up to the overthrow of the tyrant Kwame Nkrumah. Of course, there were some amongst us who knew the end was near. Such was the level of discontent among the populace that it could only be a matter of time. Rarely did a week pass without a new rumour spreading like wildfire through the workplaces and drinking spots in the capital that a coup was being plotted.'

'Humble? Huh! What about the red car?'

Patrice stared at the old lady. 'What red car, Aunty? What about it?'

Aunty Yawor stared out into the garden and didn't answer. It was impossible to know what was going on in her head.

Kekeli picked up where she'd left off:

'It's fair to say that after the military coup in Nigeria, the atmosphere had reached fever pitch. And so it is strange to report that when Ghana's day of liberation arrived, on the 24th of February 1966, the event took us by surprise. All of Accra could hear the battle rage that morning around Flagstaff House. We hardly dared believe it was true. Who was it, we wondered, who had come to save us? Who were these brave soldiers who were prepared to risk everything for the sake of their country and the freedom of their fellow citizens?'

'Ackk!' Aunty Yawor squawked. 'Ofori saw you!'

'Ofori? Aunty? Who's Ofori?'

'He saw you together. Huh! Ofori ... Ofori ...' She tailed off.

Kekeli leaned close to Patrice. 'I don't know what she's saying, but this is making her remember things.'

'Things that happened then, do you think?'

'Yes, I'm sure of it.'

She continued reading aloud:

'Colonel Kotoka came on the radio and made his now-famous announcement: "The myth surrounding Kwame Nkrumah has been broken. Parliament is dissolved and Kwame Nkrumah is dismissed from office ..." As has well been recorded, the news was greeted with jubilation and to a man the people celebrated through

308

the day and long into the night. Kwame Nkrumah may have started out with good intentions, but he became corrupted by power and had driven our country to ruin. The men who overthrew him were rightly welcomed as heroes.'

Kekeli paused for a moment. 'It's actually annoying,' she said. 'It's a first-hand account of that momentous event in our history, but it feels one-sided. My grandfather is writing his own history here, the history he wants to be passed down.'

'But it's still interesting,' Patrice said, 'to hear from someone who was there at the time. I wonder if he tried to publish it.'

'It's dated August 1979, which is not long before he died, so I guess he didn't have time for that. And it seems my father made sure it never saw the light of day.'

She read some more:

'You can well imagine, therefore, what a great honour it was for me personally that just two days after the coup d'état, a car was sent for me, whereupon I was driven to police headquarters, to the office of Police Commissioner JWK Harlley, the very room in which the National Liberation Council was formed. Commissioner Harlley happened to be an old school-friend of mine, and it was clear that he and Retired General Ankrah were in charge of the new government. It was Commissioner Harlley himself who informed me that, owing to my outstanding record and service as a district court judge, I was to be appointed to the high court.'

'Huh! You got what you wanted! But Adzo ... you didn't care.'

'Goodness, Aunty. You're talkative tonight.'

'Adzo ...'

Patrice was lost. 'Who's Adzo?'

'She was your sister, wasn't she, Aunty? It was just before the coup that she died.'

'He killed her.'

'What? Your Uncle Joseph killed Adzo?'

'Krieger killed her. He ran her down. In a red Ford Mustang. And you let him get away with it.'

'Who's Krieger?'

Aunty Yawor's eyes were darting from side to side.

'Aunty? Who's Krieger?'

The old lady didn't answer. It was like she was back in 1966 and lost to the present.

Kekeli said, 'I hope it's not too much for her ...'

She read on:

'I shall turn to the record of the National Liberation Council in due course. But let me first address one of the wilder conspiracy theories that were propagated by deposed members of the Nkrumah regime, namely that the American secret service orchestrated the coup. I am, owing to the personal friendship that existed between myself and Commissioner Harlley, able to refute that assertion, for I had that refutation from the horse's mouth, so to speak. Once, some months after the coup, I asked JWK Harlley what assistance, if any, the Americans had given. He looked me straight in the eye, as only a man who is about to speak the truth can, and said a man called Howard Bane, an apparently unimportant figure at the US embassy, had responded to a request by delivering some small pieces of equipment. That was it. A little help, yes; but hardly the orchestration of a coup d'état!'

'Well, well,' Patrice said. 'They may not have organised it, but they were involved.'

'My father was right!'

'Krieger brought the boxes.' Aunty Yawor was chomping on air. 'Ofori, remember? In his car. Bane was there. And I slipped. Remember? They nearly caught us ... We got away, but then … Ofori … Ofori …' She closed her eyes and was suddenly sleeping.

'My goodness,' Kekeli said, closing the manuscript. 'I'll leave it there for now.'

She got up and put a blanket round her aunt, then went into the house and returned with a bottle of Star.

'That was strange,' Patrice said in a low voice. 'She spoke as if she knew about that man Howard Bane, like she was there. But how could she?'

Aunty Yawor was snoring. Kekeli kissed her head and adjusted a cushion in her chair.

'How did her sister die?' Patrice asked.

'She was run over. I don't know the circumstances, but it was on the day Kwame Nkrumah inaugurated the Akosombo Dam. I assumed it was an accident.'

'Aunty said she was at the inauguration with your father.'

'I know. It's confusing. I don't think she was. My father said she was terribly upset by Adzo's death. She used to visit her grave until a few years ago. She never talked about what happened. I don't know … she might be getting different stories mixed up.'

'Yes, I wonder …' Patrice scratched his head. 'The red car she's been talking about … was it Kwaku Sarpong's or this Ford Mustang from long ago?'

Kekeli shrugged. 'Who knows? I keep wishing I'd asked my father more questions about that time. There are so many things I should have asked him.'

A ping sounded. Patrice's drowned phone had come back to life.

'A miracle!' he said.

He picked it up and saw he had new messages. There was

311

one from Kekeli and one from Josie Mwinga, both asking where he was, sent the night he lost the phone. And there was one sent the day before that, which had only arrived now. It was from Professor Henderson.

'*Mungu wangu ...*'

'What is it, Patrice?'

'A message from the American professor I met at the dam. Did I tell you about her? I heard today she died, the same day she visited the dam. Listen. She says, *Hi Patrice, nice meeting you. Just wanted you to know, that man is following me, the man on the terrace. He's here at the village. I'm sure I'll be fine but if anything happens, please tell the police. His name is Marty Drake. Good luck with your master's degree!*'

'That's awful, Patrice. What man is she talking about?'

'That's his name. The explosives expert - the bomber. He was looking at her when we went for a drink at the Volta Hotel with her students. And she's dead now. They told me at the university this morning.'

'What does it mean?'

'It means she wasn't mistaken about who he was. And her death probably wasn't an accident.'

'What?'

'The professor told me he worked at the American embassy and had harassed her at a function there. He must have recognised her and heard she was taking her students to the village, taken a boat across the lake, and then returned that night to Akosombo.'

'You're saying the man who attacked the dam was working for the American embassy?'

'We need to confirm that. But also ...' Patrice looked away, trying to figure out how to say what he had to say. 'Kekeli, I

312

think this is also the man the boys in the river saw running away the day your father died.'

Kekeli squinted at him, then stared out into the garden.

In the *News and Events* section of the American embassy website were two postings from the previous week. Patrice read them the following morning as he sat sipping his tea on Kekeli's back veranda.

One was about the death of Professor Elsa Henderson. Below a photograph of her, a brief statement read:

The US Embassy in Ghana learned with sadness of the death of US citizen Professor Elsa Henderson whilst on a visit to Lake Volta. Professor Henderson has been leading a popular exchange study program between the University of Louisiana and the University of Ghana, Legon, for the past seven years. Embassy staff have been offering support to her students and helping to arrange for the repatriation of her body to the United States.

Above that, issued a day later, was a posting headed: *Statement by US Embassy in Ghana. Dam attacker not US citizen.* Patrice raced through the text:

The US Embassy in Ghana has cautioned local media against suggesting that a man who died during the attack on the Akosombo Dam was a US citizen. The man, named in reports as Martin Daley, was alleged to have been traveling on a US passport. But the US Department of State in Washington has confirmed no passport was ever issued in that name with the date of birth supplied. The US Embassy in Ghana further draws attention to the state of relations between the United States and Ghana, as described elsewhere on the pages of the Embassy website, namely that our two countries have a close and enduring friendship rooted in our mutual commitment to freedom and democratic values.

Patrice called the embassy. He listened through the list of options and held for the operator.

'US Embassy in Ghana, how may I help you?'

'Hello, please put me through to Mr Marty Drake. He is a second secretary.'

'May I ask who's calling?'

'My name is Étienne Kabanda. I am an old acquaintance of Mr Drake's. I am passing through Accra. I try to call his number but it doesn't go through.'

'I'm sorry, sir. Marty Drake hasn't worked here for more than a year.'

'Oh, I see. Do you know where is now?'

'I believe he left the diplomatic service, sir.'

'Well, thank you for your help. Goodbye.'

Kekeli came out and sat next to him. 'Nice disguise, Patrice! What did they say?'

'He used to work for the embassy, but he left more than a year ago.'

'Oh,' she said, despondently. 'Does that mean ... Is that the end of your investigation?'

'There's one last lead. It may come to nothing. It means taking a holiday.'

'Holiday? Really?'

He smiled, seeing her face light up. 'To Western Region. I hear the coast there is beautiful.'

'It is! I would love to go. But what about Aunty? I don't think I can leave her, and anyway the Addo family will be moving out any day ...'

'Aunty can come too.'

'Oh, I see.'

Patrice took her hand. 'Seriously, Kekeli, I must be straight

314

with you. This could be dangerous. I want you to help me find this man, this Joseph Horst, if that's his real name, the man who was with Marty Drake at the Volta Hotel. I don't believe he thought they were there to go fishing.'

'Fishing?'

'It doesn't matter. The thing is, he's seventy-five and he has a sweet spot for pretty women. So I was thinking, you can chat to him, win his confidence. Then we get him to talk and clear up this whole business.'

'I can do that. Can an old man be so dangerous?'

'Maybe not him, but look at his friend. If he has others like that, well, we have to be careful.'

'Okay. When do you want to go?'

'Now? It would be good to get there before dark. We could stay tonight in Cape Coast, then move on to Western Region tomorrow and start working our way along the coast. Until we find his hotel.'

'Do you know how many beach hotels there are in Western Region? There are many, you know.'

'I know.'

Kekeli clapped her hands and got to her feet. 'Well, okay. I haven't been to Western Region for a long time. And perhaps Aunty will like it by the ocean. I'll pack our things ...'

'One more thing, Kekeli. Please see if your friend Valerie is at her office today. I'd like to pick up that envelope she's got in her safe.'

'Yes, sir! Is there anything else?'

'Well, yes, there is. Does she have any elderly female relatives?'

Kekeli shrugged. 'Her mother died three years ago. I don't know about her aunties ... why, Patrice?'

'Would she let you borrow her ID card? And an aunt's for Aunty to use?'

Kekeli smiled. 'Are you going to tell me why?'

'We don't know how this man is mixed up in all this. But it's possible he knows what happened to your father, in which case he may know your family name. So it would be good if you could use a different card ... for a few days? And you look a lot like Valerie. It's an idea I had.'

'What about you? Won't he recognise you?'

'Wait.' He turned to a small mirror hanging on the wall and pulled the bandage off his nose. 'Not without this.'

She rolled her eyes and disappeared inside. A moment later, she popped her head round the doorway. 'Anyway, how about you fix that flagpole? Here ...' She handed him a bucket containing a hammer and a screwdriver and other tools and pointed to a rickety-looking set of steps lying beneath the veranda.

Patrice took the bucket and the ladder round to the front of the house and climbed up to inspect the damage. Up close, it looked like a previous attempt had been made to repair a crack in the wood using two metal strips, but one of these had sheered in two and the other was bent over and was all that was holding the flagpole together. He figured a couple of pieces of wood to use as splints and rope to bind them up might do the job, at least temporarily; and, noticing the pole itself was hollow, a length of dowelling wedged inside would give it extra strength ...

He stuck a finger in the hole to gauge the diameter, and it touched something. He peered inside. It was a rolled-up plastic bag. Using the screwdriver, he eased out the bag and unrolled it. A scroll of paper was inside.

'Kekeli! Come!' he shouted, climbing down the ladder.

She came running out of the front door. 'What's happened?'

'Look …'

She stepped forward, looking in astonishment. 'The title deeds! We've searched every place and …' She looked them over, up and down and again. 'He hid them in the flagpole – the pole that's supported the Ghanaian flag all these years. That's such a Young Pioneer thing to do! Oh, Patrice, thank you …' She hugged him and kissed his forehead. 'I'll tell Aunty, though I don't suppose she'll know what I'm talking about. Oh my goodness, I don't believe it!'

She went back inside. Patrice found what he needed and put the flagpole back together again, and the red, gold and green flag, with the black star in the middle, hung high once more in front of George Abotsi's house.

Chapter 40

They drove to Accra once again in Kekeli's old Nissan Micra and joined the traffic jam heading for the city centre. Aunty Yawor was asleep in the back. The sun was burning a hole through the white cloud. A woman on *Joy FM* said it was 34 degrees. It felt like 50.

'So, what do you think we'll find next?' Kekeli asked, grinning at Patrice.

'How do you mean?'

'Yesterday you found your phone and I found my grandfather's memoirs. Today you found my father's title deeds. We're on a lucky streak.'

'Maybe,' he said, not wanting to tempt fate.

They went first to Patrice's hotel. Kekeli stayed with her aunt in the car while Patrice picked up a change of clothes. Heaven, the receptionist, was on shift.

'Hello, sir. Good morning,' she said impassively.

'Good morning, Heaven.'

He packed a bag and was heading out of the hotel when she called to him. 'Oh, sir, your friend is here.'

He looked round. Josie Mwinga was at the desk.

'Ma'am, good morning. Are you looking for me?'

She looked startled. 'Oh, Patrice … yes, I am, good morning.

318

I'm glad I've caught you. I was leaving a note. I didn't realise you were here.'

Patrice looked at Heaven. She was adjusting the position of her computer keyboard.

'I'm on my way to Western Region. What can I do for you?'

'Er … well, can we sit? I won't take much of your time …' They walked through to the coffee lounge with the round armchairs and thick carpet. Mwinga was wearing a loose-fitting navy-coloured gown with an embroidered collar; she'd brought a lot of outfits with her on this trip. 'I must say you're looking a lot better, Patrice. That's good.'

They took their seats. She looked troubled. He braced himself, expecting to be asked another favour – an unpleasant one, judging by her demeanour. The waiter asked for their order. Patrice said they weren't staying.

'This is difficult,' Mwinga said, avoiding his eyes. 'I wanted to tell you the other day, but you weren't in good shape. I'm leaving for Banjul tomorrow, but I won't be staying there. I'm resigning.'

'Resigning?'

'Yes, from the African Union's Human Rights Commission.'

'I see. That's a surprise, ma'am. I thought you loved your work.'

'I do like the job, Patrice. The Commission's Investigation Unit has been my life, but … something else has come up, something else has entered my life, you might say.' She was looking down, playing with her fingers. Then she looked up and with an apologetic smile, she said, 'I'm getting married.'

'Well, congratulations. That's exciting.'

'I wanted to tell you personally. And to assure you that I will speak highly of you to whomsoever is chosen to replace me, and tell them it's agreed you can take a year's unpaid leave to study.'

'Thank you, ma'am.'

'I told you before, you can call me Josie.'

'I know, ma'am, thank you. It's hard to break the habit.'

'Yes ...' She was looking down again. 'There's something else you should know, that I wanted to tell you personally also, because I know otherwise, if you heard it from someone else, you'd think I'd been trying to hide it from you ...'

She paused. Patrice had never known his boss to be shy.

'My husband-to-be ...' She smiled again. 'It seems strange to call him that, because we've known each other for so many years. But he's a well-known public figure here in Accra and ... well, he's about to take on a new job for which he suggested, and I agreed, it might be better if we were formally attached.' She cleared her throat and finally looked straight at Patrice. 'He's been appointed as Ghana's next ambassador to Washington. And I shall be going with him.'

'I see. Well, congratulations again ...'

'I know what you're thinking, Patrice. But I could never allow a personal issue to influence my professional judgement. At least, that's what I thought. Now ... now I can see that I may have been over-hasty in dismissing some of your assumptions regarding this case. You were right to raise questions about the American angle, as you put it ...'

Patrice coughed. 'Well, to a point. I may have been over-hasty in jumping to conclusions, ma'am. I found out the man who attacked the dam used to work for the American embassy, but not any longer. So ... well ... I'm on my way now to find the man he was with before, to try and wrap things up, for Kekeli, to help her find closure.'

'I'm glad to hear that, Patrice. And thank you again for doing this favour for me.'

'Thank you, ma'am. I'm pleased for you. And I will miss you. You have always … almost always, given me your full support.'

They got up and walked out of the hotel.

'Good luck, Patrice, and for goodness sake, be careful.' She spotted Kekeli and waved to her, then turned and walked to a waiting taxi.

'Goodbye, ma'am,' he called after her. But she was gone. Off to start a new life, hosting cocktail parties in Washington. He shook his head in amused disbelief.

They reached the Ministry of Women and Children's Affairs around lunchtime. They parked in the shade beneath the building and walked to the staircase in the central courtyard. A rubbish skip was planted next to it. Shouting and banging sounded from above.

Aunty Yawor looked ill-at-ease. After her stream of utterances the previous night, she hadn't spoken a word all morning. As Kekeli helped her up the stairs, the old lady glanced around agitatedly, like a trespasser checking to see if they're being watched.

They had to navigate their way round boxes and pieces of furniture in the corridor to reach Valerie's office.

'You should have called to let me know you were here,' Valerie said, as she met them at the door. She sounded flustered. 'We're living in a building site. It's terrible, it's impossible to work in these conditions. You can't have a quiet conversation. You can't even think. And the dust, it gets everywhere. Anyway, Patrice, you want your envelope …'

She went to her safe and fetched it for him.

'Thank you,' he said as he pulled out the papers. 'But wait a moment …' He searched for an email he remembered from before and placed it at the front. It was from ArizOil's CEO to Victor Mensah, and ended with the words: *We're doing what we can this end to push this through.*

'Valerie, could you use your government connections to forward this envelope on for me, to someone who needs to see the contents? Urgently?'

'With pleasure,' she said. 'And who's that?'

'The president. For his eyes only.'

'Oh …'

'He was supposed to visit me, so he owes me a favour. He can pay me back by looking through these …'

Patrice wrote a note at the top of the email – even if it didn't prove anything, it might make him think: *Mr President. Mensah's backers in the US knew what was going on. They've been behind this deal from the start.*

Valerie took back the envelope. She looked uncertain. 'I'll do what I can,' she said. 'But now, let's not stay here. Come with me and we'll have something to eat.'

On their way past the top of the stairs, she shouted at a worker who was dropping heavy-looking crates into the skip below. 'Must you do it this way? You should carry these things. You are making too much noise.'

'This way is faster,' the man said.

'Agh …'

They went to the ministry canteen. Patrice wasn't hungry and ate only dried fish and a bowl of fruit. Valerie ordered fufu and meat stew for herself and the two other women.

'I eat fufu when I'm angry,' she said, tucking in. 'Well, I eat fufu at all times, but I eat it when I'm angry because it calms me down.'

'Comfort food,' Kekeli said, and they laughed.

After lunch, they walked back to the top of the stairs. Valerie gave Kekeli the two ID cards she'd asked for. 'Look after them!' she said. 'And have a safe journey.'

Kekeli and Patrice helped Aunty Yawor down the steps. As they passed close to the rubbish piling up in the skip below, Patrice noticed something unexpected: among the old desks and cupboards and empty drawers and broken chair-legs, a label attached to the base of an Anglepoise lamp read *Property of US Government*. He looked more closely at the other items.

'Come on, Patrice,' Kekeli said, tugging on his sleeve. 'If you want to reach Cape Coast before dark …'

He turned to follow her, but as he did, a large, worn-looking book caught his eye. Gold writing showed beneath the dust on the spine. He leaned over and wiped it clean. It said *Gatehouse Log 1966*. There was no one about, so he picked the book out of the skip and took it with him.

They drove away from the ministry compound. Kekeli was complaining about the traffic. Aunty Yawor had become animated again and was muttering about men painting placards. Patrice's face was buried in the pages of the book.

'You were right, Kekeli. You said we'd find something else and we have.'

'A dusty old book. I don't know if I even want that in my car.' She put her foot down and turned sharply into the next lane.

'But this is history. *Thursday 24 February* … The day of the coup! And guess what, Howard Bane is recorded entering and leaving the embassy … one, two, three, four times.'

'Huh! He was busy that day.'

'Yes …' Patrice flipped back through the pages, not looking for anything in particular. But another entry made him stop. 'Look at this: *Saturday 22 January. 6.15pm. Steve Krieger vehicle entry with visitor Adzowor Abotsi.* Is that …'

There was a screech as Kekeli jammed on the brakes. 'My God! That's Aunty's sister, Adzo. That's the day she was killed, the day of the inauguration …' Cars behind were beeping. 'Aunty …'

They looked round. She was sleeping.

'It looks like Steve Krieger worked at the embassy. He's not described as a visitor.'

Kekeli moved off again, chased by more beeps.

Patrice read down the register of comings and goings that evening at the American embassy. 'Look: *8.15 pm. Howard Bane vehicle entry.* And here's Adzo again: *8.20pm. Visitor Adzowor Abotsi exit on foot.* And there's more …'

'She left on her own? At night?'

'Wait. *8.25pm. Steve Krieger vehicle exit.* And, nearly an hour later: *9.20pm. Steve Krieger vehicle entry …*'

'But that's … I mean, you heard what Aunty said, that Krieger killed her sister, and here, in this book … She knew. She found out what happened to Adzo. But somehow, like she said, this man got away with it.'

'If he was a diplomat, he would have had immunity.'

Kekeli was leaning over as she drove, reading the entries herself. Cars behind were still beeping. 'This book could have been the proof Aunty needed. All these years, it's been stored away in a dusty cupboard. And that Steve Krieger … no doubt he lived a long and happy life and retired to a cattle ranch in Wyoming, or something like that.'

They left Accra on the Winneba Road and headed west. They drove without stopping for three hours and reached Cape Coast before dark, checking into a small guesthouse on the edge of town. Kekeli asked Aunty Yawor more questions about Adzo and Krieger, but the old lady looked at her niece blankly, like she'd gone back into herself again.

The two women went to bed early. Patrice stayed up and drank a bottle of Star, watching boys play football on a dusty pitch across the road, under the faint glow of a nearby streetlight.

He pulled out his phone and searched for the two names, Howard Bane and Steve Krieger. There were lots of results for Bane. He was the CIA station chief, and his role in the coup against Nkrumah was cited in books and newspaper articles. According to one account, he wanted to blow up the Chinese embassy during the upheaval, but his bosses in Washington wouldn't let him. There was no mention anywhere of Krieger.

Chapter 41

Next day, they proceeded methodically along the coast. When they came to a town, Patrice took a taxi to the nearby hotels. He checked out more than a dozen, with a story that a group of German tourists had hired him to find them "a place in paradise". Some were down well-paved roads, others at the end of rough tracks cut through dense bush. They varied from five stars to one, but they had one thing in common: a golden sandy beach fringed with palm trees.

Patrice inspected the rooms and chatted with the manager or receptionist or barman, but he drew a blank. None of them was owned by an American. He ticked them off in a guidebook he'd bought in Accra. After a while, regardless of their star rating, they had begun to look the same. The only one he could remember distinctly was a simple place south of Axim, where Kekeli and her aunt had joined him for a lunch of grilled fish. He recalled Kwaku Sarpong saying he could recommend a hotel in Western Region and wished he'd thought to ask him the name.

'It looks like our lucky streak has run out,' he said as they drove out of Axim in the middle of the afternoon, continuing west. He was studying his map. 'There aren't many more hotels between here and the Côte d'Ivoire border.'

Out of the blue, Kekeli shouted out, 'Nkroful!' She slowed and pointed at a dusty signpost. 'Patrice, this is where you wanted to come all this time! We are close by ... shall we go?'

Patrice hesitated. It was one of the reasons he'd come to Ghana in the first place, but right now he was distracted. 'We can go when we come back. We've still got places to check.'

'Patrice, we're tired. You're tired too. We can take a break and start again tomorrow.'

He looked behind. Aunty Yawor was staring ahead, looking like she was in a daze. Kekeli was right. 'Sure,' he said. 'Let's go. We can see the museum and stay the night in the town where Kwame Nkrumah was born.'

Nkroful was a small town with wide streets. The Nkrumah Museum was near the centre, a quiet white-walled compound. Patrice, Kekeli and Aunty Yawor were the only visitors. A young man called Kofi, who said he was Kwame Nkrumah's relative, showed them round. The highlights were the house where Nkrumah was born and the mausoleum that housed his remains before they were transferred to Accra.

'Kwame Nkrumah's birthday is not known,' Kofi said. 'A priest worked it out to be 21 September, 1912. That was a Saturday, and that is why he was named Kwame, the name for a boy born on a Saturday.'

He pointed to a small building. 'Kwame Nkrumah's father was a goldsmith but did not live with the family, so Kwame Nkrumah was raised by his mother in this house. He was her only child. They were poor, but he was a happy child ...'

They went in the house. 'This was Kwame Nkrumah's bedroom.' There was an iron bed frame in a small and otherwise bare, whitewashed room. An outhouse contained the kitchen, with a clay stove on the floor.

Kekeli said, 'You don't imagine that such a great man came from such humble beginnings.'

It didn't take long to see the whole museum. Patrice and Kekeli walked with Aunty towards the exit. On the way, they passed a mural of Kwame Nkrumah with a quote of his below:

"The people of Africa do not seek political freedom for abstract purposes. They seek it because they believe that through political freedom they can obtain economic advancement, education and a real control over their own destiny."

Patrice took a photo. 'People forget this man was a genius. This all looks obvious now, but in those days people accepted colonialism without question. Aunty, did you hear Kwame Nkrumah say things like this?'

Aunty Yawor didn't answer.

Kofi, their guide, led them into a small gift shop.

Patrice bought a mug with a photo of Nkrumah and one showing another quote, which he gave to Kekeli.

She thanked him and smiled, and read out loud as she turned the mug in her hands: '*As long as a single foot of African soil remains under foreign domination, the battle must continue.*'

'Let them remember that!' Patrice said.

'It's strange to think he was perceived as a threat. Everything he said sounds reasonable.'

'These were things Nkrumah said during the fight against colonialism. It was his later analysis of neo-colonialism that scared them. That's what turned the Americans against him.'

Kofi took the mugs and bagged them up. 'The Americans still don't like Kwame Nkrumah.'

'How do you mean?' Patrice asked.

'They don't like him. There is an American man who brings visitors here, not to pay respect, but to say bad things.'

'What does he say?'

'Many bad things, like Kwame Nkrumah was a dictator and a thief who stole from his people. He says he was a communist who wanted to turn the whole of Africa against America.'

'He's entitled to his opinion. But he's a fool. Nkrumah gave the Americans a good deal on the Akosombo Dam. You should tell this man he's not welcome in your museum.'

Kofi kissed his teeth. 'Anyway, he comes here often, so … it is difficult. We don't have many visitors.'

'I'm sorry, I didn't mean it.' Patrice slapped the young man on his shoulder. 'It's good you're taking his money. He owes it!'

Kofi laughed. 'Actually, he stays near here. He has a hotel on the beach.'

Patrice was turning to leave but stopped dead in his tracks. 'Really? How old is this American man?'

'He is old. I don't know exactly. But he has good health.'

Patrice showed him the copy of Joseph Horst's passport photo page. 'Does he look like this?'

'That is him.'

'Where's his hotel?'

'It is close to Axim.'

"That's funny. I thought we'd seen all the hotels. We must have missed that one.'

'It's called Heaven on Earth Hotel. It is exclusive. You will not even see a sign for it.'

Patrice got directions and told Kekeli they wouldn't be spending the night in Nkroful after all.

Chapter 42

The sun was a hazy red ball and sinking in the western sky as the old Peugeot taxi worked its way down the rutted dirt road that headed south out of Axim. The only other traffic was an occasional goat. Patrice had passed this way earlier with Kekeli and her aunt, but he hadn't noticed the turnoff at the bottom of a hill, opposite a small church.

The taxi squeezed into the narrow track. Cut through the mangroves, it was more like a tunnel. Branches scratched on both sides and on the roof. It felt like they'd taken a wrong turn, but soon it opened into a clearing and they came to a gate in a high stone wall. An arched sign above announced the Heaven on Earth Hotel. An armed guard peered inside the taxi and waved it through.

The track continued to a shaded parking area next to a group of low, thatched buildings. Patrice paid the fare and waited for the taxi to turn and leave. A black four-by-four looked familiar - like the one he'd seen driving away from the Volta Hotel, heading for the lake. He walked over and took photos of the tyre-tracks in the sandy earth behind the back wheels. He compared them to the photo he'd taken at the turning point above George Abotsi's hydroelectric station. The tread was the same pattern.

330

'So,' he said, 'it was a white man but it wasn't a red car.'

A wooden arrow directed him down a thatch-covered walkway of wooden decking to reception, a thatched hut connected to other buildings by more thatch-covered walkways. He was welcomed by a young woman wearing a tight-fitting blouse made of Kente-style material and a beaming smile.

'Good evening,' she said, her teeth sparkling

'Good evening. I'm looking for a single room for two or three nights.'

'All our rooms are doubles, or we have suites on the island.'

'Island?'

She pointed over his shoulder at the view behind him: a lawn sweeping down to the ocean, palms silhouetted against the setting sun, and to one side a small rocky promontory with more thatched buildings set among a thick covering of trees.

'When the tide is high, it's an island. We have four bungalows there, which are currently vacant.'

It looked idyllic. 'How much for one of those?'

'Six hundred dollars.' She was still smiling.

'And the other rooms?'

'Two hundred with a sea view; one hundred without.'

Kekeli and her aunt could have one with. He took one without. While the receptionist was photo-copying his passport, he noticed a camera attached to a rafter. He didn't stay to ask questions and went straight to his room to call Kekeli. He told her to come immediately. It would be dark soon and this place was hard enough to find in broad daylight.

'Remember,' he said before hanging up, 'you don't know me. I'll do my best to be discreet, so Aunty doesn't recognise me. Safe drive.'

He took a shower and took a walk round the hotel grounds in the twilight. The rooms were arranged in clusters. His was on the side of a hill at the back. Others overlooked the water, most with terraces. And there was the island, with its exclusive bungalows. All around was the sound of waves lapping the sand and drawing back.

He went to the main buildings and walked up six steps to the bar, half of a large, open-sided L-shaped room, built on low wooden stilts, with bare floorboards and a thatched ceiling. At the far end and round the corner, tables were set for dinner. There were other guests: families, couples and one or two singles, mostly tourists judging by the casual way they were dressed.

He sat at a stool-like table near the reception hut. Through an opening in the whitewashed wall, he could see the receptionist in her brightly coloured top, talking on her phone. He ordered a Star. As he took his first sip, he heard a car door shut. Soon afterwards he saw Kekeli helping her aunt towards the hotel. A porter was carrying their bags.

He watched them checking in and heard Kekeli ask for a room with an ocean view. They turned to leave but stopped in the doorway. Patrice couldn't see what they could, but he could hear.

'Good evening, ladies, welcome!' It was a man's voice, high-pitched. American.

'Thank you,' Kekeli said. 'It is beautiful here. We were looking for a place in paradise and we've found Heaven on Earth! I'm so looking forward to our stay.' Patrice smiled to himself. Kekeli sounded like she'd been educated at a British girls' boarding school. 'And I'm sure Aunty is too ... the fresh ocean air will do her the world of good.'

'Well, we'll do our best to make you both comfortable. Let's show you to your room ...'

Patrice peered round the corner. The man was leading the two women down a decked walkway. He turned abruptly to introduce himself to his new guests. Patrice recognised him. It was the man in the passport photo, the older man he'd seen on the terrace at the Volta Hotel. His parted grey hair looked moist from sweat.

'Joe Horst,' he said, extending his hand. 'Let me know if there's anything you need.'

Kekeli shook the hand and introduced herself as Valerie Asamoah, as if she'd done so a thousand times before. 'Thank you,' she said. 'Are you the owner of Heaven on Earth?'

'That's one of my jobs,' he said and winked. 'I'm Horst, your host. I'll give you the most! I've got quite a life story. We should have a drink together.'

Patrice tutted.

Kekeli said, 'I should like that, but later, Mr Horst. I should like to freshen up first. And my aunt is tired after the journey.'

'You came from Accra?'

'Er, yes, but not today. We spent last night in Cape Coast. But it took us a long time to find the right hotel ... for us. When we saw this one, we knew it was it.'

'How did you find us, if you don't mind my asking? We don't advertise much.'

'It was recommended by a young man we met in Nkroful.'

'Well, what do you know? Thought they hated me in that place. Finally, something good's come from there!'

Kekeli smiled politely.

'See you later, ladies ...'

A porter led the two women to their room.

Horst lingered, ogling Kekeli's behind. A few moments later, though, the old man came scuttling back, wiping his brow, looking flustered. He walked past reception and into the bar.

Patrice looked him straight in the eye.

The man nodded and said, 'Good evening,' and walked past without giving Patrice a second glance. He headed for the bar and ordered a Scotch, downed it in one, and pointed at the glass for a refill. He was looking at his watch and in the direction of the entrance.

Patrice drank his beer, gazing out to the palms by the ocean, now lit from below and glowing golden against the night sky. He opened his guidebook to pass the time and play the part of a rich, lonely traveller searching for something meaningful. Ten minutes later, he caught sight of the receptionist picking up her phone and Horst, still by the bar, picking up his.

'They're here,' she said.

Four men came round the corner and up the six steps. They didn't look like tourists. Two white, two black, all dressed in dark Western suits. Horst approached and greeted two of them with a two-handed handshake. From the tense smile on his face, it was clear he wasn't glad to see them. He motioned for them to follow him, but not to a table. He led them into a room behind the bar.

Patrice tapped his foot, thinking. An idea came to him. He texted Kekeli, then he went outside and round to the back of the building. There was no one around. He ducked down, then crawled between the wooden stilts, shuffling along on all fours. Light from the bar and restaurant above shone through the cracks in the floorboards.

As he moved below the tables, he caught random snatches

of conversation. '... the thing I loved most about Sri Lanka was the spirituality. It's a very spiritual place, very deep.' 'Isn't there a war going on there?' 'No, not any more ...'

He made out two dark, square shapes ahead of him: water tanks. These had to be below the toilets, which were to the side of the bar. He crawled round them. There was a squeal. Two rats scurried past. A little further, he found himself below the room where Horst had taken his guests. He could hear men's voices. He positioned himself below what he supposed was a table in the middle of the room. The voices were clear – like Patrice was in there with them. He pressed the record button on his phone.

'... it's Joe, remember? Round here they call me Joe.'

'Doesn't matter what they call you, you fucked up ... Joe.'

'I didn't fuck up. It was Marty who fucked up.'

'You were working together. You were a team. And the team fucked up.'

'Marty fucked up. But what do you care? Ariz are still in the game. What I hear, the contract's theirs. They're in the game.'

'Thing is, Marty's cover's blown. State Department weren't in on this.'

'So, wasn't me that fucked up.'

It sounded like Horst was on the back foot. The man putting him on the spot was another American.

'You think stuff won't come out? Sooner or later, they're going to start asking more questions about this man who tried to blow up their dam – tried to blow up the fucking Akosombo Dam for Christ's sake – and they'll find out, and they'll say, wait a minute, this man used to work for the CIA and so did his old man buddy.'

'Christ's sake, cut it out, will you? They don't know shit.'

'They're not stupid, Joe … Micky Mouse … whatever you want to call yourself, they're …'

'I said cut it. Why are you fucking with me?'

'Because you fucked up. The plan was to scare them, not blow up the fucking dam.'

'I didn't know Marty's stuff was live.'

'You kidding me, Micky Mouse?'

'It's Joe.'

'Fuck your fucking Joe shit. You knew what he was doing. You thought you were back in the Cold fucking War. That right? You were thinking of all the things you and Bane wanted to do. You thought this is your chance to do it your way. The Bane way. You didn't get to blow up the Chinese embassy, so now you're going to blow up the Akosombo Dam.'

'You hired me. You're the one who came fucking begging. "Oh man, help us out will you, buddy?" Remember? "You're the one who knows this place, you know the people." Remember what I said? "Why come to us to do your dirty work? Don't you know how to do these things no more?" Remember that conversation?'

There were nervous coughs. A chair scraped on the boards.

'You came to us three weeks ago when you needed professionals to speed things up, turn the screw, to push the Ariz deal. And the reason you came to us was because you wanted nothing to connect the agency. Because the agency's running scared these days, afraid to do the right thing for our country when it matters.'

'Bullshit. You wanted the job.'

'I own a hotel and I got a successful mining consultancy with Marty. Why would I need the job? Look at this place,

look around you. Fucking paradise. I didn't need your job
… I was doing you a favour, that's all. I retired from that game
long ago.'

'Everyone knew you didn't want to leave. They kicked you
out because you were old. We offered you a chance to use
your skills and you messed up.'

'Marty messed up.'

'We're going round in circles, Micky.'

'It's Joe. So what you going to do about it? The genie's out
of the bottle.'

'We're going to put it back.'

'How you going to do that?'

'You're going to do it, Joe. You're going to disappear. You're
going to leave here tomorrow, go back to the States and stay
hidden. You could get back with your beautiful Ghanaian
wife … what's her name?'

'Beatrice. She left me a long time ago. You know that.'

'Well, find someone new. Just disappear.'

'I'm seventy-five. What if I don't want to disappear?'

'Then we'll disappear you, Joe. You'll have a drowning
accident, off your island. It's your choice.'

'You're kidding me, right?'

'No kidding, Micky. Anything links you to us … we can't
afford it. We're giving you a chance. We're not forgetting
you were once one of the top guys. Here's your ticket for
tomorrow night's flight to Amsterdam and here's one for an
onward flight to Washington. If you're not on those flights,
we'll come find you.'

The next words were lost under the sound of scraping chair
legs and footsteps. The meeting was over. Patrice rolled
out from under the building. Keeping to the shadows, he

hurried back to his room. He showered again to wash out the smell of rats and sat himself down. Then he played back the conversation he'd recorded. It was muffled but audible. There was nothing to identify the man talking to Horst – but plenty to identify Horst, no matter what name he used.

Chapter 43

Patrice paced around his room, figuring out the best course of action. The old man would be out of the country in little over twenty-four hours, unless he chose to have a drowning accident. He shook his head – in disbelief that people actually talked like that, and in despair at their neo-colonial depravity. Even if his recording couldn't be used in court, the security people at the Akosombo Dam would want to talk to Joe Horst. So he called John Sarpong. Then he called Kekeli.

'Where are you?' he asked.

'Hello, yes, good to hear from you. I'm away right now, in Western Region. I've brought my aunt to the coast for some fresh sea air.'

This woman kept a cool head. 'Did you see the old man, in the bar, with four men in suits?'

'I believe I did.'

'Is he still there?'

'Yes, indeed.'

'Good. Now listen, can you stay on the phone without it looking suspicious? I'll tell you what you need to do ...'

'We're about to go for a stroll around the grounds of this delightful hotel with the owner. We can speak later if that's alright. Bye for now ...'

'Kekeli, don't go with him, wait for me ...'

The acoustic on the line changed. Patrice made out clinks of cutlery and a distant murmur of voices. He heard Kekeli's. She wasn't speaking into the phone, but she hadn't hung up.

'... come along Aunty, we're going for a walk ...'

He pulled on his clothes and raced down to the bar. They weren't there. Panic struck Patrice like a punch to his stomach. He looked out across the lawn and all around. There was no sign of them. His hands shook as he held his phone to his ear. He could hear waves. He scanned the beach, but it was deserted. Then he heard voices down the line, distant.

'... so you see, I built this place up from nothing.'

'It is beautiful. Thank you so much for giving us this guided tour. I know you must be a busy man.'

'The pleasure's mine.'

'And you say this is an island at high tide? How exciting ...'

Patrice looked at the island. It was hard to make out much in the darkness apart from the shadowy trees. But he spotted some movement: three figures walking up a path, approaching the bungalows.

'... mind how you go there. Now look ...'

The lights went on in one of them. Patrice could see three silhouettes inside. He hurried to the ocean. It was impossible, with the waves so close, to hear Kekeli's conversation with the old man. He reached the bar of sand that linked the island to the mainland. It was almost submerged. He splashed across and crept up the path. As he got close to the bungalow, he heard voices and saw shadows on a veranda that wrapped around the building. The shadows were coming in his direction. He dived behind some rocks below.

'... here you've got everything, an infinity pool and the

ocean. Every luxury you could wish for. Heaven on Earth. You like it?'

'Yes, you must be proud.'

There was a pause in the conversation. Then the old man shouted out, 'No one's going to take me away from this.'

Patrice peered through a gap in the rocks. The old man was clutching the railings with both hands, looking out to the ocean. Tears were streaming down his cheeks.

'My goodness, sir, we've upset you. I'm so sorry.'

'No, no, it's not you …'

'But my aunt and I should leave you in peace.'

Aunty Yawor was sitting in a chair. She, too, was looking out to sea. Patrice wondered if she had a clue where she was.

'No, really, please stay. I need friendly company.' He turned and wiped his cheeks with his hand.

'In that case, of course.' Kekeli offered him a tissue. 'But why should anyone want to take this away from you?'

'It's a long story.'

'We are good listeners, aren't we, Aunty?'

'I was here, minding my own business … like I say, I built this place from nothing. I get a visit from these people I used to know. They said they had a job for me, could I help them? I was the only one who had the expertise, they said.' He paused and stroked his upper lip with his thumb and forefinger, as if he was considering how much he wanted to say.

'Eeek!' Aunty Yawor let out a terrifying shriek.

'Aunty! What's happened?'

'It's him!' The old lady was pointing at the old man. 'With the red car. He did it.'

'What's she talking about?' The man's tone was suddenly hostile and defensive. 'Is she crazy?'

'She's old and confused. But she's not blind. She saw you. We know who you are.'

Aunty Yawor got to her feet and swung her crutch at the man. 'Murderer!' she screamed.

The man caught the crutch in his hand and twisted it, forcing the old lady to let go. He stepped up to her. 'I remember you.' He threw the crutch on the floor and grabbed hold of Aunty Yawor's arms.

Kekeli screamed. 'Leave her alone.' She wasn't speaking like a posh English girl now. She tried to pull the man away, but he lashed out with his free arm and knocked her to the floor.

Patrice jumped over the rocks and up onto the veranda. 'That's enough! Let her go.'

'Who the fuck are you?'

'Patrice! This is the man who killed my father. Aunty saw him.'

Patrice edged along the veranda towards the man holding Aunty Yawor. 'He didn't kill your father, Kekeli. He killed your aunt. He's not Joe Horst. He's Steve Krieger, and fifty years ago he killed Adzowor Abotsi.'

'Adzowor Abotsi? Never heard of her. What are you talking about?'

'You've never heard of her? But you drove her to the American embassy on the night she died. And this lady here is her sister.'

'What the fuck? Who are you?'

'You don't remember me either? For an ex-CIA man, your memory is poor. I was sitting with Professor Henderson at the Volta Hotel the day she died. That's another death you'll have to explain when the police get here.'

342

The man was old, but he was strong. He threw Aunty Yawor to the side and charged at Patrice. Before Patrice could take evasive action, the man rammed into him and brought him down. Patrice looked up, winded, to see a raised fist. But behind it, Kekeli was back on her feet. At the pivotal moment, she grabbed the man's arm in mid-air, catching him off balance. Patrice got to his knees. Stretching over, he pushed the man's head hard against the railings. The man cried out and sagged to the floor. Patrice got on top of him and jerked his hands behind his back. Kekeli went to her aunt and helped her back onto the chair.

'Right,' Patrice said. 'This is where you confess and beg for forgiveness.'

'Patrice, how do you know all this?' Kekeli was staring at the man on the floor.

'I heard it all. He's part of this whole thing, but it was his partner who killed your father.' Patrice forced the man's arms back and up towards his shoulders. 'Isn't that right?' he said, increasing the pressure.

'Okay, okay …'

Patrice eased off.

'It was an accident. Marty didn't mean it. That's what he told me.'

'The full story.'

The old man was gasping. He turned his head to look up. 'It was Mensah and Boateng's idea. They said Abotsi was causing problems, holding things up, so they said to go and mess up his hydro station. Marty was going to plant explosives, but Abotsi disturbed him and Marty panicked and threw a switch … and the man died. That's what Marty said.'

'That's not an accident.'

'He messed up.'

Kekeli glared at the man. Her eyes could have killed him there and then.

Patrice gripped an arm tight again and pushed it back towards the shoulder. 'Is that what you call it? Messed up? Is that what happened when you killed Aunty's sister?'

The man groaned but didn't speak.

'You ran her down, didn't you?'

The old man's eyes flashed from side to side, as if they were looking for an escape.

'Admit it …'

He screwed up his face. 'She was a whore. I liked her. I took her to the embassy one evening, showing off. I had a few beers and bragged about how we were going to bring down Nkrumah … showed her the bugs we had. But Bane came back and got mad. Said I had to deal with her. Adzowor ran off … I drove, but I couldn't find her, so I waited near her house. I was going to talk to her, explain she had to keep quiet, but when she saw the car, she ran. I followed and … fuck it. I hit her, fuck it. She was running … I had to stop her.'

Patrice slapped the side of his face. 'You people! You disgust me! You kill and cause chaos. What gives you the right? Do people like you ever ask that question? Life and death, other people's, they mean nothing to you. For you, everyone is just a pawn in a game. Well, let me tell you, so are you …'

'Stop, Patrice!'

Kekeli was shouting. The man was screaming. Patrice hadn't noticed. He let go of the man's arm. He was panting, like the lump beneath him.

'Okay,' he said, 'the police can deal with him. Justice can take its course. It's not too late.'

He pulled the old man, Steve Krieger, to his feet. The old man grunted. His earlier strength seemed to have drained from him. He looked frail and more like his age. The past had caught up with him. They walked back down the path, Patrice in front with Krieger, Kekeli behind with her aunt.

A breeze had picked up and the water below was choppy. When they reached the beach, the tide had risen. The island was cut off; a narrow channel of water separated it from the mainland. They'd have to wade across. In the light reflected from the restaurant beyond, Patrice could make out a strong swirling current. He was working out how to get them all across when he saw three policemen approaching.

'Stay here with Aunty, Kekeli. I'll take this one and come back for you.'

Kekeli stood with her arm round Aunty Yawor, whose eyes were fixed on her sister's killer.

Patrice pushed the man forward into the water. Two policemen waded in from the other side. The warm sea splashed. Patrice felt the undertow pulling and pushing his legs. The water swelled up to his waist. He swayed from side to side, leaning into the flow. They were close to the policemen when Krieger jerked his arm. Patrice lost his balance – and the old man broke free. The policemen jumped forward, arms stretched, but they couldn't get a hand on him. They and Patrice watched, spluttering, as the old man swam away.

One of the policemen pointed down the beach. 'There are fishermen in the next bay. We will go with them to bring him in.'

Looking out across the water, catching glimpses of a head bobbing between the waves, Patrice realised that might not be necessary. The American was heading for the open sea. It didn't look like he meant to come back.

Patrice waded to the two women on the island. 'He gave me the slip.'

Kekeli kissed her teeth. 'He'd rather die than answer for his crimes. So much for his heaven on earth. He's going to hell.'

Patrice and Kekeli led Aunty Yawor into the water and carried her across. She was singing a song:

If you follow him,
If you follow him,
Osagyefo!
He will make you fishers of men!
He will make you fishers of men!
If you follow him ...

They reached the other side. A hotel boy brought towels and Kekeli wrapped one round Aunty Yawor. The old lady was repeating the verses. Again, it was impossible to tell what was going on in her mind. But the hint of a smile showed in the upward turn of her lips, and there was a steadiness in her eyes. Kekeli held her aunty tight and kissed her head.

The fishermen found no trace of Steve Krieger that night. Next morning, his body was washed up on the beach in front of the hotel. Patrice and Kekeli watched the police load it onto a pick-up truck and take it away. The atmosphere in the hotel was subdued, with the staff uncertain about their future.

'You look sad, Patrice.'

'I'm not sad. Frustrated perhaps, with the world.'

She squeezed his hand. 'Me and Aunty will always be grateful for what you've done for us.'

He looked round at Aunty and she smiled at him.

As they were getting ready to leave, Patrice got a call from Josie Mwinga.

'Patrice,' she shouted, in the way she always did on the phone, 'I'm at the airport, about to fly to Banjul. I thought you'd like to know, I heard it from my friend, the president has rejected the solar farm proposals, the ones backed by ArizOil. All of them. He'll be making an announcement later.'

'That's very good news. Thank you for telling me, ma'am. I appreciate it. Please pass my best wishes to your friend.'

'The president is going to say Ghana's sunshine belongs to Ghana, and any benefits from it should stay in Ghana. It's a good line, isn't it?'

'Yes, it is.' He looked to the sky.

'Good, yes, well, goodbye. Come and see me if you come to Washington.'

'Goodbye, ma'am.' The phone cut.

On the drive back to Accra, Kekeli asked, 'Do you think you'll go?'

'To see my boss, my ex-boss?'

'No. I mean, will you go to America to study?'

'That's the plan, still. Why?'

Kekeli glanced at him. 'I don't know. I was thinking, are you the academic type? Will you like sitting in the library for hours on end, reading and writing? You might get bored. Whereas here, well, I thought perhaps you liked it here?' She had that sparkle in her smile.

'Well,' he said, 'it's not like I'll be gone for ever.'

THE END

BUKAVU BLUES

A macabre murder. A country torn apart by conflict. A man determined to stop the bloodshed.

Seeing his people suffer for many years has left human rights defender Patrice Le Congo feeling weary and cynical. But when schoolteacher Aurélia Mukunda turns to him for help after a mutilated body is found in a village, he can't say no.

His inquiries take him on a perilous journey to the heart of a seemingly never-ending war that's brought death and destruction to eastern Congo.

After more murders threaten to derail a crucial peace conference, the killers abduct Aurélia. And Patrice is faced with two challenges: save the teacher and save his country.

Bukavu Blues **is the opening novel chronicling The Investigations of Patrice Le Congo, a series of crime stories from Africa with a global political dimension.**

'A blistering and eye-opening read. Highly recommended.'
Amazon Five-Star review

'Captivating political intrigue at its finest.'
Amazon Five-Star review

PALA PALA KILLER

A bitter feud. A spiral of killings. A fight for justice.

Human rights defender Patrice Le Congo is a man who'll leave no stone unturned in search of the truth.

   When the death of a park ranger in a Cameroonian rainforest is reported as a freak mishap, he has his doubts. It soon becomes clear there's been a cover-up. But why?

   As more bloodshed follows, Patrice suspects a hidden hand is at work, stirring up trouble.

Pala Pala Killer is the second novel chronicling The Investigations of Patrice Le Congo, a series of crime stories from Africa with a global political dimension.

.

"A gripping story. And credible at every level. *Pala Pala Killer* is a work of *reality fiction* - all of it could have happened - addressing issues that should be of interest to all readers."
John Stockwell, author of NYT best-seller *In Search of Enemies* and *Red Sunset - The Full Story*

About the Author

Peter Lewenstein was born in London. Before turning to fiction he was a journalist. He edited and produced the BBC radio programmes Network Africa and Focus on Africa, and travelled widely across Africa, reporting on elections, war and everyday life. When not writing, he does normal things like going for a walk or watching football. He is married and has two daughters. He is a member of the Alliance of Independent Authors.